I0846638

The Rowans

a novel

Beverly Cooper Pierce

3 Winter Island Road
Salem, Massachusetts 01970

Names: Pierce, Beverly Cooper, author
Title: The Rowans : A novel / Beverly Cooper Pierce
Description: First edition. | Salem, Mass. : Winter Island Press, 2025.
Identifiers: ISBN 979-8-9878655-9-0 (hardcover)
ISBN 979-8-9878655-8-3 (paperback)
ISBN 979-8-9925945-0-8 (eBook)
Subjects: LCSH: Puritans -- Massachusetts -- Fiction |
Self-realization in women -- Fiction |
LCGFT: Magic realist fiction | Historical fiction | Novels

First paperback edition, 2026
Cover and interior art by Alex Edwards
Interior design by Maile Black

For my sons

Tobe and Tristan

and

my wondrous great-aunt Isabel Cooper Mahaffie

The Family of Thomasin Bennett
to the Year 1750

Isaac Rowan, 1608-1674
m.
Margaret Rowan, 1612-1683

Matthew Tobin, 1598- ?
m.
Prudence Bailey, 1618-1659

Simon Bennett, 1599-1681
m.
Keziah Eliot, 1615- ?

Thomas Dane, 1624-1686
m.
Abigail Capen, 1622-1689

Priscilla Rowan 1550-1715   m.   **Samuel Tobin** 1647-1697

Robert Bennett 1642-1697   m.   Sarah Dane 1648-1718

Isaac Tobin 1574-   **Daniel Tobin** 1676-1694   **Gabriel Tobin** 1680-1716   **Catherine (Cat) Tobin** 1688-   m.   **Thomas Bennett** 1680-1735

Peter Bradbury, d. 1735
m.
Elizabeth (Bet) English, d. 1746

Walter Shepard, 1673-1728
m.
Jemima Hale, 1680-1733

Nathaniel Bradbury 1704-
m.
Martha Hale 1716-

Susannah (Bradbury) Julien 1710-   m.   **Robert Bennett II** 1709-1750

Simon Bennett II 1711-   m.   **Adah Shepard** 1713-

Peter Bennett, 1734-
Thomasin (Tamsin) Bennett, 1735-
Eli Bennett, 1743-1743
Phebe Bennett, 1745-

James Bennett, 1733-
Naomi Bennett, 1736-
Ruth Bennett, 1736-
Walter Bennett, 1738-1740
Luke Bennett, 1743-
Abigail Bennett, 1747-
Sarah Bennett, 1750-

PART ONE

West Dorset
Massachusetts Bay
1750

1

Grandmother Cat would say this when Tamsin was little – *Note the signs, dear* – and Tamsin would peer all round for a thing that surprised her or looked out of place. Leaves on the rowan trees or river birches might twist backward in a breeze, or a honeybee rest amiably on her hand. When she was little, Tamsin thought this was a game. As time went on, Grandmother might be cutting rosemary to make a vinegar scrub, or grinding seed with her mortar and pestle when, for no seeming reason, she would turn to advise urgently – *Tamsin, always heed the unexpected.*

A thing as slight as a redbird feather might blow onto the doorsill of the meetinghouse, a wisp one could easily step right over without seeing that the old minister would hurt himself cutting wood on Tuesday and not be there to preach the next Sabbath. This happened. So Grandmother Cat taught Tamsin that even a feather could point beyond itself to an event of such weight, it could wound a man mortally. "Or," she would murmur, "plague a child with fear her life long."

Tamsin heard faint words, but with no idea what they meant,

3

she put them into the growing store of questions she kept for the days when, together, she and Grandmother Cat would go upstream to forage.

ONE SUCH DAY, THE 31ˢᵗ OF AUGUST IN 1750, MARKED the fifteenth year since Tamsin was born. Dates of birth were written into the family Bible as a matter of record, even if rarely observed, but Tamsin always noted hers – in part because of the day, nearly seven years ago, when the baby Eli was born. She remembered with awe her brother Eli, born and dead within a few breaths. It struck her as she watched him come and go, that somehow she had come and stayed. The difference was a wonder to her. And so this was the day when, once a year, she would do her ordinary day's work, mindful of the puzzle that she was here at all, on this farm, in this family of Bennetts, by this stream that flowed out to the Massachusetts Bay. She was Thomasin Bennett, called Tamsin, named for her grandfather Thomas Bennett who had died on the day she was born. To Tamsin, the very fact of her life was persistent mystery.

AT DAWN ON THAT DAY, SHE WENT OUT TO THE BARN to milk the Devons with her cousin James, as she did every day, though alert this morning for anything remarkable that might touch on the question of her being. All began as usual, peaceful. The cows showed not the slightest vexation, not even when mice took the mortal risk of chasing one another round among clumsy hooves. No bucket was kicked over, no milk lost.

As she and James worked, he spoke happily of the field of Red Lammas wheat the cousins' two families had cut and stood up in sheaves. He said this looked to be another good day for drying wheat. Tamsin said this day looked fine for going upstream to forage with Grandmother Cat, and that yesterday had been a remarkably good day.

All day yesterday, she told James with pride, she had pulled stone and built fence with her Papa to clear the new rye field. James smiled. Her heart bloomed as it would when he smiled, and she turned away to the work of her hands. She would not tell him that yesterday in the rye field, she felt she heard music and imagined she danced with him.

On this morning of her birth day, the barn swallows' late-summer fledglings looped perfectly in and out the barn door. Only one new swallow, path awry, swept Grandmother Cat's rowan-wood crosses down off the beam and so plummeted with them to the dirt floor. Tamsin picked up the little bird, carried it gently to the barn door, and tossed it into flight, then went back to collect Grandmother's fallen crosses. James moved the ladder, and she climbed up to put the rowan-wood twigs, bound with red thread, back upon the beam, restoring their protection to cows, swallows, and mice.

She gave thought to the little bird that had aimed itself amiss before flying up properly in the air. She wondered, in passing, whether a tumble among rowan-wood crosses could be a sign that pointed somehow to her life on this day of her birth. She lost the thought, however, in delight that today she would go upstream in the coracle with Grandmother Cat. Tamsin was always enchanted with Grandmother's coracle, the slight vessel she saw as part willow, part hemp, part – what else? Air, she thought. With only a single broad oar, it carried them gracefully, inexplicably, away up the millstream, away from two busy, often bickering families. Today they would go to gather herbs for Aunt Adah's birth and the change of seasons. Grandmother Cat, in rowing and foraging, would tell Tamsin stories of her family, the Rowans, and Tamsin would ask as many questions as she could.

But before her wondrous day could unfold, a confounding thing happened.

· · ·

Tamsin took two buckets of milk into the house and put them on the kitchen table, just as Papa was going downstream to the mill to meet the new moon tide. She went to embrace him and bid him good morning, but in the very moment she touched him, a horrific shriek shot up somewhere, she felt, behind her. It crashed round the kitchen and seared inside her throat as, right before her, Papa splintered entirely into little shards of light, all tiny shocking stars.

Her arms now held a vast dark space where, a moment ago, Papa's sturdy form had stood. Her hands full of little pricks like stinging nettles, she felt wholly untethered from kitchen, stone hearth, and pine-board floor. Still, a rumble of common sense made her keep hold so that Papa would come back and settle again into bone and body. And so she did, and so it was.

In the next moment, as he did every day, and as if nothing impossible had happened, Papa smiled at Tamsin his kind smile and went out to the mill to make best use of a good tide.

Stock-still, she watched him go. Fearing whatever wreckage she would find of the kitchen, she turned round to look. But there were her buckets of milk. There were her cousins Ruth and Naomi scooping porridge for Abigail and Phebe, keeping Luke from rolling berries to the floor. Had they heard nothing, seen nothing? Grandmother Cat was tearing peppermint plant into a jar, Mother just going out to the garden with Peter. The speed of their steps pulled Tamsin, loose, into their wake, and she went out the door.

Wherever was Papa? She must look for him and find him of sound body. Whatever would happen, were he to split all out into sparks again, and no one there to hold the dark space? Crossing the yard, she went among the rowan trees at the head of the mill path. A rush of air swept them as if they all gasped at once, but her eyes found Papa, already well down the mill path, broad back stark white in his linen shirt. He moved at a good pace.

Tamsin followed, keeping a little distance at first, a close watch. But where the path skirted the rise of the wheat field and curved with the stream, he slipped from view. Her feet knew every rock, root, and stump of the wide path, so when he vanished, she pelted heedless till she found him.

"*Papa!*"

He turned. "Tamsin! I know, I saw it. Go tell James and Peter!"

She caught up and reached out to feel in her fingers the exact weave of the linen shirtsleeve she had sewn.

"*Papa –*"

"Go back," he said. "Tell them the gale blew down our wheat."

She shook her head, this made no sense. Her eyes searched the air around him for motes of light that might threaten more splintering.

He spoke with force. "Tamsin, that grain must dry, or by God, we'll lose it."

"Papa, are you well?"

"I am," he said, and then, "Are you?"

Her mouth opened as if to speak, but on its own, it had no answer. She studied his eyes. "Are you fevered, Papa?"

"I am not," he said. "What is it?"

"In the kitchen –"

"What?"

She willed herself to form words. "In the kitchen, there was a cry and you looked like a night full of stars."

Papa nodded slowly and waited.

"Like all the bright points in your compass," she said. "As if they all flew up in the air at once. In the dark. But Papa – *what did you do?*"

She nearly asked if this were magic, but held her tongue.

"Nothing at all, my girl," Papa said quietly. "Not a thing. But your grandmother knows a great deal more than I. You may tell her what you saw."

She nodded wordless. There was nothing more.

"As for me," Papa said, "I must get to Simon and set this good tide to grinding our neighbors' corn." He pointed up the mill path. "To the house, Tamsin. Tell James and Peter to fix the wheat. You have work upstream with your grandmother."

With a twist of a smile he added, "Mine is downstream with my brother."

Tamsin could not turn her eyes away from her Papa, even if he looked to be himself now, and real. Instead, she walked backwards up the path, keeping a steady watch. He watched her too, then walked down to the dam and crossed to the mill.

Tamsin turned and ran. Grandmother Cat would know what this was, what happened.

But when she came to the rise of the wheat field, she saw what she'd only now sped past. The night's gale had tumbled all the wheat shocks the families had worked a long day to make, cutting and binding, standing them up in the sun. There should have been fat sheaves leaning together by half-dozens all over the field, heavy heads drying in late-summer air. Instead, here was disordered gold, a crop on the ground.

Paying no mind to Papa's words for the boys, forgetting even Papa's stars, Tamsin set to fixing what she could of the families' wheat. Fabled across the county for its rich yield, if this crop were lost, there would be no other source for the seed.

She stepped from the path up the rise of the field and lifted, as she went, all the sheaves still bound. Restoring them in their shocks, she breathed to herself what Grandmother told of the Rowan women who'd saved the seed of the Red Lammas wheat. "It was my Grandmother Cat, and her mother Priscilla, and in England her mother Margaret –"

Tamsin knew there were more mothers beyond, but not their names, and from the east of the field to the west she moved, now telling the lineage to the wheat. "Remember Catherine, and Priscilla, and your Margaret who sailed with you over the sea. Catherine, and Priscilla –"

She did what she could. For the wheat still fallen, she would need a rake and ran up the path to the barn.

James was there, splitting wood at the shed. He looked up sharp and put down his maul. "What is it?"

She told him, and he said, "I'll get Peter and the rakes. You did well, cousin."

He put his arms around her. It was sweet to hold onto him until her heart and breath would settle, although they did not very much.

In the kitchen where that morning Tamsin had felt a shriek, the butter churn now made a joyful noise. Phebe, her sister four years old, hadn't the height and strength yet to work the churn, but she liked the knocking of the dasher. Playing at it now, she would do well with it soon, when it was her work to do. Tamsin smiled at her and sat down hard on a chair to wrestle with the inexplicable.

Papa said she could tell Grandmother Cat what she'd seen, and when they went upstream, she would try. But how to make words tell a thing both terrible and impossible? If she'd truly seen it, would that make it a sign? Or could it be magic? And if magic, then what was it, made the magic happen? A baneful spirit, come down the chimney, caught in the kitchen. Tamsin raised her eyes to the ceiling and corners, then wondered if it were perilous even to think such a thing on the day of her birth! But if a demon were in the house, she must tell Grandmother Cat, because then they'd all want her rowan-wood crosses to tuck in their pockets or inside their stays.

This needed thought.

Wood scraped wood as Grandmother, hands full, hitched a stool with her foot close to her cabinet, hooked her petticoat with two fingers, and stepped carefully up to put her jars on the shelves. "Where have you been, Tamsin? I'm ready."

"The gale blew down all our sheaves, Grandmother. I fixed what I could, and I told James."

From atop the stool, Grandmother Cat looked down at her granddaughter and nodded once, birdlike, quick approval.

Tamsin flushed with love. *Catherine, Priscilla, Margaret –*

"I'm ready too," she said.

2

ON THE 30th OF AUGUST, THE DAY BEFORE TAMSIN'S
fifteenth birth day, she had been clever enough to find a way to
work with her Papa through a whole day!

He had gone out in the morning to pull stone from the old
woodlot, newly cleared of stumps. The boys were not there to
help, having sailed the shallop out for a haul of fish. Tamsin,
observant, knew better than to ask. She waited till she saw Ethan
yoked, then followed the ox and her Papa out to the field that
would be rimmed with stone and planted to winter rye.

"Papa?" she said in quiet mischief.

He smiled and said into Ethan's ear, it looked like they'd not
be alone after all.

"I'll help, Papa. Mother and Phebe are in the garden. They
don't need me."

"Good, then. We can use the help, Ethan and I. We'll get the
heaviest out first with the stoneboat. You look for good flat ones.
We'll need them too."

"To wedge with the lumpy ones."

"Level as we can."

Tamsin patted Ethan's broad face and set off to study the
ground for wedging stones. This would be a very good day. To

her mind, she had never enough chances to work with Papa. Peter and James were lucky, working with him since they were six and seven. And lately, Uncle Simon was teaching the boys the more particular needs of the tide mill. Tamsin understood the cycles, natural and mechanical, that worked the mill, and would be drawn there too, given the chance, unlikely as that was.

Though never, not even once, did she ever regret her time working with Grandmother Cat, foraging for herbs, growing them, learning to make extracts and teas, poultices, needful things. A history of such knowing came down through a long line of Rowan women. But Grandmother was stoking the oven for bread this morning – Indian corn and rye, no milled wheat yet – so she told Tamsin to go off and make herself useful. That, she was pleased to do, and ran out into this rocky, rough field that looked to need her help, as did Papa.

Then came hard, hot hours of shifting, hauling, and placing stone before Tamsin saw Mother at the edge of the field with a big wooden tankard.

"Robert, Tamsin! Cider!"

"Susannah, yes!" Robert Bennett crossed the field to his wife, and gratefully, in turns, he and Tamsin swallowed the cider down.

"Ethan will need a drink too," he said, and when he unhitched the ox and led him back to the trough at the barn, Susannah took Robert's hand and walked with him.

Tamsin followed. "Papa, may I hold your compass?"

He pulled it from a little pocket Susannah had stitched into his breeches to keep it safe. "Ethan and I will be back."

Tamsin took her Papa's precious brass compass and, holding it with care, took it to the middle of the field. She watched as the needle quivered north, pointing straight into the new woodlot. Lifting her eyes from the needle, she smiled and whirled all the way round once to see in a single sweep – new woodlot, old rye field, blue sky, house downhill, barn past trees, stone fence begun, uphill, more trees, and woodlot – and there she stopped short, due north. Then she whirled once more and stopped, whirled again, stopped, whirled, stopped.

When images were swinging all round her head, she sat down on the ground, and when her eyes settled again, she raised the fine triangular blade that turned the brass circle of the earth into a sundial. It showed mid-morning. She felt it must be later, so she looked up into the sky to be sure the sundial was telling her the truth about this hot day, and it was. Squinting from the sunlight, she cupped the compass in her two hands and looked deep into it, wondering again how this miraculous thing was possible – that she could hold, right here, all the directions to all the created earth, as Papa said she could, and also tell from a little triangle pointing up to God's wide heaven just where she was in this day – in the middle of a morning, in the middle of the world.

Folding the blade down, she tucked the miracle into the pocket tied inside her petticoat, and stood to survey the field – surprised to find that in the midst of all far-flung earthly directions, she felt as if she were floating. Her arms lifted right up into the air, all on their own, and she felt light as when Grandmother Cat's brother Isaac came to visit with his fiddle, and all the Bennetts, or most of them, would dance. They would carry chairs, bench, and table out of the parlor to open up space like a field, like *this* field, and Mother, who knew all the steps *perfectly*, would show them once more. Then Uncle Isaac would play his fiddle, and Papa would go to Mother. She and Papa would face one another and smile, and begin. The children in two lines would all watch them and follow. It was a joyous time! Papa looked so happy dancing with Mother, and she smiled all the evening long.

Tamsin now, in her mind's ear, heard Uncle Isaac playing his fiddle – magically! she said later to Grandmother Cat. Indeed he played "All in a Garden Green" so nimbly and sweetly that just here in the field, she began to dance, whispering beneath the lift and tumble of his notes –

"My left hand in the boy's right, I'm to turn right. Four steps up, four back, then turn to face – James!" Her heart sang with the fiddle, "Step left, step right, turn all the way round and – 'tis James! Step again left, right, turn and –" She smiled, "Step to James. Come *very near* touching right shoulders. Step back, left, right again, turn and step –" She nodded exactly to the spot where James would be – "*near as we can,* touch left –"

Papa led Ethan to the field, and Tamsin took him the compass. They went on moving stone and making fence, Tamsin bringing good flat ones to wedge with the stones she thought lumpy, until Papa said they'd made three yards of low fence and it was time to go and eat dinner.

The boys had pulled in cod and bass that morning. Mother made her good fish soup with onions and milk and her tied-up bundle of cooking herbs. This, she had learnt to do years ago at the harbor from the one she called *Belle-mère,* the mother of her first husband, a captain lost at sea.

After taking Mother's soup, Tamsin and Papa went back out to the field to move more stone and make more fence. Come supper time, Papa unhitched the stoneboat, lifted Tamsin up onto Ethan's back, and led him to the barn.

Riding high, she stroked the ox's summer-smooth, Devon-red hide and spoke to him of his good day's work.

3

AT THE END OF THEIR DAY'S WORK, AT THE END OF supper, the youngest finished their turn at table and washing up was begun. Tamsin went to the parlor and settled herself, a window to one side, a betty lamp at the other. Across her lap she laid two linen shifts, long outgrown by Naomi and Ruth, Uncle Simon's twins. Phebe and her little cousin Abigail would wear them soon. Tamsin inspected the tucks she had basted. They were neat, and shortened each shift by a good ten inches. This evening, if she was quick and the scripture reading long, her fine running-stitch might finish one shift. Tomorrow, which she would mark as the day of her birth, she might finish the other. Then as Phebe and Abigail grew, the tucks could be let down, one by one.

She cut a length of linen thread and drew it across a lump of beeswax. This would preserve the thread through years of soap and water, but truly Tamsin did it because the feel of waxed linen pleased her fingertips.

She looked up as Papa came into the parlor, then bent quickly to her work as Uncle Simon came right behind, hurling complaints into the back of his brother's head. Tamsin eyed her needle closely, threaded it.

"That field of yours, Robert, is a cursed rock graveyard. You

15

clear it late for planting, roots will be dead in a first freeze. You've gone and lost the season, brother –"

Tamsin gave attention to a long end of her thread, wound it round her fingertip.

Her uncle fairly shouted, "The mill needs that grain!"

She tugged her thread to a knot. At the first tuck she began to stitch, careful, neat.

Papa didn't answer, but sat in the wing chair at the hearth and took the Bible from its carved rowan-wood box. He opened the book and read silently.

Uncle Simon stood over him. "And would you work that rock *on a Sabbath*? Do you court damnation?"

Divine threat made her shift her eyes from the needle to her Papa. A corner of his mouth twitched, a tart bit of smile. Her eyes flicked to her uncle, to her needle, to Papa again, and to the linen in her lap. She wove her needle into the cloth so as to make five tiny stitches at once, and her thimble pushed the needle through. She did it again, and again, and again.

The air in the parlor bore the weight of two brothers at odds, one staring, one reading. It was a mercy they'd inherited assets that spanned land and water both, as the work scattered Bennetts wide across farm, mill, and bay, even out on the marsh to cut salt hay. Still, they shared only the one good house, and not often in comfort. So these evenings of reading scripture were meant to weave the Bennetts peaceably together. And to keep even the little ones listening to the Word of the Lord, Robert had made up a game. It did indeed catch and hold the children's interest, so every evening when the family gathered, they played.

Grandmother Cat came now to sit by Tamsin and see her work. A quick nod, it was good. Tamsin was adept with her needle, having finished a fine sampler when she was twelve.

Still Uncle Simon stared down at his brother. "Your luckless reading of scripture! You turn the Word of God to child's play, and a miserable example to your own." He stalked away at last to stand hunched in his habitual place by the east door, open to salt air and thinning light. This time of day galled him, he made no secret.

"Sacrilege!"

Tamsin looked aside to Grandmother Cat, whose eyes followed her sons. She addressed the elder of the two with a smile and a raised eyebrow.

"Your game does make for chancy biblical learning, Robert."

Tamsin knew the lift of that one brow meant teasing, so she watched.

"Is that true?" Papa showed surprise. "Is it chancy then, we should listen to the children? Are we not taught to become as little children ourselves?" He whispered to his mother as if confiding, "I think of Matthew's gospel!"

Grandmother Cat laughed. Tamsin looked to her stitching and hid her smile. Uncle Simon railed from his spot at the door.

"Your *game*, Robert! Haphazard! *Devilish!* Do you know your daughter now thinks to hear music in her ear *by magic?* So she told her grandmother." He cocked his head at Tamsin. "Watch out, brother, your rocky field spawns a new Witch of Endor."

Grandmother Cat's teasing went cold. "Simon. No."

Tamsin made herself go on stitching, but when her thimble pushed the needle through five tiny folds, a sharp point pricked her hard. She pressed her thumb over the blood, flicked a look at Papa, and lowered her eyes again to the linen. She had told Grandmother Cat that Uncle Isaac's music caught her in the field as if by magic, and she danced. She wondered now, was it Naomi or Ruth this time, who had tattled to Uncle Simon? She was glad she'd not said she imagined dancing with James or, for sure, they would have told him too, and then how could she face him when they milked the cows?

Uncle Simon turned his anger on Grandmother Cat. "Your mother *Priscilla –*"

Grandmother stopped him. *"Simon!"*

Papa said nothing of a witch, but raised his voice. "Simon!

Haphazard, you say? What of the vastness of God's created heaven? Is it not possible, even chance may point to the Lord? May we not trust?"

Tamsin's eyes looked at white linen, but saw a wide night sky as if from the very middle of the dam over the millstream – Pole Star to the north, tiny lights everywhere. Once when she was little, Tamsin told Papa the stars looked as though God had sneezed on the sky. Papa said yes, he had. "As above, so below," he said. And he taught her that now there were figures in the sky, with names. Mariners knew them. What looked to be heavenly disorder, he told her, were waymarkers that sea captains trusted.

As best Tamsin could tell, Uncle Simon, a deacon of the West Dorset parish, did not trust to heaven's light, nor to the breath of God, but relied on duties he believed assigned to him by the apostle Paul. Loud and often, he would remind the Bennetts of Paul's charge that deacons were to rule their houses and children. *"Their children and their own houses!"* he would repeat, though they all knew his elder brother Robert was the family's head.

In truth, Uncle Simon's rule over his children was frightening – his anger like a cookfire, judgment growled harsh in their ears, and a willow whip to hand. Evenings in the parlor, Tamsin would track his spirit by the creases at his eyes and restlessness in his feet. This might progress to a barely controlled twitching of one shoulder, and on stormy nights a tightness in his fists. Now a breeze kicked up in the doorway beside him, lifting dark curls above his head. Tamsin saw black flames. For what looked to plague Uncle Simon unbearably were the moments when Grandmother Cat laughed at a comment of Papa's on a verse of the Bible, or worse, when the children, curious each evening how the game would turn out, sat still and rapt as Papa read.

Aunt Adah now, ungainly, soon to give birth, came carrying Abigail on one hip and leading fidgety Luke by the hand. She put them on the settle by the hearth, and herself between them. On the edge of fussing, they would soon either fall asleep or follow the game.

"Adah is wan this evening," Grandmother Cat said quietly to Tamsin. "I'll send her to bed with nettle tea. Tomorrow, dear, you and I will take the coracle upstream and cut a load of new greens."

Tamsin smiled and stitched, then stopped with interest as James and Peter stumbled into the parlor, pushing at each other in good humor. Often they sparred and tangled, but did work well together. Tamsin saw how Peter admired James, a year older, and wished her brother would give her more regard than he did. Of the two, it was James who was warm and kind with Tamsin, when morning and evening they milked the Devon cows. He listened to her as if he believed she had sense, though younger and a girl. The boys took their accustomed bench, stretching out lanky legs.

Mother came now, and Phebe skipped in to find her sister. "Tamsin, what are you doing?"

"See, I'm stitching up these two shifts for you and Abigail."

Phebe patted the linen, then turned and slid down to sit on Tamsin's feet. Mother took a corner stool.

Last to the parlor were the twins Naomi and Ruth. They pointed and poked at Tamsin's work, and laughed. Perhaps they laughed simply to see their old shifts, but often they made light of Tamsin's work. It puzzled her, sometimes saddened her. They were near enough to her in age, she thought they might be friends, but they were not. She looked to her needle. At a bark from Uncle Simon, the twins whipped round and settled to the floorboards like birds to an autumn field.

From his place in the wing chair, Papa surveyed the gathered Bennetts and smiled at his mother. Grandmother Cat smiled back, and he began.

"All here? Good then, who will tell me what book we shall think on tonight?"

James erupted with an answer. "Mine tonight! The Book of James."

Tamsin watched the boys. James avoided his father's eyes, and Peter looked sideways. Something was going to happen.

"James," he said, "Is that the one you like to speak of? The one about *lusts that war in your members?*" Peter reveled in the words, "*Ye lust and have not!* That one?"

Tamsin smiled down at the linen in her lap. Uncle Simon shifted noisily, sending James rebuke. Papa stared Peter to silence, and the boys ducked their heads, smothering their laugh.

Grandmother Cat whispered to no one, "They are so like my Thomas!"

Tamsin wished she had known him, her Grandfather Thomas who died on the day she was born, and who might have been like James.

"Very well," said Papa, "This evening the Book of James. And reading from what chapter then? What do you say, how old might one of you be?"

He looked about and found Phebe, one small hand held high, all her fingers spread wide. "Four!" she said.

"Four? Are you sure? Not five?"

"Four!" she said firmly and clambered over the twins to get to her Papa's knee, where she had learnt her numbers from the Bible.

"Right then, chapter four. Anyone else?"

"Thirteen, Uncle." Naomi spoke up. "I'm thirteen."

Ruth prodded her. "I'm thirteen *too*."

Their Uncle Robert smiled. "Good. And how many verses shall we have tonight?"

"Oh, just two, please, Robert," Aunt Adah said. "These two and I must lie down soon." One arm around Luke, one around Abigail, she kept them on the settle.

Papa nodded. "Good. Reading from the Book of James, then" – he smiled at Phebe – "chapter four" – and at Naomi, elbowed again by Ruth – "beginning at the thirteenth verse."

Naomi elbowed Ruth back.

The parlor was quiet, as the boys' joking had roused a certain interest. Tamsin looked aside at the pair of them. James winked at her. She smiled and looked to her stitching.

Papa read: "*Go to now, ye that say, Today or tomorrow we will go into such a city, and continue there a year, and buy and sell, and get gain. Whereas ye know not what shall be on the morrow. For what is your life? It is even a vapour that appeareth for a little time, and then vanisheth away."*

Several long breaths, the parlor waited.

A wash of air swept in from the bay, a sudden break in the day's heat. Grandmother cast her eyes about and whispered to no one, "There is change afoot," and to Tamsin, "Is the light enough for your work, dear? Has it gone dim?"

Tamsin looked up from her needle with a discomfort she couldn't name.

Papa scanned the parlor, saying at last, "James, what shall we make of your choice?"

"I don't know, Uncle," he shrugged. "We grow our crops, we mill. We take the shallop out to fish. We sail to Newbury and Salem, buy and sell. Is it for nothing?"

No answer came until, surprised, Tamsin heard Mother speak up from the corner with uncommon strength.

"No, James, not for nothing. Our work is everything – all to care for one another, grateful. You must know, James, how soon our lives end. The garden, the fields, the mill –" She shook her head. "They're never for nothing, James. All for love."

Tamsin thought of Mother's first husband, the French sea captain lost twenty or more years ago, and for the first time felt Mother's sadness inside her own heart. Phebe stepped away from Papa, tipped her head to look at her mother, and went to her. Mother smiled, tears wet in her face. She gathered Phebe onto her lap and held her close. "Life appears for such a little time, James, and it vanishes away."

Tamsin felt now how lost she would be if James were to die. Her eyes somehow went to Uncle Simon. Strange, he held a fist tight to his heart, a gesture she'd never once seen him make. Fading light or an unlikely breath of compassion blurred the etchings in his face. Gusts stiffened off the bay. His eyes turned and locked on Tamsin, fist flung back to pound the door hard shut. His face went tight.

"Have a care, Susannah," he said. "'Tis not fitting, a woman should speak to a man on a matter of scripture. Eve betrayed Adam. No woman preaches to my son. Sure, no papist!"

Papa stood and wheeled round. "Simon, you will not!"

"I am not," Mother said softly.

Her uncle ignored them. "Yes, the mill gets us gain, the verse says. We do well enough now, but not –" His brow low, he stared at Aunt Adah, his youngest children nested against her great belly. "Mayhap not for long. And as to this farm, brother, Massachusetts soil blooms rock."

"That's as may be, Simon. But every spring, we do clear the winter-blooming rock, and the mill brings us a fair share of West Dorset corn."

Without answer, Simon pressed his back to the wall and cast a rough look at Susannah, as if she too threatened to be with child.

How was it, Tamsin wondered, a man could be so displeased at births in his own family? This good farm fed them all. It disturbed her, too, how bitterly he invoked God's judgment against Adam for hearing Eve, when it pleased Tamsin every day how willingly James listened to her.

Wind off the bay sharpened, slapping leaves about the house, warning of a summer night's gale.

Grandmother Cat watched her second son. "Simon," she said with force, "these children are ever a blessing and a help." She looked round at all of them, and said to Tamsin, "I am tired. Come help me get your Aunt Adah's tea. Adah, Tamsin will bring you nettle tea."

Tamsin put down her work, one shift nearly done. Before her on the floor, Ruth elbowed Naomi and the two tossed her a look of disdain.

In the kitchen Grandmother Cat studied her jars, labeled and arrayed on their shelves. She took several down. "We need more yarrow," she said. "Raspberry leaves. Burnet."

"Grandmother, why did Uncle Simon call me a new Witch of Endor? Was there an old one?"

"She's in the Book of Samuel, dear. She was a woman of skill who called on the prophet Samuel to speak to King Saul, so he would understand the work that lay before him. And when he was sore afraid, she was kind to him and fed him."

"Skill," Tamsin said. "Does Uncle Simon think I am like her?" She doubted her uncle thought her skillful. Still less, kind.

Grandmother Cat put on a smile, and her one teasing eyebrow went up. "Tamsin, you are more skillful and kind than your uncle chooses to know, so we'll leave that alone for the present. Nettles."

Doubtful, Tamsin climbed up on the stool, and from the top of the cabinet where tied herbs hung dry in the dark, she brought out the nettles. In handing them down, however, she found Grandmother Cat distracted, looking away to the hearth. The kitchen held a sudden quiet. As Tamsin stepped down, a pricking ran up the skin of her neck, all the way up inside her cap. Grandmother Cat, face alight, spoke to empty air.

"Our Robert read this evening, *Life is a vapor that appeareth and vanisheth*. We know it well, don't we, love?"

She smiled wistfully, then more openly. "You see how she grows up lively and willful. So like my mother."

She looked at Tamsin with warm concern, and again toward the hearth. "There is much for her to know."

She waited, then nodded.

"'Tis near time."

4

What Grandmother Cat meant that evening, speaking into the air as she did, Tamsin was too bewildered and tired at this hour to ask. And whyever would Uncle Simon liken her to a witch who was good to King Saul? On the one hand, if he meant to judge her ill, why would he think it shameful to help a biblical king? On the other hand, she didn't believe her uncle meant to speak well of her, as he never had before.

She carried hot nettle tea to Aunt Adah and sat with her while she drank it, wondering about a kind witch in the Bible.

Tamsin had long known that imponderable things could swarm in her mind like bees on milkweed. She was unsure why these things should visit her alone, as they didn't seem to bother Peter or James, and surely not the twins. She thought her wondering must have begun early, when she was six, when Grandmother Cat first took her out in the coracle, the craft she would row upstream to forage for herbs. It was such a curious thing, different in every possible way from Papa's plain dory. The dory, Tamsin understood perfectly, even at the age of six. It was wooden, with a prow, and it moved forward through water with two long oars pressing back.

But this coracle of Grandmother's was another creature altogether, its own endless question. Hempen skin tarred over a split-willow frame, it had no prow at all, but was rounded like an egg and rested atop the stream like a featherweight basket. Strangest of all, it came to life with only a single rowan-wood oar passing side to side – *out in front* – as if all the slight vessel needed to slip upstream was the sweep of a water-broom.

Imagining this once, she asked Grandmother Cat about the water-broom. But Grandmother only shut her eyes tight and said a broom had nothing whatever to do with it. She said her mother Priscilla called it by the ancient word, *oar*. It was a sort of a paddle only. Nothing else. Tamsin accepted this, reasoning that water, when pushed, did not stay still, like ashes or leaves, but only ruffled and rippled back. She knew this from playing at the millpond.

But by the time she was eight, she knew more about water. She understood that when water fell from the headrace at the dam onto the troughs of the millwheel, it pushed down hard into the stream below. Water was the heavy weight that turned the stones to grind the grain. That being so, then how could – not a broom, of course, but a sort of paddle – *work out in front* – so the coracle would row *into* the weighty water of the stream?

As years passed, Tamsin found herself so puzzled by the coracle that she thought to abandon her questioning altogether and believe instead, in wayward reaches of her mind, that this breath of a craft was simply magical, and that's all there was to it.

Yet she knew for certain that to say such a thing aloud would be folly, especially within earshot of Ruth and Naomi. Without doubt, one or the other would speed her words to Uncle Simon, and then in the evening, whatever scripture was read, he would twist its meaning to find fault with Tamsin before the family. So she knew to bridle her unruly thoughts, unless away from the house with

Grandmother Cat, or with Papa. Or sometimes, very carefully, with James in the barn. Or as long as possible, keep her reasoning and imagining quite to herself about mysteries like the coracle, or Papa's sundial-compass that held earth and heaven together as one, or Uncle Isaac's fiddle music, so astonishing it might slip over into magic at any moment and lift her in the air to dance.

ONCE TAMSIN'S RESTRAINT PROVED WISE, AFTER MR. Joseph Briggs came to replace old Mr. Ingersoll in the West Dorset parish. Among all the interesting things that young Mr. Briggs might have preached on, he chose to speak often and with alarm on the unchristian practice of magic in Massachusetts. On one Sabbath of his particular distress, Tamsin listened closely. To follow his argument, she laid her two hands in her lap, palms up. She imagined stacking Mr. Briggs' preachments in one hand, her left hand, and weighing them up with her own observations of the world in her right.

Mr. Briggs held many opinions. Not only did he denounce as ungodly the consulting of planets (to know the fortune of a newborn, or a voyage) and the reading of palms (Tamsin looked quickly down at her own, then quickly back up again), but he also condemned the common nailing of an iron horseshoe to the beam of a barn (to keep the animals healthy and safe).

Given his opinions, she was glad Mr. Briggs did not know of the small rowan-wood crosses bound with red thread that Grandmother Cat had made. Tamsin herself had gone up the ladder in the barn and tucked them atop the beam to protect the lives sheltered under that roof. She was fairly certain Uncle Simon did not know about them, either. There had been no stormy discussion. Nor must he have seen the shadowed place where Papa had nailed up the horseshoe. At least, her uncle had not ranted on it.

Despite Mr. Briggs' preaching, however, Tamsin had with her own eyes seen him hammer an iron nail into the corner beam of the meetinghouse, right there beside the nail of old Mr. Ingersoll. Indeed, from where she sat in the family's box pew, she could see both those very nails, right now. Mr. Ingersoll had driven his iron nail into that corner beam to protect the new meetinghouse from bad spirits, and when Mr. Briggs came, he had done exactly the same thing.

Pondering the Lord's distinction, then, between the iron of a horseshoe and the iron of a nail, Tamsin was enjoyably occupied through both morning and afternoon sermons that Sabbath.

On Monday she took the riddle to Papa at the mill.

Tide was up, high water rushing across the headrace and dropping hard down to roil under the millwheel. It made a sound like a nor'easter closing in. With that came the rush, rattle, and squeak of the mill's own mechanical storm. Papa and Uncle Simon were both there, Uncle Simon upstairs on the grain floor, feeding Indian corn from bin to hopper, Papa below on the meal floor, where the turning of millstones edged ground corn out a spout, down a trough. Papa took up bits of ground meal in his fingers, rubbing to feel the texture was good, while he listened to Tamsin weigh Mr. Briggs' views of magic.

At last he laughed. "Briggs, the ninny! Tamsin, he'd best never try to dispute with you, you'd beat him hollow. And before he stoops to find fault with a horseshoe, I'd have him look again at Matthew's gospel." Over the sounds of the mill, Papa declaimed –

"Why beholdest thou the mote that is in thy brother's eye, but considerest not the beam that is in thine own eye?"

Tamsin listened closely and gave due consideration to the Lord's manner of weighing things. She felt it in her hands, a speck in one, the mass of a timber beam in the other. And as to *"thy brother's eye"* – did the Lord weigh brothers too? This bore thinking.

She did not hear Uncle Simon come down to the meal floor, but there he stood as Papa went on, "Tamsin, that horseshoe in the barn does no offense to God. Nor is it even a mote in a man's eye. But Briggs!" With force he scooped milled corn, trough to sack. "He's glad to poke another man's eye, though not clever enough to see the beam athwart both his own."

He smiled broadly. "And whether that beam in his eyes be the roof beam of a barn or the corner beam of a meetinghouse, Tamsin," he said, "the fool is dead blind either way!"

Tamsin pressed a hand to her mouth so not to laugh, but Uncle Simon's face swelled up purple. Empty grain sacks were a mess in his hand and he thrust them hard at Tamsin, shoving her backward. "Be useful, girl, fold these. And never think to mock a man of God. It speaks ill of your predestined soul." He rounded on the stairs, snarling, "As it does of your father's."

Uncle Simon's words were his ordinary bile, but what caught Tamsin's ear were the things Papa had *not* said. He had *not* said that the nailing of iron was powerless against baneful spirits. *Nor* had he said it was ungodly to call in the strength of iron against those spirits. Tamsin was glad there was a horseshoe in the barn, fixed to the beam above her good Devon cows and the oxen.

In fact, Papa had said nothing at all about magic, but only that Mr. Briggs was possessed of two eyes that could not see truth. That being so, then however could he preach on magic?

Or indeed on anything at all?

5

NOW, ON THIS AUGUST DAY THAT MARKED HER FIFTEEN years, Tamsin thought of the verse that Papa once spoke out loud at the mill. A person could be blind and not know it. Mr. Briggs could pound an iron nail in a beam to ward off evil spirits, yet preach against magic, and be a hypocrite. Therefore, she'd not believe the splintering of Papa she'd seen that morning, for later she'd seen him whole and real and ready to work the mill.

The calamity of the wheat, however – that surely did happen, near a disaster, but she'd done her best, and after her, the boys would too. So on the day she would ponder once more the mystery of her birth and life, she rejoiced to be out with Grandmother Cat, sky clear, earth firm underfoot, and soon the slip of water under the coracle's hemp skin. All would be well. Surely all would be well, as she and Grandmother were to go upstream.

For many years, Grandmother had taken Tamsin up the millstream to gather herbs for food, injuries, or ills of the seasons. Today they wanted greens and roots for Aunt Adah. Grandmother Cat had her knife to cut a sackful of dandelion greens. Tamsin had her scissors in her pocket to cut raspberry leaves and save her fingers from thorny cane. What she liked best, though, was squishing bare feet into the stream edges to pull burnet, yet another remarkable thing – for though burnet grew wet, its gift was to heal a wound by drying and drawing it closed. Together, Tamsin and Grandmother Cat would look for yarrow and shepherd's purse, and all along, they would talk.

Grandmother often told Tamsin stories of the Rowan family who had left Brampton Bryan, at the border with Wales. When Royalist soldiers had burnt their village and looted farms in a war about religion, Grandmother Cat's grandmother Margaret gathered up her family and goats, her herbs, seed of the Red Lammas wheat, and a sack of rowanberries, and brought them across the ocean to Massachusetts. Here, for protection, Margaret planted rowanberries all round her house, and the trees grew up strong. Then Margaret's daughter Priscilla took rowanberries and Red Lammas seed to the homestall she'd helped her Samuel to find. And after that, Priscilla's Catherine planted Red Lammas on the gentle southerly aspect of the Bennetts' hill. She put rowanberries in the ground by the millstream, so now the wise rowans flourished at the head of the mill path by the bridge, and on the far side of the bridge too.

GRANDMOTHER CAT AND TAMSIN WENT TO THE BARN to take the coracle, a hemp sack, and baskets down from a line of pegs, and carried them out to the stream. Grandmother always held the coracle by its rim on one side, Tamsin held the other. This morning it tilted awkwardly, though, so Tamsin dropped her shoulder to level it. Willowy and light, it floated in the air between them till they set it down in the shallows.

Then came the touchy matter of getting them both into it without Tamsin putting a foot wrong, tipping in a slosh of water. This, she had done when she was younger. At fifteen, she was still abashed at the memory, but now stepped neatly in and settled beside her grandmother, pleased to have done it.

Yet Grandmother Cat smiled sadly at her. "Tamsin, my dear,

you've grown so this summer. My coracle won't do for us another season."

"Grandmother? No!"

The thought turned Tamsin's morning to shambles again. Her heart refused.

If this were true – if this were to be her last day in the coracle with her Grandmother Cat – on the same day a whole field of Red Lammas had gone down in a wind – *and beyond that*, on the day her Papa looked to split all out into stars, *even if that didn't happen* – then nothing could ever make sense again on the face of this green earth.

So much misfortune on the very day that marked the day she'd been born here and stayed – was there meaning in this for her life?

"Grandmother, no," she said. "You will teach me how and I will row for you. I have the strength and I know the rowing of the dory, two oars." She made two fists and pulled them back. "But the coracle has only the one oar. You put it in the water *out in front* and it turns this way, and that." She made an uncomfortable twist of her hand. "How do you go *upstream* then, and not back?"

"My dear, I only mean to say, small as I am, the two of us are nearly too big now for this one bit of a boat."

Tamsin held her breath in case there were further calamity, but Grandmother Cat said nothing. She flicked her wrist, and the little craft made clever progress away from the bank toward the yarrow and burnet and all they sought upstream.

In a while, Grandmother spoke.

"When we're out foraging, Tamsin, do we ever walk a straight line to a patch of herb? No?" She rowed farther on, an oar slipping through water. "This millstream," she said, "does it run straight down to the sea? No, a stream bends one way –" Grandmother Cat turned her oar, a stroke to the left. "And it bends another," a stroke to the right. "Do you see?"

Tamsin shook her head. She saw only the riddle she'd seen all her life.

"Imagine then, dear, and your eyes may show you something new – the unexpected," she said, a lilt in her voice, a flick of her wrist on the oar.

So Tamsin let her eyes wander as they would until, of their own volition, they showed her Grandmother's strokes, not so much pushing as making slight loops. With a small turn of her wrist, Grandmother's oar formed a loop in the water to one side, and without lifting up, slipped to a loop on the other side. Tamsin let her eyes follow, and follow, and follow more until, just in front of the coracle, the loops left and right showed themselves linked, transformed into figures of eight, and then one after another, after another, the many figures of eight did not so much puzzle the mind as enchant the spirit with their seeming-unending movement in the stream.

"Heed the unexpected, dear," Grandmother said, and Tamsin saw with her heart the thing that was invisible – the point at the exact center of each figure of eight. And as she heeded one point, and the next point, and the next, each unseen to her eyes, her heart felt the way forward to the work she and Grandmother Cat were meant to do.

"Remember this, dear," Grandmother said. "Remember the feeling. 'Twill be a sign to you of your path."

And on this day that marked Tamsin's birth, the day she wondered at the mystery of her being, she kept this and pondered it in her heart.

6

GRANDMOTHER CAT ROWED ON AND TAMSIN WATCHED her, watched her loops, and thought of the unexpected. Papa had said she could tell Grandmother the unearthly thing she'd seen in the kitchen. She had heard it too. But the words would not come. Grandmother Cat spoke instead.

"Tamsin, you know my father Samuel Tobin was a clever man. He asked many questions and found his own answers. He farmed and fished and built a shallop for sailing and trading along the coast. He grew hemp and took it to the ropewalk and sail-makers in Salem. He had a hand in everything. My mother Priscilla Rowan was different. She asked few questions, but she saw everything and knew even more."

"She taught you the use of herbs and how to make the coracle."

Grandmother Cat cocked her head. "Tamsin, I do wonder sometimes whether you are more Tobin or Rowan. Like my father, you ask questions and you do what you want. But like my mother Rowan, you see more than others do."

Was that true? Tamsin watched the water twist this way and that, round the oar. Behind her eyes she knew the same confusion and turned her face to the trees.

33

In a while, they came to the low bank of the meadow, where they could step out mostly dry-shod and lift the coracle up onto mosses and grass. It was a good place, dandelions thick. Raspberry cane grew on the bank farther up, and burnet with its feet in the water. Up the rise toward the woods grew plenty of yarrow, and they knew a good patch of shepherd's purse taking over old Mr. Oliver's abandoned garden, just beyond.

They took their baskets and walked toward the hill, warm in the sun. Tamsin was both hopeful and fearful. She cast about for a way to tell Grandmother Cat what she'd seen of Papa, and she wished, in return, Grandmother would tell her of the wondrous Priscilla Rowan, who was mentioned only quietly in the family. If a thing so impossible had happened with Papa, what mischance had come to her?

"Yes, dear, 'twas my mother who taught me the use of herbs, and her mother taught her, with seeds and roots from home, and new plants here." She laughed. "Yes, my mother taught me, in ways I won't forget."

Tamsin felt a story to come. "Tell!"

"Once when I was little, I tangled myself up in poisonvine away down Dawkins Creek and the next morning woke in a fearsome fit of itching. My mother plunged my clothes in water and soap and marched me back down there in my shift to where I'd found that patch of trouble. Then she made me sit out in the briny cold water to douse the itch, while she searched the creek bank for jewelweed. When she had a great orange-flowered bunch of it, she let me come onto the bank and we pounded the stems to a mash between stones. Then she made me rub the mash all over where I itched, while she made fun of my complaining by reciting from the Psalms."

With spirit, Grandmother Cat called into the air, *"Hearken unto the voice of my cry, my King!"* She raised her arms up, baskets and all. *"My voice shalt thou hear in the morning, O Lord!"*

Tamsin laughed at Grandmother waving her arms and telling verses to the sky. But there was darkness underneath. What happened to a mother who shouted psalms for her daughter in fun?

Grandmother smiled. "She was a skillful woman, was my mother – gathering, preparing, dosing, or simply touching with her hands. Anyone who fell ill felt better for her presence." Looking away, she said, "Almost anyone."

Now spread across the hillside was a vast drift of tiny, uncountable stars. Here was the yarrow. Every single yarrow flower was a white multitude above a green stalk that sprouted little leaves, each leaf like a fine feather. Tamsin thought, if ever she could see what a single breath looked like, it would look just like a yarrow flower. Grandmother Cat moved, adrift herself, toward a patch of fine white. Tamsin followed, and there they wandered, cutting and gathering flowers, stems, and leaves into a basket.

In Grandmother's long silence, Tamsin wondered if she might be sad, thinking, as Tamsin was, of Priscilla.

At last Grandmother said, "Breathe, Tamsin. What do you smell?"

She took a long breath of the air. "Sweet," she said, "and light."

"Now the bloom."

Tamsin took short sniffs of the tiny flowers. "Sweet. Do bees make honey from yarrow?"

Grandmother smiled. "Now the leaves."

Tamsin sniffed them too. "A little sharp, clean. I feel it inside my nose."

"And how does your spirit?"

Then Tamsin understood. She was a bit less lost. Clearer, she felt some ease. "Does yarrow lift the spirit then?"

"Herbs make themselves out of earth and sky, and having done so, give their soul to the air as scent. Scent is one way that we learn their gift. And yarrow's gift?" Grandmother waited.

Tamsin looked across the hillside and was comforted. "Light. A day full of stars."

Grandmother didn't respond, but the longer they sat working among the yarrow, the lighter Tamsin felt, and perhaps they both did. Grandmother Cat spoke again.

"There's a story told in the family," she said. "Long before I was born, my father Samuel Tobin built his first dwelling over at Winnipeseekett, by the fishing stage. But then he complained that, while the place was fine for fishing, it was too rocky for planting. So my mother Priscilla – of the Rowan line, mind you – looked away across the water."

Grandmother lifted her head and smiled far over the meadow to the upland. "And she told him she saw good saltmarsh and, beyond it, some tillable land and a fresh creek. My father understood the woman she was, and believed in her sight. So he went across in the shallop and saw what she had seen, and he bought the grant of old Mr. Graffam. There they flourished, because of what my mother could see, away across the water."

Tamsin followed Grandmother Cat's eyes to the upland and sky. What had Grandmother meant, saying Tamsin might be like Priscilla? If she were, could she see far away? What was it she'd seen of Papa, right there in front of her face? But he was entirely well and at work in the mill. Had she seen nothing at all?

Now she made bold to ask, and thought before she spoke, "Grandmother, what happened to Priscilla Rowan? Was it terrible?"

For a while Grandmother Cat was quiet, cutting yarrow. "I was a little girl and it was terrible. But my mother lived to a good age." She looked up at her granddaughter. "Don't be uneasy, Tamsin. She lived well and long enough to see her children settled. She saw me in love and married to Thomas Bennett, your grandfather, who never once held the accusations against us."

"What –"

"You know you're named Thomasin for him, a good man," she said, and returned to cutting.

Tamsin did know and was glad of it, but still she asked, "What happened?" Grandmother Cat breathed in the yarrow.

"So much happened, that no one can bear to look too hard. A bitter deep winter and chill spring froze the souls of Massachusetts. My father said farmers barely hoped any longer for planting. Then a droughty hot summer dazed them. Settlers back from Maine spread fear of Indians, and a plague of smallpox came up out of Boston. Everywhere was sickening and death."

Tamsin gripped a stem of yarrow, but did not cut it.

"When loss is so great, then great blame will follow. Ministers preached fear in the meetinghouses, asking why God should punish us so. Who was it, had angered him? Neighbors suspected neighbors. In the midst of it, my mother's care was sought for sick children, and when she couldn't soothe two madly fevered sisters – no, Tamsin, not even shouting psalms to the sky – then terrible accusations were flung up."

"Who accused her? Of what?"

Grandmother Cat worked in silence now, then stood up and walked away toward Mr. Oliver's overgrown garden. Tamsin followed after her.

"Grandmother?"

"Ah, what a load of shepherd's purse is here, Tamsin. Very good for Adah after the birth." She settled herself on the ground and quickly began cutting leaves. Tamsin sat and cut leaves too, and waited. At last Grandmother spoke.

"My mother Priscilla was an uncommon woman. You see, she could read and write better than most men, and make all her remedies." She looked at Tamsin, then back to her work. "Tamsin, do you know that some folk mistrust healing?"

Tamsin did not know.

"When those who are ill become well, then some may fear by what power the healing was done."

"By what power? The herbs. Rowan-wood crosses." She thought further. "Priscilla's words. Her hands. Words and figures on linen, wrapped round an ailing part."

Grandmother Cat cut leaves in silence, then pushed her hands down flat on the ground in the shepherd's purse. "But if the sick should sicken more, then even greater suspicion will come. Accusations."

Tamsin held very still.

"Besides that, my father did well in all his trade. There's some, thought others were jealous. I don't know. I was little then, and though I saw much, it was a child's view."

A child's view. Tamsin looked closely at Grandmother Cat, who was the eldest of the family and the wisest. She thought, Grandmother Cat once had a child's view. Then she tried to imagine herself elderly and wise, but couldn't see that far.

"One day Mother spent a long morning, well before dawn till noon, baking journeycakes and her good meat pies. She sent me out to pick the peas that were ready, and I sat on the floor, shelling them. After a while, Mr. Graffam's grandson came running in with a message, a whisper that found its way along the road, mile by mile, from farm to house to farm. A constable would come that day."

"A constable."

Grandmother's voice was low. "Mother knew. She knew he'd come."

"Did you know what a constable was?"

"No, and I doubt the Graffam boy did either. But Mother told him to go home through the woods and speak to no one, and off he ran like a rabbit. Then she gathered together our baskets and sacks and filled them with all the food we had in the house and whatever was ripe from the garden. When my father came in at midday, he saw it all at once. He knew. He said, 'I'll get the boys,' and went right out.

"She said, 'Tell Daniel, bring the coracle.'"

7

GRANDMOTHER CAT STOOD UP, MOVED HERE AND there, scanned the ground for another patch of herb, a different place to sit, restless. Tamsin watched till she settled, moved to be near her, and waited.

"Mother made me help her fetch our warm wool coats and cloaks. I said to her, 'It isn't winter.' 'No, but it's near fall,' she said, and she told me we would sail over to the shed at Winnipeseekett, so we'd best take our sturdy woolens. I asked why, but she only told me to be quick. I was little help, but things got bundled together, down to the shallop. My brothers stowed sacks and baskets under the deck with the fishing nets and tied the coracle down so it wouldn't lift in a breeze. Gabe stayed behind for the animals, though he was young. He was good with them, the cows, even the ox. Then we cast off and got away."

"Grandmother, what was –"

"My dear, what that little girl knew best that day was fear and speed." She got up and moved away.

Tamsin's belly in a knot, she stayed where she sat. Lifting the basket of yarrow to her face, she breathed long and slow, then pulled three whole stalks, blooms, leaves and all. She crushed and rubbed them between her hands and slipped them in the two pockets inside her petticoats, so they would lie near her skin. A tea would do better, she knew, but at this moment she could hold the yarrow close for its power to ease cramp and – as she'd now learnt – lift spirit. She felt to her surprise that the more she attended to the herb, the more she understood it. She found herself listening to the yarrow as to a note of Uncle Isaac's fiddle, rising up from quiet. The note grew inside her, then bloomed out to surround her. With that, the fear in her belly eased. She listened with her body to the unexpected, barely heard note until Grandmother Cat called, "Tamsin."

Now with less fear and cramp, she moved closer to Grandmother's story and cut more shepherd's purse.

With an eye on Tamsin, Grandmother went on. "Isaac and Daniel worked hard at the oars, Father at the stern with the tiller. Mother and I sat close near the bow and she put her arms around me. I remember the warm corn smell of her journeycakes. I wanted to go home." Grandmother stopped. "Tamsin, are you well?"

"I'm listening."

A curt nod, she said, "We were underway. I remember asking Mother, 'Where is Peseekett?' and she corrected me, 'Winnipeseekett. It means *good water all round*. The Pawtucket named it. It's nearly an island, with good water on this side, and good water on the other side, and snug coves on both sides.' She gave me a kiss. 'And there's fish everywhere and clams when the tide is out.'

"And you know I like clams! So, though I was afraid, I knew one good thing about this journey." Tamsin saw that Grandmother wanted to cheer her, so she smiled.

Pressing a mass of fresh-cut leaves down into its basket, Grandmother Cat measured with her eye. "That's a good lot of shepherd's purse. Down to the meadow now. Burnet and greens."

They set off again down the hill, meadow spread before them. Questions wanted to tumble out of Tamsin's mouth, but she held tight to them, so Grandmother would say more of Priscilla Rowan.

"The boys worked hard to get us away past Walker's Point, where Father said we'd catch a breeze, and so we did, a good southwest wind. Father said it would be a broad reach to the cove he wanted, and somehow the sound of that comforted me. He raised the sails, and when my brothers shipped the oars, I crept back to sit with Isaac. My eldest brother, I always felt safe with him. I asked him where Peseekett was, and he pointed.

"'Your Peseekett is two miles that way, Catkin.' And he laughed. 'Peseekett! Pa's seeking it today, isn't he, Cat? Sharp as he can.'"

Tamsin laughed at her great-uncle Isaac's joke and ran a few steps ahead to the meadow. Uncle Isaac lived up the coast to Colbrook, building dories and shallops. Tamsin was glad when he came to visit. When she was little, he used to scoop her up and swing her round in the air. Even now, he called Grandmother "Catkin."

"Yes, Tamsin, your great grandfather was seeking Winnipeseekett, and he found it. His good southwest wind took us right there. When we came in close, he lowered the sails, and my brothers rowed us into a narrow cove. Daniel dropped anchor, stepped out into the water, and made the shallop fast between a tree on one side and a rock on the other. I wanted to get out and help him and splash, but Isaac lifted me high in the air, swung me round till I laughed, and landed me on the shingle."

"Uncle Isaac used to swing me in the air too!"

Grandmother did not smile. "Then my father helped Mother to step from the shallop."

Grandmother stopped still before the stream, all her lightness gone. She looked away at something Tamsin couldn't see and spoke slow. "Mother settled on a stone and pulled me onto her lap. She held me like a little baby and rocked me. Strange.

"Then Daniel loosed the coracle from the deck and laid it down beside her on the shingle with the oar, and I saw two rivers of tears in his face, such as I'd never seen. So I held on tight to Mother, tight as ever I could. He put things in the coracle. Her cloak, a basket, a sack. And he and Isaac carried the rest away up a steep bank into the woods. It frightened me terribly to see them go. Then Father sat down, and Mother told me who the constable was, and why he was coming."

Grandmother Cat gave a quiet gasp, shut her eyes tight, and held very still.

When she spoke again, she said, "Tamsin, take off your shoes and stockings, tuck up your gown. Go pull the burnet, stalk and root. I'll cut the greens."

"Grandmother –"

"Go now." She took the sack and her knife and walked away.

Tamsin wanted to go after her, but did as she was told, and went ahead to the millstream, stepping in to where she could push her nose among tall, thready white blooms. She wanted a sweet fragrance, but there was none.

She knew how burnet was to be pulled. The roots of each reached out to others like a net, so pulling was a matter of lifting one stalk and tracing its roots with her fingers in the mud. Then she would cut far enough back from the stalk to bring up a length of root for drying, while leaving root enough for the ones that remained. She had the skill and liked the mud, so she waded in and did the work. When she had a dozen burnet tossed, root and stalk, upon the bank, she went to climb out after them.

Her feet, however, refused to leave the stream, her soles sucked down to stay. Toes, on their own, worked deep into the shifting soil of the stream bed. Earth oozed wet, holding her feet, as a great wave of stream water rolled up from below, splashing and spitting round her, high in the air. All she could see were drops and sparkles of the stream and, to her horror, Papa suspended in the midst. In a second, he vanished as a wilder surge rose up and pushed hard to buckle her legs. Feet uprooted from the mud, she tumbled under sideways, struggling. Every moment when her face broke from water to air, she gasped, only to be rolled under again, again, and again, till she felt a grab at her back and felt pulled away from the churn of the water. But at that, the current dragged harder on sodden petticoats and she was under again, still feeling a grip at her back – Grandmother Cat now lost in water too.

Tamsin shouted silent fury at the stream, *No! You will not have her!*

Overwhelmed with certainty, she knew she must find an edge. *Pull.*

Clawing underwater, she gripped mud that dissolved, stone that lifted useless. She swiped sideways against water that resisted her and caught a handful of burnet. Matted roots, she commanded, *Hold. Hold now. You are for healing.*

She worked to reach behind her and got a hand on a thin body at her back, *Hold me!*

Burnet root and Grandmother held. Working her feet against roots, one hand pulling at stalks, begging *please*, she felt her head hit rock at the bank. She released burnet, flung an arm to grip rock and pulled her face up, turned to pull Grandmother and held her gasping air. She dragged her up the bank, and the two of them dropped soaking across the roots and stalks of burnet thrown there.

"*Child! What ... happened?*"

"*That.* Wave, from *below,* knocked me. *Under.*"

"From below."

"There's no tide. It's too far."

Tamsin struggled up against wet linen. Her cap was snagged in the water. She fished it out with a stick, and looked for Grandmother Cat's. Still tied at her throat, it was sopped on the ground. She untied the strings and wiped hair from her grandmother's face, helped her to sit up and cough.

"Grandmother," she said, "this morning – I saw Papa –" Words would not make sense. "Papa, in the kitchen – *he broke all into sparks!*" Her hands fluttered showing what happened. "In the air, little *stars!* And then he came back. And just now he was in the stream again – *froth!*" She flicked her fingers. Whatever was there, was gone.

Grandmother's eyes watched Tamsin and turned to the stream.

"Life is a vapor," she whispered. *"It appeareth and it vanisheth away."*

The verse Papa had read last night, the same Grandmother said to the air in the kitchen. Tamsin heard scripture say almost what she meant.

Now Grandmother took Tamsin's hands and looked in her eyes.

"My dear Thomasin, listen to me. Our eyes look outward and, most times, they see what seems true. This is right and good. But some few of us have the gift – sometimes – of seeing what is, in fact, true."

Tamsin shook her head.

"You may be one who sees."

"No."

"My dear, you saw the truth. *We are all of us, earth and water, air and light. We appear and we vanish."*

"No!"

"I believe, Tamsin, you may be one like my mother. Come." Stuck in wet linen, with difficulty, Grandmother Cat stood. "We have enough burnet. Put it in the basket. We'll go."

Tamsin shook her head, disordered, unready. "We don't have –" She looked round the meadow as if the grasses would tell her. "We need raspberry leaves," she said, a hand pressed to the pocket where she had scissors and crushed yarrow.

"I've some put away dried. We'll take what we have now and go. Pick up your shoes. Baskets."

Grandmother stood watch until Tamsin peeled soaked petticoat from her ankles and moved toward the bank where they'd lodged the coracle. Together they lifted it into the stream, and Grandmother Cat stepped in, bracing with her oar as Tamsin held on. Next the shoes, baskets, and Tamsin stepped in.

But instead of tracing the ancient stroke in the water before them, Grandmother Cat sat still. She looked deep into the stream, then up to the trees where sunlight struck leaves and shone through. When she handed Tamsin the rowan-wood oar, her eyes were bright with tears.

"You are a rowess," she said.

8

Tamsin was shaken and clumsy, but with her hands on her grandmother's rowan-wood oar, she began to feel the slip of the water, and the rowan-wood itself taught her wrist what to do. Water and wood led them downstream. Through trees to the left, Tamsin could see pieces of the field where yesterday she had worked with Papa and Ethan, pulling stone and building fence. Ahead through trees, lay the barn, and when it came into view, Tamsin's heart flooded with delight, a sensation so big, she wondered if it might be "pride," as Mr. Briggs had preached on it, though this feeling had not the coldness he described. It was more like the joy she felt in watching a fledgling, when wings mustered its first lift above the nest.

In a moment, though, Aunt Adah appeared on the bank. She stood nearly in the water, holding her great belly in two hands, straining to look upstream. At the sight, all delight fled.

"Mother! Mother, come!"

"Adah, is it pains?" Grandmother Cat called back. "Your water? It's early, dear, be careful! Tamsin, see to the coracle and baskets. I'll get Adah inside." They touched the bank. Grand-

46

mother stepped fast and dry to reach Aunt Adah. Tamsin got out quickly, lifted the baskets, then the coracle.

"No, Mother, not my pains, not me. A terrible thing, Peter said! The boys went to the mill for Robert. He fell down under the wheel. James found him. Mother – Robert is dead!"

From far away Aunt Adah was heard to say, "Oh, Tamsin!"

Every color went grey. Tamsin did not breathe but was flat on the bank, and then there was a scent of yarrow and Grandmother Cat was holding her.

"I must go, I have to go," she said, struggling up. All colors grey, she found the path.

"Tamsin, wait. Adah, get my stick or I'll fall over the roots. Tamsin, I need you."

Only Grandmother Cat's voice could stop her mad run down the mill path. Grandmother needed her. She heard that. And so she made herself go slowly, but their steps were anguishing for the speed of her heart.

He is not dead. I know. I saw him splinter into light and I saw him come back. I know his white shirt. He walked on the milldam. He is there.

Grandmother Cat spoke quietly to Tamsin all the way to the dam. Tamsin heard nothing of what she said.

Robert lay on the bank by the milldam, his bruises and cracked bones terrible, his shirt and breeches wet, streaked and blotted red. One arm and his legs bent awry. James knelt beside him, sobbing, his clothes soaked a washed-out red, his hands bright red. From the edge of the millstream to the place where Papa lay, the grass was smeared where James had drawn him up. Peter knelt by James, doubled over, his face in his hands in the grass. Mother sat unmoving.

Tamsin dropped to the ground and cried out. She stroked her Papa's face and told him over and over how she loved him and she knew God would have him, such a good Papa. Grandmother Cat took her kerchief from her neck, still wet from the stream, and gave it to Tamsin, who wiped blood from her Papa's hurt face and told him more that she loved him. Grandmother Cat, weeping for her son, sank down to hold his widow, who at last broke and wailed.

Uncle Simon stood back, stricken pale, then walked unsteadily away downstream and returned pulling the dory in the water. He told Peter to get up and go to the barn, bring back an old sail. Simon made James help him get the dory round the dam to the mill pond. Peter came back with a sail that once rigged the shallop and put it on the ground beside Papa. Simon moved as if to help lift his brother to the sail, but he couldn't. He turned away to lean and retch against a tree. So Grandmother Cat rose up. Peter and James lifted her firstborn onto the canvas, and she folded it over him. The boys carried Robert to the dory. Peter on one side, James on the other, they waded upstream, pulled him to the house.

Uncle Simon, stony, supported Grandmother Cat on the walk up the mill path, in case she should fall. Tamsin held onto Susannah and they followed. Tamsin had no memory, later, of all that inconceivable walk.

It was the night of the new moon, darkest that ever could be. The boys had laid Papa on the bed under the slant roof of the lean-to by the kitchen. In this little room, women endured their labors, babies were born or stillborn, sicknesses ended, and the dead of the family laid out in their turn.

Tamsin could not bear to be upstairs with the children, but crept down to sit alone with her Papa. She lit a candle from the kitchen and put it on the table beside Papa's head. Making no sound, she moved the low stool close to him, folded the sail back, and sat. She reached out to stroke his hands and face, waxen. Though it was August, she was cold.

"Papa, I'm sorry. I didn't know," she wept. "I didn't understand. I didn't know what the lights meant. Papa, come back. I did see you come back once."

Movement in the kitchen.

"Papa!"

Silence.

"Oh, Papa, truly I didn't know. I would have told you. I would have stayed with you, and then you'd still be here. Papa, I need you."

Tamsin put her face down beside him, muffled her sobs, and fell asleep.

At dawn, when she got up and went into the kitchen, James was asleep there, his head on the table. He woke.

"I heard you come down. You said you would have told him something, what?"

She couldn't answer. "What happened?"

"I don't know. There were branches in the pond. The wind. Some caught in the headrace. He must have tried to –" James looked away. "There's – breakage – in the wheel, in the troughs. He fell between the dam and the wheel."

Tamsin's sight went dark. She took hold of James' arm. "Thank you for bringing him up."

They held onto each other and sobbed.

That morning, Grandmother Cat and Susannah washed Robert and wrapped him in clean linen. Uncle Simon said Robert must be buried that day, because the next day he and the boys would have to thresh the wheat. After milking then, James and Peter went out to the Bennetts' burying ground to pull stone and dig a grave.

Tamsin looked after Phebe and the little cousins, wanting only to be outdoors under God's wide heaven where Papa would see her. So she took them out to the new rye field and gave them work to do. They were to pick up small rocks, pebbles even, and put them on top of the stone fence that she and Papa had begun.

She told them that Papa, Uncle Robert, would see them from heaven and be glad of their help.

Uncle Simon built his brother's coffin. From the field, Tamsin could hear him in the barn pounding his hammer with terrible force. Naomi and Ruth ran to tell Mr. Briggs that their uncle was dead, so the minister came to pray and recite a psalm. He said he would send word round the parish, Robert Bennett was killed in an accident at the mill.

ROBERT WAS BURIED AT SUNSET. UNCLE SIMON DROVE the horsecart with Robert's coffin. Grandmother Cat and Susannah rode with him, the rest walked behind. Tamsin held Phebe's hand and stayed close to James. They were followed by a dozen West Dorset farmers whose corn Robert had milled. They went out the old road to the hillside where the Bennetts were, and laid him down among them.

IN THE EVENING WHEN THE FAMILY GATHERED, UNCLE Simon had already taken the wing chair at the hearth and the Bible from its box. Asking no help from the children, he read from the Book of Matthew some verses Tamsin found painful nonsense. He read of a stone so bad that a builder had thrown it away, but then the Lord made the builder take and use it for a cornerstone.

A cornerstone!

Was it possible Tamsin knew better than God how to build a stone wall? Had He intended that wall to fail? Worse, Uncle Simon read that if a man were to fall upon that stone, he would be broken. Her hands went to fists. The Lord God did not mean her Papa to fall. How could her uncle read this rot, his own brother now broken between wood and stone? He read further, that if the stone were to fall on a man, he would be ground to powder.

To powder.

The word stunned her soul. She turned to the window and imagined her heart out in the rowan trees, so her stomach would not vomit in the parlor. Uncle Simon, vile deacon, invoking the Lord to read Papa's family cruel rubbish.

Tamsin looked to Grandmother Cat to see if she would speak, but her mouth was a thin line. She turned to Mother, but her eyes on Uncle Simon were wide and dark, and she said nothing. Nor did any of them say anything, but in silence Tamsin got up, then Naomi and Ruth, and they took the children to bed.

9

THE NEXT DAY, THE STRONGEST ARMS AMONG THE Bennetts went out to the hillock to flail dried grain upon a canvas. Unnamed feelings and forces were spent in beating a field of wheat off its stalks. Afterward, at the top of the rise, the Bennett girls tossed flailed grain into the air from winnowing baskets, and watched breezes off the bay vanish the chaff. It was the one time in the year when Tamsin felt at all close to Naomi and Ruth, when the three danced together with baskets, wheat, and salt air. This time, she felt only alone.

The wheat was scooped into sacks then, and carried across the dam to be milled, with a measure kept aside for the planting soon to come. The straw went up to the barn and henhouse. Priscilla Rowan had taught young Catherine that the pile of soiled old henhouse bedding was to be taken and dug into the bare fields, so in the week after the Sabbath, the Bennetts did this.

ON THE SABBATH, MR. BRIGGS PREACHED ROBERT'S funeral sermon. It was taken from the Gospel of John, about the raising of Lazarus from the dead. This struck Tamsin hard, as with her own eyes she had seen him break into sparks of light, then come back to his body *whole and alive*. She begged him to do it again.

This was also the day when Aunt Adah was brought to bed. Years ago, when Tamsin's baby brother Eli was born and dead in a minute, she saw him as pure mystery. He seemed like Papa's sundial-compass that made earth and heaven into a single thing to be held in wonder. But she was older now, a young woman, and she did not want to see this mystery again today.

The horsecart bumping uphill to the meetinghouse that morning went hard with Aunt Adah, so the Bennetts came away before the afternoon sermon and took her home. Susannah's brother Nathaniel and his wife Martha, up from the harbor to hear Robert's funeral sermon, came too.

The cart ride back was no easier. Aunt Adah gripped the seat tight, bracing against ruts and stones. Whenever the cart jolted, she would cry, "The baby!"

Grandmother Cat rode beside her, holding on, murmuring in sympathy, "Adah, dear, this old track is rough for you, you're so near time." She laid her hand on Adah's great belly tightened in a knot. "You feel it sharp, but your babe is in the waters, safe."

Tamsin and Susannah walked behind with the children, carrying their grief as best they could with their fear for Aunt Adah. Tamsin thought her aunt should not have gone to the meetinghouse that day, provoked though Mr. Briggs would have been at any Bennetts missing his sermon. Grandmother once said the man lacked all common sense. In Tamsin's view, he thought overly well of his sermons.

When the cart stopped at the barn, Uncle Simon lifted Aunt Adah down. Her waters broke then, pains coming hard. He carried her into the house and Grandmother Cat went in after them. He came out and went to the barn.

Aunt Martha spoke to Ruth and Naomi about feeding the little ones and said, after that, they could all go out and find flowers to welcome the baby.

Nathaniel went to Susannah and said, halting, "Sister, I want to speak with you today. I believe I can help. With what comes next, I mean to say. After Robert."

Susannah stopped him. "Nat, I must go to Adah. In this moment I can't think of Robert." She crumpled forward and pressed down a cry. Tamsin wrapped her arms around her, crying too.

"Go to Adah, sister," Nat said. "Don't worry, I have something for you."

Wiping her hands hard across her eyes, she went to the house.

Tamsin wanted to ask Uncle Nat what he meant, but he turned away to Peter and James and told them to walk with him to look at the mill.

"There will be corn to grind," he said.

"Branches in the pond," James said. "We have to pull them out. And the wheel –"

They left for the mill and Tamsin went into the house, to the lean-to where lately she had sat with her Papa.

THIS BEING ADAH'S SEVENTH CHILD, COUNTING ONE dead of fever, Grandmother Cat expected her labor to go hard and fast. She and Susannah gave Adah as much ease as they could as she sat on the stool. They stroked her hands and whispered verses of the Twenty-Third Psalm, though they never reached the verse about the valley of the shadow of death. Still, they all knew it was there.

"Tamsin, go take down the peppermint tincture from last spring," Grandmother said. "Put a spoon of it into a mug of warm water, and bring it here."

The scent of peppermint would calm and strengthen Aunt Adah's spirit for the work to come, and the whiff of apple brandy in it would help too. On into the afternoon, between pains, Mother would give her sips. Aunt Adah would sigh and rest a little. As time passed, she rested less, becoming distraught.

"Dear, now bring me a big spoon of butter in a cup," Grandmother said. "I'll work the skin, and the baby will slip through. Adah may not tear."

Pains came stronger. Adah's back needing ease, Susannah half-lifted her, helping her to go forward and kneel on the bed, her arms and head on blankets and a pillow. Susannah rubbed her back as Grandmother worked butter into the thinning circle of skin, now making way slowly for a new child. As the little head appeared, Tamsin felt she watched a sunrise, and at last the baby came, face to the late afternoon light, Aunt Adah groaning low and long into the pillow.

But the sweet face was blue and quiet, without a cry, nor even a breath. Grandmother Cat rubbed the tiny body, limp in her hands.

"Is it a boy?" Adah asked.

"A little girl, dear."

Adah turned awkwardly to reach. "Is she well? Let me –"

"Not yet."

Grandmother Cat kept hold of the babe, cord still whole, rubbed the little body and spoke to her. "Child, you are here now, you may breathe."

Watching her close then, Grandmother puffed her own breath into the little one's face – once, twice, three times. With each breath a white yarrow flower bloomed quick into the air and just as quick disappeared. Tamsin's eyes wide open, she saw them, one after another. Only then did the tiny body make a face of surprise, startle her limbs, and loose a squall.

Joyous and bright, Adah reached for the child with new strength. Grandmother tucked her into Adah's arms, tied off the cord with hemp twine, and cut it.

Tamsin held her question. Later she would ask about the yarrow. First the poultice.

Before Aunt Adah's Abigail was born, Grandmother Cat had taught Tamsin to crush burnet flowers and leaves with a mortar and pestle, add a thick pinch of the ground burnet root, and make a poultice in a patch of fresh-ironed linen. Tamsin had to go and do that now. When she returned with the poultice damp in a bowl, Aunt Adah was lying back against blankets and pillows, the babe at her breast.

Grandmother rested her hand on Aunt Adah's belly, watching for a great bleed, but as the little girl nursed, all seemed well and the afterbirth came. Grandmother tucked the poultice onto a little tear where the babe had found its way. It would soothe the pain, hasten the mend.

"Nettle tea now, Tamsin. A good spoonful, strain it well." As she turned to go, Grandmother caught her by the hand and smiled. "You've done well."

"You have, my dear," Susannah said, her voice faint. Grandmother watched her for a moment.

"You go, too, Susannah. Rest. Adah and I will be fine."

Susannah went out of the house.

Tamsin went to make the tea, an image before her of the child coming through water and blood, startling herself to life. The image resolved into another, Papa on the stream bank soaked, bloodied, and still. She cried as she hung the kettle on the fire, took down the nettles, and wondered how it was she could feel gladness and horrible pain both at once in her one body.

Silently she called, *Papa!*

Uncle Simon, just coming in, cast her a look.

"It's born?"

"Yes." And because he should ask, but didn't, she said, "A good, hard labor. A girl."

He nodded. "That's fine."

"Did you not want a boy?"

"I might. But a boy child born this day would have to be called Robert, wouldn't it?"

She didn't breathe.

"Unfortunate name to lay on one just born. I'd have judged the boy hard."

You judge us all hard, she thought. *Worst, your own good brother.*

Tamsin took Aunt Adah the nettle tea, Uncle Simon following to see his child. He named her Sarah for his grandmother Bennett, whom he remembered a little, he said.

10

Uncle Nat, Peter, and James came back from the mill and told Uncle Simon they'd pulled branches out of the pond and inspected the wheel. There were troughs badly broken. Uncle Nat said he would come and make repairs within the week, if the boys would help. James and Peter said they would. Uncle Simon turned away.

Tamsin listened, but tried not to see. She wanted only to go out and put her hands flat on the ground, so she went to the garden, as if to weed. There she found Mother, sitting down among the squash plants, holding in her hands a long pie squash. She turned it and showed Tamsin the orange streak where it had lain on the earth.

"It was ripe. I wanted to make him a pie."

Tamsin sat with her and felt under thick leaves for another pie squash ready to be pulled. "Here's one more," she said. "We can make two. He did like them."

Susannah held the pie squash close.

Soon Peter came out. He seemed to examine for a while the low wattle fence he'd woven to hold the soil shoveled thick for carrots, parsnips, and onions. Then he went to the barn and brought out more willow whips to weave in among the stakes.

Tamsin and Susannah watched him. It was pretty work, and the three settled together into a sort of calm. A current of grief was near to sinking them, but in this moment, in this sitting on the ground, holding pie squash and weaving willow, they listened to each other's silence. This was the first sign that peace would sometime come.

The second sign of peace – *a half-peace,* Tamsin thought later – was more breakage. Uncle Nat came out of the house. "Susannah, I must speak with you," he said, and walked round the garden to reach her. She did not get up. She hardly seemed to notice him, so he looked about for something to sit down on, to be level with her eyes. Nothing but grasses by the garden, he made do and sat on the ground. Tamsin and Peter stayed where they were.

"Susannah, I am sorry to tell you this now, so soon upon Robert's death, but I do believe it will be of help to you. Especially now, when you have a choice to make, if you like."

Susannah looked at him.

"Martha and I are removing to the eastward, a distance up the coast from the Casco Bay. A settlement there called Combe. There's good prospect for shipbuilding and trade, the timber trade."

Susannah said nothing.

"You see, many years ago, our great-grandfather Bradbury and a few Essex men bought the proprietorship of a large tract of land. Now there are those of us who want to go there. The land lies by a great tidal lake called somehow, Lake Abbey, and maps northward some twenty miles, a good swath both sides of a navigable river. Southward, it goes all the way to the coast and a generous slew of islands.

"Susannah, men and families have been moving to the eastward now for land, fishing, and trade, so our proprietorship has considerable value. Possibilities."

Still Susannah didn't speak. Tamsin hugged her squash, protecting herself from what would come next.

Uncle Nat went on. "I am going to leave off sailing, Susannah. We'll make one last run to the eastward, where I've buyers for the schooner. We'll settle near the coast and look to shipbuilding, as there is need and material. Timber is plentiful inland. They float it downriver, some for new settlers, but much sent in trade to England along with fish and pelts. And why should we not build our own ships for that trade? British law be damned."

They all sat unmoving, but Tamsin felt the garden turning round her.

At last Susannah spoke, choking tears. "When will you go, Nat? Not now, not soon, please, Nat. I can't lose you now."

"Susannah, my leaving is a good chance for you too, terrible as this is. I want you and the children to take my house at the harbor. You know it. It's large, it's fine. It will serve you. The meetinghouse is just there on Wharf Street, so come winter, you won't have so far to go. The harbor district has more schooling than does West Dorset. Much better for the children. For Phebe, at least."

At mention of the harbor, Peter looked up, interest dawning. Inwardly Tamsin shouted, *No!* Both kept their silence.

"And Susannah, this is important – I would advise you to keep the house as an inn and a tavern. It is large enough, and the harbor draws more trade every year. There is need for such a place, well run. My house will shelter you and the children, give you a good living."

Again Susannah asked, "When will you go, Nat?"

"October, to settle before winter. A man is building a house for us now, and furnishings will be sent from Boston. But when I leave Dorset, I will leave you well provided. And in coming to Wharf Street, taking on the house, you help me too. I will speak to the selectmen on your behalf. Approval of a license would be assured. There are fishermen who will gladly barter with a tavern. Butchers, farmers will bring you meat and milk. I will leave you with funds."

"Nat, stop, stop, please, I can't think!" Susannah raised a hand to ward off her brother's busy mind. She looked uphill and to the sky. Tamsin watched. Mother had been born at the harbor. Her whole life and her first husband were there till he was lost at sea and she came to marry Papa. For Mother, the harbor would not be impossible. For Tamsin, it was unthinkable.

"Susannah, did Robert leave a will?"

She shook her head.

"By law, you'll inherit one-third of his share of the estate. You may stay here always, if you want. You have that choice.

"But Susannah," her brother said quietly, "There will be changes here without Robert. Simon works hard, but he is not the same man."

That, Tamsin took in. A drop of bitter extract in a cup changes every sip. Now she asked, "Uncle Nat, could Grandmother Cat go to the harbor with us?"

He considered. "If she would like, surely. I'll speak with her." He looked to his sister, who gave a little nod, and he went into the house.

Tamsin still held onto her squash, imagining what might come.

Susannah sat awhile unmoving, then stood, slow and awkward. She said she would go to see Adah's baby. Peter stopped his weaving. After some minutes he got up and walked away, so silent and slack, Tamsin thought he might fade in the air. She went to sit by his willow work and considered how these fine yielding things could make something strong. She ran her fingers along the withies that were woven between stakes firm in the ground.

Naomi came out of the house and stood by the garden, looking straight at Tamsin, then wandered halfway round the garden's edge, still looking at her, now sideways. Tamsin pretended Naomi was not there. Then Ruth appeared too, waited, and walked with slow intent round the garden to her twin. They stood silent by the beanpoles, eyes on Tamsin. She glanced up quickly and down. They were swaying, uneasy, as if gathering force. More silence.

"Your Papa is dead," Naomi said, her voice wobbly, rough.

Shocked, Tamsin did not look, but kept her fingertips stroking the willow withies as they bent easily forward this side of a stake, then wove behind, hidden a moment by the next.

Naomi began again. "Your Papa is dead and burning in hell. Right now."

"Most likely. Maybe, maybe not," Ruth said. "But probably."

"For all you know," Naomi said.

Ruth started back round the garden, gathering confidence. "Uncle Robert read scripture all the wrong way." She wagged her head. "In no good order."

Naomi followed her. "Senseless patches, our Pa said."

Tamsin stroked the willow with greater attention and did not look at them. "You always played the game. You listened, every time."

Ruth kept coming. "He read the Bible backwards. Like the devil."

"And how would you know how the devil reads the Bible? You've been to his house?"

"And Pa said Uncle Robert made *jokes* about Mr. Briggs." Naomi nudged her sister forward.

"That shows he was damned," Ruth said, now at the corner of the garden, a straight shot. "He could not have done that, otherwise. *Your Papa* —"

Tamsin's fingers curled round one fine withy of Peter's, loose on the ground.

"Your Papa is burning *in flames*," Ruth pressed on, her voice quavering between terror and known fact.

"Forever!" Naomi said in wonder.

Tamsin sprang up to whip cruelty away, ran slashing at the twins as they fled. "Why do you run? Your Pa whips you! My Papa never whipped me! You deserve it, you witless evil —"

"Thomasin Bennett! Stop you now!"

Shouting sobs, Tamsin stopped.

"Let them go. Let it go." Grandmother Cat took the withy and threw it down.

"Whatever they did may well be witless, but you've no need to whip them and it will not help." Grandmother held Tamsin tight. "You have lost your precious Papa and I've lost my dear son." Her voice broke to a whisper. "We will wrestle this sorrow."

Tamsin shrugged loose from her grandmother's hold and went back to the garden to take up her pie squash. Papa liked them. She would make him a pie.

11

AGAIN THAT EVENING, FROM LONG PRACTICE, THE families found their way to the parlor, all but Aunt Adah and the baby. Tamsin felt the room full of Papa. She did not want to hear her uncle's foul choice of scripture again, but Grandmother Cat was already in the wing chair, her hands resting on the Bible in her lap. Uncle Simon went to stand over her, and she looked up at him. "I will read this evening, Simon," she said. He stumped to his place by the door.

Grandmother Cat looked round the parlor. "I am sure Robert is glad we're here, inquiring of scripture as he would do," she said. "And tonight I believe we'll need the Book of Exodus."

She turned to Ruth. "Would you remind us, Ruth? How old are you?"

At the question, Uncle Simon made a rude snort. Ruth hesitated, but did answer. "Thirteen, Grandmother. Until December."

Grandmother Cat nodded, opened the Bible. "Ah, just where we are. Reading then from the Book of Exodus, chapter thirteen, beginning –"

She scanned the page, then with a mischievous smile glanced to the ceiling. "Indeed," she said softly, and to all the parlor she

64

said, "Beginning at verse twenty. *So they took their journey from Succoth –*"

She stopped. "Who remembers what Succoth is?"

"Harvest," James said.

"Harvest, yes, like our Lammastide. *So they took their journey from Succoth, and encamped in the edge of the wilderness –*"

She looked up again to say brightly, "When I was a girl, we lived at an edge of a wilderness. My mother Priscilla would go out foraging with an Indian woman and learn new herbs. The sweet-grass at our marsh was a gift from her. So good, you see, sweet-grass not only –"

Simon was heard grumbling in his place.

"Sweetgrass not only drives away mosquitoes, but it summons those we call angels. The smoke of it carries prayers up –"

Simon erupted. "She was heathen, Mother, you blaspheme!"

Grandmother stopped and looked at the Bible in her lap, her lips tight. After a silence, she went on.

"And the Lord went before them by day in a pillar of a cloud to lead them the way, and by night in a pillar of fire to give them light, that they might go both by day and by night. He took not away the pillar of the cloud by day, nor the pillar of fire by night from before the people."

She stopped, still looking at the verses she had read. No one spoke on what they meant. Even Luke and Abigail were quiet, Phebe curled on Mother's lap. Uncle Simon stared at the floor, black curls hiding his face.

A vision came to Tamsin. Mother and Phebe, she and Peter were walking the harbor road after an autumn-red shape that looked to spawn scores of jumping flames.

Into the silence, Mother spoke. She turned to address Uncle Simon, who still stared at the floor. "Nat told me today that he and Martha intend to leave Dorset and settle to the eastward. He wants to invest in timber and shipbuilding. He has asked me to take on the care of his house at the harbor, keep it as an inn for travelers."

Her brother-in-law roused at this. "What, the harbor? Yourself?"

"The children and I. It's a large house, enough for an inn."

"No. Peter stays here. I need him."

"Peter will come to help me with the inn and care for Nat's property," Susannah said evenly.

"Nat can care for his own damn property." Uncle Simon raised his voice. "Peter is –"

"Peter," Grandmother Cat said, "is Susannah's son. He will go with her."

"I want to work at the harbor, Uncle," Peter said.

James dropped his head in his hands.

Tamsin shut her eyes to look at what she'd seen on the road. "Grandmother Cat, will you go to the harbor with us?"

Grandmother spoke simply, straight to Tamsin. "A pillar of cloud and a pillar of fire will go with you, dear."

"She stays here," Uncle Simon said with force. "It's September already. Adah will need help seeing to the children and storing up for winter. If Peter goes, there's too much for James. The girls will have to tend the animals and finish the garden."

"Grandmother –" Tamsin knew she trod unwisely to ask again. She did it softly. "Grandmother, if we must go, please come with us."

Naomi and Ruth didn't often speak unbidden in the evenings. Now both broke in. "Grandmother Cat, stay!"

"We need you for the new baby."

"The baby will need you."

Uncle Simon snatched at the thought. "More to the point, Adah will surely have more babies. She is young enough. But Susannah, twice widowed, your age, you're unlikely to get with child." He turned to his mother. "You're needed here."

James sat up, flashing anger at his father and everyone else, pain sparking off ceiling and walls. Tamsin felt it on her skin.

"Stop! Would you cut our grandmother in half like the child brought to Solomon? Let her be!"

Simon, shocked, looked about to hurl himself at James and beat him with fists.

Grandmother's cry was like a murder of crows – *"Simon!"* – a sound never heard out of her thin body, not ever, not once. It looked to rip right through her son.

"I will stay at the farm," she said quietly.

Tamsin shut her eyes tight. She still saw the four of them walking the harbor road, those flames and a horrible emptiness.

"Nat wants to leave for the eastward by All Hallows'," Grandmother said. "Susannah has a great move to prepare for, and I have much to teach Tamsin."

Ruth and Naomi looked at each other, sour.

"And Simon, from now until then, if you were to keep your peace and stop the cruelty of your daughters' tongues" – Grandmother aimed a searing light at the twins – "it would be nothing short of God's merciful work."

From that night till All Hallows', Ruth and Naomi spoke to Tamsin hardly a word.

12

Papa now some weeks gone, Tamsin was broken and saw brokenness all round her.

Mother, lost in mourning, would wander from the house into the rowan trees at the head of the mill path, watch toward the mill, then turn and cross the bridge over the stream to look down the harbor road, as if all she wanted was to go there, now. Grandmother Cat told Phebe to walk the roadside and fields with her mother. She gave them sacks to gather milkweed pods drying in September's air. Floss packed tight in the pods would fill a quilt for the inn.

Peter looked by turns crushed and eager. In the garden, his spinach withered. His parsnips were the sweetest ever the Bennetts had tasted.

Uncle Simon stamped so fierce about the house, that mice skittering in the kitchen fled to the henhouse, where there was good corn, but peril from quick beaks. Aunt Adah wept hours at a time, her breasts overwhelmed with milk. Grandmother Cat had Tamsin steam a good mess of shepherd's purse for poultices, which gave Aunt Adah relief. Still she wept.

Naomi and Ruth did their best with housework and meals,

though they squabbled about their mistakes and added to the din. Ruth said loudly they'd be glad, come winter, when the new baby was older and all the cousins gone to the harbor.

Phebe and Abigail fussed with their elders' distress, so Tamsin took them out to the stream beyond the barn and taught them to listen to the water. She sat on the bank, holding them, whispering of the stream till she felt them soften. One might fall asleep, or neither, but they did learn the stream's voice. Tamsin thought, when they went to the harbor, she and Phebe would hear those waters too.

JAMES WAS NOT WELL. TO TAMSIN, WHO KNEW HIM TO be steady, he looked shattered. One morning in the barn as they finished the milking, he said at last, "Tamsin, listen."

She waited, though they should take the milk in.

James looked away out the barn door. Tamsin saw him empty. His shirt hung on him as if there were no body inside it, but when he spoke, words whirled like a storm. "Tamsin, that scripture my father read the night we buried your Papa. Remember. The stone the builder refused was made a cornerstone. You heard that."

She did.

"Tamsin, do you know how much my father hated living in the house with your father? With all of you? It's why he rails and quotes the Bible about deacons owning houses and children. Tamsin, he hated being Grandmother's second son. Despised it."

"Then he is no longer second," she said bitterly. "Does it please him?"

"You heard what he read. A man who fell on stone would be broken, and if a stone fell on a man, it would grind him. Tamsin, you heard that?"

"No one spoke on it."

"Listen. A man who fell on stone would be *broken*."

Tamsin saw Papa, crooked and bloody at the milldam.

"Again. If a stone falls on a man –" James' voice cracked. He stared out the barn door at the house. "It will *grind him*."

Tamsin heard, *To powder*. As at a mill. She spat, "James, why would God do such a thing?"

"I don't think God did it."

"What?"

He said nothing.

"You think your father did it?" In horror and disbelief, she whispered, "Pushed Papa."

"Why else read that scripture, that night? Why, if not to tell what happened? Or threaten. He does it to us. He cracks a whip on the ground before it hits us."

"Was he there? At the dam?"

"Not when I was there."

"But before."

James shook his head. "I don't know. Ruth went to get him at the woodlot. He could have gone there after."

"After."

Tamsin sat down hard, dizzy. "James. Uncle Simon was there. I know it. I went down the path to find Papa, and he said so. He said he and Uncle Simon had corn to grind." She did not want this to be true, but it was.

"My father hated yours," James said.

"Cain slew Abel," she said.

"Tamsin, I want to go away when you go. Apprentice at the harbor. Anything."

"Have you told Peter? Or Grandmother?"

He shook his head. "Don't. He'd hurt us."

Tamsin tried to think what would happen if they told Grandmother Cat. What would she do? Papa gone, Uncle Simon was needed for the farm, the mill, trading. Whatever he was, he was needed.

"James, we have to take the milk in or he'll be out after us."

"Be careful. We'd best not spill any."

He reached out to Tamsin and pulled her up. Holding tight to his hand, she felt despair and felt everything round them, cows and barn and yard, fall away empty into black. Her legs hardly carried her as she and James crossed the yard to the house with buckets of milk, sick with fear.

13

TAMSIN'S SPIRIT WAS TWICE BLASTED, FIRST IN PAPA'S death, then in misery to think her uncle had done it, her uncle the deacon, the one who read scripture in the parlor now these fall evenings. Despairing, she did not tell Grandmother Cat, whose loss of her firstborn had turned her papery, translucent over thin bones.

Fragile as she was, however, she took hold of what was needed and spent her grief in teaching Tamsin the things she must know. So these were days of gathering herbs, flowers, berries, and roots, chopping or tearing them, drying, soaking or steeping them, making mixes of them with flax oil or beeswax or apple brandy, and storing them. Grandmother Cat gave Tamsin a day-book so she could write what was needed, how it was to be done, and how it turned out. In all, best they could, they prepared two households for fall, winter, and the start of spring. And day by day, Grandmother Cat's frame strengthened, and so she molded and changed Tamsin's grief.

Peter was most eager to be away and insisted he should go to the harbor to dig Aunt Martha's garden. He said rightly, the house had a broad lot and they'd want more tilled ground to feed the tavern. Susannah wanted him at the farm, but he argued that

72

digging soon would let him put in his carrot, turnip, and onion seed properly on the waning moon and, moreover, make the garden fit for early cabbages, come spring. He said, too, he must learn to keep an account book for the inn, and Uncle Nat would teach him, so at last she let him go.

Then James wanted to go and help Peter with the digging, but Uncle Simon made him stay. At this, Tamsin was relieved. Before the new moon, James hitched Ethan and took him out to plough new furrows in the wheat field.

ONE OF GRANDMOTHER'S FALL PREPARATIONS WAS TO cut the purple-black elderberries that grew thick by the mill-stream. She would lay them out to dry and cook them down to a syrup, a welcome sweet remedy for the grippe and catarrh that came as the weather turned. Tamsin gathered elderberries with her each fall, but now she was to make the syrup herself, enough to take to the harbor and enough to leave at the farm. For this, they needed a great load of berries, so they would spend a long after-noon filling baskets and talking. This, Tamsin wanted above all else.

The bushes grew along the north side of the millstream, where sun was still good in September. It was a comfort to be there, though it was a hard story Tamsin needed to hear.

"Grandmother," she began, stepping on purpose right between her grandmother and the baskets she'd set down in the grass. "You told me of Samuel Tobin and Priscilla Rowan and you and your brothers all sailing into the cove at Winnipeseekett, and the coracle and the cloaks and the food. What happened?"

Grandmother Cat gave a sharp shake to a berry-laden branch. "Tamsin, you'll keep a tavern with the inn. Remember, elderber-ries give good flavor to ale in winter, and you can mix an extract of the berries with an extract of chamomile greens. Put that into your ale. It will prevent catarrh."

"Grandmother Cat," Tamsin began again and, to keep her attention, picked up a basket.

Grandmother nodded deeply and began cutting bunches of dark berries, dropping them into the basket Tamsin held. "We were there in the cove, and Mother told me why the constable was coming."

"Why?"

"It was said she'd done witchery."

"Witchery!"

"Mother said no more, but kissed me and gave me to my father. I tried to hold onto her, hard as a little girl could, but she took my hands and made me let go."

Grandmother's voice caught. In a silence that was agony to hear, Tamsin breathed slowly so as not to cry.

"Then she put the coracle into the water, stepped in, and rowed out past the far point of the cove, I knew not where. I cried for her, but my father carried me away up the bank and said I must be very quiet and not worry.

"He told me Mother knew just where to go with the coracle, a safe place. He said it would be like the hiding game I played with Isaac, when I hid from him and he couldn't find me. So I understood." Grandmother smiled. "But of course Isaac could always find me."

Tamsin smiled too, tears on her face.

"And Father told me that if the constable should come, I must be brave and not sad, because all would be well. On no account, he said, was I to speak to the constable."

"Did he come?" Tamsin took hold of Grandmother's hand, and Grandmother patted hers.

"Yes, he did."

"Who was he?"

"Hubbard, his name was."

Grandmother Cat moved on to another bush heavy with berries. Tamsin put the basket down between them and began cutting bunches too. They stained her hands.

"Father carried me to the shed. Daniel was there, piling kindling. Isaac went to sit hidden and watch the tide road that leads from Winnipeseekett toward Salem Town. Daniel said Hubbard must either take his horse over that spit of wet land or else ride round the upland way. Or else swim, he said, and he laughed. Father said Hubbard was paunchy and lazy, and he'd come the easiest, driest way he could.

"They meant to poke fun, but it frightened me, Mother gone, and only a little coracle between her and the sea." Grandmother gave a sad smile. "Daniel said that when Isaac saw Hubbard, he'd come back and tell Father to be ready. With the rough track and the woods, it would take time for man and beast to reach the shed. You know what that road is, Tamsin."

She did. It crossed a narrow, wet strip, climbed up round a steep hill, then at a tight bend turned back onto Winnepeseekett. The road would have given Priscilla time to be away and gone with the coracle. The upland road, the long way round, would give her even longer.

"At last Isaac came back to say the constable and some craggy, gaunt figure had come splashing across. Father said, Good then, we'll eat when they're here, so when the two of them arrived, we were eating my mother's meat pies, and he offered them some. The skinny wretch had terrible hollow eyes that lit up and frightened me when Father spoke of the pies."

Grandmother Cat shivered, Tamsin thought, just as a very little girl would have done.

"Isaac plays the constable in good humor to make me laugh, but –" She looked away downstream, shook her head and was silent.

Tamsin looked, too, and waited. A hawk circled the meadow on the far side, tail fanned wide, sun-lit, bright.

"I remember Hubbard's red woolen breeches," Grandmother said carefully, "but not everything."

She walked away to the stream bank and sat. Tamsin followed.

"Hubbard was fat. Isaac remembers he came in breathing

hard. He told Father he had a warrant to take Mother away to Salem jail on charges of bewitching, but Father said no, she was too busy for that, she was in Haverhill, looking after some cousins. Isaac makes fun of Hubbard saying, *he'd come ten mile to find Goody Tobin at the farm and then another ten mile to come to Winnipeseekett, and he were not going thirty mile to Haverhill to find her not there!*"

Tamsin laughed and Grandmother smiled a little, but her eyes were round.

"Hubbard told Father he must bring Mother out from hiding, because of the warrant.

"Father told Hubbard he was here to fish and Mother was not, so Hubbard had best go back to Salem and get some rest. Now Hubbard was vexed and he moved in close. This I remember. Father stepped forward and then my brothers stepped in, too, and there I was, alone on a dirt floor.

"Hubbard said Father was not there to fish, and Daniel said, *We are all here fishing.*"

"Furious then, Hubbard pointed straight at me and shouted, *She does not fish! Goody Tobin is here!*"

Grandmother Cat's berry-stained hands went to small fists.

"And I was so frightened for Mother, I got up, and I walked right in front of my brothers, right under Hubbard's big nose. And I looked straight up over his fat belly and his red woolen breeches and I said to him, *I DIG CLAMS!*"

Her little fists shook, and Tamsin shouted, laughing, "Grandmother, you were so brave! Four years old!" Then she stopped because of her grandmother's tears.

"Tamsin, a child will never forget the sight of her mother rowing a little coracle out into the ocean. Off to nowhere."

After a moment Grandmother Cat spoke again. "And do you know, that wasted man with the hungry eyes – he laughed just as loud as you did. Hubbard went into a fury, slapped him hard across the face, and ordered him out."

Tamsin saw a ragged starveling lead a thin horse on the Winnipeseekett road.

"Then I remember Hubbard looking at me. He looked right down at me for a long time, and I was afraid he would take me to Salem jail for shouting at him. Later I learnt they did jail a little girl. But he didn't take me. I looked right back up at him and tried not to cry." Grandmother Cat set her jaw and didn't blink.

"Then?"

"Then his face changed. It went soft. I saw it happen, but I didn't understand it till Isaac told me later. Hubbard looked over my head to my father, and said Governor Phips' wife herself was lately accused of witchery. He said the Governor would come back soon from the eastward, and then either Mistress Phips would be examined, or else the Governor would put a stop to it all and shut the court down. Hubbard said to Father, Do you hear what I say, Samuel Tobin? If you were to know where your Goody Tobin might be, let her keep well away from me till the Governor's return.

"Then he looked down at me again, and went out and didn't come back."

"He didn't come back? Did he never come back?"

"Father gave us a sign we mustn't speak. Then after a while he talked of more supper and told the boys to get a fire going, so they went out. Isaac went to watch the Salem road again, but the tide was in, so Hubbard and the dreadful skinny man would have gone the long way round."

"And then?"

Grandmother got up and went back to cutting elderberries, throwing bunches into a basket. "It was a fearful time. For the whole county. But you know Priscilla had a long life and a good one, Tamsin. You know that."

Tamsin insisted. "Did nothing more come of it?"

"Beliefs die slow. Shame goes on. Whole families shunned one another for years." Grandmother Cat stretched her hands and looked at the stains. "Many do still."

"Grandmother, how –"

"Yes, Tamsin, there is more." But she moved away to another bush of dark berries. "Not now."

WHEN THE MOON HAD WANED TO A SLIVER, PETER WAS done with his work at Uncle Nat's and came back to the farm. The next morning, all the Bennetts but Aunt Adah and the baby gathered at the wheat field to see the furrows James and Ethan had ploughed. Each Bennett took a cup to the east end of a furrow, and Uncle Simon put a scoop of Red Lammas seed into each one. Abigail rode on James' shoulders to watch from high up. Another year, she would have her own cup and furrow. Then Phebe and Luke started out first along their furrows, followed a few steps after by James, Tamsin, Peter, and the twins, then by Susannah, Grandmother Cat, and Uncle Simon, each dropping grains of wheat, one at a time. They did this with quiet, careful attention, as this was the way the youngest would come to understand the sacred work. When each had come to the end of a furrow, they moved out to form a single great circle round the field, and watched Uncle Simon rake the soil one last time, to cover.

Tamsin turned away. In every year of her life, she had seen Papa rake the field, sweet as tucking a child under a quilt. But Uncle Simon, who believed the ground cursed for Adam's sin, moved heavily and raked earth without grace. She wondered if his unnatural opinion could stunt the wheat. She thought to observe at the next harvest and make a note in her day-book, but was hit with a fact like a slap. She would be gone. Next year she'd not be part of the Rowans' ancient custom, caring for the Red Lammas.

That day, there was one more custom still to be honored, its history from long before the Rowan family had left the farm at Brampton Bryan.

On a night of the waning moon, wheat planted, a couple would lie together beside the field in a blessing of soil and seed.

Often enough, the next spring, a child would be born, and after that in late summer the field would give a bountiful harvest. In gratitude, the Rowans would share with the village a festive portion of the season's first bread.

The Rowan farm, however, was among those burnt by the King's soldiers in the year 1644. Margaret and her husband Isaac packed then what they needed to carry on the Rowan lineage and sailed to Massachusetts Bay. There, one spring, their daughter Priscilla was born. When she was grown, Priscilla Rowan married Samuel Tobin, and a dozen springs after that, their Catherine was born.

Catherine married Thomas Bennett under a full moon in August of 1708, in time to plough a field and plant the Red Lammas seed she had brought to their union. Cat, as Thomas liked to call her, chose the south face of a low hillock by the Bennetts' millstream as holding the proper earth, water, air, and light for the Rowan family's seed. The evening of that first planting, Cat spread blankets by the field, and that night she and Thomas lay there together. Their first child, a son, was born on a bright June morning. Named for his Grandfather Bennett, this was Robert, Tamsin's Papa.

Cat told Thomas then to make an arbor of the trees on the spot, and every September since, with the planting of the wheat, one couple of the family has slept there on the earth. Therefore, this very night, according to Rowan custom, Uncle Simon and Aunt Adah might sleep under the arbor. But his demeanor was grim and Aunt Adah had the baby, so he took his rake to the barn and did not come back.

Tamsin wondered again, urgently, whether a lapse of ancient practice might harm the wheat. She wanted to ask Grandmother Cat, but Grandmother had gone to sit under the arbor and only shook her head. She wouldn't talk, not now.

14

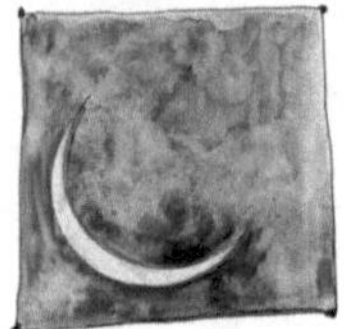

THE DAY TAMSIN'S PAPA FELL DOWN UNDER THE wheel, the moon was new and the tide was up. When next the day of the new moon came round, Grandmother Cat made Tamsin walk with her to the millpond. Tamsin hadn't gone there since the day Papa died and she held back now, but Grandmother had a purpose. She led Tamsin not down the mill path, but across the bridge to the far side of the stream. From there they squished barefoot along the narrow bank, past where the rowan trees crowded out of the woods on that side to find sun, and all the way on till stream opened out to pond.

Here the bank spread away into a meadow of tall grasses with clumps of purple Michaelmas daisies, sparks of Aaron's rod, and the soft white of yarrow. Tamsin had to turn and rest her eyes where the field was bright, as she could not face the milldam, the wheel, or the bank on the other side where James had laid Papa. But Grandmother Cat drew Tamsin near to the pond and settled down by a mass of purple daisies. Tamsin sank beside her, eyes wet, so that all she could see was watery. Grandmother cut a bunch of Michaelmas daisies and pressed them into her hands.

"Here, dear, tell me what you feel."

"I miss Papa so, Grandmother, I am lost," she said, and

80

stopped. She would not speak of the fear and horror, if it were true Uncle Simon had killed him. It was too evil a thing to say to Papa's mother.

"Yes. And in your hands, Tamsin, what do you feel?"

Tamsin made her fingers move along the stems and leaves, and when her curiosity rose, she rubbed an arm across her eyes.

"The leaves are rough and long," she said, "Shaped as if each one held onto its stem with two arms. Stems are red. Strong." She looked at Grandmother. "That's why the leaves hold on so. They have a good stem."

"They do," she said. "And the bloom?"

Tamsin put them to her nose and sniffed. There would be little scent, she knew. "Purple, yellow. A spiky bright button in the middle and dozens of petals like narrow, fine spokes to a –"

She glanced up quickly at the wheel that took her Papa, then back to the flowers in her hands.

"Yes," Grandmother said. "And its name?"

"It blooms at Michaelmas."

"It's Michaelmas now. And the angel Michael – you know this, Tamsin – he slew the great dragon, cast it right down out of heaven. So that even now, on the day of a new moon, the angel Michael is here for our courage and protection. His flower bright and fine, as you say. A shield and a sword.

"And now you must hold onto his courage and protection, dear, because I've more of my mother's story to tell."

Tamsin gripped the tough stems and thought, *I will not tell about Uncle Simon.*

"Tamsin, you know what happened at Winnipeseekett. Mother got away in the coracle. She went and tied up in a little inlet under a ledge. The constable –" Grandmother Cat pushed her hands to the ground among Michael's daisies. "The constable came to the shed, and he left. And this is the reason why he came.

"In the midst of that summer's drought and sickness, and all the fearing of God the ministers preached, it was the children most troubled in body and soul. One day Mother's care was sought for some distracted girls up to Rowley. Two sisters complained of choking and heavy weights upon their chest. Their mother wanted to blame a poor beggar widow, named Cobb, saying she would appear to the girls and stop their breath, but their father insisted the Rowan woman, Priscilla, must come and see what she could do. So my mother went and laid her hands on the girls. She put the sign of a blessing on linen and wrapped it round the chest. She gave them yarrow and sweetleaf tea with elderberry syrup, but they could hardly swallow, and nothing at all would soothe the fever. So the girls' mother sent Priscilla away, and she left there."

Grandmother Cat sat very still and took a long breath.

"Soon as she left that house, she was taken to a selectman of Rowley whose hired girl had a great story. This girl told my mother that one night as she stood at the hearth, suddenly she was thrown over backward to the floor and pinched and pricked, and was mute for three days after. She said she hurt still. She told Mother the Widow Cobb had come to the house begging, but the girl turned her away. So she blamed that old woman for her bruises and for being struck dumb.

"My mother had a good lavender salve, made as her grandmother had done before the Rowans came to Massachusetts, so she rubbed the girl's skin with it to ease the soreness. Then she saw the selectman's son hovering about the girl, and thought the injury likely his doing, and the poor widow innocent."

Tamsin considered. "If the widow was innocent, then what came of the two sisters' illness?"

"One recovered, and after some days, the other died. The throat distemper, I would think, though they didn't know it then. But the sister said she saw the Widow Cobb and my mother Priscilla come nightly to sit upon her sister's breast until her death."

"She lied!"

"And why would she lie? She didn't know the truth. And why did she not know the truth?" Grandmother asked.

"She didn't know it was the throat distemper. She thought Priscilla and the Widow Cobb made it happen."

"Yes, and why wouldn't she think that, when ministers and magistrates were rattling on about evil powers, and the girls' own mother was afraid?

"Tamsin, my mother Priscilla could heal with her herbs and her heart and the laying-on of her hands. But if a sickness were too deep and there were no healing, then her work might seem to do harm. Would that look frightening to one who didn't know?"

Tamsin nodded, and thought it best a healer should keep her healing entirely to herself. But if so, then how could she use what she knew to heal? It was a dilemma.

"Beyond that, the girl was fevered, and fever itself may cause sick visions. If she were to have a nightmare vision of weight upon her sister's chest, why not think it was my mother Priscilla, laying on hands?"

"She didn't know," Tamsin said, and felt her stomach turn because of her own visions – Papa gone into sparks and mist, or herself walking the harbor road with Mother under a crowd of flames. She didn't know how to stop her visions, any more than that girl long ago in Rowley.

She must never speak of her visions.

"No, dear, the girl didn't know."

"Grandmother, the danger in the county, then, wasn't evil spirits or the devil or witchery. It was not knowing."

"Yes, dear, it's not-knowing, does the greatest harm. Not-knowing and fear."

Tamsin in fear could hardly ask, but had to know. "What happened?"

"Terror. Accusations begot accusations. Hearing of Priscilla accused, then the selectman's hired girl cried out the lavender salve had made her skin to burn, and the selectman's wife called the girl cursed and made her go out to the barn and never come into the house. So the girl stayed outside and wept when any went to question her."

A sight flashed unwanted before Tamsin. She shook her head and tried to lose it, but there it was. "The selectman's son went to the barn, didn't he? He hurt her."

Grandmother Cat looked at her with worry. "Yes, Tamsin, I believe he did."

"And she blames the Widow Cobb. Because she can't blame the boy. She needs the place to live and work."

Quickly she caught herself speaking of a vision, and stopped.

Watching, Grandmother Cat said, "Tamsin, I think you've long known when it's safe to speak and when it's not. Heed that. Above all, think how to continue your work of heart and healing, but draw little attention and no accusation."

Tamsin let that in and let it settle, imagining how she could do her work, yet not be noticed. Do the work of a rowess, invisibly. Endangered, but safe. Do this, and be that. Her mind swaying side to side showed her the rowing of Grandmother's coracle, a broad oar looping one way and looping the other. At the exact center of each figure of eight, an unseen point showed her intention, direction.

She asked again, "What happened?"

"Widow Cobb was taken from Rowley to Salem Town, and tried and convicted with other poor souls of the county. After that, the condemned were put into a cart for the town to see and mock, and dragged to the top of a ledge."

Tamsin gave close attention to the angel Michael's daisies.

"There they were hanged from the branches of trees, seven that day. Salem watched."

"No, they didn't take Priscilla. That didn't happen. She did not die."

"There were those in Rowley said the girls were oppressed of the devil and named my mother his servant. I don't like to tell you these things, but you need to know."

Chilled at her heart, Tamsin saw something else. "Grandmother, you never go to Rowley, do you? Nor Salem. You don't go to Colbrook to see Uncle Isaac."

"No, dear. My work is at the farm. Earth and stream and rowans are my company. We understand one another."

Slowly, she took up the story again.

"At Winnipeseekett, after Hubbard left and Isaac saw they couldn't go back to Salem by the tide road, we knew they'd go the long way round, so we waited a while in the shed to be sure they were well away, and then went out to find our mother. We went back along the track, calling and searching all the shoreline for a cove where waves might have washed her in and let her hide.

"At last we found the coracle, but it was empty. Mother was gone. We shouted for her, I cried for her, we searched. Later we knew. When Hubbard slapped that vile wretch across his face and ordered him out of the shed, he went searching for Mother till he found her. She was in the coracle under the overhang of a rock, but she didn't know she'd been seen. He waited till Hubbard came, and then they took her."

Grandmother's voice was bitter. "Hubbard had told Father, keep her hidden. But that hell-cursed Judas, when he found her, he grabbed her and he took her to Salem jail."

Tamsin's fists pressed the angel Michael's daisies to her face, as if that could stop her from seeing a woman sitting on a horse before a ragged man with eyes like caves. Her hands were locked in irons.

"Father told the boys to sail home in the morning and stay there, but he ran up the track, uphill to John Lane, begged use of a horse, and rode straight to Salem. Isaac carried me back to the shed and tried to tell me Father would bring her home, but none of us knew that, not even Isaac. We sailed back in the morning to tell Gabe, but he wasn't there and the cows hadn't been milked, none of the animals fed. Isaac and Daniel and I took care of them, I fed the chickens, and we passed three terrible days alone. On the third day, Father walked home with Mother and Gabe on John Lane's horse."

Tamsin had all but stopped breathing, her fingertips cold and prickling. Now she took one long breath. "They took Gabe? Why?"

"When Hubbard went to the farm and found us all gone, only Gabe there, he took him. Revenge, suspicion, I don't know." She curled forward, hands flat in the angel Michael's daisies. "No. I do know. He took Gabe to Salem and put him in the jail, then set out for Winnipeseekett. And when his fat self and that stringy curse of a man got Mother to the jail, and she wouldn't confess –"

Tamsin waited.

"They tied Gabe, ankles and neck, there in front of Mother so she must watch him suffer until she would confess. And when he could speak, he told her no, but blood flowed to his face and gushed from his nose and his mouth."

Tamsin pushed her fists into her chest and didn't breathe.

"At last the jailer saw this would do no good, and had small pity. He loosed Gabe and let Mother go to him and lay her hands on his throat and joints to soothe him. He had pain for the rest of his life until he died.

"In this time, Father reached Salem, but Hubbard wouldn't hear him. The next day the judges questioned Mother, tried to make her confess, but she would not, having nothing to say. Then they made a midwife examine her in all her parts, but the midwife was one who had bought my mother's extracts, and said she could find no mark of the devil. So they had the jailer put her into the cart with the ones condemned and took her up to the ledge. A crowd mocked them and threw stones and followed to see them die."

Grandmother Cat's voice went faint. "They made Mother watch all the hangings that day. It was the day they hanged the Widow Cobb, from Rowley."

Tamsin's stomach rebelled. Grandmother rubbed her back.

"One of the condemned men begged for time, saying he was not yet fit to die. But the Reverend Mr. Cotton Mather himself was there, high on his horse, and refused mercy. So the poor man began to say the Lord's Prayer, no single word amiss, when the cursed Reverend gave a sign for the man to be pushed off his ladder. He strangled with 'deliver us from evil' in his mouth.

"Those who saw it felt remorse at the man's good words, believing him innocent, but Mr. Cotton Mather declared the devil may sometimes look to be an angel of light.

"And there, Tamsin, he told but God's truth. That ordained minister was the devil himself on horseback. But she never broke. They took her to jail again, alone in that cart. And she never broke."

Tamsin's sight was grey and black.

"Even so, the jailer would not let Father take her. He demanded bribes for himself and Hubbard, and some shillings for the jail, so Father told him that two sacks of Red Lammas wheat would be left at his back door, for Mother was with child and must be at home. Then the jailer and Hubbard took one shilling for the jail and let Father escape with her for the wheat."

"A child! Was it well? Was it born?"

"It was pretense, and no matter to the blackguards. They wanted our wheat."

Tamsin heard this. Cruelty and greed turned round and round in her mind like dogs, found room, and settled. The world could do this.

"Did the Governor stop the trials? Were more hanged?"

"He stopped the trials, he changed the rules of the court, he pardoned some. No other accused were hanged." Grandmother took hold of Tamsin's hands, still full of the angel's daisies.

"To the end of her long life, my mother carried the terror."

"And you," Tamsin whispered.

"But she was safe. Your great-grandmother Priscilla lived a long and a good life. There were neighbor families, still wanted her herbs and her touch. Others did not, but those were folk we chose not to see. And she was strong through all of it.

"When you go away to the harbor, Tamsin, you will be strong. You are a rowess. But you must know this about the work of a rowess. It is good, and it is perilous."

Tamsin was silent. Words echoed. Good, perilous, good. Perilous.

"Come with me, dear." Grandmother Cat got up and walked away onto the milldam.

Tamsin didn't move, but kept her grip of strong stems and listened to the stream. As a child, she would tear from one end of the milldam to the other, arms stretched out like wings. Pond to one side of her, stream and bay to the other, she was like a lightsome blue heron skimming the water. Now she willed herself to put the angel Michael's daisies down, take up her shoes, and move toward her Grandmother Cat. But a step from the dam, she stopped still.

To her eyes, the stream pushed up in the pond and threw itself hard over the headrace, pounding down like hooves on the wood of the wheel. Turning now to a deadly gallop, the millwheel cracked, shattered, and shot the air full of splinters that seared Tamsin's throat. She knew this heat in her voice from the shriek in the kitchen when Papa went all to sparks, and now she could not move for the breakage.

Grandmother stood on the dam and spoke softly to Tamsin, her tone level as a hand held out to calm churning water. "Where are the soles of your feet, dear?"

Tamsin couldn't speak.

"Tell me, where do you find your feet?"

The soles of her bare feet pressed on the earth, she felt them and not her throat.

"Good. You know what to do."

"What –"

"You feel what happened here, dear. A shade of what your Papa felt, but it's done. It's over. You found your feet. Do you see the tide running in now?"

Unmoving, Tamsin let her eyes turn downstream to a gentle lift of the water.

"It will rise easy now in the pond, then flow out to the bay.

The tide turns, the wheel turns. The millstone grinds our good grain."

There was comfort in Grandmother Cat's voice and in the working of the mill Tamsin long knew. She rubbed her fingers against her thumbs the way Papa would rub the milled Red Lammas in his fingertips to know it was properly ground.

What came next, she felt inside her body. As she stood above the incoming tide, a beneficent strength came into her feet. It lifted right up through her belly to her heart, a flow so strong it changed her very breath and lifted up into her head, or even higher. She felt this must be what maple trees know in spring when sap rises up from roots into trunk, and branches push to leaf out. When the sweetness flooded even down her arms, this was the first time her hands held the scent and gold light of a mystery she would later understand. In her mind she saw a summer day, the wide-open bloom of a flower in her hands, and a man. On that day she would remember this day and the golden what-was-it that rose inside her by the stream lifting in from the bay.

Grandmother Cat watched her. "Come," she said, and walked across the dam to the mill path. Tamsin followed, not as a blue heron, arms wide, but aware she held something new in her hands.

When they had walked the path as far up as the rowan trees, she saw they'd circled the whole of the pond. Worn though she was, she felt knit together, as if in passing through the rowans on the far side of the stream and walking all the way round to the rowans on this side, she'd come back and met herself.

15

IT HAD BEEN WARM FOR OCTOBER SO FAR, FROST SOON. Tamsin and Mother had cleared the garden and set aside what they would take to the harbor for seed, the last ears of corn, the remaining cucumbers, peppers, and a pie squash. Phebe pulled the bean pods still hanging and laid them out to dry. One morning Tamsin spent in the orchard picking up fallen apples, hooking down the ones not yet fallen, and wheeling the load of them to the press in the barn.

That afternoon Grandmother Cat said, "Walk with me, Tamsin," and Tamsin followed her from the house down to the millstream bridge. Grandmother sat and dangled her feet over the edge like a young girl. Tamsin's heart ached at leaving her.

"Sit, dear. I want to show you one more herb, the seed of it." From the pocket inside her petticoat, Grandmother brought out a small linen drawstring sack, opened it, and let Tamsin look. A score of seeds were in it, smooth and brown. Some still clung to their dried-up pods, like peas.

"What are they?"

"They may have many names. They are old and from far away," Grandmother said. "I learnt to call them 'floss,' though not like the floss of the milkweed we put into quilts. This herb doesn't flourish here, I've tried. But the name, floss, may point to *flow*. These seeds do cause a woman to flow. You understand."

Tamsin nodded.

"Years ago, when your Grandfather Thomas had a crop of hemp, he'd load the shallop and take it to Salem for trade. Once doing business at the ropewalk, he fell to talking with a sailor from a ship just docked from the Indies. The sailor showed him a pouch of these seeds and told him the Indians of Suriname found them good for the lungs and breath. Your Uncle Simon was little then and prone to wheezing and fussing, so your grandfather brought me a good supply of them.

"Now, Tamsin, note. The sailor told him to be stingy with dosing, as these seeds may be deadly. And to be most careful if ever giving this to a woman with child. An amount like the tip of your little finger could bring on a loss."

Grandmother gave Tamsin a close look.

She nodded. She understood the risk.

"The women of Suriname would use them," Grandmother said, and put the sack in Tamsin's lap. "Tuck that in your pocket, take them with you. Keep them to yourself. Should you ever need them, grind fine. Measure well.

"Your uncle's breath is somewhat better, now he's grown. I stir a pinch of powder in his cider, only when his fear seems to need it."

Tamsin heard then what Grandmother was saying – that fear could lead to a constriction of the breath, or constricted breath lead to fear. Therefore, opening the breath might open up a man's heart and spirit. Was this why Uncle Simon so reviled Papa? Tight of breath, tight of heart.

Tamsin studied the deadly, useful nubs in the little sack that was now hers. This world, rowan trees and millstream, swirled round her head and made her dizzy.

Whatever would it be, to be a rowess?

Grandmother Cat laid her hand over Tamsin's. "My dear, the moon is full tonight. Tide will rise in the millpond." She nodded downstream. "Go and walk round once more, as we did. See what you see. Go to the mill, think of your Papa."

Tamsin clenched her eyes to block the whirling. She would see nothing. Her legs had no will to them.

"Remember, Tamsin, when Moses saw the burning bush, he turned aside from his path. From that, he learnt a great deal."

"Will you come with me?"

"I have work, dear. You go." She stood up from the bridge and waited.

Leaden, Tamsin got up. "Come with me," she whispered.

"One foot before the other," Grandmother said, and watched while Tamsin crossed the bridge. She called after her, "Touch the rowans."

Passing among the rowan trees, Tamsin stopped and laid hands on their branches. "Help me," she said, then moved slowly downstream as far as the broad field by the millpond. Here she sat and pressed her face into Michaelmas daisies, still purple. At new moon, Grandmother Cat had said these daisies were like the shield and sword of the angel Michael. Now Tamsin found herself angrily pulling at the angel's daisies, then more of them, and more, and without thinking began to braid them into a purple-green rope that, after a while, coiled itself into a wreath. The making of it gave her some peace.

Standing all round were brown stalks of yarrow, too dry for braiding. Still their lightness did look like a puff of breath, and she was glad to see them. She leant over and blew softly onto one dry bloom in a clump. Pleased at the feeling, she brushed a breath onto another brown bloom, and another, and when she sat back, she was stunned to see that each had turned white and soft. Fine featherish leaves were now green. She doubted her eyes and so peered round the field. A multitude of yarrow were there, brown and dry.

Whatever had she done?

But she knew to heed the unexpected, and so picked the ones that were suddenly fresh. She would show them to Grandmother

Cat. The Michaelmas wreath, she would take to Papa. And so with a measure of courage, she went to face the wheel and found to her surprise, she could sit right down beside it. Water from the full moon tide pushed across the headrace, forcing the wheel down, round, and up again, working the mill.

"Papa," she said, "I miss you more than I can say. More than all the words in scripture. But Uncle Nat is helping us, Papa. We'll go to his house to keep an inn and a tavern. Mother and I will look after each other and Phebe, I promise. Peter is skillful and good, you taught him well. And here, Papa, I made this wreath for you from the daisies of the angel Michael."

With spirit, she added, "He threw a dragon out of heaven!"

The mill door opened.

Quick, Tamsin laid Papa's wreath where he died.

In an instant, Uncle Simon was on the dam, staring at a mass of purple flowers sinking water-soaked on the wheel. Tamsin scrambled to her feet and turned downstream, so as not to face his look of horror.

The wreath bobbed up once in the froth of the wheel, then swept toward the bay.

"I have to go," she said. "Grandmother wants me." She tried to hide the white yarrow in gathers of her gown, but she couldn't. She wanted to turn and run back the way she'd come, over meadow and upstream, but she stopped. To run back would mean not finishing the circle of the millpond, not coming round to meet herself again at the rowans.

Uncle Simon stared at the clutch of impossibly fresh yarrow. Tamsin read anger, or would it be fear? He spat words. "Know this, child. In the ordering of the church, God set the apostles first, then the prophets, then *deacons –*"

Tamsin looked fixedly down at the dam and willed the stones to become steps. When she felt they knew their part, she started directly toward her uncle. He didn't move. Though she believed he would knock her into the pond, she trusted to the stones, narrowly passed him and kept on. He stalked her to the far end of the dam, snarling at her head, "Yes, your grandmother wants you, girl, but take care. God ranks healers *far below his deacons*. Your grandmother imagines her lineage powerful, but they are ungodly weak and dangerous. Mind that when you go to the harbor, and when you fall down to damna –"

At the mill path, Tamsin ran.

Grandmother Cat was among the rowans.

"Grandmother!" she began, breathless. She would say nothing of Uncle Simon. She had the yarrow.

Grandmother smiled. "Tell me."

Tamsin took as many breaths of the yarrow as she needed. "When we went upstream to forage, we sat with the yarrow and you asked me about the parts – leaves, blooms, and scent. And when Sarah was born and didn't breathe, you puffed your breath into her face. Yarrow bloomed in the air! And she breathed. Was it the spirit of the yarrow?"

"I find that yarrow brings light into us," Grandmother Cat said. "Opens us up. Speaks of grace in the air and sweetness in the earth."

"Sarah liked it."

"It's important you practice, Tamsin. Be with the green ones, hold and watch them. Hear them as clearly as you would hear your Papa read scripture. This is yours to do." She lifted her eyes up to the rowan trees, tipped her head as if curious, and gave a nod. "We will."

She smiled at Tamsin. "You see," she said.

16

ON THE DAY BEFORE SUSANNAH AND HER CHILDREN were to leave the farm, Grandmother Cat and Tamsin were in the kitchen dividing stores of dried herbs. Some would be folded in linen and packed in a chest for the move to the harbor, the rest would go back into the cabinet. Susannah and Phebe walked all the way to Robert's grave to say goodbye, taking a sack for any milkweed pods they might find. Uncle Simon told James and Peter to go hitch Ethan and lead him out to the new woodlot. There were trees down, branches cut, he said. They needed hauling in.

This morning, too, Grandmother Cat made Tamsin cross the millstream for a third time, pass down through the rowan trees on the far side, and walk one last round of the pond.

"Do you fear it now, dear?" she asked.

Tamsin considered that Uncle Simon was intent on hauling wood today, and was glad.

"I'm not afraid, Grandmother, but I do wonder. Walking round the pond changes something in me. I don't know what it is, nor how it happens."

Grandmother Cat smiled. "Good," she said. "Courage and humility, both. Go now."

95

Tamsin ran for the bridge, but reaching it, she slowed and stopped to look down at the weathered planks she'd crossed many hundreds of times. The worn grain of the wood looked to her like the wrinkled leather of her shoes. She took her shoes and stockings off, so the soles of her feet felt every plank as she crossed. She went on to the rowan trees, resting a hand on each one, heavy with berries. In the field by the millpond, the Michaelmas daisies were faded now. Stalks of yarrow stood stiff with delicate, dry blooms.

She had begun to think of the yarrow as a sort of companion, a sweet conspirator, and she wondered, would it happen again? So she tried, and to her delight it did. Puff, one soft white bloom happened. Puff, another, then another, and more after that. When she had breathed a drift of yarrow to life, she gathered it to take back to the house as solace, she felt, for these two Bennett families about to be divided like an overgrown herb. Tamsin had learnt about dividing green things from Grandmother Cat, who once made her use a sharp knife to split a tangled coneflower.

With that, her feet found their way to the milldam, where she sat and swung them over the edge beside the wheel, facing out to saltmarsh and open bay. The new moon tide was coming in gently now, with glints of little fish and soon after a white egret, gliding low to put its stilt legs in the shallows. Egrets nested in spring in the scrubby trees on Towne Island, out where the Bennetts kept their sheep. But why should this one be here at the end of October?

Poised, a beautiful presence, the white bird stood watch for a flash in the water, darted its long beak down and brought up a silver wriggle, swallowed in a second. Another moment, another little fish, a toss of the fine white head, a quick swallow. As if expecting notice, it raised sharp eyes to the one sitting up above. Tamsin obliged with a wave and a laugh. The bird returned its gaze to the water, predatory and still, though the next quick dart came up empty. A pause, then again a sharp poke down brought up no little fish. Instead, the bird aimed a crooked look upward at the dam. Tamsin was charmed. Once more the egret shot a purposeful beak down into the shallows, came up again as quickly, and once more held a look at Tamsin.

"You are so beautiful," she whispered. The great bird dipped its long neck as if in polite agreement and, with that, poked once more at a light in the water. Bringing nothing up, at last it turned away in all dignity, held out broad white wings, and with perfect grace lifted away downstream.

Tamsin got up and scrambled down the bank to see what had so drawn the egret's pointed looks. There, just in the water was a thing small, round, and brass. Plucking it up, she saw the great bird had found Papa's compass that was lost, forgotten since the wheel had pulled him down – Papa's precious compass with the hinged blade that made it into a sundial. He always had it with him.

Papa had known by instinct the pull of the moon, the times of night and day when he had to leave the fields or his bed to be at the mill for the tide. But this sundial-compass that drew together in his hand all the earthly directions, a faraway sun, and time itself – this was a mystery Tamsin knew he pondered.

The day they'd pulled stone from the new rye field, Papa had let her hold the mystery. It was the day before he split into lights. Now here was his puzzle again, a knot of earth and sun in her hand. She looked up in case she might see the white egret, but it was gone, so she thanked the air. Tomorrow she would leave and take Papa's mystery with her.

She climbed back up the bank to the dam and examined the sundial. The hinge of the blade still worked – shadow made it mid-afternoon – and the compass needle pointed due north perfectly along the line of the dam. The millstream and stony bottom had not harmed it, had been merciful to a small miracle. Tamsin tucked the sundial-compass into the pocket inside her petticoats, scooped up her shoes in one hand and the spray of white yarrow in the other. Arms held wide, once more like a blue heron above the pond, she ran the length of the dam to the mill path.

There she sat to put on her stockings and shoes and, marveling still, took the sundial-compass from her pocket. She raised the blade again to see the shadow it cast and studied the compass, puzzled now that the needle pointed not north, but east. She tapped the brass case. The needle bounced a little but steadied again, still east.

Tamsin could hear Grandmother Cat's voice in her mind – *Heed the unexpected, dear*. After all, when Moses saw a burning bush, he turned aside from his path and found himself on holy ground. And from that, he learnt a great deal. So she got up and walked east, tending toward saltmarsh and bay.

When she had passed the low mass of blueberries, dense leaves now dark red, her feet slowed and stopped. Breeze was turning chill, clouds moving in. She listened to the air and considered the compass. The blade showed nothing of time now, but the needle still pointed east. Uneasy, she bent her face to the soft yarrow. Then holding the sundial-compass in a fist at her heart, she walked on toward the thicket of marsh elders that crowded into red cedars.

Coming close, she was met with a racket of red-winged blackbirds, their harsh *oh-a-reeyee* a din as loud as if dozens of them with their scarlet shoulders were shoving one another to claim nesting ground. But this was the end of October. Something had rattled them badly.

Tamsin's heart beat hard against the small brass mystery. Holding her yarrow close, she pressed on into the thicket. She wished now she'd taken the track that ran round the far side of the hill, the way horses hauled winter fodder from saltmarsh to barn. But she was here now, in among red-cedars, Papa's compass showing only east, and so she made her way. Branches pulled at her gown, brushed her face, and snatched her cap.

She stopped again to listen.

Life in a houseful of family had taught her that in the midst of any racketing sound, if she was quiet within and listened beyond, she might hear slivers of something else, a silence perhaps, or another story. So she stood still, waiting for what might come in the quarter-moments hidden within blackbird fuss.

Soon a thread of voice came through, and the deeper she listened, the longer the thread she could follow, until she knew it was the sound of a man wailing wild and dreadful at the salt-marsh. In this tidal place, thick grasses rooted in patches of mud shallows, no sound would carry far. The wide marsh, water, earth and grass, would be soft and compassionate as a breast, willing to receive a cry of any sort, anguish or prayer.

Drawn by the pain hurled out in the voice, Tamsin moved into the tangle of groundsel trees that flourished at the salty edge. She pressed, uneasy, through silky late flowers and poison leaves, and when she stepped from the thicket, a clamor of blackbirds flushed up in the air above the marsh.

The egret was there, poised in the water, quite still.

Close in front of Tamsin, a man was bent in pain, salt water lapping his feet. He watched the egret. At the explosion of blackbirds behind him, he stood and whirled, an upraised fist wielding a stone.

Abruptly Tamsin faced Uncle Simon. Both froze, his expression twisted. The mass of stone now held above her head sent a shaft of clarity straight down through her brow, through the soles of her feet and into the ground. A sensation filled her utterly, that years later she would liken to the will of a figurehead at the prow of a ship, a woman facing turbulent seas, pledging protection to the mariners at her back. From beneath her soles through her heart, a lightning impulse lifted to her uncle's face the spray of white yarrow. Tiny shooting stars crossed the air to breath and spirit. The yarrow blew clean through him, so that when his fierce stone arm went light, he let it fall.

Outraged, he shouted, *"Magic!"*

And when the stone itself let go, his empty hand rose to the yarrow, and Tamsin let him take it.

"Grace!" she said, surprised, and took a single step back.

Blackbird clamor stopped. Silence held over the marsh.

His jaw did not move, but she heard his words. "The Judas, I could have killed him."

Another step back. Poised to turn and bolt, she asked quietly, "Did you? Kill him?"

His sound was wild – *"I could have saved him."*

Sundial-compass tight to her heart, cry stifled, Tamsin took one after another near-invisible step back till groundsel trees brushed her neck.

"But I didn't!"

"You didn't – *what?*"

"Stop him! He fell. I didn't stop him."

Her face to the marsh, Tamsin scanned it avidly. If her uncle wanted her dead now, she wanted to see the egret first. She wanted to see its sharp look back at her.

Still her uncle didn't move.

Nor could she move, but with a sense not of her body, she knew she could melt imperceptibly to become one with a groundsel tree. So single-minded, she melted back, and when she had done it, the egret spread long white wings and lifted away.

Then a groundsel tree began the shift to hurtle a returning girl through red cedars, snatch her cap from a branch that had taken it, and push through marsh elders a living girl. Tamsin pelted hard up the mill path as far as the dam, till she knew her uncle had neither broken a tree with his bare hands, nor come after her.

There she stopped long enough to breathe, stuff the cap into her pocket, kick dirt from her shoes, and think. Was Uncle Simon at the dam, but did not push Papa down? Did not kill him, and did not save him? Her uncle believed his own children so sinful, he would take a willow whip to them.

His own brother, he called Judas. He would let her Papa die.

But what light was it, shot from the ground through her soles, heart, and yarrow, straight to his breath? *Magic?*

Grace.

Why grace?

Grandmother had told her, yarrow speaks of grace.

Papa's compass in a fist, she opened it to look. Needle pointed north, dial showed late afternoon. Surpassingly grateful for ordinary time and direction, only later might she wonder at her movement through groundsel tree. Now she went on past the mill pond, past the low hill where the Rowans' wheat hid till spring, and on to the elderberry bushes, source of her syrup now put up in jars in the cabinet, tomorrow packed in the oxcart.

17

Out of the rowan trees ahead, James strode the mill path toward Tamsin, smiling broadly, holding out to her something bright red in his hand. At the sight of it, her stomach rose. Veering into the elderberry bushes, she vomited.

"Tamsin! *Tamsin!*" When he came to her, his hand held rowanberries. "Look! Grandmother Cat will do something wonderful for you in the morning! She's to call in a whole flock of cardinals to eat the rowanberries, so they –"

She stared at his hand that was not bloody with Papa's blood, and opened her fist. His face went pale.

"Where did you find it?"

"In the stream below the dam."

He shut his eyes hard.

"James, an egret showed it to me."

He said nothing.

"A great egret, a white –"

He looked at her and snapped. "I know what an egret is."

She was stung, but understood. She'd seen Papa splintered into lights. Her arms held empty space so he'd come back. But James had grappled bodily under the wheel. James untangled broken limbs, held Papa dead, and laid him out.

Now he looked downstream, bleak as though his Uncle Robert were still caught. "My father," he said with loathing, "is a monster. Damned. Monster."

"James," Tamsin whispered, "we don't know that."

He stared at the mill.

She saw chilling flashes of Uncle Simon at the marsh. She searched her uncle's rage for one single harmless moment she could lift up and offer to James for comfort, but there was none.

She would not tell him Uncle Simon was on the dam when Papa fell. She would not tell him his father was mad. With grief or guilt or fear of God, she didn't know, but if she told James, he would be sure his father had done murder, and he would be wrong.

Nor would she tell him the needle of Papa's compass had pointed east, or that lightning exploded *up* from the earth. Something desperately wrong in Uncle Simon had changed in a flash of yarrow to his breath. But she couldn't explain it. Morning and evening, when she and James milked the cows and talked, he never once mocked the workings of her mind. But after this he wouldn't believe her, so she'd not tell him.

Dizzy, she sat down hard among the elderberries to put herself and her hands on the ground. A slow swell of unnamable *good* came up from the earth. She held still until her breath eased. When she could, she looked within to see what was there and found a sort of evenness. It was in the set of her shoulders, the balance above her heart. A beginning of peace perhaps, but no word of comfort for James. Still she loved him, and so, close as they were, something consoling and true must be said.

He sat down with her on the ground. She closed her eyes, feeling for the balance above her heart, but saw the dam instead, her uncle at the far end, dragging gale wind wreckage from the pond. Her Papa, pulling a branch wedged in the headrace, tumbled backward onto the wheel.

She opened her eyes to stop seeing.

"James, your father is fearful and he's angry. He can be cruel. But he is not Cain. He grieves Papa. He didn't kill him."

"You don't know that."

She did not say, *I see it,* because he wouldn't know how to believe her. She said, "I feel it."

"You've never felt his whip."

Tamsin hurt for him. She fingered the rowanberries in his hand to touch his palm.

"Grief may change him," she said. "What if he never takes a whip to any of you ever again? He might not. I don't think he will."

"He's not your Papa," he said and tipped the rowanberries into her hand, his eyes on her hair. No linen cap, but tiny groundsel tree flowers were stuck there by their nectar. He picked and brushed them away, one by one.

She watched his face and said, soft as she could, "James, they were brothers, however at odds. Your father is grieving. When he finds his peace, he may be a different man."

James didn't answer, but went on picking flowers from her hair. Slowly his face softened. Tamsin was moved by his touch. She liked it, and looked for the last moment he'd been happy. "You said Grandmother is calling in the cardinals. Why?"

"So they'll eat the rowanberries and carry the seed to Uncle Nat's house for you. They're to plant the Rowan line at the harbor. For you."

She hesitated. "For me."

James smiled a little, his fingertips gently tugging in her hair.

Now she wondered what he knew. Had Grandmother told him his cousin was a rowess? Did he know what that meant, though she had only a faint idea herself? Rowanberries in one hand, Papa's compass in the other, James' touch in her hair, she felt wobbly, all unready. Tears rolled up from her heart in waves. James put his arms around her and held her. In a little while, he kissed her at the corner of her mouth. A single blossom of red lobelia bloomed there. She felt it clearly, only for a moment, but never lost the memory.

After silence he whispered, "We should go back."

"The cows will need us," she said.

LATER, WHEN UNCLE SIMON CAME TO THE KITCHEN, Tamsin was wrapping stalks of Grandmother's herbs, fresh cut. She did not look up as he laid a bunch of white yarrow on the table. Aunt Adah thanked him over and over, in tones of surprise, and put them in a jar on the cupboard. He went out and was heard chopping wood until supper. When he came in, he buried his face in the mass of starry flowers. Tamsin didn't look, but she saw.

AFTER SUPPER, SHE TOOK HER MENDING TO THE PARLOR to sit between the window and the lamp. James was there, Peter beside him on the boys' usual bench. James had taken the Bible from the rowan-wood box and held it open on his lap, reading. Uncle Simon, coming to the parlor, held his hands out silently for the book. James did not move, but asked to read scripture on this last night before his cousins were to leave. Tamsin held her breath for the storm, but instead felt an odd peace in the room. Her uncle went to sit in the wing chair and waited as the family gathered.

With the Bible in James' hands, Tamsin felt a shade of Papa and looked round the parlor. James smiled and asked her what book they should read. His little brother all but leapt off the settle.

"Mine! My book! Luke!" he said, grinning in triumph.

"Very well, the Book of Luke. And what chapter? How old would someone be?" James asked, exactly the way Papa would do. His eyes turned to Tamsin as if they couldn't help it.

Softly she said, "Fifteen."

"And beginning at what verse?"

Phebe climbed onto Peter's knee beside James and showed her wide-open hand. "Four!"

James tucked her thumb into her palm. "How many?"

"Four!"

Abigail insisted, "Three!"

"Good," James said. "Reading from the Book of Luke, beginning at chapter fifteen, verse four. Reading three verses."

He smiled at Abigail, who dimpled happily at her big brother.

Phebe leant in to watch, so James moved his finger under the words:

"What man of you, having an hundred sheep, if he lose one of them doth not leave the ninety and nine in the wilderness and go after that which is lost, until he find it? And when he hath found it, He layeth it on his shoulders, rejoicing –"

A discomfited sound came from the wing chair at the hearth. Grandmother Cat turned to her son. Tamsin heard, but did not look. These were beautiful verses. If her uncle was struck by the story of a lost sheep, then she wished him the pain and joy of being found.

"– And when he cometh home, he calleth together his friends and neighbors, saying unto them, Rejoice –"

Uncle Simon gasped, heaved himself up from the wing chair, and left the parlor. James waited. The back door slammed.

Phebe poked James' finger. *"Me.* That word is *me."*

"It is," James said, and continued, *"Rejoice with –"*

He let her say it.

"Me!"

And he ended, *"For I have found my sheep which was lost."*

Right away, Grandmother Cat got up and said everyone must go to bed, because tomorrow morning early the cart must be packed to go to the harbor. There was no chance then, for anyone to remark on Uncle Simon's sudden leave-taking or on the meaning of the verses.

James did, though, catch Tamsin's eye, go light a lantern in the kitchen, and go out the kitchen door. Slipping out after him, she saw him hesitate. Uncle Simon might be in the barn. She followed him into the rowan trees.

He said to her quietly, "Whatever did you mean, my father is well? He walked out on the reading. It's his same old ferment."

"But, James, might it be a good ferment?" She smiled in the dark. "Like cider, like that. Only watch him. Watch his manner. You may see a change." She touched his hand. "He brought yarrow to your mother today."

She wanted him to kiss her again, but he didn't. He spoke of loading the cart in the morning, so she said she had to go tuck Phebe into bed and left him. Still, at the kitchen door, she stopped and turned round to go back, but the lantern moved away across the bridge.

18

Rising in a cold dawn, Tamsin and James did the milking in near silence. Soon as they were done, she went with Phebe to gather eggs. Phebe stroked the hens' feathers goodbye, but Tamsin chose three good layers and put them in a willow cage of Peter's devising. Aunt Martha would leave some of hers too. There would be enough to begin.

Peter was lifting Mother's great wheel up onto the cart. Sturdy as it was, rowan-wood, he cushioned it round with the last sacks of the spring's wool. Tamsin brought out her many jars of extracts and elderberry syrup, with Grandmother Cat's jars of pickled cucumbers and onions. She put them, safe as she could, in a front corner of the cart, padded with linen bags of seeds and beans, wrapped herbs, and sacks of milkweed pods, wadding for the quilt they would make in the winter. The floss from Suriname, Tamsin kept with Papa's compass in the pocket tied inside her petticoats.

Peter and James followed with three hogsheads of cider, two barrels of apples, a sack of onions, a dozen pumpkins, three sacks of ground Indian corn, two of rye, and one of the new Red Lammas wheat just milled. They swung up a chest packed with linens, blankets, two quilts, and a good counterpane, and another chest of clothing. Last, Tamsin put the cage with the hens up onto the back of the cart. Phebe would watch over them.

WHEN THE FAMILY WENT INSIDE TO TAKE BREAKFAST, Grandmother Cat held Tamsin and James back and led them to the bridge. She had a wide flat basket and two knives. Tamsin took a knife to the rowan trees by the mill path, James took a knife to the far side, and they cut bunches of rowanberries to put in the basket. Then lifting it high in the air, Grandmother Cat stepped about the bridge as if she were dancing, and whistled the cardinals' long, sloping *cheer, cheer* and their quick *pretty! pretty! pretty!* Warm light rose above the berries, and the first flashes of wings whipped the air red all round her. She laughed.

"They like to start with the abundance of the basket, but they'll go all over the trees."

James took up the birdsong and the flickering spread. Tamsin, enchanted, surrounded with wings, sang too, and then not only bright red, but so many soft brown, flame-edged wings flocked to the berries that the branches of the trees themselves danced under the weight of their landings.

When scores of brilliant birds, replete with rowanberries, had settled somewhat, Grandmother Cat took up their song in longer phrases and stepped lightly to the oxcart. There she turned and cocked her head toward the trees. Listening, she nodded once, and sent Tamsin and James ahead to the house to take their breakfast.

MIDMORNING, JAMES HITCHED ETHAN AND LEVI TO THE cart. Tamsin stood and watched. There was a boundary in the world between everything and nothing, and the oxen under their yoke would pull her across it. She went to Ethan, laid her cheek against his broad face, and stroked young Levi's neck.

Uncle Simon wandered seemingly aimless round the cart. Tamsin stayed with the oxen and took care not to look, but she heard him. He went near Peter and spoke under his breath. Peter would want to fish for the tavern, he said, so he would have Isaac build a shallop for him up to Colbrook, and he himself would sail it to the harbor. Then he went round back of the cart to Mother and told her he knew Martha had a good garden, but he would send provisions. James would drive down to the harbor, he said, twice a year. Milled rye, Indian corn, Red Lammas, vegetables. Mother told him she would have half the wool to be shorn, come spring, and he agreed.

Aunt Adah came out of the house, the twins did not. Good-byes were short. Peter got up at the front of the cart. James helped Grandmother Cat to step up beside Peter. Susannah and Phebe climbed onto the back, Tamsin with them. Phebe laid her hands over the cage of hens.

Tamsin looked to James, where he waited to walk behind the cart. He was eyeing his father sideways, so she knew he'd heard the words. When Uncle Simon turned to give Tamsin a quick nod, oddly humble, James was watching. He glanced at her now, brow furrowed. "You see," she wanted to say.

At the front of the cart, Grandmother Cat scanned the rowan trees and whistled one strong, swooping note. The next moment, when Peter called out, "Ethan, Levi, step up," a hundred wings flamed from the trees and danced above the oxen like a pillar of fire, all the six miles to Wharf Street in Dorset Harbor.

THERE, WITH A LAST AWKWARD TURN, THE CART passed a row of substantial Dutch-roofed houses. In the midst of them stood a large white meetinghouse. A gentleman with powdered hair stepped out, wearing bright white preaching bands under a black coat. The minister of the Dorset Harbor parish stopped to watch the driver of a laden oxcart manage the rutty street. The cart, however, was less remarkable than a great flap of redbirds spiraling in the air above it. Then noteworthy at the back of the cart was a well-favored woman sitting with two young girls.

Captain Nathaniel Bradbury's sister had come to keep a tavern.

On down the street, the oxen ceased their labor in the side yard of the house that would be a tavern, an inn, and a home. There, before the family had even stirred their legs, the crowd of cardinals settled on the ground to pick about the bounds of the property for nourishment, dropping down their rowan seed, well prepared.

PART TWO

Dorset Harbor
Massachusetts Bay
1750-1751

19

October 29th, 1750

My dear Susannah,

Nathaniel and I are to go aboard this evening and set Sail in the morning. Despite our absence, Dear, we welcome you and your precious Children to this your new Home, with thanks and with confidence in your flourishing here. Many in the town have told us how glad they are at your Return.

Peter did very fine work in my Garden and was a clever Apprentice to Nathaniel, who says he now has a good grasp of Accounts, so I do hope you will be easy in your mind in that regard. As Peter will have told you, Nat has deposited significant Funds for your use, with several of the harbor Merchants. I want to explain one in particular.

A dear Friend from my early Cambridge years, Mistress Grace Parker, has kept up her late husband's Pottery manufactory in Charlestown since his sad death. Indeed she has worked hard to improve both the Making and the Material, leaving off use of our common local clay, and preferring a superior clay from Philadelphia that fires to a more durable dish, that is, her Stoneware. I will pass over Mistress Parker's many dreadful misfortunes, but end by saying that her Manufactory is now near bankrupt, so to help her and to gather all we can of her excellent Ware, we have purchased every piece of her remaining Stock: some baking dishes, pots, pudding pans, bread pans, bowls, platters, pitchers, mugs, several chamber pots, &c. A few of the pieces I have packed to take with us to the Eastward, the rest shipped to the harbor merchant, Mr. Jonathan Somerby, a good man, also a Deacon of the Parish. Therefore, when you are well settled, Dear, do go to him and he will see the Stoneware delivered to the House. As we know, our local redware is soft, cracks and nicks easily, thus poorly suited for Tavern use. Too, I have learnt from Mistress Parker that her Stoneware does not require use of the Leaded Glaze, but Salt instead, which will lessen the risk of Colic to your family and townspeople alike. Imagine! Visiting a Tavern for pleasant company, but leaving with a knotted-up Stomach, or in some years' time even the Palsy! This will not happen in your house, Susannah, I am quite sure. Not with you and Tamsin taking good Care of All.

Do tell Tamsin about the salted Glaze of the Stoneware. I think she will find it interesting.

Nat has had his ship's Carpenter build a bar in the large parlor, and simple tables and benches. I regret to say there's not been time for the bar itself to be properly finished before we sail and take the Carpenter with us. Nat spoke with Peter about this. He is quite an artisan, your Peter, and eager to be about the work!

As to Cordwood, young Noah Southworth brings it. I know you will remember his Father. He will keep an eye, but do let him know when you need more. He has been paid. Nat also had Noah Sr and Jr dig and build the second, larger Privy to accommodate the Tavern, as I am sure you were pleased to see!

I must not forget to say that Deacon Somerby has also three dozen pewter Spoons for you and a half-dozen pewter Forks, paid on account. If you like the Forks, he will acquire more. He carries a greater stock of imported goods lately, various sorts of Cloth, and Oranges, Lemons, Coffee, &c. You'll know by now that I have left with you some large Pots and Utensils. May all this be of good use as you make your start at the Harbor.

Nathaniel says that our new House is pleasantly set on a riverside between the settlement of Combe on the coast and an upriver Headland, called Doe's Leap. It is said that a Doe once escaped hunters by taking a great Jump, and disappeared in the middle of the Air! I promise not do likewise, Susannah, but we must write to each other.

Your loving Brother and I pray to the Lord always for your Health and Prosperity. With highest Regard and Affection, your Sister-in-Law,

Martha Bradbury

SUNSET ON THE DAY THE BENNETTS ARRIVED AT THE house at Wharf Street – oxcart unloaded, possessions in order, animals and family fed – Tamsin went up to help Phebe and Grandmother Cat settle for the night. Both were worn from a long day, but Tamsin was restless and went back down. She put on her cloak and went out the big front door, turning to study it in dim light. It was framed with wide boards and had a pretty, half-round window across the top, divided in pieces, like an arc of Papa's compass. Her hand slipped to the pocket inside her petticoat. The compass was there, safe.

Papa, I need you.

Salt breeze came in from the water. Tamsin went to the front gate to gain a little distance and consider the house. Uncle Nat's was a finer place than she'd ever thought to live. This was disquieting, as it walked her one step further away from Papa. This settling at the harbor, this living among all manner of townspeople, it felt unfitting. Mother was born here, true. Her father Peter Bradbury, now gone, had been a blacksmith well regarded among sailors, and her mother, Tamsin's Grandmother Bet, was much admired for her shore plum cordial in winter and excellent plum cakes – though honored even more for her kindness to the families of sailors lost.

Mother would feel easy here, of course. But the tavern would open daily to a welter of townsmen unknown and, stranger yet, mariners who came to the harbor from far away. Some might even stay nights at the inn above the tavern, below the attic chambers that would be Mother's and Peter's and hers shared with Phebe.

At this thought of the spacious attic, Tamsin's shoulders softened and fell a good inch. She surveyed the house now with the beginnings of gratitude to Uncle Nat. Their bedchambers would be more pleasing than those at the farm, even if the tavern would be full of the town.

She let go a long breath, feeling some peace would come – *a half-peace* – and walked round to the back. Peter had spent days digging Aunt Martha's garden out wider, and Tamsin wanted to see it, if she could in faded light. She had seeds to plant, come spring, and uses for the herbs.

Grandmother Cat had said to put extracts of elderberry and chamomile into the tavern's ale, so guests would do well through winter, whether or not they knew why. Tamsin liked this thought. There were stews, too, and other dishes she could change with herbs, though her present store would not last the season. Still she would try, quietly. Now knowing the horror that befell Priscilla, Tamsin would heed Grandmother's warnings. Always note signs. Heed the unexpected. Carry on the work. Rouse neither attention nor accusation. Keep the day-book. Record the work and its effects.

Unable to see much of the garden now, Tamsin was drawn to an ancient oak at the edge of the east yard, and she spoke to it, promising to move any rowan seedlings that started up too close. She laid her hands on its bark and looked to the sky through branches not yet bare, leaves rattling in the air off the sea.

It was All Hallows' Eve, only one dark night past new moon, the narrowest sickle of light already gone in the west. Grandmother Cat once told Tamsin that after harvest, at All Hallows', the red thread between life and death was spun out so fine as to all but disappear, and the living and the dead were then as close as ever they could be. Grandmother seemed to find that a comfort, but Tamsin could not yet.

Grieving and cold, she was turning to go in, when lantern light shone through the open kitchen door. Mother's figure, lit from behind, her face in full shadow, leant so far out from the doorway, she looked to be a bow with its string pulled back taut, her arms stretched behind her like arrows. Tamsin thought her hands must grip the doorjambs tight, or else she would spill forward, or else shoot straight out into salt air.

Instead, Mother slipped back into the house and came out in her cloak. Lantern in hand, she closed the door and walked away alongside Uncle Nat's back field, then turned. Tamsin followed the lantern with her eyes until, after another turn, the light began to move uphill. It disappeared in glimmering pieces beyond the trees.

Wherever would Mother go at this hour, and why? Tamsin thought to follow her, but remembered what happened the day she followed Papa. The thought cut deep and she didn't move, but pulled her cloak tight. She knew Mother had lived in this house with Uncle Nat and Aunt Martha sometime before she married Papa. She must know where she is, even in the dark. She must know where she's going, and how to come back.

Tamsin stayed a while watching for the lantern. When no light shone through the trees, she walked round to the big front door and went in under the arc of the window that was like Papa's compass.

20

IN THE LARGE PARLOR THAT WOULD BE A TAVERN, Peter sat with James, drinking Grandmother Cat's sharp cider in near-dark. A betty lamp sat on the bar, a lantern shed light on the table. Tamsin went to look at the bar. A wall of sturdy shelves had been built behind it, and at one end a tall cabinet. An array of spindles ran from counter to ceiling, the middle dozen of which were set in a frame that could be raised and hooked above to open the bar, then lowered and latched to close it. She thought it clever, and liked the unknown carpenter for making it.

The boys were talking over ways to finish all this fresh wood, and do it soon, before the tavern would open. Proper varnish, Peter said, would be costly, but with hard work, plain beeswax could be rubbed in and would do for a seal. He would watch for pits and wear, he said, and take good care of it.

Tamsin listened, and said nothing of Mother going uphill in the night. Seeing the boys had cider, she took the lantern to the kitchen and brought back a mug to lift her spirits. When she was Phebe's age, she'd felt that Grandmother's tasty cider danced upon her tongue. She wanted that dancing now.

Peter and James discussed what they knew from the tide mill

120

about the care of wet wood, and paid Tamsin little heed. Drinking her cider, she considered the bar.

At last she said, "Why not paint then? A shade like the sun, yellow. To seal the wood and brighten the room. Think of all the winter days and nights."

Peter didn't answer, but asked James if he'd look round the farm for hives and bring whatever comb he found.

James told Peter he'd likely not come back to the harbor till spring, and glanced a moment at Tamsin.

She went on considering the bar, the wall of shelves, the neat cabinet, the many spindles. She imagined all the wood painted, then imagined it waxed, and put her mug down with a small thump.

"Peter, you're right, of course, all those pieces would be handsome waxed, though they've so many edges and dips and curves. The panels on the cabinet, all the spindles. But the spindles could be very pretty painted as well," she said. "And painting would be faster than rubbing it all with wax. We should open the tavern." *Though I don't want to.*

Peter set his jaw.

She took a swallow of cider and turned round to see dark wainscoting in dim light. "And it will be much easier working in the tavern in the evening," she said, "if there's more light." *Though I don't want to work in the tavern at all, no matter the light.*

Peter drained his tankard and got up. James caught Tamsin's eye and said he'd go out to the barn and see all was well with Ethan and Levi. He took the tankards and the lantern. Peter went to the attic in the dark.

Tamsin finished her cider and looked about the quiet room, seeing it now as a public house, the carpenter's new tables full of noisy men. Then taking the lamp and her mug, she crossed past the fine front stairs into Aunt Martha's small parlor that might soon become a meeting and drinking room for the town selectmen, or a room for lodgers to dine apart from the tavern. A folded paper lay on a desk, "Susannah," written on it. She took it to the kitchen table with the lamp and went to watch out the back door-way, in case Mother would come.

Instead, it was James who sprang up the steps with a lantern and, in dim light, all but ran her down. Steadying her with a hand, he hung the lantern on a peg, put his arms around her and kissed her on the mouth. He drew back, though not far, and she took his hands, to hold on.

"I'll miss you," he said. "I don't want to leave here. I want –" He broke off. "The farm will be bleak with you gone."

"Come to the harbor then, James, and bring us things. Bring us more Red Lammas, we surely won't find it here. Bring us our wool from the shearing. Dig me good patches of chamomile. And Michaelmas daisies from the meadow at the dam. I want to put them beside the path in front, and on every side of the house. For courage."

He smiled. "You need more courage?"

"If you find beeswax for Peter, you can bring us the honey."

"You know you're right. Paint would be better."

She shrugged. "Peter has his way of seeing. He wants to make things beautiful. But James," she said quietly, "I will miss you. I'll miss you listening to me. Peter doesn't."

"I'll come in the spring."

"It's a long time."

He put his arms around her and slipped his fingers inside her linen cap. She held him too, intense sweetness tangled with her alarm at Mother walking away in the dark. She wanted to go on holding James for a very long time, and needed to be alone with the fear spreading inside her skin. Eyes tight shut, she saw Grand-mother Cat, a small child watching her mother maneuver a coracle at the edge of a moving sea. Tamsin wanted her mother.

"I'm tired," she said. "Are you?"

He nodded. They went into the kitchen and she took up the lamp. They climbed to the attic of Uncle Nat's fine house, and he kissed her again. James went to Peter's chamber, and Tamsin to hers, a mass of feelings overwhelming her.

She lay awake listening to Grandmother Cat and Phebe sleep, listening for Mother's steps, fear rising till exhaustion let her not listen.

21

SHE DREAMT A WHITE EGRET STALKED THE NEW RYE field for little white stones, earth breaking beneath its chancy, thin legs. A fine red thread shuttled between rowan trees on the far side of the stream and the rowans on the mill path, a spidery bridge across the air. Water rushed red under the bridge to a mill wheel and out to a vast sea.

IMAGES WOKE HER.

Phebe was still asleep, Grandmother Cat pinning her gown over her stays. When she went downstairs, Tamsin got up to dress, and when she heard Mother start down as well, she went weak with relief. Mother had not disappeared in the night.

At breakfast, Tamsin's stomach was too unsteady to take even one of Mother's journeycakes, even with a spoon of her own elderberry syrup on it. Losing Grandmother Cat and James both at once would be unbearable, and it would happen this morning. It would happen now.

Grandmother sat with Tamsin and took her hands. "My dear, watch over the rowan seedlings. Move them as they need to be moved. Help Phebe to work with them. Her touch will be good

124

for them, and the rowans' wisdom will help you both with what you need to do. It will ease the change. And listen, my dear. You are a rowess. Look after your mother."

Tamsin wanted to hold onto this moment and never lose it. Her eyes grew soft as she gathered every expression, every line of Grandmother's face, drawing it into memory like putting fresh yarrow up in a cabinet before a cold winter. She listened closely, not so much to Grandmother's words, but to the sound of her voice, so that it soaked into her being in the way linden flower extract suffuses cake. Grandmother watched Tamsin and nodded, and they went out to the side yard, where Ethan and Levi were yoked to the cart. The others were there.

"Susannah, when will you open the tavern?" Grandmother Cat asked.

"In a month. We'll try to open in one month."

Grandmother nodded once, but said nothing and got up on the cart.

Tamsin saw James trying hard not to look at her, so she went to him. "I thought of something else I'll need from the farm. In the spring, bring me sweetgrass from the marsh. I want to find a spot where it will do well here. I'll make ointment."

"And save your townsmen from a plague of flies and gnats?" He put on a wry smile.

She was glad he could tease. "Yes. Dig up some patches for me. Good roots," she said.

"In the spring," he said. "Good roots." He looked into her eyes and turned away.

At a word, the oxen pulled the cart carrying Grandmother Cat and James onto Wharf Street, past the row of Dutch-roofed houses and a meetinghouse. Tamsin made herself breathe slow and deep to keep from crying out, and went round to the back of the house. The oak at the yard's edge called to her, so she went and put her face against its bark. She reached her arms as far round as she could and sobbed, holding the ancient tree.

When her sight cleared, there in morning light was Peter's

work with the garden. He had dug it longer and wider, divided in four squares. There looked to be root crops in the near square, spread with wheat straw from the farm. Tamsin bent down, took up a handful of newly turned soil, and smelled it. This would be home now. For now, this was home, and she was grateful to Peter for digging in the earth.

Thinking further on his plan to finish the wood of the bar, still doubting he was right, she went into the house. Mother was in the kitchen, cutting apples. The letter from the parlor desk lay unfolded on the table. Mother gave it to her. "Your Uncle Nat and Aunt Martha have done so much for us." Her eyes were wet.

Tamsin began to read, but Peter was speaking to Mother of his urgent need for beeswax. Mother told him softly, they were unlikely to find enough beeswax to finish all that fresh wood, but she knew where a mass of bayberry bushes grew, and if Peter could pick twenty pounds or so, there might be just enough wax in the berries to seal the bar's counter. "You could wax at least the counter, Peter."

Tamsin ventured again that perhaps paint, perhaps a shade of yellow, would brighten the tavern for the short days and dark nights to come.

Peter planted his feet and glared at his sister. Mother agreed to the paint.

"We'll get bayberry wax for you, Peter. We'll go to Green Cove," she said, and made him go out to the barn to find buckets.

In quiet victory, Tamsin called to Phebe to say they were going out.

Mother covered the bowl of cut apples with a cloth, then oddly pressed her hands flat on the kitchen table and leant over deep, as if in sudden pain.

"Mother?"

She stood up slowly. "Green Cove," she said. "Going there is very hard."

There was grief in her mother's face.

"I will tell you," she said.

22

PETER STRODE THE SHORE ROAD WELL AHEAD OF THE others, swinging four empty buckets hard as he went.

"I used to go there, to the cove," Mother said, holding Phebe's hand tight at her side. "It's just past Pulpit Rocks, protected. It opens southward." She called out to Peter, "Bayberries grow exceeding thick there.

"But Phebe, you be careful," she said. "They're to be picked and boiled only, never tasted."

Watching, Tamsin wondered whether Peter's speed came from his anger at her, or better, the eagerness of an artisan to render wax for the care of new wood. But sure, beneath any anger must be restless grief at his Papa's death. Did he know that?

Phebe carried a bucket and swung it in imitation of Peter.

"And there's beach," Mother murmured.

They walked another half-mile and, passing tall swells of granite, found an ocean scooping inland suddenly at their feet. To one side, by the rocks, was dense rambling green, to the other side pale beach, and along the landward edge of the cove, a thicket of scrub pine. Peter ran to examine the bushes. Chickadees flew up as he shouted his approval of the abundant berries. He set to picking and thumping them into a bucket, and Phebe ran after him to watch and do the same. Tamsin followed.

Susannah walked on alone toward the beach.

EXPLORING WITH A BUCKET, DROPPING BERRIES ON berries, Tamsin found her way to the shoreline. A jut of rocks pointed away toward an island. Looking all round her, Tamsin thought the cove an excellent refuge, and turned back into the bushes to a spot where she could go on picking and keep an eye on Mother.

Might she have come here last night?

Tamsin watched her walk the sand, rest on a driftwood log, then rise and walk and pick up little things.

Tamsin went to find Phebe. "Finish the rest of this bucket for me, would you, dear?"

Phebe would.

A MEANDERING LINE RAN THE LENGTH OF THE BEACH, marking the change from firm, damp sand to dry and soft, a line between dark and light. Tamsin walked that line.

"Mother, all these little holes. There looks to be good clamming."

Susannah lifted a hand, holding out white shells. "I used to come here to dig clams with the mother of my first husband," she said softly. "My *belle-mère*."

Tamsin looked at her mother's handful of shells, stared at them, and heard in her mind a thing she'd heard when she was little. At the time, it had made no sense. Mother once had a husband who was not Papa. That man had a mother who was not Grandmother Cat, but was called by a strange name.

Susannah slipped the shells into her pocket. "We English didn't use to eat clams, you know. We thought them the poorest of God's blessings, and let our pigs run and dig them up. It was the Indians who taught the English to eat clams. My mother didn't like them." Her eyes seemed to crinkle in a smile and see a distance. "I learnt from my *belle-mère* who came from an island where they ate clams and mussels." Susannah nodded across the water. "She taught me how to find them out on Flagg Island, and taught me to cook them."

Tamsin heard her mother's voice as if from far away. She sensed a threshold and took a step, a very small one, with an uncertain foot. "What did you call her? What was her name?"

"Isabelle Julien," Susannah said, as if the sounds were comforting to her ear, though entirely strange to Tamsin. "Her husband was Ezechiel Julien, from the island, the Île de Ré."

"Where they cooked clams and mussels," Tamsin said, stepping carefully.

"Yes. For a while he was minister to the French in Boston, but as their church dwindled, he brought the family here to Dorset. I asked him once why they came, though no other French were here, and he told me he knew two things only – our Lord Jesus Christ and fishing." She smiled. "There were French settled inland, but he didn't want to go there. He said our Lord would understand his desire to be at the sea.

"His son, my husband, understood too. Lost." She looked toward the water.

Heed the unexpected, Tamsin thought. This heeding made her dizzy, but she took a brave step. "What was his son's name?"

"Élias. Élie. He went to sea too."

Sharp pain in Tamsin's heart – Eli. So Mother named the newborn after her husband lost at sea. Tamsin's Eli, the one who didn't stay, but taught her to wonder at her life.

"Élie and I had three daughters. Alice, Charlotte, and Lucretia. Our little girls are in the graveyard up past Nat's house."

Now Tamsin knew. "You went there last night."

Instead of being with us, you went away to a graveyard with dead children of a dead husband. What if we needed you?

"All Hallows' Eve," Susannah said. "I went to sit with them."

Phebe came struggling, out of balance. "Mother, look at the berries! See, Tamsin, I filled your bucket!"

Susannah knelt to put her arms round her lastborn, her fifth daughter. She looked into the bucket and kissed Phebe. "You've picked a good lot of berries! How many buckets are left?"

"Peter's last and one more. Tamsin, will you come?"

Tamsin didn't answer.

"Let's go see all the berries," Mother said. She took the bucket and they shuffled through sand to the bushes where Peter still worked.

"Goodness, Peter, you've done well. Phebe, dear, stay here with Peter and help him finish this last one, then come home. Tamsin and I will take the ones that are full. Peter, would you look in the shed for the biggest tub and fill it with water? Phebe, you tip all the berries in and start them to soak clean.

"Tamsin and I will be out a short while."

Tamsin, the eldest of five daughters now, carried bayberries to the house with her mother. Beyond that, she didn't know where they were to go, but understood thresholds and was quiet.

23

LEAVING BUCKETS IN THE KITCHEN, SUSANNAH LED Tamsin out along the path that edged Uncle Nat's back field. "This is the way toward Mr. Proctor's orchard. The graveyard is up the hill road, near the top."

Tamsin tasted vinegar. *No, not the daughters, the ones who are dead, not today.*

She stopped walking. Her insides felt sick, but Mother kept on, so she made herself follow uphill. She pushed her hand into a pocket to find Papa's sundial-compass that held all the world and the heavens. On this road that she did not want to walk, she did what Grandmother and her own good sense had taught her. She looked into the trees and listened to birdsong. Her eyes foraged for herbs. She would need to know and write it in her day-book.

Spiky patch of mullein: Good, throat, headache.

Susannah spoke. "Tamsin, you've been uprooted, I know, I'm sorry. You'll miss your Grandmother Cat and the farm. But the harbor will make you a good home, I promise. I was here all my life till I married your Papa." She smiled. "I was here when I was first a mother. So I'd like you to know your little sisters, Tamsin. They would have been so dear to you.

"I will wait before bringing Phebe and Peter up to the grave-

131

yard. But you're nearly a grown woman, Tamsin. You're strong and learnèd as a healer."

She took in her mother's words.

Soon they came to a stone fence with a low iron gate, little piles of white shells on either side.

"Here," Susannah said. "The gate will cry like a tree full of crows, but never mind it. There's no one nearby to hear." She whispered, "Not even your baby sisters."

An image struck Tamsin of three little girls laid in the ground, daughters of her own mother. The shriek of the gate was a sound she'd not heard since she stood at the dam with Grandmother Cat, or before that in the kitchen. She tightened her grip of the compass.

In the graveyard Susannah turned uphill, skirting rows of graves, some marked, others low mounds. Some were very small. Near the top of the rise, they stopped at a patch of ground, white with shells. Here were three big stones in a row, not proper markers, but pumpkin-sized stones like the ones Papa and Ethan had pulled from the rye field. Susannah dropped to her knees at the edge of the white ground and took from her pocket the shells she'd gathered at the cove. Setting them gently at the big stones, she said, "Alice, and Charlotte, and Lucretia.

"They died of the throat distemper."

Tamsin did not kneel or sit, but stood back. *Mullein. There is mullein on the road.*

"When I used to dig for clams at the cove, Alice and Charlotte would go with me to pick up shells. Once, when we went home, Alice threaded some gull-pecked shells into a rattle for Lucretia, and came running to me, just like Phebe this morning with her bucket. '*Maman, Maman!*' she said. 'See what I made for Lu!'

"Élie spoke French with the girls, so they called me *Maman*."

"*Maman*," Tamsin said, trying the sound.

"Yes. Then after my three little ones died – and then Élie – your Uncle Nat and Aunt Martha took me to live with them. All I could do then was go to Green Cove and walk and pick up shells.

So I brought them here to the girls. And as days grew short, I saw that when I came in the evening, the lantern always found them because of the shells."

"You left shells at the gate."

"Yes. And I planted seedlings for the shore plums." She nodded to a thicket of red fall leaves just beyond her little girls' stones. "They've done well. You see, Alice loved plum preserves. When I cooked plums, she liked to press them down through the strainer with the back of a spoon. We did have mishaps, but she learnt not to push so hard the strainer would tip."

Tamsin pictured the strainer like a little coracle, tipping in a stream. She had done this too. A different picture came, unbidden. A field of small white stones on broken ground. A tangle of red arced over – something. Water. A white bird was there. In a moment, Tamsin felt her hand in her pocket touching Papa's sundial-compass, and the mismatched things that she saw felt familiar, somehow right.

"I put in the strawberry plants too," Susannah went on. She looked to a withered patch beyond the third stone.

Tamsin saw the strawberries would need care, come spring.

"And up beyond the shore plums, you can't see, but I put in raspberry cane.

"I busied myself," she nodded. "I thought what things the girls would like, and I planted them. I thought, when I came here to sit, there would be berries through the summer, and I'd gather them for Nat and Martha, and we'd think about the girls."

Susannah looked up at Tamsin. "I didn't know then about your dear Papa. I didn't know how soon I'd be gone to the farm."

Tamsin turned away and looked back at the rest of the burying ground. "Is – is your –"

"Élie died at sea, at the Grand Banks. He didn't come home."

Tamsin was chilled. How terrible if Papa had sailed away and never come back. At least she could sit up with him that night and talk to him and hold his hands. Now she sat down.

"Élie loved the sea as his father did," Susannah said. "So to be buried there –" She cocked her head and smiled. "It's what he would have wanted. More than this ground."

Watching the softness in her mother's face, Tamsin felt how much she had loved this unknown person who spoke another language to his daughters, who were incomprehensibly Tamsin's sisters. Mother had loved two men.

Looking away, she considered the shells from the cove and the meaning of three stones pulled, no doubt, from this very field. Tamsin knew the pulling of stone. She wondered at the strawberry patch and the bright autumn red of the shore plum bushes, so unexpected in a burying ground. And raspberry cane, unseen, thorny.

Heed them, she thought. *They might be a sign.*

Mother's life with Papa at the farm now looked to be a thick vine overgrowing deep years at the harbor, where she'd loved a stranger called Élie, and three small girls had died. Then a vision of Mother stood up before the mass of red leaves, a tangled, foreign being, complicated as bayberry bushes, with shells and plums in her hands.

24

THE NEXT WEEKS AT THE HOUSE WERE AS FULL OF WORK as the last months had been at the farm, though now without Grandmother Cat and James, and without the farm. Once after supper Phebe said they should read scripture again because she wanted to look at the words, then remembered they had no Bible.

Tamsin kept watch on Mother, braced herself for the mass of coming strangers, and tried to fix her mind on dishes she could make and improve with good herbs, for some yet-unknown number of drinkers and lodgers. And in this time, she found wonder in the tips and shoots of rowan seedlings appearing new each afternoon of a seacoast November, all round the edges of the property. She taught Phebe which of the sprouts were well placed and which should be moved, and it became Phebe's own work to lift and resettle them, telling Peter where he must break up the soil for them in Uncle Nat's back field.

Peter's heart was set on giving a sturdy, warm finish to the bar's counter, and Phebe worked with him to render the wax he needed. For days, they simmered bayberries in batches in a great pot, long used for this purpose. Every morning, Phebe would run downstairs, eager to see what green had floated up and cooled in the night, enchanted that her fingers could slip beneath the skim and lift it right up off cooled water.

ALMOST EVERY DAY IN THE MIDST OF PREPARATIONS, and well before the tavern was opened, townspeople would come to the doors, both front and back. Women came who remembered Susannah's mother, Tamsin's Grandmother Bet, and brought with them gifts of onions or a squash pie. Old fishermen, who for years had downed their ale with Tamsin's Grandfather Peter, the blacksmith, came to pay their respects and bring fresh fish to the widow they'd known since a child. Tamsin watched as each went to greet Mother. They had all known Élias Julien, the captain buried at sea off Newfoundland. She wondered if all these greetings were painful to Mother, or comforting. She couldn't tell.

One morning Mr. Benjamin Proctor, who had the orchard out beyond Uncle Nat's big field, came to the back door with an offer of barter – apples in autumn and cider through winter and spring, in exchange for meals, drink, and good company, as often as he would come to the tavern. Susannah invited Mr. Proctor into the kitchen and told Tamsin how very kind he had been to her in her first bereavement. She accepted so generous an offer, and said she would have her son Peter go to help him with the harvest and the press. Tamsin said she would surely help too, and in time Phebe did as well. It was a good arrangement for all, as Mr. Proctor was a widower and had no living children.

More men came to the house on matters of trade. Uncle Nat had left funds on account with the brewer and the butcher, so one week, one of them came round to the house, and later the other came, to ask what the tavern would need delivered, and when. The brewer said, too, he had a cousin who was a coastal trader and would keep a supply of rum coming up from Salem, if Mistress – he stumbled, seeming unsure what family name he should remember – if Mistress would like. Peter inquired as to cost, and Susannah said that would be fine.

Later, when the butcher came, Tamsin had been considering dishes that might be made for tavern dinners, and told him, to begin, she would like to have three pounds of salted beef flank and about a third that weight of suet. She had her grandmother's ancient receipt for meat pies, she said, and would make them first for the family, later for the tavern. Susannah asked the butcher what farm nearby kept a good number of cows and might sell cheese and butter through the winter. He advised her to speak with Miriam Gates. She would be at the meetinghouse, come Sabbath, he said.

Therefore, three days later, the Bennetts went to worship at the harbor parish meetinghouse for the first time, though two Sabbaths had already passed since they'd come. Tamsin was sure this would prompt an unpleasant visit from the minister and didn't want to go, but Mother said they needed to meet Miriam Gates about cheese and butter, so they had best start going to Sabbath worship. After the morning sermon, they found Mistress Gates who, as it happened, was once Miriam Varney, who had known Susannah from childhood. She was pleased to see her, and glad the tavern would be a customer for her cows. Her boy Seth could, of course, deliver butter and cheese through winter, and milk when it came in spring.

To Tamsin's surprise, the minister did not descend with the dreaded visit immediately. Instead, the day after the Sabbath, a well-dressed gentleman in a fine wig appeared at the front door. He introduced himself as Deacon Jonathan Somerby and asked for Mistress Bennett. Tamsin feared the deacon had been sent ahead to deliver the minister's reprimand, but as he had a kind look and carried a basket of oranges, she withheld judgment.

When Mother came to the door, she said, "Captain Somerby, how good to see you!"

Tamsin heard, *Captain*.

"Mistress Bennett, how do you do?"

He made a slight bow, a flicker of light in his eye.

"It was my pleasure to help your brother acquire stoneware and pewter for the tavern. I've come to ask when you'd like delivery." He appeared to remember his hand. "And to offer you this welcome. A few oranges. I'm a merchant now, shore-bound, no longer sailing."

Susannah thanked him and invited him into the tavern.

Tamsin brought a mug of cider, and when she put it down before him, said politely, "*Deacon* Somerby." She meant it as a hint. *Deacon, Mother, like Uncle Simon. Be careful.*

Mother smiled. "Tamsin, Deacon Somerby was the ship's captain who took your Uncle Nat aboard as a boy and taught him to sail."

Tamsin went to the bar and pretended to dust, in case there might still be some reproach as to Sabbath attendance, but Mother spoke of Uncle Nat and Aunt Martha now in the eastward, and the deacon expressed sadness at Papa's death. Mother said she and Tamsin would visit his shop to plan delivery of the pewter and stoneware.

Deacon Somerby would be glad to assist in any way he could.

Soon after, Susannah told Tamsin they must go to the wharves to look for the deacon's shop. Though Uncle Nat's house was not far from the wharf, Tamsin had not been eager to go. But now before her, she found busy, interesting movement, vessels and sailors from away, unloading cargo and loading up salt cod for places unknown. She was curious where they'd all come from, and seeing African sailors, wondered, were they free or else bound, as the African people were who sat in the balcony of the meetinghouse on the Sabbath. If bound, she wondered whether there were ports where they might go ashore and choose not to return to sea.

Deacon Somerby's shop was lively with trade, but he came forward quickly, with wide eyes and a smile, to greet Mistress Bennett and her daughter. Indeed, he had received Mistress Parker's stoneware and the pewter spoons and forks. Was there any other way he could be of help?

Susannah asked if he might have a good close-woven linen, fit for a quilt. He assured Mistress Bennett that he did. Tamsin chose green for the quilt top and a near-white for the backing, four yards of each. Deacon Somerby called for his apprentice and the horsecart, and said they'd load up the tableware and linen and dispatch it all to Captain Bradbury's house this day. And would there be anything else?

Tamsin looked at Mother with a glint of mischief. "Paint?"

"Yes. We'd like a light – perhaps even a bright shade of paint. To lift the tavern in the dark of winter."

Deacon Somerby somehow pursed his lips and smiled at the same time.

The deacon looks to have a secret, Tamsin thought. Then he gave her mother such a look of intrigue, she imagined he had more secrets than one.

"Mistress Bennett, I have just the thing for you." In a low tone, he said, "I have a source of fine yellow ochre pigment, what you might call a personal source." He gestured vaguely inland.

Herself a keeper of secrets, Tamsin could see he enjoyed holding whatever this one was, and whatever others he might have as well. She liked him for it, and for his good humor and his help.

"I will acquire the pigment for you, and for how large an area?"

Susannah said it would be the paneled bar, the row of narrow spindles from counter to ceiling, and the wainscoting all round the parlor. The deacon was pleased to reckon the amount of paint to be mixed, and advised purchase of several hog bristle brushes and perhaps two narrow brushes of either sea mink or squirrel hair, suitable for the spindles. He would have them ready with the ochre pigment in a week's time.

"I will put it to Captain Bradbury's account and oversee the mixing of it myself," he said, then caught Tamsin's eye. "I would teach you to mix it too, Miss, if you like."

"I would, sir!"

"I'll gather supplies," he said, smiling. "Turpentine, linseed oil, all of it. Never fear!"

Never fear! Tamsin heard these curious words with a blink of revelation – that in this moment, in this shop, in the presence of this man, she did not feel fear, even at the harbor. Whatever had happened? And looking at Mother, she saw lightness there too, threaded into long grief. Perhaps it was hope, for here were fortunate things.

Kindness. Stoneware. Yellow ochre paint.

25

THAT SAME MORNING, WHEN SUSANNAH AND TAMSIN left for the harbor, Peter had held in his hands a mass of deep green wax that, as Tamsin watched, seemed to glow from within. Peter himself appeared luminous. She wondered if day after day of rendering the bayberries had eased some knot in his being. His way with the wax was nearly reverent. She thought of Peter in the garden after Papa's death, all absorbed in his weaving of low wattle fence. She wanted to see this new work of his with wax and wood, and tell him it was beautiful.

When they returned to the house, however, the air carried unexpected sounds. Tamsin heeded them, wary, and when they went to the bar to find Peter, there was the Reverend Mr. Ferris, a substantial, perhaps handsome man in a fine black coat, minister to the harbor parish of Dorset. He had a ruddy face and a sharp eye, and his hair was well powdered, the powder having escaped rather generally across his firm black shoulders. Upon seeing the Widow Bennett and her daughter, he rose to give them a fulsome greeting with many biblical words. Peter went on urging bayberry wax into the grain of the counter, with the inadequate tool of a wood block.

Since coming to the harbor, the Bennetts had attended the

meetinghouse only twice, and then not for both morning and afternoon sermons, so Tamsin had dreaded Mr. Ferris' inevitable chastising visit, and the likelihood they'd be fined. Peter did well avoiding talk by attending to his work, but Mother would need to accept any coming rebuke.

Having grown up in a house with Uncle Simon, Tamsin knew the device of virtuous explanation and quickly considered her chances. Perhaps she could lead Mother to ask for Mr. Ferris' understanding: Such a weight of work we have before us, Mr. Ferris, Mother might say, all this settling and readying to open a tavern. May we offer you a cider? Or else: In truth, my family is newly arrived, deeply bereaved, and not fit to be with the congregation very much. Our trials have been great.

But Mother would say none of these things, so Tamsin thought instead how to distract his presence, ease him out of the house. She begged the minister's pardon for speaking, but she and her mother were worried where her little sister might be.

"She's been digging up seedlings in clumps of earth," Peter said. "Taking them out to the field. I doubt they'll live."

Tamsin took hold of the thought. "But she hopes they'll live," she said earnestly, and to the minister, "*All things are possible to him that believeth*, would that be right, Mr. Ferris?"

The minister eyed his young parishioner, nodded, and turned aside to speak to Mistress Bennett.

"Mother," Tamsin said, "we believe we'll open the tavern in two weeks, don't we? If we work hard and keep at it."

Susannah gave her a knowing smile. "We do indeed."

"Admirable, Mistress Bennett!" said the minister. He showed no inkling whatever that he should be gone, but turned to Tamsin. "With so much work ahead, perhaps you ought to go and find your sister."

The irksome man moved not at all.

In her leaving, Tamsin said to Peter that his work showed forth the beauty of the wood. She nodded politely back to Mr.

Ferris, so he might think to observe Peter's labor as well. He did not, but turned again to the Widow Bennett.

"I'll come back and help, Mother," Tamsin said, and went out.

IN A FAR CORNER OF UNCLE NAT'S FIELD, SHE FOUND Phebe mingling happily with stalks grown well over her head.

"Tamsin, see what I found! The milkweed rattled its pods at me!"

The place was thick with dried milkweed, pods cracked open. Some still showed white floss pushing out along the seam. Phebe collected these in a sack.

"More wadding for the quilt!" she said.

Tamsin told Phebe of the linen that would come on Deacon Somerby's cart that afternoon, and they picked all the floss-filled pods that were left.

"Now come see the rowans!" Phebe led Tamsin away to where she'd been planting. "They wanted to be in the sun *here*," she said.

Phebe's clarity on this point made Tamsin glad. Peter had turned over a good strip of earth for her, and a dozen seedlings were in and spread with wheat straw. Seeing them here, Tamsin saw their past. These descended from the very trees Grandmother Cat once told her had stood with the Rowan family, long before they left the farm at Brampton Bryan. Grandmother Cat told Tamsin the painful story, one spring morning upstream, gathering nettles. Now in this autumn field by the harbor, sorely missing her grandmother's voice, Tamsin would tell Phebe.

"Come," she said. She sat down and settled her sister beside her.

"A long time ago, when Grandmother Cat's grandmother Margaret was still in England, there were many hard years of war about religion and the power of the King. Margaret Rowan and her husband Isaac – our Uncle Isaac is named for him – Margaret and her Isaac had a farm by the village of Brampton Bryan, where a great castle was held by a family of godly people. But the Lady of the family had to manage the castle all by herself, because her husband was away in London, opposing the King's too popish religion, and their son was at war, fighting the King's soldiers. Then one summer the Royalists came to fight at Brampton Bryan, wanting the Lady's castle for the King.

"So Margaret went out among the rowan trees on the hill above the farm and asked if they would give her a great many of their living twigs. The trees allowing, she made for each of the Rowan family, and for the Lady of the castle, for all her defenders of the castle, and many a villager, one hundred rowan-wood crosses bound with thread pulled from her red petticoat. Margaret rowed her coracle upriver, crossed to the other side" – Tamsin whispered – "and she passed through the Royalist line without the soldiers ever seeing her at all!"

Phebe's eyes wide, she whispered back, "How did she do that?"

Tamsin remembered melting into groundsel tree at the salt-marsh. "She did it because she had to," she said, and watched Phebe's eyes until she saw her understanding.

"She knew a secret way into the castle," Tamsin said, "and she went there, time after time, to bind the wounds of the defenders and lay her hands on those who were hurt.

"And do you know, in the whole of the battle that summer, only one man in the castle died? And though the castle was badly damaged and much of the village destroyed, along with animals, gardens, and a mill, still the Royalists could not defeat the brave Lady, or take her castle for the King. So at last the soldiers went away. But soon the Lady became ill, and despite all Margaret could do, the Lady died. It was just before All Hallows' Night. And when the King's soldiers came back to fight again, this time the castle fell.

"So Margaret and Isaac put what they could in an oxcart – their two sons, her coracle, her herbs and seeds, a load of hay and three goats, and set out to find the sea. When a Royalist soldier tried to steal one of the goats, Margaret had a rowan-wood cross tucked inside her bodice, and she gave him a scoop of raw, red rowanberries mixed in honey. *And he ate it all down!"*

Phebe clapped a hand over her mouth and giggled.

"Yes," Tamsin said, clutching her stomach. "He went deadly pale, miserably sick."

"He deserved it," Phebe said.

"He did. Then Margaret and Isaac and the boys and the goats went on to find the sea at Bristol, and in spring they came to Massachusetts Bay. So now, Phebe, so much later, even here at the harbor, we have seedlings enough for a grove of rowans to keep us, the house, and the land quite safe, if ever any Royalist soldiers choose to fight again."

Phebe considered this. "Do you think they will?"

"I shouldn't think so, no. You take such good care of the seedlings."

Responsibility dawned in Phebe's eyes.

Tamsin was less concerned with the King's soldiers, however, than with the overbearing presence of a parish minister. "Shall we go see how Peter is doing with your wax?"

Phebe leapt up and managed an awkward sack of milkweed pods all the way to the house.

Deacon Somerby's horsecart was stopped in the side yard, his apprentice hefting stacks of stoneware up the back steps. Tamsin asked if she could help. He looked distracted and saw Phebe, who shifted a sack nearly her own size.

"No, no," he said, "if you dropped something, it would be on my head," and he craned his neck around his load to find the steps. Sisters followed him into the kitchen, where he set piles and large pieces down on the table, and Mother brushed off bits of straw.

To Tamsin's astonishment, Mr. Ferris himself was in and out of the pantry with Mother, giving advice and carrying weighty plates, bowls, and pans. He nodded at the girls, looking alight with a zeal for accomplishment. Phebe dragged her sack through the kitchen, forcing him to a precarious detour. Such help was surely needed, though Tamsin did not expect it of a minister. She watched his effort and thought, with some shame, she must correct her view of this reverend.

"Mother, may I help?"

Susannah looked a complete jumble. "We'll wash everything later, but just now I need it all in the pantry, and Mr. Ferris is putting things in such good order! Go and see Peter. Tell him about the paint. He has something to tell you too."

At the bar, Peter's eyes were fixed on his work, his hands pushing wax hard into woodgrain with his woodblock tool. "I know now," he muttered, "November is not the month for this. I'll do what I can, but come July, I'll do it over, when wax is more willing." Still, he looked up at his sister, cheerful enough.

"Tamsin, after you went out, Mr. Ferris looked at the counter here and asked if I'd wax the pulpit at the meetinghouse for him. I said I would, and then he said his sexton has gone to sea, and he needs a new man. He asked Mother, would she let him hire me to care for the meetinghouse, and she said yes! There will be wages, Tamsin, in lawful money! Ten shillings a month, plus five shillings for every grave dug!"

"Ha!" Tamsin laughed, though quietly. "Is that how he thinks to get us to the meetinghouse? Fair enough! Tell me, did he scold Mother? Did he make her pay a fine?"

"No, he hired me and then Deacon Somerby's cart rolled up with the stoneware, and off he went to take charge."

Tamsin humbly considered further adjusting her opinion of Mr. Ferris. "Well. Don't spend your time waxing a whole great pulpit till there's a hot summer to do it in."

"No!" he whispered. He patted the counter before him. "This wood comes first after midsummer!" Then he aimed a thumb up the street. "His bloody pulpit, maybe August!"

"Peter!"

He ducked his head and went back to work. "This isn't easy."

Phebe appeared, climbed on a chair, and sat on a table to watch.

"Peter," Tamsin said, "Deacon Somerby will have yellow ochre paint for us in a week, and all the brushes we need, so we can start in to paint the wainscoting first, and then when you've finished the waxing, we can paint the cabinets and spindles."

"But Peter," Phebe broke in, "you must still help me move rowan seedlings."

"I will, Phebe, I will, till frost. You can show me where they want to be."

For a moment, Phebe was content, but had one more requirement. "Tamsin, you won't go to school at the schoolhouse, will you?"

Tamsin shook her head. "I finished all the girls' schoolwork in West Dorset."

"Peter, will you?" Phebe asked.

"I've finished the boys' schoolwork, and Uncle Nat taught me to keep accounts."

"So Tamsin," Phebe said, "I can puzzle out words in the Bible, and you can teach me more words, and after that, Peter, you can teach me to write and keep accounts. So I won't go to the schoolhouse, either."

Tamsin and Peter sent each other a look, and Phebe saw them.

"You can teach me everything. I don't have to go to the schoolhouse," she said with finality. "Besides, there will be so much work here, you will need me. And, Peter, I can dust the meetinghouse."

"We'll talk with Mother," Tamsin said, though in truth, she knew Phebe was right.

A week later, as promised, Deacon Somerby sent his apprentice to tell the Bennetts he now had in stock all the makings for the paint, and brushes too. Peter and Tamsin went together to his shop to witness the mixing, then returned to the house with brushes, paint, and a strict admonition to use it all on that one day. The next day they watched the mixing and did the painting again, but on the following two days at the shop, they did the mixing themselves, measuring the same proportions of ochre pigment to linseed oil and turpentine, so as to make the same shade of yellow each day, and they completed each day's painting. On the fifth day, the tavern was as bright as ever Tamsin had hoped.

Peter never conceded how glad he was to have waxed only the bar's counter, and not also the shelves, cabinets, and spindles. But when he had a pleasing lump of fragrant green wax left at the end of his labors, he seemed entirely happy.

27

ON THAT AFTERNOON OF THE FIFTH DAY OF THE LAST week before the tavern opened, an elderly selectman of Dorset Harbor, Mr. Silas Manning, arrived with greetings and his dog, who paced so close to the old man's feet, it seemed he would trip, though he did not. Mr. Manning admired the new bar, drank a cider with Mistress Bennett, and then made to leave. As Tamsin was concerned he might take a spill over his dog, she went ahead to steady him, if needed, on the front steps. Safely out to the path, he turned and looked back.

"Captain Bradbury has a fine house," he said. "A handsome entry. That window above the door. He brought it from England, you know."

"I like that too. It looks like a half of my father's compass."

"Does it? Not a useful compass, I shouldn't think, only half. Still, a fine entry for a welcome to a tavern!" He went to leave, but turned back. "By the bye, what shall your tavern be called?"

Tamsin had no answer. From a West Dorset farm, they'd not considered the question, but before Tamsin could say as much, Mr. Manning walked away and stood at the front gate. There he looked down to waggle his fingers at the ground.

150

"What are all these sprouts doing here, popping up green in November?" he scolded. "They shouldn't be."

"They're rowans," Tamsin said.

The old man furrowed his brow at her and turned himself round again to face the fine house.

"The Rowans," he said. "Well, as good a name as any, I expect." Then he smiled brightly and whispered, "I'll pass the word."

With one more mistrustful look at the ground and a toss of his hand, Mr. Silas Manning conveyed disdain for the young greens' poor judgment, whatever they were, and went out through the gate.

"Caleb, come," he said. "Don't eat those."

ON THE SIXTH DAY OF THE LAST WEEK, THE BUTCHER'S son delivered salted beef flank and suet as Tamsin had asked, and in the afternoon she put the beef to soak. She would ready it for slow simmering and mincing fine.

ON THE SEVENTH DAY, THE BENNETTS CAME TO THE END of the last week of the tavern's creation. Unlike the Lord in the Book of Genesis, however, they did not rest from all their work which they had made. In the morning Tamsin baked the meat pies of the Rowan women, Catherine, Priscilla, and Margaret. Susannah stitched together two six-foot lengths of Deacon Somerby's green linen, so to make the quilt top twice the width of the bolt. As well, Peter and Phebe had their own plans in hand.

Thus, instead of Sabbath rest, Tamsin reveled in reading the receipt for meat pies set down in Priscilla's own hand after the birth of her Catherine. The words themselves were delicious to Tamsin's ear – garlic in hot butter, nuts and onions to be chopped, thyme and rosemary, bread soaked in a rich sweet cider and well squeezed out, beef minced, a good knob of suet to be rendered, elderberry preserves, and dried rowanberries stewed till soft and thick. Priscilla's pastry would bake up golden, as she had written that Catherine should, for every pound of flour, rub in three-quarters of a pound of butter and an egg, with one more egg rubbed in extra at the end. Tamsin would do just so.

She had helped to make the pies before, as Grandmother Cat had helped when she was a girl, and Priscilla before her, and Margaret before her at the farm at Brampton Bryan. But Priscilla in Massachusetts Bay was the first who knew how to write the words on paper, and she did it so the Rowan women to come would always know.

Still, even a good receipt can be improved. Tamsin thought to stir into the minced beef some greens of Grandmother Cat's lavender-flowered sweetleaf, crushed and ground with salt. She would try it often and watch through fall to see whether the herb might help stave off catarrh or inflammation of the throat. If it seemed to, then she would add to the receipt a note on the use of ground sweetleaf, and note the same in her day-book. Remembering, too, that Grandmother had advised using chamomile and elderberry extracts for the tavern's ale, Tamsin would prepare a bottle of the mixture and put it in a cabinet at the bar.

By early afternoon, every corner of the house smelt of cooked meat and a heady blend of rosemary, onions, and berries, and when Tamsin pulled the pies from the oven, they were golden as the new-painted wood of the tavern. She knew then, she would make these pies again, at least for the lodgers who would stay in the bedchambers upstairs. Perhaps she would make them for the selectmen too, who would hold their meetings in Aunt Martha's parlor, now with a round table in it. And certainly for Mr. Benjamin Proctor who bartered his apples and cider for dinners, friendship, and ale. But above all for Deacon Somerby, who had found light for Uncle Nat's hall and given Tamsin such assurance – No fear.

That same seventh day, the Sabbath, was also the day of the new moon, a day of passage from an ending to a beginning. So that afternoon of the seventh day, Tamsin gave Mother, Peter, and Phebe the first of the Rowan women's meat pies that were made in that house. Peter brought to Mother one fragrant, sleek-moulded candle, come from thick bayberry bushes at Green Cove. And Phebe brought to the table the happiest, most robust rowan seedling she could find, planted in a new stoneware pot, one of many good stoneware pots now piled in the pantry.

And there in the kitchen, Susannah thanked her children for all they had done through this grievous time. Embracing all three of them at once, she cried, and they held her too.

"*Maman*," her eldest of five daughters said quietly. "*Maman*."

THE NEXT DAY, THE LAST MORNING OF NOVEMBER, Tamsin let three drops of her elderberry and chamomile extract fall from the blade of a knife into a mug. Over it, as a trial, she poured a pint of ale from a cask the brewer had brought to the tavern. Mother, Peter, and Phebe all tasted it and agreed the tavern's ale should be served just this way, for as long as Tamsin's store of the extracts would hold. Next year, they would ask the farm for many more baskets of elderberries, and Tamsin would plant chamomile to make as much of the mixture as she could, perhaps enough to last a tavern's winter.

Susannah stoked the oven and baked bread all that day.

Peter worked with Mr. Benjamin Proctor, pruning trees and raking the ground, and brought three casks of cider out of Mr. Proctor's cellar. When one was lodged in its place on a sturdy shelf behind the tavern bar, the rest in the pantry, Susannah told him to go round and find the selectmen of Dorset Harbor. Say the tavern would be open to them for dinner the next day, cider and ale, bread and a pumpkin stew. Tell them they're most welcome to come. She said Peter must extend the invitation also to Mr. Ferris, as he had been so kind in helping to put the stoneware in order and, of course, had hired Peter as sexton for the meetinghouse.

"I'll let Mr. Proctor know too," Peter said.
Just then, at mention of the selectmen, Tamsin remembered Mr. Silas Manning's promise to spread word that the tavern was to be called The Rowans. So she told Peter, as he was inviting the guests, he must use that name.

"The Rowans!" Susannah said, looking round as if testing the fit.

"The Rowans," Peter said, a bit testy. "We need a sign then. There's no time."

"But the rowans!" Phebe said, and scooped up her potted seedling from the table. "We can be the sign tomorrow! I'll watch at the gate and hold my rowan in this pot. Like this!" She tucked it in the crook of one arm and cocked her head.

"You see, Peter," she said with dignity, "You are sexton of the meetinghouse, and I am sexton of the rowans."

Tamsin laughed, delighted. If Peter's meetinghouse were a place of Christian teaching, then the rowan trees were a store of ancient wisdom, never built, but grown up out of the earth, and watching across time. Young as Phebe was among Rowan women, Tamsin saw her sister knew the truth.

THUS, ON THE FIRST OF DECEMBER, ONE MONTH FROM the day the oxcart had taken Grandmother Cat and James away to the farm, Tamsin and Susannah set to roasting, scooping, and mashing three big pumpkins for a stew with carrots, onions, garlic, and generous tosses of rosemary, sage, and thyme. They used only enough cider so the stew would be pleasingly thick and not slop from men's bowls.

Stew done, Tamsin was jumpy and needed to be out.
"Mother, shall we ask Deacon Somerby too? He was so kind. Shall I go and ask him?" She edged to the door and took down her cloak.

"Yes, go and see if he'll come."

She was down the steps, near out of earshot, when Mother called from the door, "Tell him we hope he'll come."

NOT LONG AFTER NOON, PHEBE PUT ON HER CLOAK, picked up her rowan in its stoneware pot, and went out to the front gate to await the tavern's first guest. This turned out to be the elderly Mr. Manning, dog at his ankles. Tamsin, uneasy, on edge, watched from the porch as Phebe opened the gate.

"What's this, child? Why are you carrying that pot?" Mr. Manning demanded.

"We don't have a sign to put up yet, so we are the sign today." She lifted up the pot and nodded at the house. "This is The Rowans."

"So I heard," he replied.

"And," she said, embracing the pot, "I am the sexton of all our rowans."

"Sexton of The Rowans, no less!" he said, with a wave generally toward Tamsin on the porch. "Indeed a tavern is a sort of meetinghouse, I grant you that." He brightened. "And like a meetinghouse, it could be said to house the spiritual! I trust the spirits are good?"

Cheered by his joke, Tamsin went part way to meet him. "Oh, yes. Our ale is especially good!"

"Well, then, I must go in and have some," he said, as another selectman, a hefty fisherman and trader Mr. Joshua Dingley, arrived, followed by a third, the weaver Mr. Dominicus Oakes.

"Joshua!" Mr. Manning called. "I hear The Rowans' ale is excellent! Shall we go in and try the claim? Dominicus, let us have a pint!" He turned to Tamsin and said in her ear, "We granted your mother the license for a good reason, you know!"

His ragged eyebrows went up in glad anticipation, just below the white hairs flying loose from his wig. "Caleb, come!" And they went in, man and dog, neither of them tripping over the other.

Tamsin and Phebe bade welcome to Mr. Dingley and Mr. Oakes, Phebe with lively pride, Tamsin more restrained. The men laughed at Phebe wielding her pot, and with bright eyes greeted Tamsin. When she turned away, they followed her into Captain Bradbury's house.

She did not want to be looked at. These first guests behind her now, these men looking, following her – she dreaded them. She would be watched by men who might say to one another, this Bennett girl was, you know, a Rowan – yes, of *those* Rowans.

Grandmother Cat had stayed safe at the farm, but here Tamsin had to forget who she was, in order to be who she was, the rowess. *Hide the rowess,* she told herself. *Do the work.*

She went on and showed the guests to the table with the pot of pumpkin stew, a pan of fresh bread, new stoneware bowls and pewter spoons, and when all the selectmen asked for ale, she retreated behind the bar with relief. There she took three mugs, and at the far end, out of sight, let three drops of elderberry and chamomile extract fall into each mug from the tip of a knife.

Peter's work was to tend the bar, so he filled the mugs with ale and took them out to the selectmen, now settling with their bowls of stew, Mr. Dingley praising the taste of spiced pumpkin. Susannah went out to welcome them and receive their compliments on the handsome ochre-yellow bar. As she told them how hard Peter had worked to wax the counter, Mr. Ferris arrived. His impressive voice announced that, indeed, he had hired this hard-working young man as sexton, and wasn't that a stroke of luck? They all agreed it was, and commended to him the stew and ale. Mr. Proctor was next to appear. He hailed Peter from the doorway, thumped a basket of apples on the table, and made inroads into his dinner.

Tamsin went to the kitchen to cut another pan of bread, glad to step away from the pile of voices. The men's noise was ordinary, she knew, but in days to come, it would grow louder and beat upon her ears. She took more bread into the tavern, then returned to the kitchen with Mother. She sat in peace at the hearth, feeding a small fire, stirring the stewpot hung above it.

Mr. Ferris loudly wished the tavern keeper to join him at table, have a mug of this remarkable ale, and tell him of her plans for the tavern. At the kitchen door Mother said she regretted, but she could not sit, as she had work in the kitchen, so instead Mr. Ferris brought her his empty bowl and went to the pantry. Surveying there the arrangement of all things, he asked if it were true, Mistress Bennett planned a separate dining and drinking room in the small parlor? A fine prospect! And were there bedchambers upstairs? He stopped himself. That is, he said, had she told the harbor merchants they must send travelers to this exact house on Wharf Street for good food and rest?

Susannah admitted she had not gone to the merchants to ask this favor, and Mr. Ferris promised to do so on his pastoral rounds this very week. In her retreat at the hearth, Tamsin heard Mr. Ferris' thoughtfulness with alarm. The house would be ever busier.

"Mistress Bennett," he added confidingly, "I may dine here often myself. You may not be aware, my wife is sadly deceased in childbirth, and I am ill-suited for cooking."

At that instant, the last of the day's invited guests, Deacon Somerby, came in a rush through Aunt Martha's parlor and stopped short at the door to the kitchen. Finding Mistress Bennett, he expressed sincere regret if he were late – then looked blank for a moment at the sight of Mr. Ferris standing at the pantry. Quickly, however, Deacon Somerby's expression went to pleasure.

"I have been delayed by my apprentice," he said. "You see, he tried to deliver some oranges and a remarkable blue and white Nanking porcelain chamber pot to you, Mr. Ferris, but found you neither at your house nor at the meetinghouse. And now here you are!" The deacon smiled broadly. "So I regret not bringing with me the oranges and such an excellent Nanking porcelain chamber pot, Mr. Ferris. I congratulate you on the purchase! Would delivery tomorrow suffice?"

With a discomfited look, Mr. Ferris agreed it would.

Then, no doubt kindly, Deacon Somerby covered what might have been an embarrassed moment for the reverend by presenting a gift of six linen towels to Mistress Bennett. "Something of use to a new tavern keeper," he said. "We are all very glad you're here."

Quiet by the hearth, Tamsin looked from one gentleman to the other and back again, seeing a stir in the air between them.

"Ah!" Mr. Ferris exclaimed, pulling a significant piece of iron from a coat pocket. "Mistress Bennett, I must give your fine son this key to the meetinghouse! Please excuse me!" And he swept past Tamsin to return to the tavern, calling out, "Peter, young man!"

Tamsin got up and followed in his wake to see there was bread enough and stew hot enough to serve the deacon. Carrying the pot back to replenish it at the fire, she saw, in passing, where Peter put the meetinghouse key. *Note the signs,* she thought, without quite knowing why.

Susannah led the deacon to the tavern to show him the light and warmth of his good ochre paint. Tamsin, following with a pot of hot stew, barely avoided dumping it on Mr. Ferris as he threw a look at yellow wood and pushed past her, heedless, to get another pint.

The robust Mr. Dingley went to the bar as well to compliment Peter on his ale. He asked about its bracing taste. "It comforts me, it does, without so much dulling of the mind. How is that?" he asked.

"I hope it pleases you," Peter answered with a glance at Tamsin, who would later write a note in her day-book as to the effect of elderberry and chamomile extracts in ale – at least, as described by a large man who worked the coast. Would the effect differ, she wondered, for a slight man whose work was finer and quieter, on land? She went to wipe a table that did not need wiping, so she could observe the weaver Mr. Oakes. She came to no conclusion, however, as suddenly Phebe danced in at the front door and set down her potted rowan with a flourish.

A remarkable figure presented behind her.

29

THE TAVERN WENT SILENT AT THE SIGHT OF A ROTUND little man with a sweet, expectant smile lighting his face. Dressed in black, he wore white linen preaching bands that marked him immediately a man ordained. His wig appeared to waft easily about his head, an airy, powdery halo, and while his right eye lit happily upon the innkeeper coming toward him, his left eye wandered with what seemed aimless abandon about the space.

"Mother? Please, this is Mr. Lamb. He's come from Boston and from England, and he needs a place to stay."

"I beg pardon, Mistress. I am Reverend Mr. Gideon Lamb, and I was told by this delightful sprite at your gate that I might find lodging here for a few nights. Would that be true?"

His voice was surprisingly high-pitched, though not at all unpleasant. Tamsin thought he spoke musically, clear as a fiddle sings, in a way that made her want to listen to him, if not even dance. She thought of Uncle Isaac.

"Mr. Lamb, you are most welcome!" Susannah gestured to Peter and her daughters, saying, "These are my children. We are all glad to help." She cast a look at Tamsin. The bedchambers above were not ready. Tamsin moved toward the stairs.

"Please join the gentlemen for dinner, sir. May I bring you ale or cider?" Susannah asked.

Peter's eyes met Tamsin's.

"Cider would be excellent, Mistress, thank you!"

Peter nodded slightly. Tamsin took Phebe's hand and drew her upstairs, where they sorted through Aunt Martha's linens and made up a bed for the inn's very first guest. Phebe knew where the good stoneware chamber pots were stowed by the kitchen door, so she went down the back stairs to fetch one. Before nightfall they would bring up wood, lay a fire, and warm the chamber.

In the evening, the Reverend Mr. Lamb took his supper in the dining room that was once Aunt Martha's small parlor. Tamsin brought him a plate of the bread left from dinner, a wedge of cheese, and a baked apple, and he said, if he might, he would now have a mug of that ale the men enjoyed earlier, so Tamsin went to the bar and prepared it as she had before.

At his first taste, he turned to Tamsin with a slow smile. "Elderberry!" he whispered. "You did this, didn't you?"

She smiled back.

"Do you know," he said, "my mother kept a tavern, and when I was your age, I served there, just as you do."

"Today is our first day," she confided. "We were at our farm until a month ago. My father died and then my Uncle Nat gave us his house for a tavern."

"I am very sorry to hear of your father. Do you like it here?"

"I miss my Grandmother Cat and my cousin James. And the millstream. And my Devon cows." She felt her eyes wet. "And Ethan. Our great ox since I was little."

Mr. Lamb listened closely. "Miss Bennett, it's not a small or an easy thing that you do. My father died too, and then a devil of a stepfather came and went. My mother's tavern was in a crowded cathedral city where every night I drew wine for drunkards. But in this harbor town" – he took a swallow of his ale – "your elderberries will do much good."

Under his cloud of a wig, Mr. Lamb's left eye seemed always to gaze far away, as if, in addition to what his straight-ahead eye might perceive, he explored steadily for something that others might not easily find. In this, Tamsin recognized her own experience of seeing unusual things, her solitary visions, and she tended toward trusting him. Moreover, he seemed to know what Grandmother Cat knew – that elderberry extract in ale would keep tavern guests in health.

Mr. Lamb tipped his mug all the way back to finish it. Susannah came to take away his plate, now barely crumbs.

"Do you know," he said, "I spoke with your estimable Mr. Ferris, and asked him if I might be honored to give his parishioners a sermon on the Sabbath. He welcomed it."

Susannah smiled. "And what will you preach on?"

"I have preached in churches in Boston these past months, and to multitudes – many thousands – at the Common under the open sky. But as it's turned cold now – Advent, you see – I think in this sacred season I must take the Word indoors, into the meetinghouses outlying. I will preach on the coming of the Lord! I will preach on the season of Advent!

"I do know, Mistress Bennett, that your ministers here don't observe the seasons and holy days of the church year, is that not so?" He appeared to wilt. "Not even the birth of our Lord at Christmas."

"It's true, Mr. Lamb, though the family of my first husband were French Huguenots and did celebrate Christmas. *Le joyeux Noël.* Sadly they were rebuked by a Boston judge, but it will do me good to hear your sermon."

Here was one more revelation for Tamsin to put with all the others. Mother had openly celebrated Christmas.

. . .

So on the Sabbath, Mr. Lamb preached the afternoon sermon on the expectant weeks of Advent. From the Bennetts' box pew, a spot for which Uncle Nat had paid a goodly sum, Tamsin had a fine view of both Mr. Lamb, preaching high in the raised pulpit, and Mr. Ferris, seated below in the deacons' pew that faced the congregation. Mr. Ferris, unmoving but for watchful eyes, scanned his parishioners as if keeping account.

"Thou Christian," Mr. Lamb began with a warm and intimate look, as if he saw the soul of each and every one present, "I address thee in this tender waiting-time that is our present season of Advent – this treasure that leads us unto the most joyful recognition of the birth of Christ." Mr. Lamb's hands held the edges of the pulpit as if it cradled the newborn Jesus already, or as if taking gentle, but firm possession. His tone did not brook doubt. "This precious time of waiting hath been esteemed our divine duty by *most who profess Christianity.*"

At that, Tamsin eyes slipped to Mr. Ferris. She thought he winced. Mr. Lamb went on to enlarge upon a Christian's proper feelings in contemplating the birth of the Lord. Preaching with passion, with no written words, he portrayed for the congregation all the wonderment and devotion, even the horror, that he found fitting to these expectant weeks.

"When we consider the love and condescension of the Lord Jesus Christ in submitting to be born – especially as he knew how he was to be treated in this world! That he would be *despised, scoffed at!* That he would be treated as *the off-scouring of all mankind!* Not at all as the Son of God that he was!"

A great intake of Mr. Lamb's breath conveyed infinite awe. A pause hung light in the air. A large and holy gesture evoked the opening of the heavens. "No, when we consider these things, we are made to attend – to expect – to listen with care! – for the coming of our dear Lord Jesus Christ –"

Mr. Lamb now listened so intently and so long to every shuffle and shift in the whole of the meetinghouse – indeed it seemed, in the whole of Essex County, and in all Massachusetts –

that no parishioner wanted to be caught so much as breathing, and all held still, drawn into the simple act of listening by the power of Mr. Lamb's attention.

"And when the fullness of time is come" – his hands made a surprise in the air – *"Christ comes!"*

Phebe jumped.

Mr. Lamb preached in so thrilling a voice, with such expressive gesture, that Tamsin found she must place her hands flat on the seat of the pew to keep from turning aside, time and again, to see what it was that Mr. Lamb's divergent eye saw, that could impel such enchanting speech.

"He comes, not in *glory*, not in *splendor*." His tone mocked *glory* as dust. Tamsin heard *splendor* as henhouse straw.

"He comes not like one who brought all salvation with him. No! But he was made of a *woman*." He nodded, and each woman knew honor and trust. "He was born in a *stable*." Men who knew the earthen floors and muck of their barns took his meaning.

"Our Lord was cradled in a *feed trough! Oxen his companions!"*

Tamsin was certain Mr. Lamb's wayward eye swept to her exact spot in Uncle Nat's box pew. She believed it winked at her, and that he remembered Ethan.

After half an hour more, Mr. Lamb came round to address the proper Christian forms of waiting and celebration. "My brethren, read of the sufferings of our Savior! Sisters, be inspired to pray! And know this – that when you spend your time in cards, or dice, or gaming of any sort, you do not celebrate aright! Nor in eating and drinking to excess!" Mr. Lamb continued in this vein, at last tempering his exhortations with comment likely easier for the parish to hear. "No, I do not oppose the eating and drinking of good things! But avoid excess. I beseech you, avoid indiscretion. Give particular regard to your behavior at this time!"

In another hour, Mr. Lamb reached the zenith of humility and delight. "Oh, amazing condescension of our Lord Jesus Christ, to stoop so low and poor for our sake. Therefore, dear

Christians, go and ponder throughout Advent, what love is this, what great and wonderful love is here, that the Son of God should come into our world!"

Even after he stepped his presence back from the pulpit, his passion still held the air. No parishioner stirred until a dog whined to go out.

AFTER BREAKFAST AND A SETTLING OF HIS ACCOUNT with Peter, Mr. Lamb nodded farewell to Tamsin. His plan, he said, was to spread the Word in a different parish each Sabbath of Advent, and perhaps speak of the Lord in pleasant taverns midweek. Before Christmas, he would find his way back to Boston for the winter and set out again to preach in the spring.

"Be of good courage, Miss Bennett," he said. "I will see you again."

30

THE WINTER OF 1751 WAS LONG REMEMBERED AS
relentless, no suitable time for the opening of a tavern. A fero-
cious January rainstorm gusted in from the southeast, lashing
square at the wharves, and cold, snowy nor'easters piled in there-
after. Were it not for the excellent location of Captain Bradbury's
house and the rare, beguiling taste of the ale on offer at The
Rowans, the tavern might not have been there for the return of
spring. As it happened, even with winter's limited work at the
harbor, townsmen and coastal traders continued to appear, often
bringing squash, corn, fish, or wild fowl for barter. These, the
widow Susannah Bennett and her daughter Tamsin would trans-
form into tavern dinners the next day, and so week by week, The
Rowans survived.

Tamsin reveled in this hotchpotch of ingredients, providen-
tially come, and tried to match the day's gifts with some mix of
spices and herbs for the tavern-goers' warmth, peace, and good
health. Only partly by chance, more by choice, this allowed her to
stay longer in the kitchen, rather than going into the tavern under
the eyes of rowdy men. Still, the work of serving was inevitable.

Often enough, a coastal trader or even a local man would
rudely pretend friendship where there was nothing of the sort,

167

call her by endearments or improper words, and pull at her to make her sit with him. She missed James' goodness and his touch. She wanted him with her. Some evenings she could stay clear of the looks, words, and hands, though other evenings gave more trouble. On these occasions Peter, tending bar, would most often hold back from interfering. Tamsin knew he was loath to offend even a rude patron for the sake of the trade, but usually some sober enough gentleman would rise to help her disentangle, and peace would return, somewhat.

One evening, however, a trader from Marblehead caught her by the waist as she took him a rum and held her so tight she couldn't push free.

"Sir, I have others to serve. You must let me *go*." She shoved hard against his shoulder.

"Hah! You'll serve me, girl! The rest can look to their own!" He made a rude snicker, and other men, enjoying her plight, spewed laughs. Given their encouragement, he snatched her linen cap and threw it to the floor. Hairpins scattered, a dark braid fell loose down her back. One man gasped, others whooped their pleasure.

Noah Southworth, supplier of the Bennetts' cordwood, came quick to her side, gripped the trader's wrist with the work-scarred fist of a woodsman, and twisted it back from Tamsin like an unwanted shoot off a tree. She fled to the dim end of the bar as the trader bellowed rage and pain, hauled back his free fist, and landed it three times square and hard in Noah's face. Reeling bloody, Noah fell backward onto the hearth in such an arc that his head hit stone, insensible, and one wool-clad arm flung wide over an andiron. His bare hand hit red embers.

Selectman Joshua Dingley clutched the nape of the trader's jacket, manhandling him out to the street, as Tamsin flew past them to go to Noah. She dropped to the hearth, grabbed a heavy woolen sleeve, and pulled him away from the flames eating his hand. Noah roused screaming.

Men who had found Tamsin's struggle funny now cried horrified at Noah's burns, but she held his arm like a baby. She held it still to look at his hand, feeling not dismay, but compassion rise like a tide in her body, gather at her heart, and flood to her mind and palms. Compassion made her eyes see unexpected things. She knew to heed.

She saw Grandmother Cat by the millwheel, a tide lifting in from the bay. The swell of the tide pressed through earth into her feet, and moved up through her heart and mind. Then and there by the mill was the first time her hands were made to bloom with light as they did now, laid on Noah's burns.

More came, unexpected.

Beneath Noah's cries, she leant to his ear to speak softly. "Noah, all will be well. Listen to me, I tell you, Noah, you will cut wood again."

Her hands lifted gently away from the burns. His voice quieting, she heard a familiar sound, the rush of water. Overcome with a warm scent of sawn wood, she was made to see the turning of a great wheel, and she whispered, "Noah, listen to me. Do you know that you are to have a sawmill? Do you hear it?"

A shiver ran down his arm.

"Noah," she said again, "Listen. I tell you, one day you will build a sawmill."

He went still. In a moment, he drew his arm back from her, braced himself with it, and sat up. He looked at his hand and at Tamsin. The hand was clear of burns, clear even of the scar of a bad boyhood gash from a ripsaw.

Two drunken sailors were rendered cold sober. One shouted, enraged, "Damn me, look at that!" Curiosity roused across the tavern.

Noah stood, face pallid and bloody, holding his hand up like a lamp in front of him.

Everyone saw it now.

Men rose from their tables. Words rippled, cries crossed the air. Agitation grew as men watched the woodcutter stagger dazed through the tavern and out.

Tamsin scrabbled on the floor for her cap and hairpins and escaped to the kitchen to coil her braid, cover it, hands shaking at the confusion they'd set loose. When she slipped back behind the bar, men were hunkering to their tables to mutter dark things, and drink. She shook her head mutely at Peter. He nodded once and went out with a pair of rums and a cider. Over and over, she wiped down the counter, the bottles, and the taps of the casks, looked at her hands, and listened for what she could hear – the rumble of unsettled men and the sibilance of the name, repeatedly, *"Priscilla."*

Old ones told the names they remembered, those of the accused and those who'd done the accusing. A few elders told younger men of Tamsin's great-grandmother. It was the work she did up to Rowley, they said. Others had stories from Salem. One man said Priscilla was pulled in a cart with all the condemned up to the ledge, but though every other prisoner in the cart was hanged from the trees that day, peculiarly she was not. Whatever could have saved her, he had no idea, so near to her end. Another said his mother was there and saw it, but never did tell how Priscilla Rowan left that ledge alive. A third said he had the truth from an honest Salem gossip – The devil sent a swarm of greenhead flies to plague the horse, hurtling cart and witch back to her farm where no man dared pursue. The orchardman Mr. Proctor's voice rose to shame a tableful of rattled men. Another voice growled beneath him, the woman was said to be with child, but none was ever born.

Fright roiled Tamsin's gut. She clutched a cloak and fled to the privy to empty her fear, railing at herself for what she had done. She was the rowess Priscilla Rowan Tobin's daughter's son's daughter – likely a rowess herself, whatever that would mean – and she must have better sense than to endanger her family with a public healing. Worse, she had given Noah Southworth a vision of the sawmill that was to be his.

Fool! Witless girl!

Now even if drunken men should forget what they saw, Noah Southworth would always know.

No more visions, girl. No more telling of visions.

She made herself go back to the tavern as though there'd been nothing deadly. At the dark end of the bar, she set up a half-dozen mugs, dropped her extracts into each, and filled the mugs with ale. With a direct and eloquent look, she pushed them along the bar toward Peter, who went out and freely served the ale of The Rowans to a tavern of edgy, dangerous men for their greater joy and peace. Tamsin readied another half-dozen, and when Peter had taken those, she made up six more. Then she took a pint for herself, extracts liberally added, and held back behind the spindles to observe the tavern's wider temperament. She watched for the thickness of the air and the changes in men's shoulders. She composed what she would write later in her day-book on the effects of elderberry and chamomile as served in ale this night to a mess of men stirred deep with suspicion and fear.

AFTER THIS, IN HER DESIRE TO AVOID THE TAVERN, Tamsin found she could help herself and help Peter, too, by taking on part of his work as sexton of the meetinghouse. Thus, on Monday afternoons, Peter would reach down where he'd hidden the meetinghouse key. Tamsin had seen it, low in the cabinet at the far end of the bar. She and Phebe would don their cloaks, go a little way up the street, and enter the meetinghouse at the side door. Phebe would run and skip throughout, dusting the box pews, while Tamsin would wipe sills and sweep floors, taking special care with the ashes fallen from parishioners' sooty winter foot-stoves. Mr. Silas Manning, privileged as a selectman, would often bring Caleb to cold Sabbath meetings and rest his boots on the dog's warm back. No one minded Mr. Manning's privilege, though in the course of a long afternoon sermon, Caleb might quietly express restlessness by passing water upon the floor. On occasion, Tamsin had to return to the meetinghouse with her rosemary vinegar and a stiff bristle brush.

Once Phebe showed Tamsin a wondrous discovery she had made in the balcony where the African people sat. Outlines of boats were carved with a knife into the wood on the insides of two box pews. Each had a single mast rigged fore and aft, and a bowsprit long enough for two or even three jib sails, all carved full of wind, fat as three-quarter moons. Contemplating the jibs, Tamsin felt them yearning, and her heart swelled to match their lift.

"Sloops," she breathed.

Phebe said she wished she could draw such boats during Mr. Ferris' long sermons, and worried that soon there would be no more space left for carving on the insides of the pews. Then more boats would have to be carved on top of these beautiful boats and one would not see them properly.

Tamsin did not answer Phebe, but was moved by the fleet of full sails and imagined being with them wherever they would fly.

SUSANNAH AND THE GIRLS PASSED THE BITTER WINTER, too, by adding to the inn's supply of warm bed coverings. Her great wheel had come with them when they left West Dorset, so she could spin half the farm's wool, but the Bennetts' loom had stayed at the farm, so Tamsin and Phebe carried Mother's skeins to Mr. Dominicus Oakes to make a coverlet, which he turned out in a pleasing overshot weave.

Beyond that, Tamsin and Susannah spent morning hours, when they could, seaming three edges of the green linen top of a quilt shell to its white backing. Each chose a corner to start, and they stitched their way round toward one another, eighth-inch by eighth-inch. In the evenness of their rhythm, every few inches Tamsin would glance up to look at the mother she now knew as a complicated soul. Unsettled, she thought of what Mother had taken her up the hill to see, three fieldstones for three little girls. She imagined Mother's thoughts would turn that way too, and was aware of moving stitch by stitch closer to her. When at last their threads met halfway, they turned the shell so that all the raw edges were inside, and set themselves to marking and stitching twenty parallel lines, straight across the linen toward the fourth, open edge. As Tamsin's needle pointed through at the very end of each line, she had a curious sensation as if jumping off a tiny, rough cliff.

The parallel lines made channels for Phebe to fill from her sacks of milkweed floss, by now well dried out. She pushed the wadding in with a smooth stick, evenly as she could, and when she had finished wadding each channel, she basted it shut and went on to the next. When Phebe was done, Tamsin seamed the full length of the quilt's fourth side, faintly relieved when all cliff edges were turned and finished.

The quilt was completed before the return of spring. It was done even before thawed ground permitted the sinking of a post at the front gate, upon which a handsome sign would be hung, showing the figure of a tree. Peter had drawn it with sticks he turned to charcoal in a pot in the hottest bread oven he could stoke. Then he painted it with narrow squirrel-hair brushes and bits of paint from the shop of the most helpful Deacon Somerby. The sign showed a rowan tree, windblown.

Phebe had watched Peter's transformation of mere wood sticks into charcoal for drawing, and asked if she might have some. He obliged his sister, who did not say why she wanted them, though Tamsin had a thought. When next they went to the meetinghouse to dust and sweep, Phebe took black sticks out from a fold of linen and whispered, "Look, Tamsin! Now they won't have to draw with a knife!"

She took them up to the balcony and left them in two box pews.

On the Sabbath, Phebe did not sit down right away in Uncle

Nat's pew, but stood for a little time, looking up to the balcony, till she nodded and sat down. Tamsin smiled at the joy in her sister's face. For herself, she sat thinking of full jibs and the yearning onward.

31

A COOL MORNING IN MAY, TAMSIN WAS IN THE GARDEN pulling young beets and greens, when a stream of creaks and rattles was heard, then a sharp "Ethan, Levi, whoa." And there occupying the side yard was the ruddy bulk of two oxen hitched to the Bennetts' cart, come from the farm.

"Grandmother Cat!" Tamsin cried out, and more softly, "James!"

Phebe leapt from the back steps. "Ethan!" She threw her arms round the massive neck of the elder ox, and cried, "Levi!" She hugged the neck of the younger, then climbed up on the cart to embrace her grandmother.

Peter and Susannah spilled from the kitchen door, calling out welcome. Peter scooped Phebe from the cart and lifted his Grandmother Cat to the ground. James jumped down, greeting his Aunt Susannah first and then his cousins with warmth. When he came to Tamsin, his feelings were plain in his face.

"I brought your patches of Michaelmas daisies," he told her. "They're new, but the leaves have come up thick. They'll do fine. And chamomile. And sweetgrass, long roots. I'll plant them."

"Thank you. I'll help," she said, remembering a touch of red lobelia beside her mouth.

175

Grandmother Cat took Susannah and the children in her arms, one by one, looking in their eyes. Tamsin felt Grandmother's embrace both frail and determined, as if she had folded grief into her bones.

She walked away to the back of the cart. "Come, these cheeses need to go to the cellar. Be careful with that one sack, it's fresh nettles."

Susannah lifted it gingerly. Peter took in the rounds of cheese.

"These baskets. Asparagus from upstream yesterday. Rhubarb pulled this morning. Would you tavern-keepers like to make some pies?"

"Yes!" Phebe made a little jump.

"Here's one last sack of last fall's wheat."

Susannah carried the nettles in, Tamsin the baskets, James the milled wheat, and all came back out to look at the rest of the sacks, stuffed full and wedged in the cart on a bed of wheat straw.

Susannah asked, "What's all this?"

"All that. Wool from the shearing. You'll have no lack of spinning, Susannah! Work for a summer."

"We have a full summer's work already," Susannah said with feeling.

"Are you busy? It goes well?" Grandmother asked. She eyed Tamsin, who said nothing.

"Exceeding well," Susannah said. "The tavern is lively."

Tamsin pressed her lips together and hefted a sack of wool. She and the boys carried sacks to the attic where the great wheel had its place in the south chamber. James and Tamsin came back to the cart for the Michaelmas daisies, chamomile, and sweetgrass.

"I loaded a heap of wheat straw for your henhouse, but we may want to use some over the sweetgrass. They're just thin tops and roots now," James said, and showed her a score of plants between layers of damp linen. "We'll get these into the ground."

"How is it? At the farm."

James folded the linen back over the sweetgrass. "I don't want to be there. Where shall we put these? They need sun."

"Uncle Simon?"

"He's – I don't know – quieter." James looked at her directly. "You said he'd be better. How did you know?"

Tamsin lifted her shoulders, wordless, and turned to nod at the back field. "There's good sun there. We can spread them out. They'll fill in."

"Ethan and Levi need water." He unhitched them and filled the trough from the well.

Tamsin took the damp linen out to the field, and James followed with a pitchfork. He broke the soil, she planted, and they watered the sweetgrass, working close together. She wanted to touch the shoulder and hands beside hers, but in open field she did not. Nor did he reach out to her.

Phebe ran to find them. "Tamsin, you have to go in and see Grandmother Cat. She's asking for you."

"I will, dear. Can you help? There's wheat straw in the cart on top of a big canvas. If we drag that canvas out here, can you spread straw round the sweetgrass? Then the seedlings will stay damp and we'll know not to walk on them."

Phebe set off at a run toward the cart, but stopped short. "Oh," she said, "Tamsin, Uncle Simon is here."

She and James stood still.

Running a few steps farther, Phebe stopped again. "He sailed a new shallop here that Uncle Isaac made for Peter!" She marveled, "It has *rowan-wood oars!*"

When Tamsin went into the kitchen, three mackerel and a bass lay gutted on the table. There were voices in the tavern. Dreading, she went through. Grandmother Cat was on the settle by the hearth, her face full of happiness. Mother, at the bar, drew cider. Uncle Simon stood in a far corner of the room in his hunch of a posture that Tamsin used to read as warning, but Peter strode from his uncle toward Tamsin, his face alight.

"Tamsin, Uncle Simon is here! He sailed from Colbrook in a shallop that Uncle Isaac built, and it's to be mine! I can go out and fish for the tavern!"

Uncle Simon looked about himself, as if surveying the changes wrought in Nathaniel Bradbury's large parlor to make it a tavern. His face had a mild expression, perhaps pleased with himself. It was not a face Tamsin had seen on him before.

When he met her eyes, he froze. She felt the same mystery she had at the saltmarsh when light leapt from the yarrow in her hand and disappeared in his breath. It stunned him still, she could tell.

Grandmother Cat patted the settle beside her. "Tamsin, come here and sit by me."

Tamsin embraced her again, kissed her cheek, then quick had to let her go as Phebe, running in from the field, landed on her grandmother's lap.

A sideways look, Tamsin saw Uncle Simon move to a window. Susannah took him a mug of cider. "Simon, thank you. Peter's fishing will be such a help," she said. "We do get some fish as barter, but to have more for the stews will go a long way."

Simon nodded at Peter. "He handles a shallop like an old sailor. He'll do fine."

"I do many things, Uncle," Peter boasted. "I tend the tavern, I work with Mr. Proctor in his orchard, and I'm sexton at the meeting-house now."

"Grandmother," Phebe said. "Tamsin and I dust and sweep the meetinghouse too. And sometimes," she added with an indignant edge, "Tamsin has to scrub the floor in Mr. Manning's pew with vinegar because of the pee."

"Phebe –" Tamsin reproved.

"You what?" Peter asked.

Grandmother laughed. "Phebe, who is Mr. Manning and why does he pass water in the pew? Is he ill?"

"He's a selectman," Tamsin said. "And, Phebe, I don't believe he's the one who passes water. It's Caleb." To Grandmother Cat, she said, "His dog."

"His *dog?*" Uncle Simon said in the offended voice of Deacon Bennett of the West Dorset parish. "His *dog* comes to *meeting?*"

"It's just that Mr. Manning is old and his feet are cold, Uncle," Phebe explained. "So he rests them on Caleb. He told me."

Susannah spoke up quickly. "Do you know, I think there may be men coming for ale and dinner soon. Perhaps we might think less about Caleb and more about beets and fish." And she went out to the kitchen.

"Phebe," said Grandmother Cat, "I started a fire in the oven. I doubt it's ready, but let's go cut rhubarb and make a pastry." Grandmother Cat took Phebe by the hand and went out after Susannah.

With the scandal of water on the meetinghouse floor, Tamsin hoped Mr. Manning would not, by ill luck, come in for dinner anytime soon. In fact, not trusting Uncle Simon's composure, she hoped Mr. Manning would not come into the tavern at all today. Instead, several mariners came up from the wharf, and James came in from the field. He said he would plant the Michaelmas daisies now, if Tamsin would come and tell where to put them. She looked to Peter, asking wordless, would he serve the dinner? Peter nodded at James, and so they went out.

Of the five patches James had cut, they put the two largest inside the front gate, took two more to frame the front steps, and laid the last beside the kitchen door. With pitchfork and shovel, they broke and lifted earth, planting the angel Michael's protection at every entrance. And Tamsin felt stronger, knowing the courage she would have at hand when she needed.

WHEN JAMES WENT OUT TO HITCH ETHAN AND LEVI, Tamsin went with him for at least a few sweet words, but Grandmother Cat called Tamsin to the garden. She told her that Simon, by some good fortune, had become a changed man. He'd brought a bunch of yarrow into the house last fall, she said, so good for breath and spirit, and the yarrow had stayed fresh all through the frozen white of that January. Even the children, she said, were the better for it.

Tamsin was glad and embraced her. She knew Grandmother was right about the yarrow, and never told her of the encounter with Uncle Simon at the marsh, or the stone in his fist, or the rush of light he'd cried out as magic, that somehow she called *grace*.

Too late for more words, she and James tried not to watch each other's eyes, but nodded once as Ethan and Levi turned toward Wharf Street.

32

THE NEXT MORNING, TAMSIN AND PHEBE WENT OUT TO survey the plantings. The sweetgrass revived well under the strewing of the wheat straw. Phebe would water the chamomile again. The young greens of the Michaelmas daisies were already thick, and when Tamsin pressed her hands down among them, she felt their strength. Peter came out, wanting his sisters to go with him to the wharf to admire his shallop.

The moment Tamsin saw it, Grandmother Cat's voice was in her ear, retelling the escape to Winnipeseekett. Now, a lifetime after, Uncle Isaac had built a neat shallop that Peter could handle on his own. She imagined that as Uncle Isaac built this good boat for Peter, he thought about the one that two boys had rowed hard offshore on the day a constable came to take their mother. At Winnipeseekett, the little girl who was Grandmother Cat had faced the fat man in his red breeches. Tamsin heard the voice of a brave child speak up clear, right beside her –

"I dig clams!"

She held back a sob. Today she would take her little sister and go dig clams.

. . .

THE TIDE WAS OUT WHEN SHE AND PHEBE TOOK OFF shoes and stockings to walk barefoot at Green Cove. Tamsin put Papa's sundial-compass safe in her shoe at the edge of the pitch pine scrub, then took four wooden buckets and a rake down to the damp sand where clams burrowed. The buckets soon filled.

Not at all ready to leave the Cove, however, Phebe bolted to the water and jumped with both feet into the thin edge of a wave slipping away. Tamsin sped and jumped likewise, then held still to watch clear water slide away from bare feet.

The tide was turning, coming in.

She snatched up her gown, petticoat, and shift as best she could. A dozen small waves crumpled over her ankles, each tracing a different arc in the sand before it vanished. At the next wave, she jumped the breaking edge and landed in the swell. Phebe did too, soaking linen to her knees.

"Wait," Tamsin said. Lacy white water resolved to a transparent sheet and slid away. "Are you on land or in the sea?"

Phebe looked down. "I'm on land," she said. "On the sand!"

When a taller wave rolled in, Tamsin let go all her gathers of linen, flung her arms into the air and made a silly jump straight up to come down in exactly the same place. Phebe threw her arms up, laughing, and did the same.

"Now! Are you on land or in the sea?"

Phebe looked to her feet. "I'm in the sea!" she said.

Tamsin held up a finger. "Now wait!" She stayed very still. When the wave pulled back, she asked again, "Truly, Phebe, are you in the sea or on the land?"

"On the land!" she said, liking the joke, and as another wave rolled in, she jumped clear over it and splashed with hands and feet both. Triumphantly soaked, she crowed, "But I landed in the sea!"

The wave thinned and was gone. Tamsin pretended surprise.

"But I see you on the land!"

She kept on, delighting in a game such as one Papa would have made up, had he been here. She thought of a riddle to ask him. If his sundial-compass could show the whole arc of heaven and a full round of earth, then how could land and sea be two different things? They must be all one, like earth and heaven. A wave swept her ankles, washed away, and came back. If a threshold can move, then where are we?

Even more, where was Papa? Where was that edge?

Phebe's feet danced this side and that. She kicked through the tops of the waves, making droplets in air. Tamsin skipped the foaming edge too. Together they flicked and played at the boundary.

With rake and full buckets, they went back where they'd left their shoes in the shade of the pitch pine scrub. Tamsin put down her buckets and scooped handfuls of dry pine straw, thick on the ground. She put her nose to the ancient scent, looked deep into the sandy thicket, and thought it a fine retreat.

"Mr. Lamb! Did you come to find us? We have clams for dinner!" Phebe's voice came from the road.

Tamsin hurried to put on stockings and shoes, grabbed up her buckets. "Mr. Lamb, you came back!"

"Of course I did. Did I not tell you I would?" He looked at her with his straight-ahead eye, then looked into the buckets and smiled his beatific smile. "You've dug a great many."

"Yes!" Phebe said, putting stockings and shoes on her feet. "And Mr. Lamb, we hopped in the water and found that if you stand still in one place, you can be in the sea and on the land, two places at once!"

His eyebrows lifted, his wig wafting higher in a light breeze. "Ah, what a puzzle!" he said. "What astonishing girls you are! I have much to learn from you."

Tamsin smiled, pleased and a little embarrassed before the preacher. "We should go home. We have to wash the clams and make a stew."

They walked back to the house together, Mr. Lamb carrying the buckets and saying he'd just been at the tavern, hearing praise of Peter for his skill at fishing. "Of course," he said, "Matthew's gospel does tell us, Peter was a fisherman." His voice drifted lighter. "Yes, he was a very good one."

Tamsin glanced at Mr. Lamb walking beside her, and wondered again what it was he saw with his eye that looked always away, somewhere else.

33

THE OVEN WAS HOT AND THE HOUSE SMELT OF BAKING loaves. With the sack of Red Lammas brought from the farm, Susannah again made her good thirded bread of Indian corn, rye, and the family's own wheat. Also, a few times of late, Tamsin had used Red Lammas for the Rowan women's meat pies. Word of their savor had spread south to Marblehead and north as far as Newbury, so the tavern was now much frequented by coastal traders. The reputation of the inn drew distant mariners as well, ship's captains and first mates from England, when they came to Dorset Harbor to load dried cod.

This day for dinner, Tamsin would stew the clams and bake them in pies with the mix of herbs that Mother liked, her chervil, chives, and parsley. Mr. Ferris had said he liked that, too, so he might come in and stay for dinner, as would Mr. Proctor. And of course, Mr. Lamb would take dinner, having just arrived. Tamsin and Phebe went directly to the kitchen to wash the clams in several waters. Tamsin put them over a fire to stew. Phebe went out front to tend her young rowans.

Indeed Mr. Ferris did come in, and early, at that. Tamsin went to the bar and took care to put three drops of her extracts into his mug before the ale.

185

"Oh, Mr. Ferris," she said, "Mr. Lamb has come back. He's gone upstairs, but I expect he'll be down soon." She waited for a response.

With a slight grimace, he swerved off to stare out a window. Recalling his pinched look during Mr. Lamb's Advent sermon, she added, "Mr. Lamb should be taking dinner – "

"I heard you."

Pleased with her observation, she said quickly, "Excuse me, sir, I'll just go and keep on with the pies. Clams today. My mother's herbs." She went back to the kitchen, curious whether he would stay for the clams and herbs, or leave and slight Mr. Lamb.

Peter came in. He'd had to dig a baby's grave that morning. He looked dark and moved slowly to the tavern. Mr. Lamb came down from his chamber and put his head into the kitchen to compliment the new quilt on his bed, and see what had become of the clams. His face brightened. "I will enjoy some of that pie!"

"Oh, Mr. Lamb, Mr. Ferris has come in. I think you'll find him in the tavern."

Mr. Lamb expressed pleasure in this, and went to the bar for his cider. In a little while, he returned.

"Tamsin, I believe I will take my clam pie in pleasant solitude in your dining room. I thought I might find Mr. Ferris in the tavern, but he is not there."

"Isn't he? Phebe will set a place for you in the dining room then. Let me call her."

"No, no, I know where she is. She's in front, weeding about the sprouts in the yard. I asked her what they were and she told me a great tale of their history!"

"Did she?" Tamsin answered, heart alarmed. Phebe must learn what's safe to say, and to whom, and what could bring danger. Tamsin must tell her, not to frighten her, but so she knows. Just enough.

"Yes, wondrous! I said at the shore, I have much to learn from you remarkable girls. I'll go and mention you'd like to see her." And he went out.

Rolling the pin firmly over a ball of dough, smoothing it to a near-perfect round, Tamsin made her hands and heart steady. Mr. Lamb seemed earnest and kind, though a churchman. What would Grandmother Cat make of him? Whatever would Margaret of Brampton Bryan think, her farm spoiled by Royalists?

Phebe came to the kitchen and said Mr. Lamb had gone out to see Mr. Ferris at the parsonage, and what was it Tamsin needed?

Looking into her sister's bright face, Tamsin was chilled. Mr. Lamb had gone straightway to the parish minister. What would he tell him? A story of rowan seedlings planted by charmed cardinals? Extracts of herbs concealed in ale, and for what purpose? And what then?

Priscilla. Accusations, questions, jail. Shaming from the pulpit. Loss of Peter's position as sexton, and her work and Phebe's. Loss of The Rowans, tavern, inn. And what of Mother?

She took her sister's hand and drew her away to the back door, while keeping an eye that no one came into the kitchen.

"Dear sweet Phebe," she said, "There is something you must know that may not make sense just now, but one day it will, and so you must listen."

And so she did.

"You see, there are certain things within our family that have belonged to us for a very long time, and we take care of them because we use them to help people."

Phebe nodded. "The mill," she said. "Papa used to take good care of all the wet wood. Uncle Simon too."

Tamsin was grateful for the thought. "Yes, like the mill, and we hold these things close and don't speak of them outside of the family, because they're not simple things to understand. Another would be Grandmother Cat's knowing of all her herbs and her healing."

"And the cardinals!" Phebe said. "I told Mr. Lamb how she sang to them, and they –" She stopped. "Should we not talk about the cardinals either? Or the rowan trees?"

"It's best we keep all such talk within the family, among, shall we say, Grandmother Cat's grandchildren."

"James," Phebe said firmly. "Ruth and Naomi?"

"James, yes, though I don't believe Ruth and Naomi have an interest."

Phebe shook her head. "I don't think they do."

"No. But do you see what I mean? We keep these things close among ourselves."

"And not even Mr. Lamb?"

"Likely not even Mr. Lamb," Tamsin agreed. "Now, would you set a neat place for him in the dining room? And careful as you can, careful as a precious granddaughter of your Grandmother Cat, would you take the first of the clam pies into the tavern?"

And Phebe did.

In a little while, Mr. Lamb stood in the kitchen doorway, his sweet face clouded, the white halo of his wig gone limp. "I am here, Tamsin, and ready for my pie. May I have a pint of your ale?"

Tamsin found it difficult to meet his eye, the straight-ahead one, and she feared what the other might see, but she took a big piece of clam pie into the dining room and went to the bar for his ale. She hesitated a moment to add the drops of extract, but felt it would be dishonest to do otherwise, so she mixed it as usual and took it to Mr. Lamb.

"Tamsin," he said, "I am sorely disappointed."

She took a single step backward toward the kitchen.

"Your Dorset Harbor parish is not what I would have hoped."

"Isn't it?" She thought of her Michaelmas daisies for courage. She reached for the bravery of a four-year-old child looking up at a constable. "Is there something we might do?"

He smiled sadly. "Your pie and elderberry ale will work wonders, my dear. But I lament that your parish minister has forbidden me absolutely to preach at your meetinghouse this Sabbath, this Whitsunday, when we rejoice to celebrate the magnanimous descent" – a large, eloquent gesture to the ceiling, Mr. Lamb now seemed to revive – "Yes, the descent of the Holy Spirit upon our Lord's disciples in a wind like the beating of wings from heaven, a glorious day, remembered liturgically in my Church with the vibrant lifeblood shade of red!" All his ten fingers fluttered about the dining room. Tamsin saw birds.

His brow aloft, his wayward eye alight, the straight-ahead eye lit upon Tamsin, as if happy in a secret joke. "The lifeblood red," he said. "It does put me in mind of your busy cardinals!"

"Cardinals," Tamsin said.

"So very many of them! All escorting you here to the harbor! Remarkable! However did she make such a thing come to pass?"

"She." Tamsin shook her head once, as if she had no earthly idea what he meant.

Both Mr. Lamb's mismatched eyes were bright at once. "Your dear sister painted me a great picture in the air! How extraordinary of your grandmother!"

Grandmother Cat. Danger now. Fear in the gut.

"Tamsin, I should so like to have seen her miraculous tribute to the Holy Spirit!"

Holy Spirit. Tribute. Tamsin could only nod. It took her many seconds to understand. Then awash in gratitude, she was able to whisper, "Ah! Then perhaps you will, Mr. Lamb, one day."

"Now," he went on, "what I have done in Boston, of course, is to preach out of doors, in some wide-open place where many hundreds and hundreds of people might come. Very many African people come, and sailors from everywhere in the world! A great space where all are able to hear me. Is there such an open space here, would you say?"

Weak still, nearly mute, she pulled her wits together and made herself answer. "Near the fishing stage. Past the meetinghouse, out beyond the last houses. That way. There is a field."

Mr. Lamb's unexpected honor to her Grandmother Cat overwhelmed her. What was it he needed?

Whatever she could do to help this good man, she would do.

34

OVER THE NEXT DAYS, MR. LAMB TOOK HIS DINNERS
and cider and ale in the tavern, and told all who came that he
would preach in the field by the fishing stage on the following
Sabbath, which was Whitsunday, a marvelous day for preaching,
he said, though parishioners had not heard of this before and
thought it likely popish. He would begin early, go on for some
hours, and preach again after dinner. When Mr. Ferris came into
the tavern during these announcements of Mr. Lamb, he would
take his drink to the kitchen, peruse the pantry, and talk to Susannah, all of which discomfited Tamsin.

The discord made for ticklish decisions round about the
parish, whether to attend morning and afternoon sermons at the
meetinghouse to hear Mr. Ferris, or hear both sermons at the
fishing stage with Mr. Lamb, or first one and then the other. And
if that were the case, then which was to come first and which
second? Susannah said to her children that they would go to the
meetinghouse as they should in the morning, and after dinner go
to the fishing stage, because Mr. Lamb was their lodger. Tamsin
understood, but had thoughts of her own.

· · ·

THERE WAS A CLOUDED HALF-MOON WHEN SHE ROSE IN her shift, donned her bedgown, and went downstairs to wrap in a dark cloak. She fetched from the cellar a certain supply she still had from the farm. With a sack of it, she went out to the back field and called the sloping *cheer cheer* she knew from Grandmother Cat's voice, and then the *pretty! pretty! pretty!* that she herself had sung among the rowan trees by the millstream. She heard rustlings above, and walked on through the fields behind a row of Wharf Street houses. Ducking back among the sumac, she made her way past the parsonage and meetinghouse, then to the end of the street. Still she heard wings, and kept her eyes on the path. There was a granite outcrop that Mr. Lamb might like for a pulpit, so she went there, and all round over dewy, wet grass, she flung wide her dried rowanberries for Mr. Lamb's red Whitsunday and the delight of red birds.

"Now," she spoke into the air, "you must be patient, and wait for him to come. Wait for your berries to be good and wet, or else they'll make you ill. Wait for the people."

There were small sounds in the grass, but most of the birds settled in the trees. She left them and fled silently back along Wharf Street in the light of the half-moon, willing herself unseen all the way to the house and to the attic.

IN THE MORNING, SUSANNAH SAID AGAIN THEY'D GO TO the meetinghouse to hear Mr. Ferris. For Tamsin, the hard seat of the pew was even more unforgiving than usual, as her mind already went to sunlight, salt breeze on her neck, and grass under her feet. She wanted to be with the brave and curious souls now venturing to hear a sermon out beyond the fishing stage. She imagined bolting from the meetinghouse to run and see cardinals circle the air over Mr. Lamb's head, but instead pressed her hands flat to the wood pew.

On this strange, split Sabbath, however, no one in the parish had to wait long to learn what happened. Vivid accounts, thrilling, alarming, landed of a sudden, even in the meetinghouse. Mr. Ferris had only begun to read the pages of what he meant to preach that morning.

OUT ON THE GRANITE OF THE OPEN FIELD, MR. LAMB'S clear voice had risen to tell of God's infinite love for sailors come up from the harbor, Africans who'd come past the meetinghouse, and eager townsfolk. All were stunned, at once, to be in the midst of a living miracle! Cardinals uncounted streaked the air, and the preacher, hands to the sky, cried awe-struck, *"the flame-red doves of the Holy Spirit!"* He preached on, as red and red-tipped wings dropped to the grass, mounted up, swooped, dropped, and rose again. But still more shocking, at the pinnacle of Mr. Lamb's transcendent sermon, he had an attack of painful wheezing. When he collapsed on the granite, three men carried him posthaste to The Rowans and upstairs to a chamber where he pointed. Others pelted to the meetinghouse, crashing shamelessly in on Mr. Ferris' sermon. All four Bennetts rushed to The Rowans, and a good number of parishioners took the chance too, whether or not there would be ale on the Sabbath.

TAMSIN, AT THE LOOK AND SOUND OF MR. LAMB, KNEW what she must do.

"Peppermint tea," Susannah said.

"With sweetleaf extract," Tamsin said, then made Phebe sit with Mr. Lamb and hold his hand. "Watch both of his eyes," she whispered. "Talk to him gently, and don't stop." And she rushed for the linen sack of seeds from Suriname, that Grandmother Cat had called "floss." With a speed she never even noticed, she took her mortar and pestle, pounded and ground a seed down fine, and returned to the bedside as Susannah came with a teapot and glass cup. Tamsin had no idea how little to use, but it must be very little, so she put a pinch into the cup, poured some tea, and with difficulty helped Mr. Lamb to sip.

It took time. When he'd finished the cup, she listened to his breath, gave him a second pinch of floss in more tea, and listened again, anxious if he would need still more. Slowly the wheeze released, his face softened, and everyone breathed more easily.

"Thank you," he whispered. "I am asthmatic, you see. This has happened before. It will happen again."

Tamsin's tears were of glad relief, but fear as well, that someday Mr. Lamb could die of this.

Susannah took Peter and Phebe downstairs to the tavern to look after a crowd of men now settled in, thirsty not only for news of Mr. Lamb.

TAMSIN SAT WITH HIM THROUGH THE AFTERNOON, listening to his breath. He drowsed, woke, and drowsed. She spent the time puzzling about his wandering eye that seemed to take in so much more than would be possible if his two eyes were more disciplined. She considered, not for the first time, that his vision must be like hers, showing him diverse things that must somehow be put together with his straight-ahead sight.

Once when he woke, she asked him a question.

"Mr. Lamb, may I say – when you went to see Mr. Ferris, I feared you'd gone to tell him what Phebe said to you about my Grandmother Cat and the cardinals and the rowan seed. You see, for a long time, as far back as I know, my Rowan family has been mistrusted, blamed, truly almost killed, only for seeing what we see, and healing where we can heal. I don't know why, when healing and helping are the Rowans' whole work. Those of us who can write –"

Should she mention Priscilla? No.

"You see, we keep note of our herbs' effects, so that in time we learn more. My grandmother's mother Priscilla –"

She stopped.

"But time and again, attacks come. Do you understand it?"

Mr. Lamb reached for his Bible, turned pages toward the end, and read: "*Andres Israēlitai, ti thaumazete epi toutō, ē hēmin ti atenizete hōs idia dynamei ē eusebeia pepoiēkosin tou peripatein auton.*"

He smiled at Tamsin then, as if he expected she would rejoice to have her answer. She waited and he read from the facing page: "*Ye men of Israel, why marvel ye at this? Or why look ye so earnestly on us, as though by our own power or godliness we had made this man to walk?*"

Still Tamsin waited.

Mr. Lamb spoke carefully. "Tamsin, some people will see what you Rowans do, and marvel at it. They will believe that you presume improperly, arrogantly, to take on the Lord's work. They will be confused, and think you very wrong. Some will believe you do this work not in the Lord, but through poisonous, persuasive, dark forces. They will judge you damned. Some will simply watch you, envy your knowing, and oppose you for no other reason than simply to take you down.

"Is any of that true, Tamsin? Do you presume?"

"No."

"Do you meddle in dark forces?"

"No!"

"Are there those who envy your family?"

She hesitated. "I have heard, some may."

"Yes, Tamsin," he said. "Never doubt it. Some do." He reached for his day-book, tore out a page, and began to write. "Commit this verse to memory in Greek and English both, so that if ever you must defend yourself, you will do it in the words of Luke the Apostle, in the common Greek of the Book of Acts."

"Must I defend myself?" she asked, and a spark of Mr. Lamb's attention lit his wayward eye.

He nodded once. "You've already done so, Tamsin. What do you remember?"

She saw fearful men in the tavern, and mugs of her ale in a line on the bar.

"And you'll defend yourself again, in word and deed."
She looked at the paper. "*Andres…,*" she murmured. "*Andres Israël –*"

She doubted such curious words would help, however biblical, however old. What she wanted for her beloved Grandmother Cat, for Priscilla who had been so hurt, for Margaret who had fled an old world, and for every rowess before and to come – what Tamsin wanted was simply for the lineage to be safe in the work of seeing and healing.

"*Ye men of Israel,*" she asked, "*Why marvel ye at this?*"

35

UPON HEARING OF MR. LAMB'S RECOVERY, SOME WHO'D been at the meetinghouse were disappointed, finding it an unlucky failure of divine judgment. They were glad when he went away. Others – those who'd seen Mr. Lamb send vibrant words like living birds into the air – these witnesses rejoiced in his health. Even years later in the tavern, Tamsin would hear certain men say they were lighter in spirit ever since that sermon in the field and the flight of those birds.

Indeed, that Whitsunday led to an unseen breach that niggled at certain persons of Dorset Harbor, none more deeply than Mr. Ferris himself. His sermons became darker, his presence more frequent at the tavern. While he preached fervently against drunkenness and disorder, he took ever more pints of The Rowans' ale, together with his favored drink, called a stone fence. It was a stiff mix of rum and cider. So often did Mr. Ferris ask for this that Peter quietly took to calling him Mr. Fence.

In the midst of noonday ales taken with a stone fence or two, the minister might find his way to Susannah's kitchen to survey the current arrangement of the pantry. At times he'd shift around plates, pots, and jars to satisfy some new opinion, while lamenting to her the sad death of his wife, buried in the graveyard. Susannah and Tamsin kept silence on these occasions, and after a while he would leave for the parsonage.

Still, as June went on, Tamsin saw her mother more disturbed by these intrusions into the kitchen. Then Susannah would speak to Tamsin and Phebe of all the good new wool upstairs that needed to be carded and spun and, after preparing the tavern dinner with her daughters, she would retreat to the attic chamber, to her great wheel, and take Phebe with her. There Phebe would card and Susannah would spin through afternoon until sunset, making up skeins of perfect yarn to take to Mr. Dominicus Oakes, who wove them into blankets for the inn.

Sometimes when Mr. Ferris came to the kitchen, Susannah would simply leave the house. She might fill a watering can and walk out along Uncle Nat's field to the uphill road, and Tamsin knew she was going to see her little girls and water the berries.

In time, Tamsin took on Mother's disquiet. Mornings when there were no guests for breakfast, she'd run out to Green Cove to sit in solitude on the rocks that jut out past the bayberries, or else make her way in among the pitch pines and bury her hands in the scent of pine straw.

One morning when days had passed without rain, she went out early, filled two watering cans, and carried them uphill. The shriek of the gate aired again the sound that tore through the kitchen, the morning Papa split into lights. Still she went in, bade good morning to her sisters and watered their berry plants. On leaving, she did not close the gate, but took the cans back down to the shed, took an empty sack, and ran to Green Cove. There she gathered dry straw from the pitch pines into the sack and ran it up to the graveyard. By her sisters' graves, she spread needles all over the strawberries to shade the moist soil. When she left, she closed the gate.

That afternoon, she went to the attic chamber where Susannah was spinning wool and told her what she had done.

Her eyes filled with gratitude. "Thank you, Tamsin. It does comfort me that you know them." She smiled. "Perhaps in the morning I'll go there with Phebe and Peter. They should know their sisters too."

THE NEXT DAY, AS TAMSIN WAS MAKING UP A FISH STEW for tavern dinner, Peter came in somber, Phebe in tears, and Mother with new peace in her face. Tamsin stooped down to hold Phebe, who wept, "Tamsin, they died. Alice and Charlotte and Lu, they all died."

"I know, dear, they're in another land." She rubbed Phebe's back and kissed her cheek. "Did you see the strawberries and the shore plum bushes Mother planted for them?"

Phebe nodded. "And the raspberry cane."

"And the raspberry cane," Tamsin said. "Come now and help me cut potatoes for the stew."

She looked up at her mother, who gave a trembling smile. A few days later, Susannah went again to her daughters' graves to water the soil beneath the pine straw.

AT LAST LETTING GO OF HIS INCURSIONS INTO KITCHEN and pantry, Mr. Ferris instead took to appearing in the dining room when the selectmen met to consult on town matters. There, he pushed to address, that very month at the quarterly town meeting, some lamentable spiritual declines in Dorset Harbor. Easily heard in the kitchen, he denounced incidents of excessive drink and the flouting of curfews. He decried the sinful relations of some who'd recently stated their intention to marry – and, still worse, the vile sins of those who had not.

One noonday, Susannah, clearly vexed, told Tamsin that, as Mr. Manning's Caleb was sloppy and prone to passing water in the meetinghouse, she did not approve of his presence at the selectmen's meetings, and she thought to tell them they must meet elsewhere. Tamsin assured her that, should Caleb stain the floor, she knew very well how to clean it, and Mother wasn't to worry. Still, something alarmed her beyond what she could bear, and she disappeared to the attic. Tamsin believed she'd gone up to her great wheel and the peace of her spinning. She hoped so.

AFTER DINNER AND WASHING UP WERE DONE, TAMSIN went to Peter at the bar and told him softly that she would go up the road to water the strawberries and bring some back, as Mother was unhappy and this might please her. He nodded, so with watering can and basket, she went.

The sound of the iron gate still hurt. "Papa!" she whispered and went through.

Then, just inside, she could see something wrong. Approaching her sisters' stones, she stopped. Some animal had dragged something, or dragged itself, right across the strawberry bed. Much of Tamsin's pine straw was scuffed aside and pushed uphill, plants pulled askew and pressed into the soil. What was this?

Could a raccoon and her kits have done this, or would they only eat the berries and be gone? But there were berries here, ripe for the eating. Tamsin picked and put them into her basket. She fixed the plants' runners and roots as best she could, and watered the soil.

Pine straw had been pulled away from the bed, and she went to look past the shore plum bushes, if there were an animal dead or injured. None was there, but the shore plums had branches broken, and some raspberry cane looked trodden. Around the bed, she scooped what straw she could and returned it to the plants. She would bring more from the cove. Then she picked up the basket and left, closing the terrible gate.

SHE FOUND PHEBE IN THE BACK FIELD, WEEDING AMONG the sweetgrass James had brought from the farm. Tamsin had already made up one batch of the ointment. The smell of sweet-grass took her so near to him, she felt his touch.

James, come soon, today, tomorrow.

She let Phebe choose a few berries from the basket and carried the rest into the house, to the attic. When Mother saw them, she did not stop her spinning, but only shook her head. Tamsin felt her overwhelming sadness. Time and again, Mother had lost so many who were precious to her. Perhaps later she would take yarrow tea. So Tamsin took the strawberries down to the dining room and offered them to the selectmen, just finishing their meeting and their cider. All congenial and pleased, they passed the basket round the table, joking and picking out particular berries, and Mr. Ferris did too. He even dropped some on the floor for Caleb.

36

In the past spring, when James and Grandmother Cat brought provisions and new wool, Grandmother had hinted her worry there'd not be enough trade for the tavern to stay open, but Susannah, who knew the harbor, knew there would be no lack of work. Now in August, Tamsin saw the wharves constantly busy. The tavern flourished. Gardening, fishing, cooking, serving, and cleaning filled every day, and the blessing of wool in the attic chamber made Phebe card enough to keep Mother occupied at the great wheel. All of Susannah's children worked at the meetinghouse too, and in Mr. Proctor's orchard.

So one morning in the kitchen, when Tamsin said it had been nearly a year since Papa's death, they all stopped short, stricken again with the grief they daily put aside. Phebe threw her arms around Tamsin's waist. Peter went into the tavern. Susannah, holding her heart and her stomach, went out the back door and was heard retching.

That day, that very same day, Grandmother Cat and James came again with the oxcart, bringing pullets, pumpkins, herbs, and sacks of new milled rye. Grandmother looked closely at Susannah, lowered her brow and pursed her lips. Later she told Tamsin her mother was over-weary, her skin parched and pale.

"She is unwell, dear, and unhappy. How does she eat? Have you more of the dried nettles? You must cook them up for her, and dandelion greens as much as she will take. Pumpkin stew. Eggs. Do you have beef? Send her to bed nightly with a posset – hot milk, ale, nutmeg, cinnamon. Do you see?"

She did, and promised.

When James said he wanted to see how the new Michaelmas daisies and sweetgrass were faring, Tamsin slipped out, walked round the house with him and into the field. Sweetgrass had rooted well. Soon, Tamsin said, there would be enough growth, she could make a batch of ointment. She showed him the rowan seedlings that Phebe and Peter had moved, and then took him to the far edge of the field, into the tall milkweed.

In the midst of late summer stalks, James put his arms around Tamsin and kissed her on the mouth, and kissed her again. She told him how much she missed him. They stayed happy awhile in the milkweed, talking quietly and quickly. She knew they must go in.

"Tamsin, I want to come to the harbor soon. I don't want to stay at the farm. The mill is good, I like the mill. But I always think of your Papa. Tamsin, of the men you know in the tavern, are there any that might look for an apprentice?"

She gave a small, bitter laugh. "They don't speak to me of their work, James. They drink and make noise and –" She stopped short, looking back to the house.

"Drink and make noise and what?"

"I keep myself to myself as I can."

"They trouble you."

"Some. They reach for me, speak coarsely. But no, I don't know if any would take an apprentice. If my Grandfather Peter were still living, he would teach you blacksmithing!"

"They reach for you?"

"They've had too much to drink and show too openly what they want. Peter tries to keep watch, but –"

"Who does this?"

"I stay away, James. I hear as little of their business as I can."

"If I were here, they'd not be reaching for you." He held her tight.

"I assure you," she laughed, "some would try. But as to work, ask Peter. There may be another blacksmith at the harbor, glad to have you."

But Tamsin knew Uncle Simon would never let James go. A signed paper was needed, a bond, and Uncle Simon would never put his name to such a thing. In any case, would James leave Aunt Adah and the little ones, even if he could? They needed him.

"Tamsin, would you come back to the farm? I'll inherit my father's part someday. Peter can come back for the part of your father's that didn't go to your mother. Would you come back?"

He did not say, "Marry me," though, loving him, it was what Tamsin believed would happen. But Mother needed her, and she couldn't leave, not soon.

"I must go in and put out the dinner." Her fingertips touched his cheek. "They'll wonder where I am."

She kissed him and ran to the house. She would think on this later, as she often did.

When James came in, Tamsin was carrying stew and bread into the tavern. He hovered at the bar, near Peter. Tamsin thought he might speak with Peter about work at the harbor, but instead he seemed to watch men's hands as she passed them by. When she took a cider to Noah Southworth, she saw him cast a look at James. James returned the look.

IN THE AFTERNOON, HE WENT TO HITCH ETHAN AND Levi to the cart. Tamsin promised Grandmother Cat she would cook beef and greens and spice pumpkin stews for Mother, and then had to grieve their parting all over again. Still harder for her was the stoop of James' shoulders as he walked round the cart, climbed up, and drove the oxen onto Wharf Street. The memory hurt her heart all evening as she worked, and long into the night when she couldn't sleep.

Would she and James be together someday, with Uncle Simon needing him, and Mother needing her? If they were to marry, she thought Uncle Simon would be glad of it, to keep all the property in the family. He would think it wise business.

But Mother – Tamsin had never spoken to her of her feelings for James, but she felt somehow Mother would not want this. She was a daughter of the coast, not the farm. She'd married first a man of another country, a son of French parents, and she'd loved them all. Mother seemed at home, not so much in the round earth of Papa's compass, but in a world thrown wide open to the sea. She'd never forbid Tamsin to marry James, but neither would she hope for it.

Every day now, Tamsin did as Grandmother had told her. She cooked good things for Mother, watched her, and saw how little she ate. She refused beef and eggs, did less of the cooking that once pleased her, and went to the attic to spin.

ONE MORNING, RETURNING FROM HER REFUGE ON THE rocks at Green Cove, Tamsin found Mother sitting on the back steps, doubled over, vomiting on the ground. She wiped her mouth with her apron. When she sat up, she was pale, eyes round and dark as if she looked at a moonless night. She had been crying.

"Mother." Tamsin sat down and held her. "You're worn, you're wrung out empty. Grandmother said you must eat. Whatever you'd like, let me make it for you."

Her apron was a knot in her hands. "If I were empty, Tamsin, I would be glad, but I am not." She turned away, retching. When she could, she said, almost unheard, "I've not wanted to tell you this, but I have no choice now. I am with child."

There came a space of time. Tamsin couldn't tell how large it was, but all it held was impossibility. In that space, she heard over and over the thing Mother had said, which could not be true.

"Mr. Ferris has seized and disgraced me."

More time. More impossibility resolved slowly into images, then fact, then horror.

Pine straw dragged. Branches broken. Raspberry cane, down.

"Mother."

"He tried to persuade me. He told me Adam was tempted by Eve in the garden, and I had tempted him with my plantings. I denied him and he forced me."

Susannah's body convulsed. She covered her mouth to stifle sobs. The sound of smothered pain was unbearable. Tamsin held her mother tight till she came to rest.

"He told me I must keep the secret because I am an innkeeper and widowed, and would be called a whore. He said I would lose the tavern, ruin our living."

The inn was empty today, but there would be a tavern dinner to make. Phebe had gone out in the shallop with Peter. They'd return soon with fish to be gutted and cooked. A minister of God might come for his dinner. Tamsin would gut him like a fish. She would use her fingernails and caustic herbs.

"Does he know?"

Susannah shook her head. "I hoped there would be no child. Then, God forgive me, I prayed it would be lost. I've miscarried before, but I still have it." She hardly breathed. "It will destroy us."

Tamsin gripped her mother's hands. "It will not."

Susannah turned her dark eyes to the field. "I think to go to the cove and fall from Pulpit Rocks. Leave the tavern for you and Peter."

"Mother!" Tamsin felt dizzy. Black trees circled her.

"You would do well. You would teach Phebe. Grandmother Cat would come."

Tamsin held tight to her mother to make the trees stop. "No. You will not think this."

Susannah pushed back with a hellish look. "The sin of dying by one's hand is terrible. But worse, Tamsin, would be to leave you in poverty and shame. That is not why Nathaniel trusted us with his house."

"Mother, I will not permit this. I will not let you. I will hitch myself to you like Ethan to a stoneboat. I will be your stone. I will make you pull me with you wherever you walk."

"Tamsin."

"I will sleep tied to you in your bed."

Susannah tried to get up. Tamsin held her wrists.

"If, God forbid, you go off Pulpit Rocks, be sure you will take me with you."

"My daughter. Then we will all of us go down. You deserve a good marriage, not this."

"No." Tamsin pressed a hand hard to the stays laced tight over her mother's belly. "You will lose this. We will lose this," she said, her certainty harsh.

It was the last day of August, marking the sixteenth year since she was born.

"Listen to me. I am a Bennett, but I am a Rowan. I am a *rowess*. Grandmother Cat said it, and I know it. I think of Priscilla Rowan. When they called her a witch, she kept to her work. And Margaret. Her village bled in battle, but she crossed the siege line over and over and over. Mother, we will go to that line. I tell you, I am a rowess."

Tamsin watched her mother's eyes till she saw the meaning go deep enough.

Susannah whispered. "Not here. I will not do this here, not in this house. Nathaniel's house."

Tamsin gave a nod. She saw the angel Michael throw a dragon over the edge of heaven and knew the edge where they would go.

37

THE FIRST DAYS OF SEPTEMBER HAD BEEN DRY. TAMSIN opened her palms to the sky and begged, *please hold, we have work.*

She went to Peter and told him Mother was unwell. She was upstairs at her wheel and would not come down today. She said, tomorrow being fair, she would cook pumpkin for Mother's breakfast and take her away from the tavern. Today, she and Phebe would bake bread enough for two days, and early tomorrow start a stew for the dinner. Peter would have Phebe's help all day. Would that be enough? He agreed.

That night, Tamsin stitched a small sack of fine linen with flat-felled seams for the poisonous powder that would keep her family safe.

THE NEXT MORNING, PHEBE WAS ALIGHT WITH THE same spirit that let her brighten the front gate on The Rowans' first day. Gleeful and serious, she explained to Tamsin that Peter would carry from the kitchen whatever she couldn't manage, and she would go among the tables to take cider, ale, and rum to the men. And, she noted, the stone fence to Mr. Ferris.

Her hands were adept with the rye and Indian corn bread that took only stirring, so Tamsin was in the kitchen to stoke the oven for bread, cook pumpkin for Mother, and take what she would need for the day, peppermint brandy tincture and a mug.

Alone upstairs, she took Grandmother Cat's sack of floss from the chest, and with mortar and pestle, ground five seeds down to a grit, then to a powder, and spooned it into the sack she'd made with strong seams. She would give Mother the floss in small pinches in water, and wait for the cramping as comes at the start of labor. She wanted to ask Grandmother Cat if this would be the right way, but in truth Tamsin didn't know whether Grandmother had ever used floss for this purpose. So she would go ahead, watch for the effects, and heed the unexpected.

She pushed the sack deep into the pocket inside her petticoat and brought out the sundial-compass.

Papa, am I doing right?

No answer, she put his compass in the chest and took out scissors, a length of hemp twine, and all the clean linen cloths she wrapped round herself to catch her own flow. She took a charcoal of Phebe's and wrote a verse the length of one cloth, though she did not have it in the common Greek.

These things she carried out to the shed, put them in two clam buckets, and took down the rake. She filled a jug with water from the well and put the jug into a third bucket. Uncle Nat had left a pile of sailcloth patches on a shelf. As Papa was laid out on a sail by the millstream, Tamsin took two patches and folded them around the jug. For clams, she took another bucket.

She didn't know how long the day would be, nor whether the tides would be right for the work at hand – high enough at the rock pools to wash away blood, low enough for clamming. She remembered the day Mr. Lamb had surprised them at the cove, and prayed no man would appear. But Mother would be hidden from the road by the height of Pulpit Rocks and the mass of bayberries, and Tamsin had the rake and empty bucket, a reason to be there.

Now she went to see that Mother was eating her pumpkin,

and not laced in her stays. Simple as possible, Mother should wear a shortgown over her petticoats today, no pinning a bodice to stays. Tamsin would find her a shawl to cover.

THEY WALKED THE SHORE ROAD IN SILENCE, TAMSIN with the buckets, Susannah stiff, restrained, a hand sometimes rising to her belly till she would let it drop limp. Tamsin watched and wondered if this showed dread or grief or only enduring.

Past the Pulpit Rocks, they stepped into thick sand. Susannah stopped and looked to the beach, hand at her belly.

"Mother?"

"I've lost so many. My girls played here." She looked to Tamsin. "At the farm I lost your little brother."

Tamsin saw the miracle of Eli, born and dead.

"And the ones I miscarried."

"Come." Tamsin went to the bayberries, to the narrow passage between dense green and the base of Pulpit Rocks. She made her way toward the water, pushing sideways at times, an eye on Mother. Leaving the buckets under bayberries, she took her linen cloths and climbed out on the narrow jut of rocks. There were mornings she sat here on a certain rock that was sometimes dry, other times edged round with a spiral of salt water. She found it comforting, enchanting. She wanted this peace for Mother and spread her folds of linen out to a mat.

She helped Mother settle, took off her shoes and stockings, and lifted her feet into the shallow pool. She made her way back over the rocks to the buckets where, all unsteady, she sloshed water into the mug. Trembling fingers dropped in the smallest pinch of powder and swirled it, trying not to spill. Afraid to climb over rocks now, she bared her feet and used the strings of her pocket to tie up her petticoats. Gripping the mug like a holy cup in two hands, she waded knee-deep and held it up to Susannah, whose restraint cracked. She stifled a cry and with shocking ferocity drank all of it at once.

Tamsin's eyes flashed to the top of Pulpit Rocks, where she caught sight of an anguished woman dropping from there onto the spit of ragged stone that pointed to the sea.

Susannah pushed the mug back at Tamsin.

"More."

Tamsin shook her head. "I don't know what will happen with this much."

Susannah pushed her hands into her belly and stared at the water. "After twenty waves," she said, "I want more."

"Call to me," Tamsin said, and waded back to the bayberries.

She took up the rake and a bucket and went where the sand was damp and dark. If she moved a bit away, Mother might find some peace in being with the tide. And if Tamsin could find little holes in the sand and work the rake, it might give order to a frantic heart. Pray heaven, no man comes by the shore road today. She must distract him. Cut him off.

Ye men of Israel. Over and over she heard, *Ye men of Israel.*

If a man were to come, who would it be? Pray not the damned Ferris, *ye men of Israel.* Would he keep away from her? Would it be a farmer, *Ye men?* Some trader afoot? Angel Michael, may he see only a girl clamming and pass by, leave her alone. *No, ye men of Israel, she is not that girl who serves at the tavern. She is not a girl keeping watch on her mother, no Rowan daughter, for sure no rowess.*

Would he speak to her, question her?

Ye men, why marvel ye? I do this because I must.

Scanning the sand for little holes, she picked up white shells and smooth stones and put them in her pockets. A few clams in her bucket, she waded back to where Mother sat looking at the sea.

Susannah shook her head.

Tamsin went to the bayberries, poured more water into the mug, and dropped a larger pinch of floss. Susannah swallowed it back.

"I'm finding clams," Tamsin said.

"Twenty more and then another mug."

"Clams?"

"Waves."

"A hundred."

"Sixty," Susannah said. "No, thirty. Then another mug."

Tamsin nodded and went back to the beach. "Call out when there's cramp."

Nothing yet.

THE WEAVER MR. OAKES WALKED THE ROAD, A BUNDLE on his back. Tamsin made as if she'd not seen him and, to prevent greeting, walked into the water and lowered herself. Never would he approach a girl sitting to pass water, and he went on.

There were more clams and many more waves before Tamsin dropped thick pinches of floss into the mug and sat with her mother to watch the effects. She felt like the blade of Papa's sundial-compass, unmoving on a rock, marking the arc of the sun. Before bed tonight, she would write long notes in her day-book.

First aching, then cramping, waves grew. She helped to pull Mother's petticoats and shift out of the way, and brought her the mug with brandy tincture. Red pushed out first onto white, then one small thing, a birth, and another, an afterbirth. She folded these things in their cloth and put them aside. Then more blood, Tamsin watched closely, then less, then less.

Susannah stood up in the pool of water. Tamsin folded the red cloths into a bucket and helped her mother step back to the bayberry bushes. They unpinned her shortgown, untied her petti-coats. She held up her shift and walked into the water to wash.

Tamsin carried across the rocks the small burden and the bucket of red cloths, watched her mother, and watched the road. When Susannah came out of the water, Tamsin folded the length of cloth where she had written words that were truthful, even if not in the common Greek.

"Woman, hath no man condemned thee? She said, No man, Lord."

Tamsin wrapped it as a girdle round and beneath her, and made it secure by tying her petticoats. Susannah pinned her short-gown and took up her shawl.

"Mother," Tamsin said, "the little one."

Susannah didn't respond.

"Mother, shall we bury the little one in the sea, like Élie, or in the ground, like Papa?"

"Here. In the sea."

She went back to the rocks, to her stockings and shoes.

Tamsin laid a patch of sailcloth on the sand by the bayberries, set on it a circle of white shells, and unfolded the cloth that held a little pear-shaped being. Shocked with grief, she pushed her hands into the sand and heard the voice she knew. She wanted her Grandmother Cat.

Heed the unexpected.

So observing her love, she studied the little one and its after-birth. She marveled at the cord, a fine, strong thing with a light like the inside of a shell. She thought the cord brave, and cried as she took her scissors to cut it. Then, more gently than was at all possible, she placed the little pear-form in the midst of the shells and surrounded the shells with a circle of smooth stones. As she folded the shroud and wrapped it round with hemp twine, she whispered a verse she'd always found sad and irresistibly exciting. It made her think of the coracle.

"And when she could not longer hide him, she took for him an ark of bulrushes, and daubed it with slime and with pitch, and put the child therein; and she laid it in the flags by the river's brink."

She walked into the sea, along the jut of rocks, and laid the swaddling low. The tide was pulling now, so she looked to the strip of green and grey across the water and imagined the little one, who could not be truly born, carried all the way over to settle in a shroud in the marsh grass, there at the edge of Flagg Island.

38

That very night was just one night shy of the full moon. This was both lucky and alarming.

Tamsin left her bed when the house had been silent for a time, Phebe's breath quiet and even. She took clothing downstairs, dressed in the dining room, dark blue jacket, darkest red petticoat over another and the shift. In the tavern, she went to the low cabinet at the far end of the bar. She felt there for the key, slipped it into the pocket tied inside her petticoats, and went out the kitchen door to the shed. No lantern, she knew which bucket was which. The first was empty. Two held yesterday's clams in salt water. There would be chowder this afternoon, Mother's *chaudière*. The fourth bucket held the bloody cloths underneath the jug. She took out the jug, splashed a little water on the cloths, and took up the bucket.

Moonlight helped. Her steps were soft, crossing the fields behind the next houses, but back of the parsonage and meetinghouse, she stopped. The sumac thicket would hide her, but she couldn't pass through without stepping on sticks on a night when, if she were heard, she could be seen. She went round behind the sumac, beyond the meetinghouse, doubling back as far from the parsonage as she could. Dangerous, the key was for the

214

side door, and this faced the parsonage. Perfect silence. Not the steps, nor the lock, nor even the handle of the bucket must squeak.

She knew which tread was weak and stepped over it, put the bucket down without a sound, and retrieved the iron key from her pocket. But in tracing the lock with her finger, she let the key fall, and in groping to find it, knocked into the bucket. She dropped off the steps, away from the moonlight, and crouched tight in shadow, praying the foul minister slept deep.

A voice called out from Wharf Street. "Mr. Ferris? That you? Somerby here. Did you take a fall?"

Deacon Somerby, far too kind a man, apparently took full-moon walks. Tamsin begged him in silence, *please go away.* Footsteps approached with a swing of lantern light. She didn't dare move to see where he stood.

"Ferris? You all right?"

Voice too near.

Bloodroot, she remembered. *Bloodroot flower folds in at night.* Tamsin spoke to bloodroot, folded inward, gave thanks.

"Lost your key here."

Do not touch the key! Do not!

"I'll leave it for you to find."

Silence, followed by a mutter like "Raccoon." Or it might have been "Rum again," either way a sign Mr. Somerby's curiosity was sated. Footsteps left.

Tamsin listened and breathed for a long while, hearing nothing in the air, not an owl, not a cricket. When she unfolded her being, she could just see the shape of the iron key on the second step. Rising slowly, she picked it up, took the bucket by its rim, and made the key open the door only enough for a slender young woman and a clam bucket to slip through.

The door closed.

Footsteps firm, inaudible, Tamsin walked the center aisle straight to the pulpit. *"Ye men of Israel,"* she said, low and bitter. *"Ye bloody men. How dare ye bloody marvel?"*

To the left of the pulpit, narrow stairs rose to the height from which Mr. Ferris would preach this day. Tamsin climbed them to the top. There at the pulpit, she looked out in fury over box pews and balcony. *So this is what he sees. He feels this height.*

"*Andres Israēlitai!*" She hurled her voice into the dark. "*Ti thaumazete epi toutō?*" And she took the bloodied linens with the astonishing afterbirth and unfolded them on the floor beneath the pulpit, laid it all right there at his feet. Floorboards bare, the vividness would soak in before red turned to dark. A scent would spread on the air.

LATER THAT MORNING, IT WAS SAID THAT AN ANIMAL, A raccoon perhaps, had gone beneath the meetinghouse and died there, and even though the young sexton Peter Bennett was sent under to find it, the offending carcass never was retrieved. Perhaps it was only a dead rat in a wall, some thought, since the smell abated within a week.

As for Mr. Ferris, he announced to the congregation at the end of the morning sermon that he was obliged to travel to Boston for a ministerial meeting the next day, and so on that Sabbath there would be no afternoon sermon. He advised the reading of Holy Scripture at home, and left for his meeting posthaste.

That week, word came to the selectman Mr. Manning that Mr. Ferris had received an urgent call to a pulpit in the Leeward Islands and had sailed with a schooner out of Boston. He wrote to Mr. Manning that he would graciously leave his small pastoral library for his successor, though sadly for the spiritual care of the parish, no new minister was soon found.

In the absence of preaching, the merchant Deacon Somerby saw to the Sabbath reading of scripture in the meetinghouse. He had a fine voice for it. Peter Bennett, with frequent help from his sisters, continued to be paid for his work as sexton, Tamsin taking special care of the floorboards in Mr. Manning's box pew.

During the week after Mr. Ferris' departure, she scrubbed another patch of floor three times with rosemary vinegar and twigs of fresh pine, to chase evil spirits. She could not remove the browning stain soaked into raw wood, but she did not greatly mind this mark. Instead, for the first time, she asked the rowans round the house to give her six live twigs. This they did, and she bound them with red thread into three crosses. She affixed them with pine pitch to the pulpit, high up on the inside, where they could not be seen unless one went to one's knees, looking up, which she thought an unlikely posture for a minister. Never again did she climb those steps to clean that floor, but filled the meetinghouse with the purging sound of furious laughter, recalling the sight of a minister tripping over his feet and falling on his baggage in a rush to reach the wharf.

SUSANNAH STOPPED ATTENDING SABBATH MEETINGS AT this time, remaining instead at The Rowans. As no new parish minister was found for a good while, and as the selectmen were devoted to the tavern, no serious question was raised, no fine levied. In truth, she was hardly seen in the tavern either, keeping herself mainly to the attic. Mornings, she would go down to put on breakfast for any lodgers and start to prepare a dinner, but before tavern opening, she would retreat upstairs to spin or sew. Because Phebe reasoned she had no need for the schoolhouse, Susannah gave a great deal of time to teaching her reading and stitching. When Grandmother Cat came with James to bring provisions and herbs, Red Lammas in autumn, new wool in the spring, Susannah would go downstairs to be with them and return to the attic when they had gone.

Tamsin missed her mother's presence in those years, but as a young woman and a healer, she understood the pain and need for refuge. Thus, Tamsin would take yarrow or lavender tea to the attic each afternoon and a posset each evening for good sleep. She watched with care for signs of a coming peace. Phebe's eagerness for learning thrived with her mother's attention, and Peter never questioned his mother removing herself somewhat from the daily work of the tavern. It gave him – most fittingly, he believed – a growing responsibility for the business.

If Deacon Somerby felt perhaps that Mistress Bennett should attend at the meetinghouse to hear his Sabbath readings, he never said so, but from time to time brought to Tamsin small delicacies for her mother from his stock of imports, and asked her to convey his respects. Tamsin, always moved by his kindness, was still profoundly grateful that when she had folded into shadow that night at the meetinghouse, he'd not inquired too closely into the sound and movement, but had walked away.

39

ON THE DAY BEFORE ALL HALLOWS' EVE, LATE IN A chill and overcast afternoon, Mr. Lamb appeared in the dining room at The Rowans, peeking into the kitchen with an impish smile.

Tamsin looked up from cutting onions. "Mr. Lamb! Welcome!"

"Hello, my dear!" His very wig appeared to lift in delight. "I've come to see you good Bennetts at an auspicious time! I believe you told me once, 'twas All Hallows' when you arrived at the harbor to keep this excellent tavern?"

"It was, Mr. Lamb, exactly. May I bring you something to drink?"

"I would find me a place to sit, dear, and," he whispered as if thrilling to a conspiracy, "I have missed your remarkable ale!"

She went to the bar to fetch an ale with the proper extracts, and when she returned he had settled himself in a chair in the dining room doorway.

"Ah, thank you! I have just now come from the town of Sawbridge, do you know that place? To the eastward, Casco Bay. And I heard from the minister there that your Mr. Ferris has departed from the Dorset Harbor parish. Is that so?"

219

Tamsin took care to straighten the corners of her mouth. "He went to a ministerial meeting last month and never came back."

"Did he? Most peculiar. Is it known why?"

"He announced his visit to Boston one Sabbath morning and went away."

Mr. Lamb's brows knit downward, an uncommon expression for him. "Has he been found? No, never mind that," he said quickly. "And how is your good mother?"

"Often at her wheel," Tamsin said simply. Then, lest she seem worried, she smiled. "Phebe cards a great deal of wool, you see."

"She would, yes," Mr. Lamb said, while a light in his wayward eye suggested he heard something Tamsin had not said.

"Have you had a preacher here since Mr. Ferris went away?"

"Once Mr. Richard Woodbury came down from Durham, but he was not well received. Most Sabbaths, a deacon reads scripture."

Peter coming in from the tavern, Mr. Lamb perked up.

"Saint Peter! How is your fishing?"

"I've had luck, sir!"

"He brings in excellent fish," Tamsin said, "And tomorrow we'll have beef. Will you stay? I'm making meat pies in the way the Rowan women have always done. My Grandmother Cat's family."

"Ah, your Grandmother Cat!" Mr. Lamb said. "Astonishing woman! I honor your meat pies, Tamsin!"

When she went to relieve Peter in the tavern, Mr. Lamb went along to be sociable, and met with two who had come in for a late day rum, Deacon Jonathan Somerby and the selectman Mr. Dominicus Oakes. (Tamsin saw that the kind Mr. Oakes did not meet her eyes. He might remember an impropriety he'd seen of a young woman alone at Green Cove, though in fact that was not at all what he had seen.)

"Why, Mr. Lamb!" he said.

"Welcome again to Dorset Harbor, Mr. Lamb!" said the deacon heartily. The deacon and Mr. Oakes looked at one another for the briefest of moments. Mr. Oakes nodded, and Deacon Somerby observed, by the bye, that tomorrow was the Sabbath.

"Mr. Lamb," he said, "I expect you've heard we have no minister in the parish at present."

"I have heard of your sad condition."

"By chance, might you preach here tomorrow? Mr. Oakes and I will gladly put out the word. We'll go house to house, and announce your coming."

"Gentlemen, of course I would preach. It will be All Hallows' Eve. My church rejoices in all the departed saints and believers, an immense cloud of witnesses gone before us!" Round and above the halo of his white wig, his hands evoked eloquently a sky full of faithful beings.

Deacon Somerby and Mr. Oakes showed an uneasy concern with the air over Mr. Lamb's head. Tamsin thought they might regret their impulsive request, as the parishes of Massachusetts avoided All Hallows' in the same way they denounced Christmas. But Tamsin understood the day, because Grandmother Cat observed it every autumn with deep feeling, to remember her Thomas. Every year she told Tamsin that the red thread between life and death would spin out thin at All Hallows'. The dead might visit the living, and the living speak with the dead. Perhaps the deacon and Mr. Oakes feared that an All Hallows' sermon would call the dead in, a perilous wicked practice. They finished their rum in haste and left.

Word of Mr. Lamb's return did spread effectively, however. All of the Bennetts went to the meetinghouse – even Susannah, just that once. Box pews and balcony, the space was near full for both sermons of the day, and Mr. Lamb's words were found entirely rigorous and moral. The Holy Ghost, he averred, knew only too well the low nature of licentious people (*the rat Ferris*, Tamsin thought) and thus inspired our forefathers to set down in writing the stories of the saints, the holy men and women who counted service to the Lord their noblest purpose. Mr. Lamb told the parish that on the Eve of All Hallows' and the Day of All

Saints, we honor not only the those whose stories were written before we were born, but also those good souls who even now walk beside and inspire us.

Mr. Lamb's straight-ahead eye beamed blessing directly from the high pulpit down upon Mother, Tamsin was sure of it. *Precious Maman!* Tamsin reached for her hand.

THE NEXT DAY, BECAUSE MR. LAMB WAS STILL AT THE Rowans, the tavern was unusually busy, both dinner and late afternoon. Susannah retired upstairs soon as she could, taking Phebe with her. Tamsin and Peter cleaned up at the end of the day, while Mr. Lamb sat by the fire. When Peter went upstairs, Mr. Lamb still sat in contemplation and asked Tamsin if she would take a cider and sit with him, as he had a question for her. She would.

"Tamsin, have you committed to memory the verse I gave you, on the true source of healing?"

"I have it in English. '*Ye men of Israel, why marvel ye at this? Or why look ye so earnestly on us, as though by our own power or godliness we had made this man to walk?*' And I practiced the Greek, rolling out the pastry."

"Practice it more, and we'll say it together before I leave. My dear, your humility together with your strength will protect you."

Saying nothing will protect me, she thought. *Saying nothing at all of a rowess.*

Sunset was long past and the tavern dim, but for the fire at the hearth and the glow of a betty lamp at the bar. Mr. Lamb faced that way, though his wandering eye contemplated the hearth. Tamsin could always tell which of Mr. Lamb's eyes he attended to at any moment, and just now she saw a shift from his leftmost eye considering the fire to his straight-ahead eye aimed at the bar. Curious, she turned.

A thin, dark figure, ragged of outline, appeared leaning there, silent, unmoving. It seemed to look away out the window, so there was no face to see, though the form alone was frightening. She could see the betty lamp right through it, and turned back to the fire. Still Mr. Lamb's gaze was to the bar. Empty tatters? Did he see it? She looked at him, and he at her. He touched a finger to his lips.

"Yes, 'tis quite an education, isn't it, to work in one's youth in a tavern? One meets so many people, all shapes. Starving or fat. Hard tales to tell. A tavern is a point on one's path, you see. One's passage. Mine, for instance. I come here to the inn, find what I need, a good meal, respite, peace. I lay down my fatigue, perhaps a grief or two. Or a great guilt. And I go on."

Tamsin turned to look again. The figure had not moved, but she sensed it listening.

"Dear girl, might there be one more of your excellent meat pies still in the kitchen?"

A whispered "yes."

Mr. Lamb gave an encouraging nod. She didn't move. He repeated it with a look from both his eyes at once. That, she felt clear as a nudge, and so moved gingerly to the kitchen.

She put one of the Rowan women's meat pies on a plate, and went to the safety of the bar to put it down before the withered thing. It turned slowly to the pie, then raised to Tamsin an eldritch face. There was an odor of swamp wood. Where once had been living eyes were deep caves. They looked to her as if to ask a question.

Barely breathing, Tamsin heard a sound rise up out of silence, a word. "Yes," she said.

Empty eyes bent so intent a gaze on the pie, they might have taken it in whole.

Tamsin let herself out of the bar to go and sit close to Mr. Lamb.

"Indeed, a tavern's a fine place for sustenance. And giving up the dirt of the road," he said, "before going on."

As they watched, the being in his rags moved to the window. There he waited a moment, dissolved in dull sparks, and was gone.

Silence.

"What was it?" Tamsin whispered, shaky.

"Only a lost soul at All Hallows' who sought his peace." Mr. Lamb gave a little shrug. "Perhaps forgiveness for a great wrong, long ago. And a particular Rowan woman's meat pie."

Tamsin didn't understand the use of her meat pie to so wretched a one, so long past eating, but she was glad if it meant forgiveness.

Mr. Lamb got up to the fireplace then, shoveled the ashes, and banked the fire for the night.

40

NEXT MORNING AT BREAKFAST, MR. LAMB SAID HE would walk to the Second Parish, West Dorset, and visit the minister Mr. Joseph Briggs. Perhaps Mr. Briggs would welcome him to preach next Sabbath at the Second Parish meetinghouse. He'd heard it was admirably built upon a hill with fine prospects all round. Returning to The Rowans in the afternoon, he took the day's fish stew in the dining room, and told Tamsin regretfully that Mr. Briggs had not permitted him to preach.

Tamsin did not say, *Papa called Briggs a ninny.*

"Though never mind," said Mr. Lamb. "I had a glorious walk today in our Lord's creation!"

THROUGHOUT THE DAY, TAMSIN WAS HAUNTED BY THE memory of the ragged being that may have come for sustenance or forgiveness or peace. Wanting to ask further, she told Peter she would serve in the tavern that evening, so he could rest, and as she expected, Mr. Lamb took his ale in company with the tavern-goers after supper. At closing time, she gave Mr. Lamb another mug of her ale and asked how it was he'd known the reason for the gaunt thing's presence.

"But you spoke to it, did you not?" he asked. "What did you say to it?"

"I said 'yes.'"

"'Yes' to what? What was the question?"

Tamsin waited, listened. "He was grieving terribly. There was something he'd done. I heard a voice, 'yes.'"

"And so you told him –"

"Yes," she said, and was quiet.

"Mr. Lamb, what if I were to want forgiveness – or peace – for something I had done?"

"Do you?"

She shook her head.

"Are you sure?"

Say nothing, she thought, and said nothing.

"A mystery, then," Mr. Lamb said, and Tamsin could see the spark shift from his straight-ahead eye to the one that saw things by wandering.

"Do you know, Tamsin" – his voice, always expressive, went low – "There was an old Scot who came to my mother's inn and had something to tell, only he couldn't tell it, which distressed him. So I sat him down alone in the chimney corner, took him his ale and went away, and he told his tale to the fire."

Tamsin looked at the fire and said nothing.

"It's late, my dear. 'Tis fine, if you'd rather not speak. Time to close?"

So she went into the bar and lowered the frame of ochre-painted spindles that secured the front, and she latched it. For a moment she rested her hands on the counter's smooth wax, and looked at them.

"I am a healer," she said quietly, "and I see things that others don't."

She glanced at Mr. Lamb through the spindles. His one eye was shadowed, the wanderer looked to the fire.

"I am a rowess, Grandmother told me. I know edges, thresholds, the crossing of lines." She wiped the counter down, wiped drips from the bottles, and cleaned the taps of the casks.

"Crossings are not what we think," she said. "I know this from Margaret Rowan who crossed the siege line at Brampton Bryan for the Lady and her people."

Stooping to swab the floor where drops of apple cider had fallen, she went to her knees and mourned. "It was formed like a pear, and sweet, and I wrapped it in sailcloth and shells. I put it in the waves and it broke my heart."

When she stood up, she looked into the cabinet for her extracts. What would need replenishing?

There was more she had to say about thresholds, and when she had said it all into the cabinet, about the luminous cord she'd cut and the afterbirth she'd laid under the pulpit, witness to Mother's suffering, then she told her gratitude to the angel Michael, went out of the bar, locked the door, and pocketed the key.

Mr. Lamb was still there, considering the fire with his divergent eye, but Tamsin saw when its spark of clarity slipped to match the other, and both his eyes saw her straight.

"Yes," he said.

IN THE MORNING, MR. LAMB ASKED TAMSIN TO TELL him again what it was that Saint Peter had said to the men of Israel, when he spoke of the divine source of healing. She understood he meant her to respond in the Greek, and so she began, "*Andres Israēlitai....*" She went on as far as *"eusebeia,"* godliness, and there she had to stop.

"*Eusebeia,*" he nodded, then finished the verse slowly so that she said it with him.

PART THREE

Dorset Harbor
Massachusetts Bay
1752-1763

AFTER SUSANNAH WENT WITH TAMSIN TO GREEN COVE to let go of the one who could not stay, there were years she kept mostly to the attic. Tamsin took more of the kitchen work. Some mornings, Susannah would come down to put on breakfast for any lodgers and start to make dinner, but before men came to the tavern, she would retreat upstairs to spin or sew, and teach Phebe her reading and stitches. When Grandmother Cat came with James to bring new wool, cheeses, nettles, and rhubarb in spring, or sacks of milled grain, dried herbs, and squash in fall, Susannah would come downstairs to be with them and return to the attic as soon as they'd gone. She no longer went to sit at her little girls' graves, so Tamsin and Phebe tended the plants and picked the berries and plums.

Whenever tavern-goers asked Tamsin about her mother, she let them believe that Mistress Bennett was simply occupied with the inn, which was true enough. Still Deacon Somerby asked after her and brought gifts of oranges or ground cocoa with cinnamon. Tamsin always carried Mother's notes of thanks to him at his shop.

Eventually, the parish found a new minister. Mr. Stevens was a pleasant young man who, it was noted with either approval or concern, had graduated from Yale, not Harvard. After that, Susannah went sometimes to the meetinghouse, though she was still rarely seen in the tavern. Peter and Tamsin did well on their own, even if Tamsin remained uneasy with commotion and rude men. This was especially true on days when Peter had to go and dig a grave, when the tavern work fell mostly to Tamsin, though Phebe was blessedly more capable every year.

ONE SUMMER MORNING PETER WAS AT THE GRAVEYARD, Phebe in the attic with Mother, Tamsin in the kitchen paring apples for sauce. Noah Southworth came with cordwood. He stacked it by the shed and brought an armload into the house, offering to stoke the bread oven if she needed. Short-handed, Tamsin was glad of the help, until he stayed well after the task was done, and his purpose seemed otherwise.

"I mean to ask –" he began.

Tamsin fixed her eyes on her paring knife and an apple. There was work to do.

"I want to know – in the tavern, the night I burnt my hand, why did you tell me I was to have a sawmill? What made you say that?"

"Did I? I hardly remember. You were in such pain. I expect it was to comfort you." She smiled. "Give you something better to think –"

"Pain, it disappeared." He flicked his fingers in the air. "How did you do that?"

She shrugged. "You see, it wasn't that bad. Truly, it was nothing."

"But it was that bad."

She stripped a red spiral from an apple. He watched her.

"Tell me, did you see me with a sawmill? You said you heard it."

Tamsin rested her hands on the table and looked at him, heart racing. "Did I?" She felt faint. Danger again. "Or did I ask if you heard it? It would be for you to imagine, not me."

His voice dropped. "You know you saw me with a mill. How did you do that? Miss Bennett," he asked, "what are you?"

She couldn't speak.

He looked to the ceiling as a woodcutter might look to gauge which way a pine would fall.

"Miss Bennett," he said, "will you marry me?" He lowered his gaze to her face, eyes dead earnest. "Work the mill with me." This was not a question.

Stricken by the look of a handsome man she'd always liked, she felt the danger. This was either a proposal from the good heart of a neighbor long trusted, or a demand from an ambitious man who knew just enough to claim her by veiled threat.

"I do thank you, Mr. Southworth, but I am sorry, I cannot. You are a fine man, but my work is to help my mother."

His eyes now cast about as if he had misplaced a tool. Tamsin picked up another apple and hoped he would leave, but he started again.

"Miss Bennett, after the night you healed my burns, did you know that men in the harbor told dark stories of your grandmother? That she goes out and lays her hands on folk? Even men. And whether it's for good or ill, no one knows till later."

"Oh no, that could never be my Grandmother Cat! She hardly ever leaves the farm." Tamsin tried to smile. She knew he meant Priscilla, but if she corrected him, he'd catch her knowing what she shouldn't. He would trap her. She slipped the knife inside the peel of an apple. It was an old story he'd heard, and it was true. What else did he know?

Noah rambled. "Folks say she travels the county, here and there. Day and night. They've seen her. Some say, flying. She went to "

Flying. Tamsin put the apple down, pared pure white but for the red flare at the top. She couldn't core it, as the knife was now uncertain in her hand.

"That is rank nonsense. My grandmother never leaves the farm but to come here with James and bring provisions for the tavern. Vegetables, cheeses. Wool. Herbs." She could not stop her mouth. *She should not have said herbs, she would not say extracts.* "Our bread. Do you like our bread, Mr. Southworth? It's Grandmother and James who bring the wheat, the Indian corn, the rye. You stoked the oven. Shall I make my thirded bread for you?"

Noah came close. "Your cousin," he said. "James. Do you intend to marry him?"

Tamsin froze at the question.

"Miss Bennett, what skill do you have, that you see a thing as hulking as a sawmill that doesn't exist?"

"Skill, what skill? I make applesauce!" She forced herself to laugh so she could breathe.

Fool! Never tell a man what you see! Priscilla once told her dear Samuel she saw farmland across the water, but he was her own trusted husband, no woodcutter in a tavern.

Noah cocked his head. "So I mean to ask –"

"Mr. Southworth, I am sorry, there is nothing more to ask. Don't we both have work to do?" She tried to smile and took up another apple.

He didn't move. "Miss Bennett, what if more talk were to go round the harbor about your grandmother? Or about you?"

Tamsin's hand became intensely aware of the paring knife.

"Why did you speak of a sawmill? What possessed you?"

Possessed?

"I ask you," he said straight to her face. "What is it you always drop in your ale, Miss Bennett? I see you. I watch you."

Her hand with the knife made no move, but he flinched.

She mocked him. "And I ask *you*. What do you remember hearing the night you burnt your hand, whether or not such a thing was ever said?"

"You said I would have a sawmill. That I would build a sawmill."

"And do you want that?"

"Yes."

At once, she saw the awful fist of the Marblehead trader pounding Noah, doing him damage. She stabbed the apple with her paring knife and forced it at his face. "Then you will build a sawmill and you will leave my family alone."

He jerked back, snatched the apple off the knife, and held her eyes while he took a long, slow bite, then went to the door.

"Mr. Southworth."

He turned back.

"If men tell dark stories about my grandmother – or about me – then why do so many of them come to the tavern?"

He looked at her, smile crooked. "They like your –" He paused, and went out the door. "Ale."

LATE THAT NIGHT, ROUSED AND AFRAID, TAMSIN WENT down to the yard in her bedgown and spread her arms wide against the ancient oak. She felt Eve there, naked beside the tree of knowledge of good and evil, and Noah, naked on the other side with an apple bitten deep. She saw him, charcoal in hand, clever plan for a sawmill drawn on a scrap of wood.

42

Susannah kept her retreat in the attic for most of three years. Spring, summer, and fall afternoons, if the sisters had been to the graveyard, Phebe would take berries or plums upstairs, in case Mother would have some. But she always refused until, one spring day of the third year, she picked three strawberries from the bowl Phebe held out to her. Then Tamsin thought to take her to the cove to walk and dig clams, and so one day they went. That fall, Susannah made her mother's plum cakes again and carried them out to the tavern, where they were met with huzzahs.

In the spring of the fourth year, Susannah wanted to go with Tamsin and Phebe to her little girls' graves to see the first of the strawberries. The patch had now spread, with long, well-rooted runners. It gave a surprising yield, so she had Tamsin and Phebe go with her to the wharf to take a basket of berries to Deacon Somerby, in gratitude for his thoughtfulness all this time.

That summer, five years since Captain Nathaniel Bradbury's sister had come to keep a tavern, Susannah settled back into the work and was heartily welcomed.

Some had murmured her absence was a matter of female illness, but upon her return, she seemed well, and this was largely forgotten.

For Tamsin, however, the year became one of unexpected, unsettling things, even turbulence. Later, when she looked back to the beginning of it, what she saw was the movement of rowan-wood oars in salt water. The oars were the ones Uncle Isaac had carved for Peter's shallop and, as it happened, they fit gracefully into the locks of Uncle Nat's dory that was stored in the barn. Tamsin thought later, this was a sign she had missed.

On a June day of that year, she greeted a young sea captain, come to take the tavern dinner – Mother's *chaudière* that afternoon – while his sloop awaited a load of salt cod. He had a pleasing figure, upright and trim. Captain Christopher Hawes must have enjoyed the dinner and ale, and the sister and brother who served him, for he decided he would stay the night at the inn, and not aboard his sloop moored in the harbor. The *Curlew* he called her.

In the morning, he came down to the kitchen doorway to ask Mistress Bennett about yesterday's delicious soup. She told him she used a certain mix of herbs to cook fish and mussels with cream and wine. She had learnt it from her mother-in-law, her *belle-mère* who was from France, from the Île de Ré. The captain responded warmly that he knew that island, as his brother's wife was from Brittany. He asked, too, about the taste of the tavern's ale, with its darkly sweet edge.

"That is my daughter's doing, Captain. She has a great way with herbs and plants of all sorts." Susannah smiled her love at Tamsin, cutting up sweetgrass at the kitchen table. "The strawberries she grows are most healing to the heart."

Tamsin was moved by her mother's words, and surprised at her saying something so private to a lodger. Perhaps he reminded Mother of her young captain, Élie. Tamsin slid a glance toward

Captain Hawes in the doorway, in case he showed any discomfort. He did not.

Instead he regarded Tamsin with interest. "Is that so? Plants. I wonder if you might help me."

To Susannah, he explained, "I've just come from Nova Scotia, and some days ago spoke with an old seaman at Grand Pré. When he heard I was sailing to Massachusetts, I must tell you, a very keen look came into his eye. He told me of a rare tree in Dorset Harbor – sailor's-grace, he called it. He said it grows all but hidden in a place called Hallett's Cove, and nowhere else. At least, it grew there once upon a time. He's a very old man.

"Mistress Bennett, do you know where that might be?"

She gave a slight nod. "I believe it grows there."

"The old man told me the tree blooms in June, and if I were to come here, I must find it. He said, once you've seen it and breathed the scent of the flower, it will stay with you to the end of your days. In fact, he told me that when he dies, the memory of that bloom will be all he wants for his peace."

"I do hope that's true," Susannah said softly. "My first husband saw it."

The captain took this in. "Where is Hallett's Cove?"

"To the west, past Green Cove. A narrow inlet with a creek that bends north, hidden, as you say." She turned to Tamsin. "You've seen that inlet from the water, you know it."

"Would you allow her to go with me, as a guide?" the captain asked.

"I would go, Mother. I want to see it."

Susannah looked at the captain, then nodded once. "My brother's dory is in the barn. Tamsin, have Peter bring it out. Though one oar may be broken."

PETER AND CAPTAIN HAWES TOOK THE DORY TO THE shore. Tamsin went to the shallop and brought up the rowan-wood oars Uncle Isaac had made, and she and the captain set off westerly. As he rowed, he told her of his seafaring family, his father a shipbuilder at Falmouth in Cornwall, his uncle a shipmaster, his brother captain of an East Indiaman. When they passed Green Cove, Tamsin told him of the good clamming there, and the bayberry wax Peter and Phebe had rendered for the counter at the bar.

The captain spoke of his ports and his cargo. South from Nova Scotia, he had loaded pipe staves at coastal towns along the eastward, then come for his salt cod at Dorset Harbor. All this he would carry to Lisbon in Portugal, where salt cod was much in favor with the Roman Catholics, and pipe staves were made into wine casks. The casks, he said, filled with madeira, would go to all the countries of Europe, and their colonies too.

While they talked, Tamsin watched the ease and rhythm of his rowing until she knew she'd been watching too long, so she looked down into the salt water he stirred with rowan-wood oars.

He said, after Lisbon, he would carry casks of madeira to England with oil, salt, oranges, and figs. There he'd rest awhile at his brother's house in the country, then set off again for Nova Scotia with a load of English woolens and Portuguese fruit, wine, and – he smiled – more salt.

"Supplies for the British and salt for the cod. Their cod ships to England," he said. "Mine goes from here to Portugal."

From here. If he sails this route, might he come back?

He said he found Nova Scotia a fertile and beautiful country, and spoke well of the French settlers, now ruled uncomfortably by the British.

His voice sounded warm to her. There might be a woman there he loved.

She looked away to the shore, and when she saw the inlet, she told him. He rowed the dory back behind a spit of rocky land, and when she found the creek, he rowed that way too. Tide was low and the creek shallow, so the dory could not take them far. Instead, they took off shoes and stockings, left them, and stepped into the creek's wet edge. He pulled the dory up the bank, and they set out to find a tree with blossoms one would remember until death.

The walking began mucky and slow. Tamsin went first. Pitch pine bordered what looked to be a very old path, boards once laid across it, now mossy and split. Captain Hawes followed. After a while, the path widened in a stand of river birch. She watched for what grew there. Bloodwort and wild ginger, useful roots. The air was less salt, more sweet.

The captain walked beside her now, first in silence, then saying thoughtfully, "I'm reminded of a place my mother once took me when I was a boy."

"Where was that?"

"In the west of Cornwall. There's an ancient spring in a woodland, thought sacred to a long-dead hermit. Saint Madron. This path reminds me of it. Folk with pain or injuries would go there for healing."

This was of interest.

"My mother knew the place because girls would go to the spring to ask when they would marry."

This too was of interest. "And did the spring tell them?"

"I don't know. My mother was married at the time."

Tamsin laughed, wondering to herself, if a bloom of sailor's-grace were to be as revealing as a spring in the west of Cornwall, would she ask?

"Also," he said, "a woman with child would go to the spring and pray to survive her coming birth."

Every woman's prayer. "It doesn't sound like a spring sacred to an old hermit."

The captain laughed. "You are most perceptive, Miss Bennett."

She smiled.

"My mother went to the spring, not for the hermit Madron, but to find *Modron.* In Cornwall, the Mother of the Earth."

Tamsin glanced at him sideways.

"Truth be told," he went on, "the reason folk go to the spring is for Modron, her healing. It's all for Modron."

"Oh. How does Modron heal then?" she asked, as if it were of mild interest.

"A supplicant goes into the water to make a prayer, then comes out, walks three times all the way round the spring, and sleeps that night on the bank."

"Three times!" Tamsin had never thought to ask Grandmother Cat why she had to walk round the mill pond three times.

"Three times," the captain affirmed. "So that's what I did."

Tamsin nearly laughed, *So did I!* – but stopped short and held her breath, lest it slip out.

"I was eleven, about to go to sea with my uncle for the first time. So Mother took me to the spring of Modron to ask her protection – and I felt it." He looked at Tamsin. "A wind came through the woods from four directions at once and embraced me. And all these years, she's protected me."

Tamsin understood this and was moved, but didn't dare respond from the knowing of a rowess. Too great a risk. "I'm glad," she nodded, and turned abruptly where a glint of creek slipped under the heart-shaped leaves of wild ginger.

Her bare feet followed water in the earth and came to the shallow bowl of a spring hidden in rock and fern. There she stopped, for just beyond stood a wondrous grove of trees, a weaving of fine trunks and branches with leaves twisting on stems, light to dark to light again as if in a breeze she couldn't feel. She took a step forward. Smooth bark gave the impression of a glaze over blue-gray porcelain. Another step, and so many iridescent beetles appeared creeping among twined branches, the trees looked to be full of living, perceiving eyes. Thus she knew that she herself was being watched as she saw, set among the leaves, the blooms of sailor's-grace.

She stepped close, but the blooms, sensing an approach, tilted and slipped away, elusive. Quickly she stood back beside the captain to observe their habit further, as once she had studied yarrow and the underwater roots of burnet. When she held out her hands to show she had no knife, the blooms came to rest, and when she went near to a single bloom, it settled at the level of her heart, even bending to her, letting her look deep as she wanted.

Its wide, round openness was a pool of sheer light. Fine gold threads and nubs sprang at its center. When she lowered her face to the scent, it was her hands that remembered first, and only then the rest of her.

She stood at the milldam with Grandmother Cat over glints of an incoming tide. An uprising into her feet filled her hands. At the time, she'd thought this was like sap in a March maple. But now her hands cupped together in the same open form as this bloom, so full of a rising mystery that the little gold fountain at its center lit two more like itself in the palms of her hands.

Beside her, Captain Hawes watched. He hardly breathed. "I understand the old sailor now."

Tamsin looked into the wide-open vessel of her hands, unsure what to do with all they held, so she extended them to the captain and he rounded his hands beneath hers. There were no English words for the stream that rippled through her body then, but a circle of gold light flamed round him and his face lit astonished.

43

THEY ROWED BACK TO THE HARBOR IN DEEP QUIET.
Tamsin saw colors around her more vivid than ever she had imagined. The slip of rowan-wood oars through salt water felt to her as
if fluid light ran over her shoulders and down her arms. When she
could bring herself to glance at the captain, he looked like open
sky. The lines of pewter buttons on his blue jacket were starry. A
thought of stars moved her hand to the pocket that held Papa's
sundial-compass, and she felt again where she was on the earth.

At the harbor, Captain Hawes beached the dory on the
shingle near the ropewalk, away from the shallops and traders,
and helped Tamsin to step out. She was uncertain of foot.

"Are you well?" he asked.

"When you've been long at sea, Captain, how do you feel
when you step across onto land?"

He smiled. "It takes a little time. It needs a sort of listening of
the body to the ground."

"Listening," she said, and remembered leaping the shoreline
with Phebe. "Might it also be dancing?"

Of their own volition, her hands slipped to the form of
sailor's-grace, little fountains in her palms. The captain lifted his

hands to cradle hers again, and they stood in palpable communion until she felt another's eyes on them. She looked up.

At the near end of the ropewalk, an African child sat on the ground, watching. Now seen, he looked about himself, got up, looked toward the road and waited, then approached them, halting. He had a limp. He wiped tears from his face, as he spoke to the captain. His hand went to the back of his head. Tamsin examined it and laid a hand there. She scanned the water for what boats were in sight, and spoke urgently to the captain, who surveyed the ropewalk and road as if a storm loomed. When he spoke, the boy was attentive, nodded once, and returned slowly to the ropewalk.

The captain rowed the dory around to tie it up by Peter's shallop, and Tamsin walked to the inn, pondering her hands, the blooms of sailor's-grace, Captain Hawes, and the Mother of the Earth in Cornwall.

SUSANNAH WAS ALONE IN THE KITCHEN. TAMSIN TOLD her about the blooms of light that Élie must have seen long ago, but she said nothing of her hands, or of the captain's. Instead, she asked if Mother remembered the loutish man from the harbor that some in the tavern called Deadrise when lolling in his cups. The one who kept the ropewalk, she said, and had the African child Neddie. Neddie had come to the captain at the harbor. He'd been badly beaten – again, he said. He told the captain he liked the pretty sloop and begged to hide aboard and get away. The captain said he could not be heard to allow it, but neither would he search the sloop, he said, *before casting off early tomorrow with the tide*. So if Mother were to hear in the tavern about a boy missing from the harbor, she needn't worry. It would be Neddie, and he would be on his way to England.

"I'm glad you told me. I would have thought far worse. Captain Hawes is good to take him."

"He told me, when he first went to sea with his uncle, his

mother took him to a spring to ask the protection of the Mother of the Earth. So he'll protect Neddie."

Susannah smiled. "He's a man like your Papa. You like him, don't you?" She didn't wait for an answer, but went on, "Grandmother Cat and James were here today. They brought nettles and rhubarb, cheese, and sacks of wool James sheared on the island."

"Tamsin!" Phebe struggled in from the yard, managing too many cabbages for her arms. "You missed Grandmother Cat and James! Here are the cabbages." Somehow she got them, all seven, onto the table without any rolling on the floor. "I have to boil them. I told James you went out in the dory with the captain, and he went to the harbor. Did he find you? He came right back and they left. Will you help me draw water for the cabbages?"

In a tangle of unlooked-for joy, mystery, and confusion of the heart, Tamsin went out to pull water up from the well.

BEFORE DAWN, SHE PACKED A BASKET OF FOOD WITH poultices of burnet and a jar of cooked rowanberries for the inflammation. She gave it to the captain, who said his mate had been told to expect young cargo and put him safe below. The *Curlew* would sail to Lisbon and, after that, Falmouth in Cornwall, where the captain said he knew of work for Neddie. He would go then to his brother near Truro before making the crossing again to Nova Scotia, and after Grand Pré, he would come back, he said, to Dorset Harbor.

Tamsin heard him clearly. He would come back. They said their goodbyes, and she watched him stride with purpose toward the wharf. She wondered now, how she would hold together in one body such happiness and uncertainty, her feelings for a man she'd always loved and desire for this captain from Cornwall who honored the Mother of the Earth.

An image came to her of Phebe wrestling seven cabbages, complicated, impossible.

· · ·

THAT DAY, TAMSIN COOKED DOWN GRANDMOTHER'S nettles and boiled the rhubarb with sugar. These were good. Soon, however, she found that when she tried to card James' wool, the fibers worked themselves crosswise and went all knotted for her, though Phebe did well enough with them. Tamsin's spinning went still worse, the yarn turning lumpish and fragile in her fingers. She tried long and earnestly, but could not be proud of the skeins she took to Mr. Oakes. He wove that summer's wool into a warm blanket that at last Tamsin had to put into a chest and take out only on the bitterest of cold winter nights, because every lodger who slept under it woke in the morning unaccountably confused and unhappy.

44

ONCE IN THE TIME OF SUSANNAH'S LONG RETREAT,
Uncle Isaac had come to the harbor from Colbrook and brought
his fiddle, which delighted the young Bennetts and lifted even
Susannah's spirit. He played indoors for the family and outdoors
on the steps of The Rowans, thrilling the air above Wharf Street.
Tamsin told him that when Mother was better, they wanted to
dance at the tavern as they had at the farm. And so it was, that in
the August after Tamsin and Captain Hawes had gone to find
sailor's-grace, a coastal trader brought word from Colbrook that
Uncle Isaac would come to play for a dance at the end of
September, when his work had slowed. Susannah sent back a
letter, saying the Bennetts would gladly have a dance at the tavern,
and would invite the West Dorset family, especially his sister
Catherine.

Tamsin thought of Michaelmas, as it was at the end of
September. With great reason to honor the angel Michael who'd
helped her throw a dragon down from the meetinghouse pulpit,
she told Mother she hoped the dance might be on his day.
Though not knowing exactly why, Susannah wrote that to Uncle
Isaac too. And so it was.

. . .

One afternoon late that month, Susannah and Tamsin were in the kitchen scooping and stewing pumpkins. When Tamsin turned round for no particular reason and saw Captain Hawes standing in the doorway, she believed him a vision – his wind-weathered face, cocked hat, brown hair tied back in a queue, his blue jacket with pewter buttons like stars – so vivid had her inner sight become, in remembering him. She wanted to go to him and take his hands, but felt the uprising in her body that would happen if she did. Instead, she pressed her hands to her apron and whispered despite her disbelief, "Captain Hawes."

"Mistress Bennett, Miss Bennett, I am happy to see you for many reasons, but at this moment I have one reason quite urgent. I have a man aboard the *Curlew* who, I believe, needs your help. He's ill. I've brought him and his niece here from Grand Pré. The British are preparing to exile the French south into these colonies, and I believe a transport ship would be the end of him. May I bring him and his niece to you? I'll gladly pay their costs."

"They are French? Yes, of course, bring them here," Susannah said. "Tamsin, go with Captain Hawes and look at the man's condition. Phebe and I will see to a chamber."

"A man is bringing him now, Mistress. I thank you heartily."

Tamsin followed the captain out to see a sailor carrying an old man up Wharf Street. From a distance, his frailty was clear, and as she approached she saw his pained breathing, a strain in neck and face. A young woman about Tamsin's age followed. A sack slung over her shoulder clanked with what might be pots or tools.

"Miss Bennett, here are Pascal Dubois and his niece Josette." Relieving her of the sack, Captain Hawes said, "Mademoiselle, we have a place for you and good care for your uncle."

The girl watched wide-eyed as the very last of their possessions now looked to be confiscated by the British, but Tamsin took her arm. "There's not far to go. We'll go together."

• • •

Pascal Dubois was washed, dressed in a clean shirt of Peter's, and put to bed at the inn. Josette sat unmoving at her uncle's side. The captain spoke French, Susannah some as well, and Josette spoke passable English, so Tamsin understood the man had been feverish for many days, with sharp pains in his sides. His ribs hurt most upon coughing to clear his throat, thickly blocked. Tamsin brought peppermint and chamomile tea with honey and elderberry extract for both uncle and niece, adding for the uncle some drops of Grandmother Cat's sweetleaf tincture. Through afternoon and evening, Josette gave him sips of tea and spoonfuls of a garlic broth Susannah made, and he rested. Tamsin carried up a supper of bread and cooked greens for Josette, then helped her pull out the trundle bed to settle and sleep.

That night, Tamsin woke to the sound of violent coughing and cries of pain. Pulling a bedgown over her shift, she ran down. In half-moon light, she found the old man convulsed and gripping his sides. Josette was at his face, soothing him, *"Mon oncle."* Captain Hawes sat behind him on the bed, firm hands on the old man's shoulders. Tamsin went to his feet, where, of their own accord, her hands took on the form of a wide-cupped bloom. Fine light fountains sprang from the centers of her palms. She laid one hand on top of his cramped feet, the other at his soles, and light moved into him from the folded blossom of her hands. Muscle by joint by muscle, contraction and convulsion let go, so that at last his throat opened to his breath.

Tamsin withdrew her hands, looked into them discomfited, and fled to the kitchen to make a peppermint tea. There she found to her distress that, just now, her hands could not manage the stoneware. They held such light that the mass of fired clay refused her and gave her stark warning.

Girl, have you done this again? A constable will come.

Tamsin saw Priscilla, her wrists in irons, seated on a horse, a ragged dark figure suffocatingly close at her back.

Captain Hawes, come to the kitchen, caught Tamsin just as she fell and carried her to a chair at the table.

She showed him her hands. "It's hard to make tea with these."

He cupped his hands gently beneath hers. "Hard to make tea," he said, "yet they save a dying man."

He made the tea and poured some for her in a glass cup, watching as she took sips.

"Miss Bennett," he said, "may I see you a while tomorrow? I've brought something for you from England. From China."

Tamsin put down the cup and pressed her palms to her lap. "I'll ask Mother. I think so."

When they went upstairs, he carried the tea and took it to the old man and his niece. Tamsin went to the attic. Phebe was asleep, undisturbed. Tamsin lay down, warmth and light still flooding her hands. She laid them at her heart to learn how it would feel.

In the morning Captain Hawes came to the kitchen door to thank Susannah and Tamsin for their care of the Dubois, uncle and niece both, and to ask Susannah if he might see her daughter a while in the course of the day. He had some plants for her, he said, that his brother had brought from China and cultivated with success in England. The captain thought they would do well at Dorset Harbor and, if Tamsin agreed, he would help her to plant them. Susannah glanced at Tamsin, who with a little smile made her response clear. Susannah nodded in return and told Phebe that she was to help Peter that day.

As Phebe set breakfast for the captain, Tamsin went upstairs with bread and a thin pumpkin stew mixed with her extracts. Both the old man and Josette looked far better than they had the night before, though still disordered and lost. Tamsin said they must rest and not worry, because all would be well. They were safe. When she came down, Captain Hawes was going out to fetch the plants from his sloop, and she said, if she might, she would walk part way with him, as she had errands at the harbor.

"Then you'll see the *Curlew*," he said, and as they walked, he told her about it. "Few sloops trade across the ocean, but she carries a good cargo and moves sweetly along coastline." He gave a wink. "She hides well on coastline. Shallow draft. And in open ocean? She's fast as I need her to be." He said quietly, "She has four mounted swivel guns and carries gold, Lisbon to Cornwall. Falmouth." He whispered, "She outruns pirates."

Tamsin felt sparks of alarm, but said lightly, "I am glad she does." Then looking about, she asked, "Captain, what's become of Neddie? Do you know?"

"I took him to England, to the Falmouth ropewalk. I watch out for him. He does well. On the crossing to Lisbon, he was a good help in our little galley. On one fine day, I let him stand a watch at the helm. You would have been pleased, Miss Bennett, to see how tall he stood."

They shared a smile and said nothing more.

Now at the harbor, Tamsin gave a small gasp at the sight of the *Curlew*. A single-masted vessel, fore-and-aft rigged, she had a square topsail and a graceful bowsprit rigged for two jibs. "Indeed she looks fast, Captain. She is quite beautiful."

"May I show you aboard?"

"I must get to Deacon Somerby –" She stopped short. "Captain, by the bye, there will be a dance in the tavern tomorrow evening. If you are able, you must come. Do you dance?"

The captain assured her that he danced, and hoped he might partner with her sometimes.

Tamsin smiled, saying, "Of course, if Josette and Mr. Dubois would like to come downstairs, they are very welcome. My Uncle Isaac is a wondrous fiddler. I believe some of my family are coming from West Dorset as well."

The captain gave her a little bow, and she went on to see Deacon Somerby, who lit up at the thought of a dance at The Rowans. "You know, as an importer," he told Tamsin, "I have business in Salem and Boston, and have been to many dances, most enjoyable. Do please give my cordial regards to Mistress Bennett and thank her for me. I shall be there."

Tamsin felt the light in Deacon Somerby's greeting, and as she had on the first visit to his shop years ago, again she found him interesting. A man of moonlit walks. A keeper of secrets.

RETURNING TO THE HOUSE, SHE FOUND CAPTAIN Hawes out by the garden with Phebe, studying what seemed to be three unusual sticks in a bucket of water. One by one, Phebe plucked them up to show Tamsin. Each stick looked much like a skinny person with arms flung up in the air and a spray of spiky legs. Phebe performed an imitation of each, to the captain's glad amusement.

"Tamsin, these are going to be rose bushes," she said. "And you're to decide where they belong."

The captain asked her, "Shall we walk and look for hospitable places?"

"Phebe, would you go tell Mother and Peter, Deacon Somerby will be happy to come for the dance? Yes, Captain, let's find where these creatures want to be. What do they like?"

They walked first a full circle of The Rowans. When the captain spoke of soil and sunlight, Tamsin remembered stoneware and the fountains in her hands. She restrained them, would not form them into a blossom, did not dare to look at them. The captain said his brother had found these roses most adaptable as to soil, doing well in both rich earth and sandy.

Tamsin's fingers closed protectively over her palms. She took this into account. If roses could be indifferent as to their earth, then perhaps when light came into her hands, she could still – for the sake of the tavern – endure the weight of stoneware.

As to light, he said, they like openness. They do well even in rough conditions and wind. Tamsin liked the open air of the bay, reveled in coastal winds. She wondered, Green Cove?

They came round again to the front walk. Tamsin went out

through the gate, turning to look back toward The Rowans. "Shall we put two here? At the road, one on either side of the gate? It faces south to the sun and catches the wind."

Captain Christopher Hawes stood on the front walk and looked toward the sea. His attention rested on something, or perhaps someone, a young woman who flourished in sun and wind. He didn't answer her.

"Captain, don't you think so? Or –?"

"Yes, Miss Bennett," he said. "I do think so."

She went to bring pitchfork and shovel from the shed, and he drew two more buckets of water from the well.

Having planted and watered two sticks that would one day overwhelm the road and gate with an intoxicating scent, they considered the one remaining stick.

"Green Cove," she whispered.

The captain nodded and went to fill the water buckets again.

As they walked the shore road to the cove, Tamsin considered where this third root and stem might best grow. Aloud, she said, "I don't know yet. I believe I'll know when we're there."

Though her question had been silent, the captain seemed to understand the answer, for when they came to the cove, he stood on the shore road while she stepped into thick sand and went to the water's edge. She turned toward the bayberry bushes, then to the jut of rocks. Turning to the sea, she looked across to Flagg Island, where she hoped a small shroud had settled in the marsh. On this side, she would plant a stick that would grow into a rose.

She turned to Captain Hawes, where he stood at the road, watching her. Whatever it was she felt with him when he cradled her hands like a bloom of sailor's-grace, she felt it again now. "There," she said. "Where you are."

The captain dug a hole beside the shore road, Tamsin planted the root of the rose, and he watered it.

When it was done, he walked out onto the beach. "This is where you come clamming."

"Yes," she said, and laughed happily. "And where Phebe and I dance across waves."

The captain went to where the sand was dark and firm. "Will you dance with me?" He held out his hand. "Do you know the minuet?"

She did not, so just there at the edge of land and sea, he taught her the figure. "One, *two*, three, four, five, *six*, one, *two*, three, four, five, *six*...."

They practiced a dance he made up in the moment – stepping to one another, circling, right hands lightly touch, turn, then left hands, release ... and turn to step away at last for six counts.

Or twelve, he said, depending on the music.

By the end, circling, barely touching his hand, she was flushed.

"Sometimes the first dance of an evening is a minuet," he said, and watched for her response.

She smiled.

W HEN T AMSIN AND C APTAIN H AWES RETURNED TO T HE Rowans carrying buckets, shovel, and pitchfork, Uncle Isaac was coming up from the harbor.

"Tamsin, my girl! What have you been digging and watering, and in whose good company?"

"Uncle! This is Captain Hawes. He's staying at the inn and brought us some rose plants from China! Captain, my Uncle Isaac Tobin, boatbuilder and fiddler, and brother to my Grandmother Catherine. Uncle Isaac, she's coming tomorrow for the dance. It will be such an occasion!"

"It will," he said, a dubious eye upon Captain Hawes.

"Mr. Tobin," the captain said, "might I make a request even before the dance begins?" At Uncle Isaac's curt nod, the captain went on, "Would you happen to know 'Mr. Lane's Minuet'?"

Uncle Isaac showed a warmer interest. "Let me put down my pack."

By the time Tamsin and the captain had put tools and buckets back in the shed, fiddle music was already delighting the air above The Rowans. In the side yard, Captain Hawes said quietly to Tamsin, "Do you hear it?" and he stepped the figure. "One, *two*, three, four, five, *six*, one, *two*, three...."

Looking to see no one was watching, Tamsin stepped it with him.

45

MICHAELMAS FELL ON A MONDAY. PHEBE, BY HERSELF, took on the making of tavern dinner, while Susannah and Tamsin made apple and shore plum cakes for the dance. They would put out cheese and bread, too, so on the morning of Michaelmas, they baked pans of rye and Indian corn, hoping that when the family came later from the farm, they would bring sacks of new-milled Red Lammas.

Tamsin took dinner upstairs to the Dubois and said they were very welcome to come down to the tavern for cakes and music and dance in the evening. Josette translated her uncle's glad response to the offer of cakes and music, and said she hoped she would be asked to dance.

"WHOA. ETHAN, LEVI, STAND."

Tamsin heard James' voice as if it were in her heart and felt his red lobelia kiss beside her mouth. Whether this gave her more pleasure or distress, in the moment she couldn't think.

The oxcart stopped in the side yard, Phebe ran out to meet Grandmother Cat and James, Tamsin following more slowly, eager to see them and deeply unsettled. She was still more unset-

256

tled upon seeing Ruth and Naomi, come for the dance. In five years, the twins had not been to the harbor, but the dance had brought them now. Tamsin buried a muddle of feelings in her relief at seeing sacks of Red Lammas.

Late afternoon, with tavern-goers made to leave, the many hands of the Bennetts took tables out to the yard and moved benches to the walls, opening up space for dancing. Tamsin stayed busy in the kitchen and laid out food in the dining room. Mr. Manning arrived early, so Phebe brought him first to view the spread of cakes – his compliments to Tamsin! – but to Phebe he said, "I am sorry, I did not bring Caleb this evening. He is getting quite elderly, and I did not think he was much up to dancing."

"Oh, Mr. Manning, I'm sure he'll be better with a nap."

"But I do hope to have one dance with you, Phebe. A round dance, perhaps, with not too much walking in it."

"Of course, sir! Come, shall I bring you an ale or a rum?"

Tamsin was full of love for her sister, who had taken to tavern-keeping far better than she had herself. Now a gabbling knot of guests came, the weaver Mr. Oakes and his wife, and Mr. Dingley, the fisherman, and his wife. On their heels, several others arrived, the minister Mr. Stevens, and the orchardman Mr. Proctor, with two jugs of his new cider. Tamsin welcomed them all and retreated upstairs, with the excuse that she must let lodgers know that Uncle Isaac would soon play.

She tapped at the door of the Dubois, gave the message, and returned downstairs to hear the sliding tension of a fiddle being tuned. Deacon Somerby arrived and gave her a broad smile. "Thank you for the invitation," he said. "What a joyous evening. Where might I find Mistress Bennett? I've brought her some chocolate."

The deacon would find her in the kitchen, Tamsin said, and stepped out the front door for a last few peaceable moments, or perhaps to see if Captain Hawes might come back from the *Curlew*. His salt cod was to have been loaded this afternoon. In the morning the *Curlew* would sail.

Tamsin felt a sensation in her heart as if being pulled and tightly stretched. Between what and what, she didn't want to think, though she knew that a thin, insistent note of a fiddle cut across an ache in her being. She looked into her hands, where the middles of her palms felt as though fountains would burst through her skin. She pressed both hands to her heart to calm them and dim the pain. Her gaze fell to thick patches of Michaelmas daisies by the steps and patches by the gate. All of them, James had planted.

"Miss Bennett! Has your uncle begun to play?" Captain Hawes made haste along the road.

"He's tuning his fiddle now, I believe."

"Then I must have a word with him." Reaching the steps, he asked softly, "May I have the first dance with you, Miss Bennett? A minuet."

She could not look into the captain's face and refuse, so they went inside. Tamsin held at the door of the tavern, while the captain made his way across to speak to the fiddler. Thereupon, Uncle Isaac raised his voice to ask everyone please to step back: The first dance would be a minuet.

Captain Hawes and Tamsin were in opposite corners of the tavern as Isaac Tobin's fiddle sang the opening notes of "Mr. Lane's Minuet." She had to repeat the count of six in her mind to keep to the figure, and could not turn her eyes away from the captain, lest she miss which direction to go. But he signaled her impeccably with his eyes and a gracious hand, and Uncle Isaac's music moved her spirit as it had at the farm. So closely did she watch the captain, she saw no other person in the tavern, and the music rose through her to lift her arms as his were lifted. Watching his steps, matching hers to his, she felt as she had when his hands rounded beneath hers at Hallett's Cove.

When Uncle Isaac ended the tune with a last longingly held note, the two dancers had stepped twelve counts apart from one another, so that in the fiddle's silence Tamsin felt suddenly exposed. Not to be alone, she turned round to face the captain, and he, putting one foot forward, gave her a slight, formal bow. Without thought, she bent her knees in the slightest of curtsies, and in this tiny gesture, felt grace.

The surrounding selectmen and tradesmen, wives and daughters, broke silence with surprised remarks and a little clapping. Whether surprise came of pleasure or disfavor, Tamsin did not want to know, but fled to the dining room to see that all was in order there, and then to the kitchen, where Mother came to find her.

"Tamsin, that was very well done. You learnt it from Captain Hawes, of course? I must ask you, dear, when and where did you dance together?"

"After we planted the roses at the gate, we planted the third one at Green Cove." She did not say she thought to plant it there for the little one lying, no one knew where, across the water. "I told him, when Phebe and I go clamming, we dance in the waves. So he asked me to dance with him and he taught me the steps."

In the tavern Uncle Isaac began "The Chirping of the Nightingale," a round dance for as many as would fit the room at once. Tamsin hoped Phebe would guide Mr. Manning to the floor before his ale made it impossible.

"Did anyone go by on the road and see you?" Mother asked.

She shook her head. "I think not."

"Tamsin, be careful. I let you go to Hallett's Cove to help the captain, but however good a man he may be – and I do believe he is – nevertheless, it takes little or nothing for a watcher to conjure stories of shame about a woman, out of ignorance or unkindness. A jealous eye, a sinful or a stupid mind, there are many in the world. Many in this very parish, I will tell you for certain."

Then Mother suppressed a smile and broke out in a laugh, as if with a memory. "Tamsin, my love, truly! Dancing with a man at Green Cove!" But her laugh trailed into one long, steady breath, and she spoke seriously. "Dancing by the sea. No, dear, only imagine the stories that would be spun round the parish. Not just to stain your good character, but mark you for suspicion. Remember your Grandmother Cat, and her mother –"

Tamsin and Susannah were startled by the captain's appearance at the kitchen door.

"Pardon, Mistress, I only wanted to see if Miss Bennett is well."

"She is, Captain. Your minuet was quite beautiful. Still, I must ask, Captain, that you be careful of her good name."

His bow was both proper and contrite. "Miss Bennett's good name is of the highest importance to me, Mistress, I assure you."

Susannah considered him and smiled. "Then let us all dance, shall we?"

She led the way back into the tavern as Uncle Isaac drew his bow to begin "The Beggar Boy," and Captain Hawes asked Susannah if he might have this dance with her. She said he might.

Tamsin stood back, looking for James, but didn't see him. Peter had kindly asked Josette Dubois to dance. She was smiling for the first time in Massachusetts, her eyes bright, and they joined, longways for six, with Mother and Captain Hawes, Naomi and Mr. Proctor. The Oakes, the Dingleys, Phebe and Deacon Somerby made up another set. Mr. Dubois had found a bench to rest upon, and Grandmother Cat, settled beside him, observed his condition. Tamsin went to see if she could take him either *bière* or *cidre*. He asked for *cidre*. She glanced at Grandmother, who nodded permission, so she found her way past the dancers to the bar and drew him a mug of cider, adding several drops of her extracts of elderberry and chamomile.

Taking the mug to him, she looked into the dining room. James was there. She wanted to speak with him, wanted to dance, so she went to him.

"I've been looking for you."

"You danced well with the captain."

She smiled. "I would dance again, were you to ask."

"It would be nothing so elegant."

"But pleasing?"

He regarded her. "I don't know."

Deacon Somerby came in then to consider the cakes. "Later," he said. "I will have some of these fine cakes later. But just now, Miss Bennett, would I interrupt if I were to ask for a dance?"

"I would enjoy a dance, sir. Shall we see what my uncle will play next?" Turning back to James, she said, "Yes, I will dance with you. We'll find each other."

Tamsin and Deacon Somerby joined together with five couples, forming longways. When Uncle Isaac took up the tune, "I Loved Thee Once, I'll Love No More," her thoughts went painfully to James, and after the simple lead up and back, her attention faltered. Instead of waiting for Deacon Somerby's walk about her, she matched his movements and bumped into him halfway, bungling the step for him and attracting sour notice. But the deacon danced so sprightly and caught her lapse so cleverly, he made it into a two-hand turn to let her recover, and she smiled as if at a simple mistake.

At the end of the tune, several things happened at once. Partners honored one another with bow and curtsy. Deacon Somerby asked in a low voice, "Miss Bennett, may I have a word with you this evening?" Tamsin gave a quick nod, puzzled, as she felt a demanding pull at her elbow. Her first thought was of James, but it was Ruth, hissing in her ear, "Introduce me to Captain Hawes now. I want him to ask me to dance." Deacon Somerby winked and turned to ask whether Tamsin's kind grandmother would favor him with a dance. Tamsin, to satisfy Ruth, made a show of looking about the tavern for the captain and not seeing him, when by luck a small commotion erupted suddenly, and everyone turned to see what it was.

With a cry of pleasure, Tamsin made Ruth's hand let go and threaded her way to the door as Phebe called out, *"Mr. Lamb!"*

46

"Why, the Misses Bennett! What is happening? A dance at The Rowans! Look, Antony, what we've happened in upon! How fortunate!"

Just behind Mr. Lamb, clumsily bearing baggage and a hefty wooden box, was a young man instantly notable for his deep brown eyes and mass of red hair. While Mr. Lamb's wig was finely powdered and wafting as in a light breeze, this young man's head was curly and thick to the point of boisterous. For watchers in the tavern, the two made a remarkable sight.

Uncle Isaac, however, drew the watchers back, skipping into the first notes of an Italian rant, so that all who had stopped still and mute, sprang into movement. Men scrambled to ask women for the dance, formed in circles of eight, and joyfully had at it.

"Tamsin and Phebe, my dears," said Mr. Lamb, "This is Mr. Antony Wingate, from Burnham. We are traveling to New Jersey, where he is to study, and I am to give a course of sermons. Antony, the Misses Bennett, the most delightful ladies you will ever meet! And this Miss Tamsin Bennett," he added too loud, "is exceeding clever with her use of herbs!"

Tamsin gave Mr. Lamb a small, urgent shake of her head, of which he took no notice.

"And here is their excellent mother! Mistress Bennett – my young friend Antony Wingate, on his way to the College of New Jersey to study for the ministry. Would it be possible for us to stay the night with you?"

Susannah assured Mr. Lamb that his usual bedchamber was open. Her daughters would show the gentlemen upstairs and see that all was in order, the trundle made up. "Then do please come down, if you will. Come eat, drink, and dance with us."

Looking entirely happy at the prospect, the gentlemen proceeded to their chamber.

Tamsin stopped Phebe as they came downstairs. "Dear, a favor. James is out of sorts. Would you please make him dance? I know he'd dance with you."

"He'd dance with you first! You always –"

"You first."

But in the tavern, James was already dancing, smiling, helping Josette through the steps. She looked as if she'd never in her life thought to have such pleasure. Uncle Isaac's fiddle sang "All in a Garden Green." In a stony field in memory, Tamsin danced with James again, as Papa led Ethan back to work.

She needed the comfort of her grandmother and went to sit with her, by Mr. Dubois. Grandmother Cat took her hand and said of the old man, "He is very frail. We must take good care." Tamsin smiled across at him and nodded.

When Uncle Isaac touched bow to strings for the melody of "Childgrove," Captain Hawes came to ask for a dance, and Mr. Proctor asked Grandmother Cat. Making a square of two couples, Tamsin felt – in this moment, in this music and movement – a little eased in her heart, perhaps more certain where her feet were to go.

· · ·

AT THE LAST NOTES, DEACON SOMERBY CAME TO Tamsin and asked, not for a dance, but for a bit of her time, perhaps in the kitchen with cider and a cake or two. Tamsin was glad to fetch the ciders and retreat to a peaceful place.

"Miss Bennett," the deacon began, "I must be presumptuous, and I do hope you will forgive me, for I have only your dear mother's good at heart."

Tamsin listened.

"I have been aware of her absence from the tavern these last few years and am greatly cheered by her return. And here I tread most unsafely, I know, but there were certain things...."

He gave close study to the plum cake in his hand. "At the time of Mr. Ferris' sudden departure from this parish, you'll remember perhaps that, as we lacked a preacher, I undertook to read scripture from the pulpit on many a Sabbath.

"By the bye, I would thank you for your part in caring for the meetinghouse, all the dusting and attention to the cleanliness of the floor. Under a difficult circumstance." He waited. "Ashy foot-stoves and all."

The deacon's mention of floor and foot-stoves made Tamsin think of Mr. Manning's Caleb, but then it struck her what he might truly mean. She had gone back to the meetinghouse three times that week to scrub the stain.

"With the scripture reading, I became aware," he said with a small, crooked smile, "how very uncomfortable it could be to stand there at the pulpit all those hours, preaching and praying. So – it's unlikely you would know this, of course – but after two Sabbaths of, shall we say, that awareness, I took a thick piece of Turkey carpet that had come to me from England, and I affixed it there to the floor under the pulpit." He laid his hands side by side on the table, a piece of Turkey carpet on a floor, and he looked up at Tamsin as if to give comfort. "You see, I thought it might help."

In a flash, Tamsin saw the deacon on his knees behind the pulpit, tacking down carpet, looking up to see – she took a swallow of her cider – three rowan-wood crosses bound in red thread.

"That is most generous of you, sir."

Had he seen them? He gave no sign. Even so, he had protected the family from the stain. Wittingly or not, he'd been moved by the magic of the rowan-wood crosses, as a man of open spirit would be.

"I was very sorry that just round then, your good mother withdrew from tavern-keeping, and so I left little things here that I thought might please her. Oranges and so on. Figs once, I believe."

"They did please her, sir." Tamsin had to blink tears.

"I am very glad. You see, I have honored your mother for many years." The deacon stopped. He didn't seem to know what words would come next. "And I would like to tell her so, although I don't know if it would please her to hear it. And I would in no way distress her."

At last Tamsin understood, and she smiled, tears on her face. "Deacon, would you be asking my permission to address my mother?"

"Yes, Miss Bennett, I believe that is what I am doing."

"I cannot speak for her, sir. But I do know that she has always found you most kind, from our first days at the harbor. And after a good deal of time resting, spinning and sewing and teaching Phebe, she is quite well."

"Thank you, Miss Bennett. Then perhaps I'll go and ask her for a dance. I did see that she danced with Captain Hawes. Who seems a fine young man, I would add."

"My mother has always liked to dance, as long as I can remember."

"I believe so," the deacon said with a wistful smile, and went into the tavern, where Isaac Tobin was about to play the poignant and graceful "Heart's Ease."

Tamsin went to the back door to cry deeply in gratitude for her mother's healing and the deacon's goodness.

The next time she went to the meetinghouse to wipe sills and sweep floor, she would climb the pulpit steps to see the piece of Turkey carpet. It would be more beautiful than she could have imagined, and she would look for the three rowan-wood crosses, high up inside the pulpit. She would find them still there.

In a moment, she was startled, though not unpleasantly, to hear Mr. Lamb's clear voice at the kitchen door. "Tamsin, is that you? Are you well?"

She went to tell him she was very well, as just now she was, and then saw that his traveling companion was there too.

"Miss Bennett," said the ebullient, ruddy-headed Mr. Wingate, "I wondered if I might have a dance with you before I go off tomorrow to bury myself in my studies. Might I?"

When she said he might, Mr. Lamb smiled and followed them into the tavern. For the last three dances of the evening, Tamsin's partners were Mr. Wingate, Mr. Lamb, and again Captain Hawes. The last dance was "Dargason," one that always delighted Tamsin, for it looked to be (what she would say to no one but Grandmother Cat, and then only quietly) magical. All the dancers and their partners formed into one single line that, with a figure of side-steps and turns, brought each dancer face-to-face with every other dancer, one after another, *twice*. It was as if everyone had the chance to greet to every other one happily, graciously once, and then again a second time to bid farewell, a perfect evening's end.

Once at the farm, watching "Dargason" from the kitchen door, Tamsin had thought this single line of steps and turns to be, itself, visible music, alive in the smiles of faces and rhythm of bodies. But this evening, the stepping and turning were all confusion. Her heart's pleasure in dancing with the captain flashed quick to heart's commotion as she turned to James' beloved face and felt again his first red-lobelia kiss beside her mouth. She turned then to a surprising wariness in the eyes of Josette Dubois – something hidden – followed by the precise stepping of Mr. Oakes and that of his wisp of a wife. After Mr. Stevens and Naomi, Mr. Proctor and a sour Ruth, Tamsin turned to see wondrous love in Grandmother Cat's face, and turned after that to Mr. Lamb, whose wig fairly bounced with good humor, and then to purest delight in Phebe's eyes, before what seemed a question on the brow of the bright autumn-haired Mr. Wingate. Discomfited, Tamsin was relieved to turn to the jollity of Mistress Dingley and, after that, her rotund husband who liked his ale with Tamsin's extracts. Tonight, even turning to her own mother in dance was not a simple thing, as Susannah had only now turned away from the deacon who might this evening have confessed his love – but when Tamsin turned to face Deacon Somerby himself with the side-steps, his eyes were smiling a warm secret.

This figure of "Dargason," she felt – a single line to be crossed over and over and over again by each dancer – she felt this figure was meant to let every complicated soul find its own particular steps, turns, and steps, right up to a last brave and proper turn. She rejoiced for the deacon and her mother.

47

Captain Hawes stayed the night at the inn, though the *Curlew* would sail early. His cargo of salt cod must get to Lisbon by the holy day of All Saints, he'd said with a smiling boast that the *Curlew* could do it.

Tamsin woke before dawn to give him breakfast and be with him a short while. He took his journeycakes and coffee in the kitchen. She gave him apples. He put them in his canvas bag, stood and slung it on his shoulder as if he were ready to go, although he wasn't.

"Miss Bennett," he said, "In the little time I've been here, you've shown me such miracles. Someday perhaps you'll let me show you wonderful things in distant places."

Tamsin read his eyes and pressed the palms of her hands together to contain their light. Even her happiness was painful.

"I'll come back soon as the *Curlew* will bring me," he said. He listened for a moment to the inn, still quiet. "Then, if you will, Miss Bennett, I would speak with your mother. I have strong relationships in trade, and every chance to do well in the world."

Tamsin took a slow breath so tears would let go from her voice. "I'll be glad of your return, Captain. I'll care for the roses. And when you're farther away than I can imagine, as far

268

away as the stars on your jacket," she smiled, "your roses will be here."

He covered her hands with his. "Think of it this way," he said. "Between us, there will be only one ocean. It's just that you and I are in different ports. It won't be so far then."

He took and kissed her palms where the fountains lifted up, and Tamsin kissed his mouth.

When she walked out with him to the sticks of roses they'd planted at the gate, the air was all fog, every leaf and stone wet.

"I'll come back, Tamsin."

"Godspeed, Christopher."

"Go inside now," he said.

She made herself turn away up the path, then turned back as he made his way through grey air over Wharf Street.

WHEN GRANDMOTHER CAT AND PHEBE CAME TO THE kitchen, Tamsin was pulling apple dumplings from the boil. Susannah appeared soon, followed by the twins and the boys. Meeting no one's eyes, James went out to feed and water the oxen.

"I spoke with the captain last night," Grandmother said. "I told him Mr. Dubois needs steady care and the inn is not the place for it. We'll take them with us to the farm and put him by the kitchen. Josette can sit with him. I'll look after him."

"Good, she can milk the cows with James," Ruth said. "I've had to do it ever since Tamsin left."

"Sometimes I do it," Naomi said.

Tamsin heard Ruth and thought how like Uncle Simon she was, or Uncle Simon of the past. "What if Uncle Simon won't –?"

Grandmother Cat's eyes flicked to Tamsin and stopped the question. "Simon will accept and welcome them. He has a bent toward Christian charity."

Naomi mouthed silently, "A bent."

"A good Samaritan, then," Susannah said. "Do you know, years ago when I was a girl, the minister of the French church in

Boston came with his family to settle in Dorset. In Boston he once preached so moving a sermon on the Good Samaritan that Reverend Cotton Mather himself took care to have it published. Mr. Mather welcomed the French Protestants."

Tamsin smiled at Mother, knowing who the French minister was, and his son her Élie.

Grandmother Cat froze. "Susannah, when I was a girl, the foul Cotton Mather went to the ledge at Salem where innocents were hanged, and when a condemned man prayed, the devil Mather told the constable to push him off the ladder. The man spoke the Lord's Prayer and his neck broke. My mother was there. She saw it. We Rowans know, to our grief, the fickle charity of the Church."

Kitchen struck mute, Susannah nodded humble agreement. Tamsin poked dumplings down into the boil. Vile, these ministers.

"The good Captain Hawes, however, left me thirty shillings to care for two French exiles in need of help," Grandmother said. "Simon will accept it."

Tamsin left the kitchen to take breakfast upstairs and told Josette they were to go to the farm for her uncle's healing. They would go with the cart this morning, soon. Josette, joyful at the prospect, translated their good fortune into French.

Tamsin felt her relief that she'd not have to risk another evident healing in the inn, and went downstairs, confused at her response.

WHEN UNCLE ISAAC APPEARED IN THE KITCHEN, HE WAS met with general clapping and delight, and dug into hot dumplings. Upon hearing the cart would leave for the farm soon, he said he would sail his shallop that way too, because he wanted more time to bother his little sister. He lifted Grandmother Cat off her feet, whirled her once round in the air, then put her gently down. Her eyes shone, and she took two apple dumplings out to

James, hitching the oxen to the cart. Shortly, Uncle Isaac, the Bennetts of West Dorset, and the Dubois of Grand Pré all left for the farm. Naomi and Ruth looked not best pleased to go with Josette, so they sailed with Uncle Isaac.

No words had passed that morning between Tamsin and James. She felt her spirit hollowed out. She swept floors. She and Peter were moving tables and benches when Mr. Lamb and Mr. Wingate came down for breakfast. Tamsin felt in no way sociable, not even for the dear Mr. Lamb, but bid them good morning and served them with courtesy. The young man's hair looked like a tumble of autumn leaves. Had he no comb?

Mr. Lamb spoke eagerly of their travel to New Jersey. Mr. Wingate told Tamsin of his origin in the town of Burnham to the north, and the schooling he was to begin, farther south. In coming years, he said, he would pass back and forth this way, and might sometimes come back to The Rowans.

Tamsin did not want to listen.

Mr. Wingate said how immensely he'd enjoyed last night's dance and Mr. Tobin's fiddle.

Tamsin smiled and wanted to go to the kitchen.

Mr. Lamb went on to praise Tamsin to Mr. Wingate, not only for her skill with herbs, but her ease in uttering an important verse of the New Testament. Mr. Lamb beamed at her. "The Book of Acts, chapter 3, verse 12, isn't that right, my dear? And in the common Greek!"

Mr. Wingate gave Tamsin a glance sharp enough to put her on edge. Did he know that verse? Did he condemn a woman for speaking Greek? Or did he wonder why a source of healing should matter to her, be it human, divine, or dark? She excused herself to the kitchen.

Much as she honored Mr. Lamb, she was greatly relieved when Mr. Wingate brought down their bags and his wooden box. Curious, she wondered but did not ask, was it books for his studies? They left for the wharves.

· · ·

Before the tavern opened at noon, Peter went to sweep out the meetinghouse. Phebe went with her dustcloths. Tamsin made pear pudding for the tavern, and Susannah started her mother's favored receipt for shore plum cordial, so it would be ready for straining by the new year. Tamsin, peeling pears, craved this quiet time with her mother, who stirred sugar by spoonfuls into brandy.

"Captain Hawes went out early. The *Curlew* sailed," she said.

Susannah was silent.

"He said he'll come back as soon as he can."

Still Susannah was quiet. Tamsin kept on.

"Mother, when he comes back, he would like to speak with you."

"I did think he might," she said. "What do you think?"

"I like him very much, Mother. I would accept him."

"Let me say to you, dear, marriage to a ship's captain, to any man of the sea, is a difficult thing. Months alone, waiting to hear of loss."

"I do love him."

"He is a good man, dear. Pray for him. When he comes back, we'll see."

After Michaelmas, as days grew shorter and cooler, Tamsin kept the roots of the roses moist so they would take hold before winter. When she could at low tide, she would go to Green Cove with a bucket of well water, the rake, and sack. There she'd water the stick of a rose by the shore road, drop pitch pine needles on the wet ground, and walk out to the beach. At first she only stood looking over the one ocean that lay between her and Christopher, and tried to imagine how far the *Curlew* had sailed. Then she'd scoop some of the ocean into her bucket and find the little holes that pointed to clams in the sand. She'd wield the rake and put clams into the bucket's bit of ocean. On leaving the cove, she'd gather handfuls of pine needles and put them in the sack, returning to The Rowans with a bucket of clams in salt water for Mother's *chaudière* and a sack of needles for the sticks of roses at the gate.

By All Saints' Day, air and earth were cold enough that Tamsin no longer watered the sticks. Clams were burrowed down, but a low tide on the afternoon of All Saints' called her one more time to Green Cove, so she walked as far as she could to the ebbing water. There she took Papa's compass from her pocket and raised the fine sundial blade. Holding a center of the world in her cupped hands, she looked to the arc of God's wide heaven and reflected on Modron, Cornish Mother of the Earth. She prayed heaven and earth would see Christopher Hawes to his safe return, then folded the blade down and put Papa's mystery in her pocket.

Oddly, however, on that afternoon of All Saints in the year 1755, birds in every tree round the cove suddenly cried out and struck with their wings as if the air itself were a predator. Tamsin, at the edge, felt a sensation like a swell – not in her feet now, but a billowing pressure that rolled above the water and pushed at her heart, so that her body swayed with the force. Some distance out, a long wave lifted, turned lacy and subsided, then reappeared closer in, followed by a tall, ragged wave farther out, and another after that, and another, each one rougher, more disordered than the last.

A tide that should have ebbed away, now fought the pull of the moon and bounded onshore, confused. Wrong as this was, Tamsin felt worse coming. In her sight, stones appeared to fall from the sky – not hailstones, not ice, but stones real as those she'd pulled from a rye field for a wall. She reached to her pocket, felt Papa's compass, and ran for the road. On firm ground, stones already gone from the air, she watched the ocean hiss and spit as far up as the pine scrub, as far as the stick that would one day flourish as a rose.

48

AFTER ALL SAINTS' DAY PASSED, THE WAVES OF THE Atlantic bowed again to the bidding of the moon. Tamsin walked daily from The Rowans, past the sticks of roses, to the cove. At water's edge, she held her palms to the sky and sent out the light that rose up through her to the *Curlew*, captain and crew. As they must now have sailed north out of the port of Lisbon, she no longer saw the sloop on an eastward course or at a single point on the face of the earth. Instead, she imagined the *Curlew* heading toward the coast of England with near-infinite possible tacks, the sloop's location a vast field of waves.

Having sent out light, she stepped the six-count figure of the minuet Christopher had taught her, leaving a dance of footprints along dark sand.

SO PASSED A FEW PEACEFUL WEEKS BEFORE ONE Sabbath morning Tamsin's heart was rocked by an announcement at the meetinghouse. James Bennett of the West Dorset parish and Josette Dubois of Grand Pré in Nova Scotia had made known their intention to marry. Banns were being read that day in the parishes of Dorset. Therefore, if anyone knew of an impediment to the union, he should speak. Throughout the sermon, Tamsin's heart struck in her ribs like the clapper of a huge bell. It so weakened her, that after dinner she went to bed, and not to the afternoon's preaching.

She had not seen James since the side-steps and turns of the last dance at the tavern, but his turning away now was a loss she could not have imagined. She'd always felt he was beside her, even when he wasn't, and now he wasn't at all. Tamsin knew she had turned away, too, but even so, felt a child's fresh, unfathomable loss. James was to be married. And Christopher had cast off to sail the ocean.

That evening after supper, her hands and heart wanted work to do. Her heart and hands wanted the work of kneading dough. They wanted to make bread that would rise through the night. They would knead light into the dough and it would rise. She would use Indian corn and rye, and as James had brought the Red Lammas, she would use wheat too. She would make Mother's good thirded bread. Her heart and hands would make it, one-third rye, one-third corn, one-third Red Lammas. She would make two loaves and knead into the bread her love for two men.

TWO NIGHTS LATER, SHE SHOOK AWAKE ON A FULL-moon night when incredibly, not only her heart, but The Rowans itself violently rocked. The attic felt untethered around her and she gripped the bedstead. Phebe called out, tried to reach her, but fell from her narrow bed. Tamsin pulled her up and they held one another tight while the house shuddered as if death had come knocking. The next day the earth trembled again, and again. By the end of it, hundreds of cod and even a few whales floated dead offshore. Stone fences were scrambled onto fields. In Dorset Harbor, three chimneys had failed, so men formed work parties to collect fallen brick, repair, and rebuild them. Uncle Nat's house had come through safe. Most of The Rowans' excellent stoneware survived, but glassware at the bar was in shards.

For months after, ministers railed at congregations for public drunkenness and secret sin that had called forth God's ire and rocked the earth. But Tamsin heard the accounts published in Boston and carried by coastal traders, blaming fluids and vapors under the face of the earth. With pressure, these could push to the point of exploding. She knew what was inside her and believed this to be true.

In the meetinghouse, Mr. Stevens preached on the terrible power of God's judgment and announced for the second time the intentions of James Bennett and Josette Dubois of the West Parish. He said again, any impediment to the marriage should be made known. Containing her own explosive vapor, Tamsin forced her hands to grip the wood of the pew and did not shout an impediment.

Before long, at the time of the new moon, the coastal trader who brought rum and news out of Salem docked with yet another disaster to tell, and he took his rum and story to the Bennetts.

He said that on the first of November, only four weeks ago, the earth had quaked savagely under the ocean. As it happened, this was All Saints' Day, he said, so in the city of Lisbon in Portugal, Catholics were gathering for the holy day. Horribly, then, churches tumbled their steeples and stone walls down on worshippers below and those in the streets. Then the shocked ocean threw its body against the port, swamping ships by the score, and drove upriver, drowning thousands. Fires leapt among fallen buildings, and winds drove hellfire hard through what was left of the once fine city of Lisbon. He caught his breath. And had the Bennetts seen that freak low tide that, instead of ebbing, surged a frothing mess on the shore, some weeks back? It was the same day, he said. That same flood that swamped Lisbon rolled back over the ocean and struck into coves here.

All round Tamsin, a world shredded. At her shriek, the rum

trader who had so relished his story froze cold. Susannah and Peter went and wrapped their arms around Tamsin to bind her together, keep her from flying apart in pieces. Wildly she called, *"Christopher! Christopher!"* as if she could summon him back from Lisbon. Phebe hurled herself at Tamsin, too, crying in horror that her sister was so undone and Phebe's friend, the captain of the roses, would be dead.

The rum trader stood dumbstruck at the vastness of grief he'd visited on this family, and he rushed out of The Rowans, as if he could outrun the sound and pain of such breakage. He never did come back to the tavern with rum from Salem. For all the Bennetts knew, he never traded in rum again.

Phebe worked the tavern that day with Peter. Susannah took Tamsin to her chamber in the attic, where she sat with her and held her. Phebe brought chamomile tea and bread with honey, also a dab of lavender salve on a scrap of linen for Tamsin to breathe.

The next day was the Sabbath. The Bennetts did not go to the meetinghouse that day, and if Mr. Stevens announced for the third and last time the marriage intentions of James Bennett and Josette Dubois, the Bennetts did not hear it. Instead, Tamsin ate bread and milk in the attic, then went down to the kitchen and quietly made dinner, feeling every step and each movement as though her flesh pressed against thorns. She did not go into the tavern the next day. Talk would be all the terrible news of Lisbon. She ate pudding and went to the attic as soon and silently as she could.

She wanted Mr. Lamb. He had gone to New Jersey to preach, but he was a wanderer, so there was no way to know what parish he might be enlivening now. It was the beginning of Advent. Somewhere he would preach on the mystery of the waiting before Christmas. In moments when Tamsin's grief slipped toward hope, she imagined Advent might bring word the *Curlew* was safe, having sailed toward England before Lisbon fell. She imagined the *Curlew* crossing a vast, unknowable ocean before arriving at a port, a single point from which news could come that the *Curlew,* her captain and crew, were safe. And so, through Advent, Tamsin walked each day to Green Cove, let the fullness move up through her feet, her whole body, and sent light from her palms to the space over the one ocean. Christopher would know that beacon, she was sure.

But word of the *Curlew* did not come, nor did Mr. Lamb.

ON A COLD DAY IN JANUARY, JAMES AND JOSETTE WERE married at the farm. Deacon Somerby was so kind as to drive Susannah and her children there in his horsecart. He and Susannah rode in front, while the children sat sometimes in back, wrapped in blankets, sometimes walked to move their limbs.

Going into the house again after years, Tamsin found welcome warmth and sharp pain. She gave James her sincere wishes for his happiness, and hard as it was, wished Josette happiness too. She sought comfort in seeing Aunt Adah's good health, little Sarah blooming, and Uncle Simon less bitter. As for the twins, it was broadly hinted that Mr. Stevens, minister to the Dorset Harbor parish, had come to visit the farm after the tavern dance, almost certainly to see Naomi. Ruth was thin-lipped at the suggestion.

Mr. Briggs, minister to the West Dorset parish, came to officiate at the wedding. Tamsin took no joy in seeing him again, the one Papa called a ninny.

Most painful of all was Papa's great absence, and even though Grandmother Cat held her close and talked to her softly, Tamsin had a wild eagerness to leave the farm. So she went for her cloak and told Grandmother she would go out to the barn to greet Ethan and Levi and see her red Devons. When they left for the harbor at last, Tamsin walked with her grief and remorse all the six miles to The Rowans, well back of the cart.

. . .

THROUGH WINTER, TAMSIN DID NOT GO TO THE COVE. She held a kind of stillness, not expectant as in Advent, but cold and covered, a white field. Susannah watched her every day and, one day in the attic chamber with the great wheel, she stopped spinning and Tamsin stopped her mending. Susannah waited, then spoke.

"My dear, do you remember what I said to you when you told me that you danced your sweet minuet with the captain at the cove? I said you must be mindful and not give cause for anyone in the parish to speak of you ignorantly or shamefully. Do you remember? Because there are those, all too willing to speak ill, especially of a woman."

Tamsin looked at her mother. He is gone. Why this, now?

"I want to tell you two more things that are true. You know that I like to dance."

Tamsin heard without answering.

"Before Élie and I married, we met sometimes at the cove, just as you and the captain did. You went there to plant a rose, I went to dig clams. Élie came to find me when he could, when he was ashore, and we would go and sit among the bayberry bushes, where no one could see us. Of course it wasn't proper, but he was so long at sea, and we wanted to be together.

"But one day, we did not go among the bushes. We were on the beach." Susannah had a wistful look. "Élie would go to Boston for trade and visit friends of his father's, who took him to dances with them, so he danced very well. The day we were on the beach, he taught me figures of the dances he knew. He taught me siding," she said, and showed it with a forward slip of her right shoulder. "He taught me the two-hand turn, and the hey – "

"'Dargason' ends with a hey," Tamsin said, alive to the last tune Uncle Isaac had played at the tavern.

"Yes. And Élie taught me the dos-à-dos, and a figure called the kiss. Here." A light finger touched her cheeks, one and the other. Her voice dropped. "And then I saw a man walking away along the shore road. I don't know what he saw, but for weeks and months, I expected gossip to run around the parish. By some miracle, there was none, ever. I never knew who the man was, nor ever heard one single word of shame. But he could easily have spread untruths and caused long difficulty.

"That is one thing I wanted to tell you, dear. And here is the other that I know."

Tamsin listened closely now.

"Only four years and seven months after we married, Élie died at sea. My dear Tamsin." Susannah took her hands. "Your dance with the captain at the cove was an act of trust and love. You see, death comes soon, but those beautiful steps will always live. Whatever else may happen, you'll always know that you danced on the sand with the man you loved. No tide will ever wash that away – no biblical flood, no hellfire wind, no break in the earth. It will always be true, that at Green Cove you and your Captain Hawes stepped round one another, dancing. True, always."

Beside the great wheel in the attic chamber, Susannah and Tamsin held one another, then continued to spin and mend.

WHEN SPRING CAME, TAMSIN WENT OUT AND WORKED the garden. She pushed her hands down into the warming soil and felt its movement. She let her heart love the roots and greening of her herbs and, out by the front path, she spread her fingers among the new leaves of the Michaelmas daisies. Later, at gate and cove, she watered the roses that this season would grow to be more than sticks.

49

ONE MORNING TAMSIN WOKE TO FIND PHEBE SITTING, impish, on top of the chest in their bedchamber, her eyes close to the sampler Tamsin had made years before at the farm. She turned the framed linen toward her sister. "Tamsin, how did you do this? I'm ten, and I know all my stitches now. I want to make one."

Tamsin looked at the work she had made in a different life. She had meant it to picture the farm.

"Do you miss it?" Phebe asked.

Tamsin nodded.

"Do you want to go back?"

James was married. "No."

Phebe fingered an arc of five round forms, satin stitch.

Tamsin got up. "We should get dressed and go down. Bring it, if you want."

SUSANNAH WAS IN THE KITCHEN, COFFEE MADE, HASTY pudding started. Tamsin went to keep the pudding stirred. Phebe tucked herself by the hearth and studied the sampler.

"Mother, I want to make my sampler."

"Then do."

"When Ruth and Naomi made theirs," Phebe said, "they only made letters and numbers, with their names at the bottom."

"I thought for a long time what I wanted to make," Tamsin said. "I wanted to stitch what was important, and beautiful."

Phebe's fingers traced blue ripples. "The millstream."

"I started with those rows of chain stitches all the way across, and then I made the millwheel in chain stitch, too, so it would look to be all one flow with the stream. Except, of course, the wheel is tall and round and black."

"Why black?" Phebe asked.

The question startled Tamsin. *Black for Papa dying underneath it*, she thought, though when she did the stitching, he was still alive. She wondered, was the black wheel another sign that she'd missed?

"Black because it's wet," Phebe said reasonably.

Tamsin sped her stirring of the pot and pointed Phebe elsewhere. "That green curve is our hill. Then on the hillside I made our wheat ripe, all yellow stem-stitches and seed-stitches."

"Because the wheat is all stems and seeds," Phebe said.

"And this grey-green bundle on the hill – "

"That's the arbor," Phebe said.

"I tried."

"It looks like the arbor."

A gladsome voice chimed from the dining room door. "Good morning, Mistress Bennett! The Misses Bennett! I believe I smell coffee!"

Mr. Wingate had arrived yesterday, traveling north from New Jersey. It was a long way, he said, so he would rest a few nights and spend the Sabbath at Dorset Harbor.

"Good morning, Mr. Wingate." Susannah smiled at her lodger. "Please sit down and we'll get your coffee and pudding. Phebe?" He retreated to the dining room.

With a cheery "Good morning, Mr. Wingate," Phebe took him his breakfast and a pitcher of syrup, and returned to peer further at the sampler. Susannah took him coffee.

"This is my favorite part," Tamsin said. "Five moons in a curve above the hill, all in satin stitch. It took weeks."

Phebe touched the round forms, one by one, right to left, done in black and yellow. "New, waxing, full, waning, new."

"Because it's the moons that make the tides that turn the wheel," Tamsin said.

The kitchen dropped silent again until Phebe read along the bottom edge, below the millstream, "*A fountain of gardens, a well of living waters.*"

Dying waters, Tamsin thought. She ladled pudding into bowls and called out, "Peter?"

"From the Song of Solomon," Susannah said. Her voice caught. "Phebe, do you remember when Papa used to read scripture?"

Phebe gave a short nod.

"When I could choose which book he would read, I always chose the Song of Solomon. *A bundle of myrrh is my well-beloved,*" she smiled.

After Élie, Mother loved Papa. After Christopher, Tamsin didn't think she could love another man.

Phebe read: "'Thomasin Bennett, Age 12, July 10, 1748.'"

"I'm almost eleven. I'm going to stitch rowan trees into mine. And a verse from the Song of Solomon. *Tamsin!* Don't drip on your *sampler!*" she scolded, and carried it out of the kitchen. "I'll get Peter."

LATER, TAMSIN WAS TAKEN ABACK TO FIND THE tousle-headed Mr. Wingate standing at the dining room fireplace, contemplating her sampler, propped on the mantel.

"I'm sorry," he said. "Phebe asked me to put it up, do you mind?"

Tamsin shook her head.

He went on, "It's remarkable. The moons."

She looked at the beautiful moons she had made and saw

them as he might, unnatural, unaccountable, perhaps wicked. "A whimsy, a fancy only," she said.

He eyed her with a sharp interest that frightened her, and continued to study her needlework. "The Song of Solomon," he nodded.

She fled up the back stairs.

As it was the Sabbath, Susannah hospitably invited him to sit with the family in her brother Nathaniel's box pew. To Tamsin's deep discomfort, he was pleased to accept.

The next day, he caught a trader up the coast to Burnham.

Weeks, then months passed, and Tamsin went often to Green Cove, digging clams for her pies and Mother's *chaudière*. She went to tend the rose and, at the edge of the water, held her palms to the sky. The movement of warm light up through her feet was at times so fulsome, her hands ached with it. Once when Phebe was with her, she asked what Tamsin was doing, so Tamsin taught her sister how to feel what was happening beneath her feet, lifting all the way up to gather in her heart and mind, then moving out through her palms into the space over the one ocean. Soon Phebe was busy showering her rowan saplings with light and warmth from the fountains in her hands. She told Tamsin they liked it.

With Tamsin's care, that summer the roses at gate and cove branched and leafed in jubilant spirit, pushing hundreds of firm green buds to open up a color and fragrance hitherto unknown in the parish. Seamen coming ashore found The Rowans more by scent than by the sign Peter had made, so after that year, the tavern was commonly called The Roses and Rowans. Peter never did change the sign.

Phebe's rowans grew tall, flowered, and bore their masses of berries. Cardinals by the score came to gorge on them in the fall.

Peter made a batch of charcoal sticks for her and brought out wood scraps from the barn, so she could draw the rowans and cardinals she saw, and plan her sampler. She made drawings upon drawings, but did not begin stitching. For Peter, Tamsin gathered bayberries at the cove, so he could smooth the scratches made by a lively trade at the tavern bar.

Still the *Curlew* did not sail to Dorset Harbor.

Thoughts of Captain Christopher Hawes wore deep paths in Tamsin's mind. She thought of him at the cove and sent out light from her hands. She thought of him when she would heft a stoneware teapot. She thought of him in the meetinghouse and looked up to the balcony where the African artists made drawings of sloops. She wondered if they asked where young Neddie had gone, as she went to the sea for Christopher.

Surely authorities at the English port of Falmouth would know whether Captain Hawes' sloop with her cargo of madeira and gold had arrived and cleared Customs. The captain's brother, himself captain of an East Indiaman, would know if his younger brother's vessel had been written off as lost. But whatever it was that happened, unbearably, no one in Cornwall knew that word should be sent to an inn at a fishing port on the Massachusetts Bay.

So for Tamsin, it was possible that he had died at Lisbon; it was possible he had decided not to return to her; and it was possible that some third thing was true, and she would never know what it was. She grieved every day that she'd not thought to make him a rowan-wood cross bound with red thread, as her great-great-grandmother Margaret had done for so many at Brampton Bryan.

Through the seasons after that first Michaelmas dance, Deacon Somerby took his dinners more often at the tavern than at his house, and more often in the inn's dining room than in the tavern. Tamsin noted this and Mother's answering smiles when the deacon came in, so she spoke with him warmly and served his dinners with care. He asked Tamsin once whether she expected her uncle Isaac Tobin might return in the fall to play another dance at the tavern. Tamsin hid sharp pain. Even if Uncle Isaac were to come, the captain would not be here to dance with her. James might, or he might not. Still she wanted Uncle Isaac to bring his fiddle to the harbor again and said she'd speak of it with her mother.

"I remember your mother from a very young woman," the deacon said. "Even before her first sadly brief marriage. She did like to dance."

Tamsin took his empty plate and mug away to the kitchen, but stopped short and turned back. "May I bring you another ale, sir?"

At his nod, she left and returned. Setting the mug down before him, she paused.

"Deacon," she began, "You spoke of my mother liking to dance."

He gave a smile Tamsin thought a little poignant, a little mischievous.

"Once upon a time –" She stopped, and began again. "A long time ago, would it be possible –?"

She looked through the kitchen door and then back to the deacon. She began again more firmly, "Once, a man walked the shore road ... "

His smile grew. "She saw me, did she? I always wondered."

Tamsin whispered now. "She saw you, but she didn't know –"

He spoke quietly. "Who it was."

"Or what he saw."

"Then shall it remain a secret?" He tipped a subtle forefinger toward Tamsin and then to himself. "Between us?"

50

ON THREE SABBATHS IN THE MONTH OF SEPTEMBER IN 1756, Mr. Stevens announced at the meetinghouse the marriage intentions of Deacon Jonathan Somerby and Mistress Susannah Bennett.

Mr. Lamb, on stopping through Dorset Harbor, heard the news with delight. Would the wedding take place at the tavern? Would there be a dance? He promised to return. Uncle Isaac did indeed pack his fiddle and come from Colbrook to play. Mr. Stevens officiating, Mr. Lamb offered heartfelt prayers at the beginning and at the end. Then as it happened, Mr. Wingate arrived at The Roses and Rowans on his travel south to New Jersey and delighted in the music and dance.

Grandmother Cat, James, Josette, and the twins came, bringing a cartload of autumn provisions with fresh milled rye, Indian corn, and the family's Red Lammas. Tamsin felt the pull of an ache at her heart and made herself busy storing the things they'd brought. After the wedding, when Uncle Isaac took up his fiddle, though she glanced at James, he would never look in her eyes, but danced with Josette, and whenever Josette turned her face to Tamsin, the air kicked up a sharp wind. Grandmother Cat, who noted signs, drew Tamsin away to speak to her about

287

teaching Phebe the things she must know, because Phebe, Grandmother said, was a granddaughter too, and might yet be a rowess. Bearing the ache in her body, Tamsin understood. She danced that evening with her new stepfather Deacon Somerby, her dear friend Mr. Lamb, and Mr. Wingate.

AFTERWARD, SUSANNAH LIVED AT HER HUSBAND'S FINE house and continued to work at innkeeping with her children. James and Grandmother Cat still drove the oxcart to the harbor in autumn and spring each year. Josette came once more, but before a jealous nor'easter struck, Grandmother Cat's wisdom and the bulk of two oxen pointed the cart back to the farm. Within the year, Josette had a baby girl named Beatrice, and after that did not come to the harbor.

Tamsin said nothing of her feelings about James' baby, but Grandmother Cat watched her face and told her again, Phebe was old enough now, Tamsin must devote time to teaching her all she knew of herbs. So Tamsin took Phebe up along the hill road to the woods and graveyard, and out along the shore road, to forage. She taught her sister all she had learnt from Grandmother Cat years ago at the farm, the making of tinctures, extracts, and poultices for wounds, birth, and milk-swollen breasts.

Josette gave James a second baby, a little boy, Pascal.

Tamsin taught Phebe everything, except for one thing that she did not tell her. She taught Phebe how very fine she must grind the floss that came long ago from Suriname for easing the breath, but said nothing of its mournful use. Someday Tamsin would tell her this too, but she could not do it now.

On a fall day when Phebe was twelve, Tamsin did, however, tell her the whole story of their great-grandmother Priscilla. Phebe was out in the back field, drawing in charcoal on wood the shapes of rowan trees, berries, and fat cardinals. Tamsin went to sit with her. She had to make Phebe understand, a trusting young girl must learn to be spare with her words about the Rowan line.

Above all, she must never speak of the light that moved through her body to fountains in her hands. She mustn't say that light rises up in her like sap. She must know that mortal danger once threatened their Grandmother Cat's own mother.

"Phebe," Tamsin had to say plainly, "this could happen again."

Phebe listened, nodded solemnly, and said she understood.

THROUGH THAT WINTER, TAMSIN WATCHED AS ROWAN trees and clutches of red berries took shape across Phebe's square of stretched linen. Come spring, on a waxing moon, the days when Tamsin prepared the kitchen garden and planted new greens, Phebe finished her sampler. Peter made a frame and hung it above the dining room mantel. The afternoon when Tamsin saw it complete, she gave a whoop of delight edged with a reservation.

Phebe eyed her sister. "What's wrong?"

A phrase of King Solomon's poem wrapped among the roots of the rowan trees – "*The time of the singing of birds is come*" – and just above it, a line of plump cardinals pecked the earth, trailing deposits of little brown knots, a stitch Phebe had long practiced to do neatly.

"Nothing's wrong, only – my dear sister and sexton of the rowans!" Tamsin pulled Phebe to her and embraced her. "You give such high honor to the droppings of birds!"

"Tamsin," Phebe said firmly, "you said not to talk about the family and not about my feet or my hands or sap moving in the trees, and I haven't." She pointed at her sampler. "The cardinals kept us safe. They ate and they carried and they planted rowan seed for us, so there they are. And that verse is in the Song of Solomon, just like yours. It's in the Old Testament, Tamsin. They can't take us to Salem jail for that."

"No. No, my love," Tamsin said, "they can't."

· · ·

STILL, DESPITE PHEBE'S RESTRAINT, WORD DID somehow spread round the parish, that Tamsin had a deep knowledge of herbs. It may have come from her stepfather, so proud of the family that had become his, late in life.

More and more often Tamsin was called upon to ease the illnesses of parishioners or fix their injuries. She was called even for some births, though she was unmarried. Those who asked for her care thought her especially wise with her mixes of extracts, but the truth of it, Tamsin knew with growing certainty, was more in her hands than her herbs, and she was in no way eager for this to be cried out.

What frightened her most was the way Noah Southworth still looked at her. His eyes too bright, he seemed to hint he knew something about her more scandalous even than the light in her hands – a secret of value to him and threatening to her. She was afraid that when he built the sawmill, as he was sure to do, his pride and a few ales in the tavern would loosen his tongue. Lustily, he'd tell drunken men that not only could Tamsin Bennett do healings with her hands, she would feed men's mouths with apples. He would tell them she saw invisible things, and rouse them to call her a fortune-teller. There would be bold looks, invented stories, and demands that she tell them what girl they could have, or if they'd return safe from sea. She'd be cried out as a witch, her family thrown out of the tavern.

Because she would not marry Noah. He'd not yet built the mill, but she saw looming peril and withdrew as much as she could. She avoided attending to burns or broken bones. The effect of her hands, she feared, would be too plain, so in these cases she sent word she could not leave the tavern. Surely someone else could apply a salve or a splint.

But if it was a matter of a child with the throat distemper, or a babe in the womb unwilling to come down, she would always go, and her hands always soothed the little one and shifted that which needed to shift. In these cases, then, she would praise the sick child for her strength, or the mother in labor for her clever body that knew the best way to give birth. Then the one who suffered knew something good of herself, and Tamsin returned unsuspected to the place she now called, in her heart, The Roses and Rowans.

MR. LAMB STILL PASSED THROUGH DORSET HARBOR, traveling to the eastward or back to Boston. Each time he came, he and Tamsin would recite together, in the common Greek, Saint Peter's words on the divine source of healing, until she could say it all in Greek, herself. Twice each year, Mr. Wingate came to stay at the inn, a few nights in May on his way up the coast to Burnham, and some nights again in September traveling south to his college at Princeton in New Jersey. He always carried books, which Tamsin quietly found of interest. Whatever day he arrived, he would stay till the Sabbath and then go to the meetinghouse with the Bennetts.

Deacon Somerby sat at the deacons' bench below the pulpit, so Susannah continued to sit with her children in her brother's box pew, Mr. Wingate with them. One time he'd walk there with Peter and discuss his uncle Charles Wingate's orchards in Burnham. Another time he'd walk behind with Phebe and compliment her on the health of her rowan saplings. Once she explained to him that her sister had taught her how to use her hands for this, and stopped to offer a moment's demonstration. Tamsin held her breath and didn't look, but was deeply relieved when Mr. Wingate said only that this looked to be a fine sort of blessing. Late that night in the attic, she had to tell Phebe once again she must always, without fail, remember the terrible things that happened to their great-grandmother Priscilla. Phebe promised to try.

After chatting with Peter or Phebe on the way to the meetinghouse, Mr. Wingate would manage most often to slip beside Tamsin in the pew. He told her he liked hearing Mr. Stevens' sermons, though he himself was Presbyterian and not Congregational. Even so, he said, a good sermon was a good sermon, no matter. He looked forward to preaching, as he would graduate from the seminary in 1762.

To Tamsin's relief, he never questioned why she had learnt by heart Saint Peter's words on healing, in both English and Greek. Nor did he ask about the effects of Phebe's hands on the flourishing of her rowans, nor about the five moons Tamsin had stitched in her sampler, so over time she felt easier in his presence. She took somewhat less exception, then, to the red riot of his hair. Instead, when passing behind him to clear the table at dinner – or even more, while sitting beside him in the box pew – she restrained her hands from reaching up to smooth the disorder, or from burying her fingers within it, just as she liked to spread her fingers among the spring leaves of Michaelmas daisies.

As years passed, evenings at the tavern, he would speak amiably with the Dorset Harbor selectmen, mention his studies and the coming year of his graduation, and then either sail north to Burnham, or else go with a coastal trader to Boston and on to New Jersey.

It did not escape the eyes of the Dorset Harbor parish that, on every occasion when Mr. Wingate attended Sabbath worship, though only twice a year, he sat by the side of Tamsin Bennett in her mother's presence. The parish as a whole, and certain regretful men in particular, came to the only possible conclusion. Miss Bennett was betrothed to the young Wingate from Burnham. In only a matter of time, their intentions would be announced.

Tamsin was not unaware of this assumption and, while it wasn't true, nor would it be, she found it increasingly useful. Men in the tavern still looked upon her with pleasure, most townsmen properly enough, others with a more desirous eye. Seth Gates who kept the dairy with his mother was a good man, a hard worker, but his interest would not be returned. The undoubtedly handsome Noah Southworth still supplied the Bennetts' cordwood and still kept his bright, frightening watch on her. Best she could, Tamsin stayed a distance from Seth and Noah, and did nothing to discourage the general belief that she and Mr. Wingate had an understanding. The unspoken pretense gave her, she thought, some harmless protection, until the month of June in the year 1762, when it did not.

That spring, Mr. Wingate completed his studies at the College of New Jersey. The selectmen of Dorset Harbor liked the engaging young man who had a good education and no pulpit as yet. They'd known him for a half-dozen years now and were in need of a schoolmaster for the parish, so they took him on and agreed to pay a small monthly sum to The Roses and Rowans, so the inn would give him lodging and meals.

After all, as it was quietly understood, he and Miss Bennett intended marriage.

51

Mr. Wingate arrived in June with a bag and a chest and the same wooden box that Tamsin once thought might hold books. She learnt soon that it did, which interested her, though her interest was complicated by unease at his coming. It made her reckon with her years of quiet dishonesty in allowing Dorset Harbor to imagine a connection between them. Still more shameful was the chance he might think this too. Did he believe they would marry?

They would not.

On the day he was to arrive, Tamsin left the house. She asked Phebe to start the tavern dinner, while she would ready Mr. Wingate's bedchamber. She'd go up to the graveyard then, water the strawberries, and pick some for fritters. But there at her little sisters' berry patch, she simply sat on the ground with her watering can and basket, turned her palms up in her lap, and looked at them. She knew their inclination. She knew the times when, against her will, they were on the edge of reaching up to calm the wilds of Mr. Wingate's madder-red hair.

She did not love him, so how could it be, her hands had a will so different from her own?

These last years, Tamsin's heart still took her to Green Cove to tend Christopher's roses, then go to the line that curved and moved incessantly between land and sea. Some days, she took Papa's sundial-compass from her pocket to watch the needle swing. Never once at the cove had it shown due north, landward, as it should have, so instead she would pose it a question: If the *Curlew* were still sailing, where on this one ocean would his beautiful sloop be? Day to day, the answer changed. Tamsin would lift her hands then, consult her feet and heart, and send light from the fountains in her palms out over the wide, unknown ocean.

No word ever came back.

Seven years after he set sail, was it pure folly to think of him still?

Beside her sisters' graves, she filled her basket and watered the ground, then walked back to The Roses and Rowans to help with the tavern dinner. For those who came to the dining room, there would be strawberry fritters.

Mr. Wingate arrived in the evening. Phebe welcomed him, set a place in the dining room, and took him fish stew and bread. Tamsin said she would stay in the kitchen to wash up, and Phebe went upstairs.

When he had eaten, Tamsin passed behind him to take away his bowl. She had an impulse to lift one hand up behind his head, just for a moment, to try what she would feel. There was restlessness in the air about his head, and in response, a warmth rose from her heart into her hand. She paused there and felt his attention shift, as if his eyes had turned, as if he felt something too. Later, when he'd finished his fritters, she brushed her hand through the air behind him once more and, this time, when she reached to take his dish, he lifted it up to her, grazing her fingers with his.

"Thank you," he said. "That was delicious. I am glad to be here."

Tamsin felt his touch keenly, and her eyes slipped from his face to the loosened wrap of his neck stock. She wished to unwind and retie it properly, but of course she went to the kitchen.

THROUGH THE SUMMER, MR. WINGATE TAUGHT A FEW lessons at the Dorset Harbor schoolhouse and went round to West Dorset and the village at Rocky Bay as well, to make up a little for the previous year's want of a schoolmaster. He would not start in earnest until the fall, however, so he took to helping Peter with the fishing and relieved him some evenings at the tavern bar. Uneasily then, it fell to Tamsin to teach him the mix of extracts that must be dropped into each pint of ale. She told him it was to give flavor. When he listened to her with no hint of suspicion, she was a bit more at peace.

One night, as it happened, he looked about the tavern and said he'd never seen a place so crowded with men who were not thick with coughing and spit, or red in the eye, or worse. So that night before she slept, Tamsin added Mr. Wingate's observation to her notes headed, "Effects of the Extracts of Elderberry and Chamomile, when used regularly in Ale at a Public House," and she smiled.

AT SUMMER'S END, MR. WINGATE WAS TO BEGIN HIS full round of teaching, but told the Bennetts he would continue to help however he could, as he was sorry the selectmen compensated the inn so feebly for his fine board and lodging. Mr. Proctor's apple harvest had begun, so Mr. Wingate worked when he could with Peter or Tamsin or Phebe to hook the apples down, haul and barrel them, and keep the cider press working. He continued a few evenings in the tavern as well, as Peter sometimes went to Colbrook to work with Uncle Isaac on his dories and shallops.

IN THE YEARS SINCE SUSANNAH HAD MARRIED DEACON Somerby, many in Dorset Harbor had come to expect that Isaac Tobin would appear every Michaelmas to play for a dance at the tavern. He'd never yet disappointed them, and in this September of 1762 he came again. All the deacons and all the selectmen and their wives gathered. Sadly, Mr. Manning had died the previous winter. Caleb, losing his position as warm footstool, soon followed. The new selectman was Noah Southworth, not only cutting wood now, but planing it smooth in the mill he himself had built as Dorset Harbor grew. Tamsin avoided his appreciative looks, and when she had to dance with him, gave him no chance to question her. There was nothing more she could say.

Many of the West Dorset Bennetts came to the dance that year, even Uncle Simon and Aunt Jane. Grandmother Cat came to sit by her beloved brother Isaac while he played. Ruth came, betrothed as she was to the dairyman Seth Gates. Naomi was there, too, now married to Mr. Stevens and living at the parsonage on Wharf Street. Her demeanor toward Tamsin was less scornful than before, though never warm. James and Josette did not leave the farm for the dance. They had three children now, and Josette was with child again.

When Tamsin thought of James' babies, she would curl subtly forward over her heart, and when she could, retreat to the cove. There she'd put her face into the roses, grown thick along the road by now, and breathe until the scent washed through her despair. Later in summer, she would pick the fat red berries that followed the blooms, and study them. She hoped these were a sign that someday something round and very real would come to her. A baby. Perhaps Christopher's.

Then she would go to damp sand and leave bare footprints in circles where the two of them had danced, or else press herself deep into the bayberry bushes by the rocks and watch the sea. On these days, she did not take Papa's sundial-compass from the pocket inside her petticoats, nor lift her hands up to the sky, in case this would send sadness to Christopher, wherever he was.

THAT EVENING WHEN UNCLE ISAAC CAME TO PLAY HIS fiddle, Peter and Mr. Wingate, whom Peter had begun to call Antony, took it in turns, one drawing ale for the guests, while the other went out on the floor to dance. Whenever it was Peter's turn to be at the bar, Mr. Wingate would try to partner with Tamsin, generally missing out to Noah Southworth or one of the selectmen, who hadn't the fussy work of dropping extracts in ale. Once seeking Tamsin, Mr. Wingate found her out on the front steps, avoiding Noah and the others, so they stood together in the cool air and did not dance.

The moon was just shy of full, and Tamsin was thinking of the first time she had walked out this elegant front door on a fall night, a dozen years earlier. The moon had been hardly there that night, the barest blade edge of light, sinking. Mother had gone away up the hill road, and the next day Tamsin had learnt she had three little sisters buried in the ground. Having worked with Mr. Wingate for some months now, she'd come to like him as a good and lively man, so she told him the story of her first day at her Uncle Nathaniel's house. He listened closely, and said it was a sad story. Still, she didn't tell him about the flurry of cardinals and their busy planting of the rowan seed in the yard. Nor did she tuck the crumpled ends of his neck stock smoothly inside his waistcoat, as she wanted.

Uncle Isaac's fiddle was singing the poignant tune of "Childgrove," then swung into a spirited "Newcastle." Mr. Wingate said he must go back to the bar, so Peter could find a partner and dance. As Tamsin stayed there at the steps, she was startled to hear Grandmother Cat's voice, not at her ear, but clearly inside her own head, saying with gentle humor, *"Dear one, heed the unexpected."*

Tamsin, surprised into heeding, located a slight catch, a small knot within herself. This was the moment when she learnt she was, in fact, sorry that Mr. Wingate had left her on the steps and gone inside to the bar. So she bounced a little to the rhythm of "Newcastle," listened enchanted to "Heart's Ease," and then went in to dance with Mr. Wingate when Uncle Isaac played "Mad Robin," a dance with many turns and the crossing of lines.

52

THAT FALL, FOR TWO MONTHS, MR. WINGATE ROSE
early most mornings to go and teach at the meetinghouse in West
Dorset. Then through four months of winter, he had only a short
walk up Wharf Street to the Dorset Harbor schoolhouse and a
mercifully short walk back in the afternoon, to warm his hands
around a hot ale flip with apple brandy and an egg. When Tamsin
made the flip for him, she sprinkled both nutmeg and drops of
her elderberry extract, as the schoolhouse was far colder than the
tavern and she thought of his health. Come spring, he had to rise
early again to take his breakfast and walk the shore road over to
Rocky Bay, where he taught April and May at the Third Parish
meetinghouse. It was a pleasant, if sometimes slow and spring-
muddy walk, both ways.

One Thursday afternoon in May when Tamsin and Phebe
were to set a tub of wash to soak overnight, Tamsin went to Mr.
Wingate's chamber to gather up his sheets and spread fresh ones.
While not meaning to intrude, she did see two things of interest
on his table. One was a comb, carved simply of horn. She smiled
to remember that, early on, she'd looked at the disorder of his
head and wondered whether he owned such a useful thing. In

300

spite of all evidence, it seemed he did. The other item was a large book bound in blue boards. It tempted her, and she picked it up.

Inside was a title – *The Preceptor: Containing A General Course of Education*. Below that, in two columns, were listed a dozen subjects, the first, "Reading, Speaking, and Writing Letters." Tamsin also saw "Astronomy," a word Papa had used when speaking of stars, and "Drawing," which she knew would excite Peter and Phebe, if only she could show it to them.

She called down the back stairs. "Phebe, come up and help me with these sheets." In a moment, Phebe was at the bedchamber door. Tamsin was turning pages. "Look at this! Look at these beautiful drawings! All sorts of shapes, and birds! And how to draw eyes, and mouths, and feet –"

On the next page, she came to a picture of a well-muscled man in a state of utter undress. She said nothing, but Phebe exclaimed for them both as Mr. Wingate came to the chamber. Tamsin whirled and shut the book.

"Oh, Mr. Wingate, I'm sorry! We were taking up your sheets and I saw your book! I thought it looked very –" She stopped.

"Interesting," he finished for her.

"Yes." Her face was hot.

Phebe, ever her curious self, said, "Mr. Wingate, there is a picture of –"

Tamsin broke in, "Of the most beautiful bird!"

Phebe looked at Tamsin and back to the schoolmaster. "When I planned my sampler, Mr. Wingate, I drew dozens and dozens of cardinals."

"Then you must borrow the book. There will be ideas for drawing more." He smiled.

Tamsin gave that a moment's thought and knew she had to clear her mind, feel her feet on the floor, or else look out a window. "Our father used to talk to me about astronomy," she said.

"You must read that, then. He would be pleased."

"He would. But surely you need the book." She held it out to him.

He didn't take it, but looked at it for a moment and then back to Tamsin. "I won't need it until late Monday at the soonest. I received a letter asking me to go to the eastward, to the parish at Sawbridge. Their minister died three years ago, and with none yet to take his place, they fear God's disfavor. I'm to go and preach to them." His fingers bothered the linen wrapped at his neck. "They may call me to serve there."

Tamsin watched his disquieted brown eyes.

"Mr. Lamb preached to them and gave them my name. I'll sail with a trader tomorrow morning."

Phebe nodded at a paper in Mr. Wingate's hand. "Is that the letter?"

He forced a smile. "So you see, please keep the book till Monday at least."

Tamsin felt a familiar, sharp frailty wrapping around, inside her skin. He might not come back. "Perhaps you should take the book with you." She turned her eyes away as if to scan the chamber. "Will you take your things?"

"No."

"Tamsin," Phebe said with some insistence, "go and draw a pint for Mr. Wingate. He's so kind to let us borrow the book. I'll take care of the sheets. And the book." She took it.

Tamsin thought Mr. Wingate had a look of relief. Was he glad to think of leaving Dorset Harbor for his first pulpit? Or only pleased at the thought of an ale. Heart uneasy, she went down the front stairs to the tavern, and he followed her. As she put drops of her extracts into a mug, he began to speak, but stopped and said nothing, so she gave him her good ale and went to the kitchen.

HE ROSE EARLY IN THE MORNING. TAMSIN HAD MADE coffee and journeycakes, some for breakfast and some to pack for his day. When he came down to the dining room carrying his bag, he was all in disorder, his hair alive like a fire, his neck stock roughly tied. Tamsin took breakfast to him at the table. When she passed her hand by the back of his head, the air was busy, as if a dozen chickens pecked at her palm.

When he had eaten, she took his plate to the kitchen. She listened up the back stairs for sounds of stirring, then went to the front stairs. Quiet.

She went to Mr. Wingate. "When will you preach?"

"I'll speak to the men of the parish tonight, and preach twice on the Sabbath."

She said to him simply, "Mr. Wingate, I hope you will excuse me."

"Of course?"

"Have you a comb in your bag? Your hair is quite – lively, in fact – and I think to calm it a little. You'll be in the wind on the water, surely, but perhaps your hat –"

He took the horn comb from his bag and let her take it. First she worked gently with her hands about his head, to calm the air itself till the sensation of pecking chickens would resolve. With the comb then, she civilized a rowdy head.

He stood, and she handed the comb back to him. "You might perhaps use it again before you preach. It would do well with your fine sermon."

She smiled, surveyed the rest of his appearance, and thought of the parish that would watch him closely this evening, his neck stock inexpertly wrapped – out of kilter, she might say.

"Mr. Wingate, do you have proper preaching bands to tie at your neck?"

"I am not yet ordained, Miss Bennett," he said, then whispered, "Honestly, I fear I am altogether *im*proper."

"Then, Mr. Wingate," she whispered back in conspiracy, "for the propriety of your preaching, may I be improper as well?"

She thought he might blush, but he did not, so she untied and unwrapped the stock from about his neck, smoothed the fine white linen as best she could, and wrapped it snug round his neck again, keeping it close inside the collar of his shirt. She hoped to seem beneficent, even motherly, but in a part of herself, inside, that was not at all what she felt. At his throat, she neatly tied what Peter, a sailor, would call a reef knot, and felt Mr. Wingate's eyes watching her as, most improper of all, she tucked the ends of the stock smoothly inside his waistcoat.

"There. Now you're proper."

"Am I," he said.

If he seemed unsure he wanted to leave now, still he did pick up his bag with the journeycakes in it and make his way down to the wharf.

THAT EVENING, AFTER SUSANNAH WENT HOME WITH the deacon and Phebe was washing up from the tavern dinner, Tamsin went up the back stairs to their chamber. Phebe had left Mr. Wingate's book on the chest and Tamsin opened it. She thought, perhaps, to read about astronomy.

ON MONDAY EVENING, A COASTAL TRADER RETURNED Mr. Wingate to Dorset Harbor. Tamsin had already closed the bar when he appeared in the dining room, looking worn. She smiled to see the windblown mess of his head and brought him a pint of ale with her extracts.

"Would you like to eat? There is some of my mother's *chaudière*."

He smiled and sat at the table.

Passing behind him now, Tamsin brushed her hand through the air – it was calm – and set a bowl down before him. She went to the kitchen to let him take his supper in peace.

"Miss Bennett, this was most restorative." He stood in the doorway with his empty bowl.

Tamsin took it from him. He did look better. "What did you think of Sawbridge?"

"The question is rather, what they thought of me."

She hoped he'd used his comb. "What did they think of you, then?"

"I would say they approved of my preaching. Miss Bennett, in the book that you and Phebe like, *The Preceptor*, a Reverend Mr. Mason takes many pages to describe the most effective manner of preaching – a minister's voice, his volume, his cadence, pauses, gestures, even his gaze."

Mr. Wingate's gaze felt warm upon Tamsin.

"Mr. Mason goes on about these devices that his parishioners found moving, to touch what he calls –" And here Mr. Wingate stopped short, but said at last, "'the avenues to the heart.'"

Tamsin's hands remembered the untying and tying of the white linen of a neck stock. Her hands understood the avenues to the heart.

Mr. Wingate made a wry face, dismissing the lessons of the Reverend Mr. Mason.

"Miss Bennett, through silly practice, I've become skilled at gestures and looks that I would call empty. So you see, the parish thought me a fine preacher."

"But," she protested, "when Mr. Lamb preaches, his looks and gestures are clear and expressive."

Mr. Wingate smiled. "Whenever Mr. Lamb speaks, his movement comes from the heart. Not from a book."

"Then you must learn to speak from the heart," she said.

"I will, Miss Bennett. I will do that."

Late the following afternoon, Tamsin was serving at the bar, as Peter had gone to Uncle Isaac at Colbrook. Susannah was baking, Phebe with her in the kitchen, mending Peter's shirts, which were rather the worse for his days hefting lumber at Uncle Isaac's boat yard. Phebe appeared with her mending at the bar, however, and told Tamsin quietly that Mr. Wingate had come to the kitchen to speak with Mother, and Mother had asked Phebe to take her work upstairs.

Phebe was wide-eyed. "What could it be?"

The sisters looked at one another, and Tamsin felt a chill.

"It must be about Sawbridge."

"Do you suppose they've called him to the parish?"

Tamsin thought of the evening before. "He said they liked his preaching. I expect they called him."

With a dark brow, Phebe carried her mending and her questions to the attic. Tamsin spread her hands flat on the waxed wood of the bar's counter. She felt for its stability, and poured a little apple brandy into a glass.

IN THE EVENING MR. WINGATE CAME TO THE TAVERN for a pint and drank it slowly, until all the other men were gone. When he stayed to help Tamsin sweep the tavern and close the bar, he said to her, since they worked so well together, perhaps she might call him Antony, as Peter did.

Intensely aware of the rhythm of her heart inside her stays, she nodded and spoke a soft "Antony."

When they'd finished the work and banked the fire, he asked her to sit with him, and they sat together on the tall-backed settle.

"Miss Bennett –" he said.

"Tamsin," she whispered.

This seemed to disorder his thoughts, and he stopped.

"The parish at Sawbridge has voted to call me –"

Tamsin was afraid to know what turn her life would take next. She did not want to lose Mr. Wingate – Antony – as she had lost Christopher, and James.

"I am pleased for you. They did well to have you go and preach."

"But I hope not to go there alone. Tamsin, I hope you might go with me."

So here it was, the choice. Would she go with this man her hands loved? To another strange place to do her work and doubt her safety? Would Christopher never come back?

"Will you consider it?"

Tamsin looked to deep brown eyes. "I will consider it."

Tamsin did not sleep that night, but got up at first light to go silent down the back stairs. She ate a piece of Mother's fresh corn bread and went out to the shed. Mother would come soon from Deacon Somerby's house. Phebe would make coffee when Mr. Wingate –

Antony, she meant. When Antony came down.

She wanted to be out.

Taking rake and buckets, she walked the shore road to the cove, birdsong in trees all the way. She wanted to go where land and water lapped one another, and dig there. Or she might sit a while in the pine scrub first, where she could not be seen, or push in among the bayberries. Instead, the first thing she did was to put her face into the roses now spread by the road at the cove. Their scent brought Christopher so close as to be unbearable.

She walked away from the roses, pushing her feet through loose sand toward Pulpit Rocks, and slipped into the narrow path between bayberries and granite. She stowed rake and buckets in the bushes and climbed on the jut out to sea. She wanted to sit where Mother had been when she lost the one that had to be lost, and wondered what it was she might now lose and gain in making the choice before her. Taking off shoes and stockings, she put her feet into the same spiral of salt water where Mother had rested hers. She looked across to the marsh at Flagg Island, then farther out to the line that marked the edge of ocean and sky.

Papa's sundial-compass was in her pocket. She drew it out and held it on the flat of her palm to see where it would point this morning. The needle swung northerly with a quick clarity that seemed to her almost joyful. Any ordinary compass would point north, but most days Papa's wavered eastward or paused sometimes in the south. So she gave close attention now to her feet in the saltwater pool and to her heart, and when she was sure, she lifted her hands and sent light northward.

Ebb tide now, she climbed down from the rocks to damp sand, took up rake and buckets, and went to find the little holes, signs of burrowed clams. There they were. She worked the rake down carefully among them and felt into wet sand as if she could see with her fingers. Grandmother Cat would call this *heeding*, she thought. So she heeded with her fingers and didn't turn to see the man walking the shore road to the Third Parish meetinghouse at Rocky Bay.

WHEN TAMSIN HAD TWO BUCKETS OF SALT WATER nearly full of clams, Phebe came. Tamsin gave her the rake to help, and soon they were done, though Phebe was in no way ready to leave. Running to the water, she jumped a lacy edge to an impressive splash. There she held still, watching thin water slide back, waiting for her next chance to jump.

"Tamsin! Remember? Where am I? On land or in the sea?" She jumped.

Tamsin smiled and waited just long enough. "I see you on the land."

Phebe took a long, determined leap toward the water and looked back, arms akimbo, hems wet. "No! I landed in the *sea!*"

Tamsin ran to the water's edge and, with a wild, great leap, landed knee-deep. "No, dear Phebe, *this* is landing in the *sea!*"

And she strode back toward sand, gown and petticoats soaked to her knees.

"Wait," Phebe said with dignity. Tamsin waited.

She took to skipping every wave, one side to the other, back and forth. At last Tamsin joined her, so together they danced the edges, laughing, one to land, the other to the sea, back and forth, till Tamsin stopped.

"There," Phebe said. "You landed on the land."

Tamsin bent her head to consider the sand under her feet and walked deeply out into the next wave. She searched the fine line of the horizon a little while, then turned and looked northerly over the land to the sky.

THE WORK OF CLEANING CLAMS FOR STEW WAS A painstaking matter, lest grit be left to annoy the teeth. Susannah thus had ample time, after sending Phebe out to the garden, to question Tamsin.

"By chance, did Mr. Wingate find you in the tavern last night?"

"He did. He stayed to help me close down."

"And did he speak with you?"

Tamsin knew where Mother was tending and took a long breath to know whether she was ready to answer. "He did ask me to marry him."

Susannah waited and, as Tamsin said nothing more, she asked, "Had you an answer for him?"

"I told him I would consider it."

"And your feelings?"

This, Tamsin could not answer. "May I have this evening and tomorrow entirely to myself?"

Susannah agreed she might, so that after serving the tavern dinner, eating, and washing up, Tamsin went to Peter at the bar and asked if he would please help her, in the morning, take Uncle

Nat's dory to the harbor and let her have the rowan-wood oars from the shallop.

He would.

Tamsin went out the fine front door then, to weed among the Michaelmas daisies, the rowans, and the roses bountifully spread at the gate. She looked at the healthy suckers sprouted up from the roses' roots, and knew that if she were to go to Sawbridge with Mr. Wingate – *Antony* – she would dig some of those. She would take Michaelmas daisies for courage. Above all, she would need rowans.

She ate no supper, but went to the attic, and when Phebe came up, feigned sleep, although she was wide awake.

<h1 style="text-align:center">54</h1>

PETER HELPED HER WITH THE DORY IN THE MORNING. She set off alone.

Working the oars of a dory in the harbor differed greatly from the singular way of handling a coracle in the millstream, but Tamsin had learnt about dories from her Papa, and as a child had watched rowing skillfully done. Now she brought to mind the captain's rowing of this dory with these same oars to Hallett's Cove. She felt her back and arms at one with his, and their union moved her smoothly, precisely, to that inlet and creek. She took off her shoes and stockings and pulled the dory up at the bank where the captain had done, eight years before, then followed the creek to its spring and the remembered scent.

Approaching, she saw again, these were not trees that grew up and presented themselves like birches or even rowans. Rather, they wove and danced in the air, playing with shade and light. Still she knew from before, that if she went close to one of the blue-grey trees and showed her hands, it would go quiet enough to let her hold a single light-cupped bloom.

No, she heard Grandmother Cat's voice, *not hold, but heed.* And so she did. She went near and reached out to one, cupped it in her bodily hands, and contemplated the broad white petals with the fountain of gold threads and nubs springing at its center. The fragrance that lifted from this one generous bloom led her to an edge of what seemed a vast space. Yesterday, out on the jut of rocks, her hands had sent light high, unexpectedly north. Was he altogether gone?

In her ordinary kitchen awareness, or garden, or attic, she never felt he was dead, only that he was not presently at Dorset Harbor. The old sailor at Grand Pré had said, all he needed for peace at his death was the memory of a bloom like this. Once, the captain had cupped his hands beneath hers. He knew the bloom as well. Had he come upon a choice at sea, to die remembering sailor's-grace, or return to Tamsin? Had he welcomed death?

She kept holding and heeding the bloom till she had learnt from it all she could, and when she let it go, it returned to lilting and flickering in the air. As she walked back along the creek, the air's scent turned from sweet to salt, ground going soft again with salt water. Her bare feet left prints in the earth.

Against an ebb tide, arms sore, back stiff, she worked with the wry thought, what sort of a rowess am I? Handling the coracle in the millstream was a delight, but working the dory against a tide was not. She didn't row to the wharf, but put in at Green Cove. She pulled the heavy boat up by the bayberries and lay down in warm sand to ease her back. One bird sang. She let its clear song soak into the pain, and slept.

When she woke, an expanse of damp sand had opened, and when she stood to see thin waves, the wide space asked her to dance. Her feet knew the minuet, so she stepped out into space – one, *two*, three, four, five, *six*, one, *two* – turning, spiraling her footprints this way and that, till she came to a center. She held there, then left her circles and went to the water's edge.

With Phebe, she would joyfully have leapt back and forth, but her soles wanted earth now, so instead, she walked till she found herself abruptly at the rocks where Mother had labored years ago.

Tamsin looked at her hands that had done the swaddling and the letting go. Now they went to hold her belly, and she turned shoreward.

Sitting in the sand beyond the dory was the man who had asked her to call him Antony, and then asked her to marry him. When she saw him, he stood, a wild aura flaming up about his head. She went to him, moved by the light that shone round him, and smiled at the tatty condition of the stock at his neck. She recalled Deacon Somerby, how he'd once seen Mother and her Élie dancing at the cove, so she cast a look along the shore road. No one there, but still –

She took Antony's hand and drew him to the narrow way between the bayberries and Pulpit Rocks. There, grey-green leaves crowded a frame around his red-gold head and struck Tamsin with his vivid beauty.

"Yes," she said, "I will."

In a hidden path known to Dorset's lovers for a hundred years, Antony kissed her. She lifted her hands to feel the singing light about his head, then loosed the ends of his stock from inside of his waistcoat and took slow pleasure in unwinding the wrinkled linen from his neck.

"Your hands are a wonder," he said. "What is it?"

She didn't answer directly, but said, "You feel different, one time to another."

"And now?"

She reached again to the light and movement she felt in the space around him. "Full. Real." She said from her heart, "Alive."

The linen stock lay simply on his shoulders now, so she took gentle hold of it in her two hands and drew him to her. Feeling him as close as she had long wanted him to be, she knew the warm, insistent ache again and the wet that seemed her own tide.

Before long, Antony drew back to look toward the road beyond the bushes. He looked to the sea, and up to the top of the granite high above Tamsin, as if a watcher might be there peering down. There was no one. "I do like this place," he said.

"Pulpit Rocks," she said.

"Is it!" He looked up. "What a pulpit! Only imagine the bombast that could be preached from there!"

"And what would you preach?"

"Ah, sweet Tamsin," he said, "I would preach from that same biblical book that you and Phebe stitch into your samplers. I would say, *Thy lips are like a thread of scarlet, and thy speech comely."* He kissed her mouth. "I would give my parish fair warning of your strength and tell them that *thy neck is like the Tower of David, builded for an armoury."*

His mouth moved to her neck, and she felt only the granite at her back kept her standing.

"Though I might forbear to tell them," he murmured, fingers brushing aside the white linen at her bodice, "that *thy two breasts are like two young fawns, twins of a doe, which feed among the lilies.* That I might not say, except to you in our bed."

"You know Solomon's Song," she said softly.

"So do you," he said.

They stayed a while longer between the granite and the leaves, speaking of Antony's call to Sawbridge, to the eastward. Moment by moment, Tamsin took in more of what was to come – that she would leave Mother, precious Phebe and Peter, and The Roses and Rowans. She would go farther from Grandmother Cat.

"Antony, I should go back to the house and tell them."

As she went out from the cover of the bayberries, her eyes fell on the captain's roses, where two visions overlay and obscured one another. Images slipping in and out made her dizzy, like a girl whirling in a field with a compass. She reached for a bayberry branch and Antony's arm to hold perfectly still, until colors and forms would resolve.

One vision showed delight in planting the stick of a rose, in walking the road with a captain not yet called Christopher, meeting Uncle Isaac's protective look. In the side yard, a young woman stepped a minuet. Then vivid colors pushed to the fore, a large house painted blue as a July sky, chimney broad and red-brick, rowans and roses in bloom. A small redheaded boy.

She swayed.

"Are you well?" Antony held her.

"Well enough," she said, and let him steady her. "I'd best go back alone. Would you take the dory?"

Antony pulled the dory to the water. Tamsin watched and waited. He rowed out past the jut and turned toward the harbor.

Crossing sand to the shore road, she buried herself once more, face and heart, in the roses, took the scent deep into her, and walked the road home, wiping tears with the backs of her hands.

Trees were silent.

55

Mother and Phebe were in the kitchen, Phebe feathering egg white over biscuits for the tavern dinner. Tamsin went to embrace her in a loving, anxious hug, which Phebe returned, then took a quick step back.

She flicked her feather in the air, saucy. "Where have you been?"

"I was at the cove. I missed your leaping."

Susannah watched her daughters. "Tamsin?"

Tamsin enfolded Phebe again. "Mother, Phebe sweet, I'm going to marry Antony."

Phebe gave a look as if this were nonsense. "You aren't! He's going away to Sawbridge, I think! A trader brought a letter. It's in the tavern." She went to get it, but Antony came in with it, in hand.

"Tamsin, they've called me to Sawbridge. Now," he said. "They want me now."

Tamsin shook her head.

"I have to go. Two deacons write to me." He brandished the letter. "I knew they've had drought, but now fires may blow in from the west. Since the old minister died, they've not filled their pulpit in three years. They fear divine anger and want me now."

Susannah laughed outright. "You're to fend off the wrath of God? Is that all?"

He gave a wry smile. "And not even ordained yet. Not even a Congregationalist. Imagine their salvation in the hands of a Presbyterian!"

Susannah put the first pan of biscuits in the oven. "It's not for their salvation, Mr. Wingate. It's their crops."

"I'll do what I can. I'll pray. I'll find a trader and go tomorrow to Burnham, see my uncle, then on to Sawbridge."

"Tomorrow," Tamsin said.

"Tamsin, you can't go!" Phebe said. Her dismay said, *Never!*

"No, dear, not tomorrow." Tamsin held her again. "There's a great deal to do before –"

Susannah snatched Phebe's feather and busied herself brushing egg white over another pan of biscuits. "There's a very great deal to do before a wedding, Phebe. Spinning, sewing, quilting –" Her voice broke, but she went on. "My good husband, such a kind merchant, will help. Pots, pans, stoneware." She smiled at Phebe's distress, her own eyes wet. "Tamsin will be all fitted out to go to housekeeping."

A CHILL WIND CAME IN OFF THE WATER THAT EVENING, and the drinkers of Tamsin's ale and her hot ale flip stayed long. She and Antony worked the tavern together, and when the last had gone home, they closed it down. Antony shifted chairs so she could sweep dirt, crumbs, and wood bark to the fire.

"I need to tell Uncle Charles I'm off to Sawbridge. He'll speak to the Presbytery about my ordination, end of summer in Burnham, I would think. Shall we be married then?" He kissed her. "Would you be married at the harbor or at the farm?"

The choice confused her. "I want at least a dance here, if Uncle Isaac will come."

Antony's brow furrowed.

"You don't mind?" she asked. "You like to dance."

"I like it very much! No, there's something I need to tell my uncle. There's discord in the parish."

Tamsin stopped sweeping.

"Because I am Presbyterian, when I am their minister, the parish will come under the Boston Presbytery. Till now, they've been Congregationalist and managed all their own affairs. Most of the voting men want to have me, but the son of the old minister has a loud voice and wants no Presbyterian blotting his father's pulpit. The deacons wrote to me that a few other men now side with him and won't pay toward my settlement. The parish has given me £100, though that's only half what Sawbridge gave to settle old Mr. Briggs thirty years ago."

"Briggs?"

"The old minister was Mr. Mather Briggs. His son who objects to Presbyterians is Mather Briggs, Jr."

"The minister at West Dorset is Mr. Joseph Briggs."

"Joseph is the younger son of the old man. Brother to Mather, Jr."

"My father thought Joseph Briggs a fool. Whole sermons, he would rail against magic."

"Waste of a sermon."

"A ninny, Papa called him."

"His brother is worse – bitter soul, a hothead."

Her heart raced. How quick would word fly from West Dorset to the eastward? It would be shocking, rich gossip – the new minister's wife a daughter in the line of the accused Priscilla Rowan, whose daughter was a widow of old Thomas Bennett of that moon-guided mill.

Then Tamsin recalled, of course, she would go to Sawbridge with her married name. No Rowan, no Bennett, but Mistress Antony Wingate, Tamsin *Wingate*.

Still – doubtless the ninny would write the hothead to spread his rancid news. Tamsin stared at the floor, the broom, the wave of grit and leavings at her feet, and angrily swept the mess. Every day of her work, she knew stories of Priscilla were unforgotten, gathered like cobwebs in corners. At any misstep, they could fly into the air and stick in men's eyes. She did well at her hiding, but the stupid Briggs who preached on magic would gladly spill to his brother, to the eastward. He would.

And which would more wildly alarm a Congregational parish in time of drought – a Presbyterian in the pulpit or a witch in the parsonage? They'd believe they had both.

"Your prayers, Antony, had best bring rain. You never want to be the one blamed for a burnt field. Never so much as a singed hen."

He laughed. "I'm not above praying for hens."

She took up a poker to push embers back and sweep over them a tavernful of bark and dirt. She knew how to do this, cover a hot danger and save it for later.

"Uncle Charles paid all my schooling. He won't leave us alone in this," Antony said, and kissed her. "I promise you a good house."

"I'm not concerned about the house," she said, and went to stow the broom. "Do you think Mr. Lamb would come?"

"To our house?"

"To the wedding."

Antony smiled. "To a dance. I'm sure he would come!"

He took a lantern to light the way upstairs. She doused the lamps, locked the bar.

THE NEXT MORNING, ANTONY LEFT WITH A COASTAL trader carrying barley to the malthouse at Burnham. Tamsin unmoored, her hands led where she needed to go, and she followed them. For three days, she made the Rowan women's meat pies.

Rendering suet, cooking beef, softening garlic and onions in butter, she listened for any faint sound that might be the Rowan voice of her Grandmother Cat. *Heed the unexpected,* she heard.

Mother and Phebe moved about the garden and kitchen as

usual. Tamsin was aware of them, but her hands worked rather with a rowess presence. Her great grandmother Priscilla was there. She laid her hands over Tamsin's and said, as if to reassure them both, *I lived, beloved. It was terrible, but I lived. Here I am.* Under Priscilla's hands, Tamsin chopped and cooked nuts with elderberries and rowanberries, rosemary and thyme. They soaked dry bread in cider and together their hands squeezed it out. They stirred everything at once into the largest iron-legged pot on the hearth. Listening still more deeply, Tamsin found her way back along the rowess line to Margaret who had carried on her healing in a village twice besieged. Every day for three days, Margaret came to watch Tamsin rub eggs and butter into Red Lammas flour in a stoneware bowl. She advised and comforted as Tamsin rolled rounds of pastry, dolloped them with meat, and pinched them tight.

Susannah and Phebe saw to the baking of them every day, and let Tamsin be alone with her work.

AFTER TWO DAYS, A COASTAL TRADER CAME TO THE tavern asking for dinner and a pint in exchange for a letter he bore from Antony, written from Burnham. Tamsin served the trader her ale and a meat pie, and another meat pie when he had finished the first.

Antony wrote that his Uncle Charles would have the Boston Presbytery fix the date of his ordination for the last Sunday of September. He wrote, too, of his uncle's displeasure with Sawbridge offering a paltry sum for his settlement. So affronted was Uncle Charles, that he himself put another £100 toward the amount. So Antony rejoiced to have all summer and sufficient funds to build Tamsin a good house before his ordination, before their wedding, before the cold season to come.

In his letter Antony mentioned as well, by the bye, the remarkable look of his uncle's dining room, newly painted by Uncle Charles himself a shade of deep sky-blue, with pigment he had imported from Prussia. Might Tamsin be pleased to have a dining room in sky-blue?

Antony would have gone on to Sawbridge by then, so Tamsin waited to respond till a mariner who came in for dinner said he would sail to the eastward next morning and would be willing – for a supply of apples and those last two meat pies – to put in at Sawbridge and carry a letter to the meetinghouse. She wrote to Antony that night.

She asked him how could he ever build such a house in a summer – £200 in his pocket! – all while writing sermons, preaching, visiting, and praying intently for rain. Who would help with the building? It would exhaust him utterly. As to the rain, she advised him to pray twice daily out of doors, morning and evening, directly under the sky. Perhaps there were parishioners who might see and join him there. She advised that he pray with his palms turned upward to the heavens, in an attitude both expectant and grateful – as one works with herbs, she wrote.

On considering further, she asked if he might look to see if the threshold to the meetinghouse were dusty. In that case, he might take a cup of water from a flowing source, a stream perhaps, and sprinkle it at the threshold with a good biblical verse. Her great-grandmother, she wrote, would sometimes shout verses of the psalms to the sky! Tamsin did not recommend he shout, but perhaps speak quietly. She was sure there would be a psalm good for rain. And if a broom were to hand, one might sweep the water on the threshold. Though on second thought, use of a broom might be unnecessary, ill-advised. Best leave the water sprinkled as it was.

If rain were to fall, however, where would he lodge till the house had a roof? Was there an inn or a kind parishioner? Tamsin closed by noting that she had never seen a blue-painted dining room, nor any sky-blue paint at all, but would trust to Antony's good judgment.

At dawn she carried her letter to the wharf.

Before dinner, an oxcart pulled into the yard.

56

Tamsin was out cutting parsley to stew with the day's haddock, when she heard the long creaking sounds she'd known since a child, and turned with an open heart. Grandmother Cat was here, with James. Phebe in the kitchen heard it too, and leapt down the steps.

"Phebe!" James called. "Your summer's worth of carding is here!"

A mass of wool shorn from their sheep on Towne Island was covered over with an old sail, weighted down with sacks of newly milled Red Lammas. Tamsin was relieved to see this, as she had used the last of the tavern's wheat on the days she made the Rowan women's meat pies.

Up on the cart, Grandmother Cat held a linen sack lightly on her lap. Tamsin helped her down, and when Grandmother opened the sack, she saw a cloud of white and green. Fresh elder-flowers, with their stems! She embraced Grandmother and laughed.

"Phebe, what an afternoon you'll have! Come look!"

Phebe left off greeting Ethan. "Elderflowers! Fritters!"

Tamsin watched James shoulder a sack of wheat into the house. Peter, coming back from the shallop, hefted another.

Phebe went straight after them to dig into the new Red Lammas and make a sweet batter for the flowers.

Tamsin stayed outside with Grandmother Cat, as she had things to tell her, and when James and Peter came back for more sacks of wheat, she drew Grandmother away to the garden.

"What is it, dear?"

"Grandmother, Mr. Wingate – Antony – has asked me to marry him, and I've told him I will."

A smile bloomed in her grandmother's face. "He is a good man, Tamsin."

"He has a call to the parish at Sawbridge in the eastward. He's there now, preaching and building a house. He'll come back in September to be ordained and then we'll be married."

"And go to Sawbridge," Grandmother Cat said.

Tamsin made a grimace.

Her grandmother held her. "All will be well, my dear. And when you have your firstborn, I will come. You'll be married in September?"

"Antony will be ordained at Burnham, the last Sunday of the month." She smiled. "I want Uncle Isaac to come and play for a Michaelmas dance again."

A spark lit in Grandmother Cat's eye. "And where will you be married?" A corner of her mouth twitched. "Do you know, dear, how late the moon wanes this September?"

Tamsin's eyes grew round with understanding. The family would plant the Red Lammas.

Grandmother regarded her intently. "Might you and Mr. Wingate come to the farm?"

"We might. We could," Tamsin said.

Grandmother Cat considered. "Would your Reverend Wingate understand about the arbor? He would be ordained by then. Would he agree?"

"I've begun to advise him," Tamsin said.

Grandmother Cat's smile dimpled.

"I gave him a proper way to pray for rain in the eastward. They have drought."

"Did you have him sprinkle water at a threshold? At the meetinghouse itself?"

Tamsin had mischief in her eyes. Grandmother Cat laughed in delight.

"He is a most fortunate man, Tamsin. Has he any idea of the rowess that he marries?"

"He loves me. But no, not quite yet. I don't think so."

"You'll do exceeding well for him."

A slow smile lit Tamsin's face. "I told him to find a psalm," she said, and Grandmother clapped her hands.

In the kitchen, in the afternoon, Phebe dipped lacy fritters in sugar and presented them to the family with pride. Everyone took up an elderflower by its stem and nibbled sweetness, murmuring thanks.

"James," Grandmother Cat said, "we have news to take back to the farm. Tamsin and Antony Wingate are to be married at Michaelmas."

James raised his eyes from his fritter and looked round the kitchen till he found Tamsin busying herself with a stewpot at the hearth. She heard his pause before he said, "That's good news, Tamsin, I am glad for you. He'll stay on in Dorset as schoolmaster?"

"He has a call to a parish in the eastward. He's there now."

"Tamsin believes they'll come out to the farm to be married. On the last day of September, it seems." A lilt of meaning in her voice, Grandmother added, "The moon will be on the wane, you see."

James looked at her, nodded as if he heard something not quite spoken, and turned back to Tamsin with a quirk of a smile. "Thank you, Tamsin. It will be a fine year for the Red Lammas. Good roots," he said.

"Good roots," she answered.

So he remembered digging up the sweetgrass then, that first year. Her eyes wet, she turned to the stew.

"Does he know already?" James asked. "About the arbor?"

Tamsin shook her head.

He teased. "Would you like me to tell him?"

Mother and Grandmother Cat watched, smiling. Phebe looked impish. Tamsin wished this talk were not taking place in the kitchen. She would never face an elderberry fritter again.

"I'll tell him," she said.

"Well." Phebe cocked her head. "He *did see the arbor* you stitched in your *sampler*," she said, as if this were all Mr. Wingate would need to know upon marrying into the Rowan line.

Tamsin gave Phebe a dark look and turned to Peter. "Does the tavern need more stew?"

He pushed his weight off the doorjamb and went to look. "When I'm at Colbrook, I'll tell Uncle Isaac, there's a dance."

Grandmother Cat called after him, "Two dances. One here, and then dancing at the farm."

James stood, gave Grandmother a nod, and they went out to the oxen and cart, Susannah with them. Phebe disappeared quietly. Tamsin expected she'd gone to the attic to study the sampler and consider the nubble of stitches a twelve-year-old girl had made to understand a sacred earthly custom of her Rowan people.

57

July 11th, 1763

My Dearest Tamsin,

I hope that you and your Family are all well and not suffering the drought that is here. My stay at Sawbridge is – as you knew it would be – wearying and hard. I take up my Calling and the labor of building us a House. Yet the work does nourish me, Soul and Heart.

As for the House, I am fortunate to have the very best of help, a Master Builder who knows far better than I how to proceed. I worked once with a crew to raise a long barn for Uncle Charles, and built myself a small Shelter with a fireplace on his land, but my skills fall far short of the House that we build for you! Mr. Mather Briggs, Jr., whom I mentioned as one who would not pay any part of my settlement, has one he calls a Servant – a Man enslaved, to speak the truth – who is expert in building, and himself built the Sawbridge Meetinghouse. But now the curious twist of events is such that – although Mr. Briggs refused to pay my Settlement – I must now pay him for the skills and labor of one he believes his Property. 'Tis a tangled World. A third man completes our crew, a parish-

327

ioner, a sometime boatbuilder and trader, who also gives me Lodging at his house, so you need not worry about rain and roof!

At all events, my twice-daily Prayers under the Sky have not yielded more than a few clouds, nor many prayerful Parishioners either, although the master builder, whose name is Hadrian, does often pray with me. I was interested to see, Tamsin, that he does what you advised and opens his Hands to the Sky in prayer. The Earth continues dry. I hope that he and I, we two may soon do some Good.

Although the Parish does not come out to pray with me, still those who attend at the Sabbath do seem moved by my Preaching, so all is well. A trader will take this Letter at least as far as Portsmouth in the morning. I must close and seal it now.

Yrs always in God's Love, Protection, & Blessing,
Antony Wingate

July 26th, 1763

My dear Antony,

I pray heartily for your Well-Being in the midst of all you must do. We are in good health, and have had Rain. Streams run as usual and the well has water for our needs. I hope there has been Rainfall in Sawbridge since your letter.

Last month Grandmother Cat and James came to us with a cart load of new Wool and eight sacks of our Wheat, which put us all in mind of this coming September's Planting. According to the phase of the Moon, this will take place just after you and I are to be married. From long ago in England, my Family has had a custom of working all together to ready the soil and sow the Wheat. Antony, if we may be married on the day after our Michaelmas Dance, then shall we wed at the farm & help with the Planting?

The amount of Wool is such, Phebe and I put ourselves to

carding every day. Mother spins daily for hours, and we carry Skeins upon Skeins to Mr. Oakes, who makes us fine blankets. I believe he has sent cloth to my Grandmother at the farm as well. For what purpose, I cannot say, although I believe it will be for our House. And yesterday Deacon Somerby brought me five yards of a sweet white Linen with pretty red stripes to make a dress for the dance and our wedding. He is so very kind to us.

Have you seen Mr. Lamb? If you should, please tell him there will be a Dance again at Michaelmas, and a Wedding the next day, September 30th. Would you like for him to marry us? I should be very glad if he would.

When you can, write to me a little about our House. It seems very long before I am to see you again, but a Joy when I do!

> *Your most loving*
> *Thomasin Bennett*

August 18th, 1763

My Dear Thomasin –

What a wonderful Name you have – Thomasin. Tamsin is sweet, but to my ear, Thomasin speaks of your Strength. You will recall I said to you once, 'thy neck is like the Tower of David.' How fortunate I am to have found such a Help-meet! Elsewhere in Scripture, your name reminds me of Doubting Thomas, the Apostle unconvinced of our Lord's bodily Presence after His Death. But my Love, I have no Doubt whatever of your Faith. Nor, I must say, of your wondrous bodily presence.

But I sense too your ease in looking beyond appearances, even into things Unseen. What is it you feel in the Air about me? Most Men would find this disturbing, but I marvel at it. It will be a joy and a mystery, my Thomasin, to be with you life-long.

You ask for Mr. Lamb. He passed through Sawbridge some

weeks ago. He may be preaching at Yarmouth now, but will come back this way, as he is to preach at my Ordination. I'll gladly ask him to go to The Roses and Rowans at Michaelmas, and dance, and marry us after that. Yes, let's go and help to plant your dear family's Wheat. Who knows, but what we may do the same in a Field of our own one day?

Our house rises with Hadrian's plans and skills. He knows Masonry as well. He has based a stout Chimney in the cellar and built it up past the ground floor with seven Flues! Two for the Kitchen, one each for Dining Room and Parlor, and three for fire-places in the Bedchambers above. Of note, Uncle Charles has sent us a great quantity of his Prussian blue Pigment. I am unsure what to do with it all.

Sawbridge continues hot, the soil dry. Animals are watered from the bends in the River now. Called the Nowhere River, its name is more accurate by the day. Together with Hadrian and the third man of our crew, I now pray Morning, Noon, and Evening. I would ask you, Tamsin, please to do the same. The sole Mercy is this – there have not been Fires.

I send you my Love, Dear One, and hope for our reunion as soon as may be,

By the Grace of Our Lord,
Antony Wingate

September 2ⁿᵈ, 1763

DEAREST ANTONY,

Every day I think how soon you're to return to Burnham and be ordained, and then we'll be wed. Mr. Stevens reads our Intentions at the meetinghouse for the first time this Sabbath and then twice more, so to finish before the day of your Ordination. (I laugh to think of his fear that, should some Objection to our Union arise, it had best be known before you are ordained! I imagine his wife, my irksome Cousin Naomi, put such a thought into his head!)

My dear, I regret we cannot leave the Inn to go to Burnham, but I know you will tell us about the event. Do you think I might prevail upon Mr. Lamb to give his Ordination Sermon in the tavern one evening? I will ask!

We have had a letter from my Uncle Nat and Aunt Martha, who settled years ago at Combe, eastward of Yarmouth. It was Uncle Nat who gave us his house to be an Inn and Tavern. They have most generously ordered furnishings, a dining table, six chairs, and a bedstead to be shipped to Sawbridge from Boston. Another kind Gift appeared here. You recall Noah Southworth who has the sawmill. He made me a fine dough box the height of a table, with four sturdy legs and a lid. Did he once tell you an old story that I pulled his Arm from a fire and healed his Hand? It's not quite true, but he likes to tell a good story and made the dough box as a Joke, as if in thanks. It will be useful in a kitchen that has two flues!

Aunt Martha will also bring me fall and spring-bearing Plants of all sorts from her gardens at Combe. I am glad you want to learn our way of planting the Red Lammas. We have a day of working all together, and that night you and I are to have the Honor of staying in the Arbor above the field to keep watch, long a Rowan family custom. Also as to planting, I must dig suckers from the Roses to take with us, and rowan seed or perhaps even Saplings, if they will travel well. I must speak with Phebe on this.

I pray for rain, imagining I am there alongside of you, Antony, our Palms to the Sky. I hope to hear the fields are wet at last, and not a single Hen singed!

Praying too for your safe return, Dear, and sending you my Love,
Yr Tamsin

September 10th, 1763

DEAREST TAMSIN,

We work hastily to finish the House before I am to leave for Burnham. There is much yet to be done. But my news is that last night we had a long, fine, steady, welcome Rain, and the Parish is now in good spirits, believing I had something to do with it!

I did at last, as you suggested, sprinkle a little river water at the threshold to the Meetinghouse – alone, no broom – and say verses of a Psalm. I went to number 147. I'd little or nothing to do with the rainfall, of course, but am glad enough to let the Parish think so!

Mr. Lamb will sail with me to Burnham on the 22nd for my Ordination on the Sabbath. I must stay another day at Burnham until the Deacons from Sawbridge have gone back, but on the 27th, my dear Tamsin, Mr. Lamb and I will sail to your Harbor. We'll dance all together with delight on the 29th!

Then comes, I must say, a very long Day – travel to the farm, our blessed Wedding, the planting of a crop of Wheat, and then keeping night watch at the Arbor – all on the one day of September 30th. Tamsin, I do understand it's an Honor to be asked to watch over the new Seed, but must we? After our long Separation, would it not be better to enjoy one another on our Wedding night? And sleep, as the next morning we are to sail to Burnham for a night, and then on to Sawbridge?

May I suggest that your Cousin James might be honored to watch over the Seed, whilst you and I take with Pleasure to a Bed? I do not mean to be ungrateful, but why this seeming Honor on our Wedding night of all nights? May I protest?

Looking forward to being with you always, Tamsin my love –
       Yr Antony

September 16th, 1763

ANTONY, MY LOVE, BE AT EASE. TRULY, WE NEED NOT take part in the Planting, if you don't wish, but to pass the night under an Arbor – this would not be a burdensome thing.

All will be just as you would like!
Yr Loving Tamsin

58

ON THE TWENTY-SEVENTH OF SEPTEMBER, THE DAY Antony was to come back with Mr. Lamb, Tamsin opened her eyes, sun dawning in the back field. From the height of her attic window, she could see the field as a quilt of earth, and saw signs of her years on Uncle Nat's land. She'd long tended the garden that Peter dug before they came. The patch of sweetgrass James brought long ago from the farm had rooted blessedly wide. She'd made the ointment against gnats and mosquitoes many times over. Beyond there, Phebe's lines of rowans, the ones she'd moved round from the front, were now thick with berries, welcoming cardinals. After a hard frost, the berries would be fit to cook, although by then, Tamsin would be gone. Here was a pang, and loss. Farther over, where the field was still half-wild, tall milkweed rustled. Tamsin had often gone there with Phebe to pick the pods that were split open, showing the white inside.

Sometimes, she had gone there with James.

Today was the day Antony would come back. She rolled over to get up and dress, make breakfast, but found Phebe sitting on her narrow bed, watching Tamsin in silence, tears making long lines down her face.

"Oh, Phebe!"

Tamsin went to hold her and Phebe sobbed. "I don't want you to go. You should stay here and not go away. The eastward is too far, and I'll never see you again."

"You will see me. I'll come back, and you'll come see me." Tamsin held and rocked her in her arms. "Peter will bring you in the shallop, and you'll bring me sacks of Red Lammas. Whatever would I do without you and Red Lammas?"

"You'll take some from the farm and plant it there yourself. And I put rowan sprouts in pots, so you can take them with you and grow them and be safe from the Royalists and have berries. You see, you won't need me at all."

"Oh, Phebe!" Tamsin cried now too. "I will always need you. I'll always miss you!"

They held one another until they both stopped crying, and Phebe said they had to make breakfast and a tavern dinner, and be ready for Mr. Wingate to come with Mr. Lamb.

"Tamsin," she asked, "do you remember when we told Mr. Lamb how we could be in two places at once? Do you think we can?"

PETER WAS ALREADY OUT FISHING. PHEBE WENT TO DIG clams because, she said, Mr. Lamb liked them. Tamsin wanted to dig in the earth, cut potatoes and onions. Mother's *chaudière* would hang in a pot over a fire today, warm welcome, because today her Antony would come with Mr. Lamb.

And they did, and everyone sat up late that evening in the tavern, drinking cider and questioning Antony about the parish and the house where, in a matter of days, Tamsin would be its mistress.

ON THE TWENTY-EIGHTH OF SEPTEMBER, SUSANNAH, Tamsin, and Phebe made a tavern dinner and began the baking of apple and shore plum cakes for the dance the next evening. Peter and Antony worked with Mr. Proctor, picking and milling apples for the winter's cider. Uncle Isaac sailed his shallop from Colbrook and brought his fiddle. Mr. Lamb visited Mr. Stevens to be sure the marriage intentions had indeed been read three times at the meetinghouse, and to inquire if he might have the honor of preaching there on the Sabbath. Every task and mission met with success. Intentions had been read, and Mr. Lamb was engaged to preach. Uncle Isaac, given supper and a pint, fiddled rants for the pleasure of the tavern, and Tamsin prevailed upon Mr. Lamb to deliver once more the sermon he had given for Antony's ordination at Burnham.

His text was from the Book of Hebrews, he said. In thrilling voice, he exhorted the young reverend always to match his faith with the devotion of the elders of the Old Testament – *"so great a cloud of witnesses!"* As he invoked this ancient company, his upraised eyes and hands located them hovering about the tavern's ceiling, and when the drinkers of Tamsin's ale looked up to see of whom he spoke, he gave public notice, he would preach at the meetinghouse on the Sabbath.

ON THE TWENTY-NINTH OF SEPTEMBER, THE MORNING of Michaelmas, Peter and Antony moved tables and benches to the yard. Tamsin cut stalks of lavender and laid them on the mantel and sills, then slipped out along the shore road to the cove where, not by chance, Antony met her between the bayberries and granite. She did not take time to unwind his stock now, but he brushed his lips along her neck, murmuring, "Sweet Tower of David," until she assured him with a laugh and a whisper that tomorrow on their wedding night, though they would watch over a field of Red Lammas, all would be as it should.

When they left the bayberries, Antony went back to the house. Tamsin walked the hill road to the burying ground to bid goodbye to the sisters she hadn't known, but had come to love.

In the afternoon James drove the horsecart with Josette and

Grandmother Cat to the harbor. Uncle Simon and the others would stay at the farm and ready the field for planting.

THAT MICHAELMAS DANCE WAS JOYOUS AND DIFFICULT for Tamsin, her last at the tavern. She stepped the figures of many dances with Antony, and partnered with Mr. Lamb, whose two eyes, alight, danced unusually well together that evening. She danced with Noah Southworth and thanked him again for the handsome, sturdy dough box he'd made. At the last notes, with a bow and a look that slipped from her face to the linen at her bodice, he leant close to her ear and thanked her for, as he said, "that good apple you thrust at my mouth on a knife." The kind Mr. Oakes happened to note her sudden blush and stepped in to dance with her, followed by Mr. Dingley, whose good humor she would miss.

At last she danced with James, who took her hands, looked into her eyes, and in every two-hand turn, swung her close to him. She did not look round to see if Josette were watching, but danced with Mr. Proctor and every other man as long into the evening as she could. Then wobbly of heart, she went to the attic before Uncle Isaac could end with the weaving steps of "Dargason," the dance she felt to be all about greeting and farewell.

SHE WOKE AS PHEBE WAS HURRYING TO DRESS AND GO down to make breakfast for an inn full of family. Then Tamsin rose, and Grandmother Cat as well, helping Tamsin into her stays, her petticoats, and the new gown, the fine white linen with pretty red stripes.

Pinning the bodice, Grandmother said, "I have something for you that will be quite beautiful with your gown."

"What is it?"

"Later," she said.

Tamsin went downstairs to see Antony bringing in a glorious

bunch of Michaelmas daisies. Full of smiles, he wore a new coat and breeches of deep green. His neck stock was spotless, neatly wrapped and tied in a handsome knot, his wild red hair held back in a queue with a strip of soft leather. Her private wish was to take his hand and walk right back out to the bayberries.

WHEN SUSANNAH AND DEACON SOMERBY ARRIVED, ALL the Bennetts, Uncle Isaac, Antony, and Mr. Lamb were in the midst of their coffee and pudding. Mr. Stevens and Naomi came as well, though at the sight of Tamsin's gown, Naomi stiffened. She offered good wishes, took Mr. Stevens' arm, and assured Tamsin that the Reverend would be at the farm in time for the wedding. They were gone in a minute.

Tamsin was unconcerned. If Naomi chose to delay their arrival, it would pose no problem, as Mr. Lamb was to officiate. The more pressing question was the loading of two shallops with all that would go with her to housekeeping — chests of linens, blankets, quilts, and clothing, boxes of pans and pots, her choice of the good tavern stoneware, a half-dozen English pewter mugs, and the dough box of Noah Southworth. That, and six sturdy buckets of soil, in each of which Phebe had tucked three lithe, little rowan sprouts to plant round the bounds of the yard at Sawbridge. All this was carried to the wharf on James' and the deacon's horsecarts, then loaded, well balanced, onto Uncle Isaac's and Peter's shallops.

Tamsin watched her brother. He'd said little about her marriage and her leaving, but saying little was his usual way. Still, he looked low this morning and moved slowly. She asked Mr. Lamb please to sail with Peter and take up an oar as needed. She feared Peter would have a hard day after the wedding, sailing up the coast to Burnham to deliver, with Isaac, all the boxes of her housekeeping. At Burnham they would have a short, painful goodbye and he'd sail back to the harbor alone. The work of the tavern would weigh on him.

Phebe seemed to know this too. She stayed near Peter, saying what good work she would always do to help him, and loaded her pots of rowans so they'd not be in his way. She sailed to the farm with Peter and Mr. Lamb.

James drove his horsecart back to the farm with Josette, and Deacon Somerby drove Susannah, Tamsin and Antony. For now, for six miles to the farm in the Deacon's horsecart, Tamsin sat snug as she could beside Antony and held his arm, first to express her love, then to steady them both as the road went rutty, and last, as the cart drew near the farm, for strength in facing her memories. The cart stopped in the farmyard just as Uncle Simon led the ox Levi back from plowing new furrows in the wheat field.

At the sight of her uncle, Tamsin said nothing. He had not with his own hands thrown her Papa under the millwheel, but neither had she forgotten the groundsel tree and red cedars that concealed her hurtling back from the marsh. Uncle Simon had not killed her, but he had watched her Papa die.

Now he bent his eyes to the ground, looked up once to nod, then led Levi away.

Deacon Somerby and Susannah went into the house, but Tamsin took Antony's arm and drew him to walk with her down-stream, her first steps on the mill path since the day she sang with the cardinals.

59

Every step on the path fetched up memories more vivid than she could take in, let alone tell. Rowan trees on both sides of the stream marked the beginning and ending of three rounds of the pond Grandmother Cat had made her walk. So familiar was the path that even now, she knew she could run heedless to the mill without ever turning an ankle on a half-buried stone. The stream still rippled, stitch upon stitch, as she'd put it into her sampler, though the meadow on the far side was even more lush than memory, thick green, gold Aaron's rod, the angel Michael's tall purple. She knew the white, however. Just there, she'd puffed her breath onto dry, brown yarrow and transformed not only the blooms, but what she knew herself to be.

"What do you see?" Antony asked.

What could she tell him? She nodded across the stream. "The Michaelmas daisies at the tavern come from over there. James dug them up and brought them to me in the first year." She smiled at the man she would marry. "For courage."

"And so you have it," he nodded.

This pleased her. This man, though educated as a minister, could learn to honor the spirit of a flower.

· · ·

THE FAMILY WERE GATHERED AT THE WHEAT FIELD. Aunt Adah and her children, Luke, Abigail, and Sarah, who was now thirteen, and Josette with little Beatrice and Pascal, all waited for James to give each a cup of Red Lammas to bear along a furrow.

Tamsin took Antony to meet them. He watched fascinated as they took their cups up along the eastern edge of the field. Each child chose a furrow to walk, Aunt Adah and Josette taking two that were unclaimed. There was one left to James, but after portioning out wheat, he turned to Antony to offer him a cup of the Rowans' ancient seed.

"But this is yours to do," Antony protested. "It's your line."

"Yours to do now," James said to Antony, and looked at Tamsin with unmistakable love.

Antony turned to her, a question unspoken. When she looked up the rise of the hill to an arbor of river birch, his eyes followed hers. And so it was, without a word, he held a hand out to James to accept the cup of grain, and went to the edge of the field, to the furrow where no one was yet. At a sign from James, first the children, then Adah and Josette started to walk, then Antony did too, matching his pace to theirs. Tamsin stood with James, her eyes wet, and watched.

When seed had been dropped the length of every furrow, the family formed a circle round the whole of the field, and Tamsin went to Antony. Gently, James raked the first furrow, starting east to west, then the next furrow west to east, and on up the rise. Tamsin saw James put the Red Lammas to bed as sweetly as ever Papa had done. At the end, the family walked up the mill path to the house for dinner, but Tamsin took Antony's hand and drew him away.

"Downstream," she said. "The milldam."

Well as she knew the path, she trembled now as they walked, and when she stepped up onto the dam, she did it carefully, as if testing either the dam or herself. A tide was pushing through the water gate into the pond. She made herself cross the dam and stopped still at the wheel, Antony at her side.

"This is where Papa died," she said. "He fell down under the wheel."

Antony gave a low moan. "Poor man."

She looked downstream and at the bank below, then drew the sundial-compass from the pocket inside her petticoat. "After he died, I found this. Down there at the edge. He always had it with him."

The needle showed due north.

"It still works," Antony said.

"A great white egret was fishing there and tried to pick it up."

The egret showed it to me. He meant to. He made me see it.

She slipped it back into her pocket and spoke of something else.

"When I was little," she said, "I would run here, one end of the dam to the other, arms out wide. I wanted to fly over the water like a blue heron."

"And did you have a blue gown flying out behind you as you rose up in the air?"

She smiled. "I never quite rose up, although I always thought I could." She glanced sideways at Antony to see his response. He was smiling.

She looked to the incoming tide, as though a great white egret might swoop in for fish. Water from the bay lifted and pushed upstream, stirring the millpond with a force she felt in the soles of her feet. She felt it as clearly as she had years ago, like sap rising in a maple. But now it felt more like light rising through her being in waves, lifting and filling till her hands, of their own accord, rose and formed a bloom wide as those at Hallett's Cove.

Antony watched her.

She looked at her hands and shook her head. "This happens sometimes," she said. She didn't know how to explain. "As when sap rises."

Antony was quiet.

Her hands held still, cupped. She searched for words. "Or as if light could shine not only down from the sun, but up from the earth."

He said nothing.

At a loss, she said at last, although this would make no sense, "There's a flower at Hallett's Cove called sailor's-grace."

"It must be very beautiful." Antony cupped his hands beneath hers. "Is the rising light what happened when you pulled Noah's arm from the fire and saved his hand?"

This caught her short.

"He told you."

She waited for Antony to be alarmed, afraid, but he lifted her hands and kissed them.

In a corner of the parlor, unbidden, Uncle Isaac brought out his fiddle and began the sweet melody of "Heart's Ease" at a gentle tempo. Eyes closed, he played as if to himself. Tamsin watched him. When he opened his eyes with a slow smile, they were smiling at one another. She put a hand to her heart and bowed her head. He answered with a nod and picked up the pace. Antony took her for a single-hand turn.

Mr. Lamb, like an actor in a play, took the fiddle as his cue, rose from the settle, and stood at the hearth. Mr. Stevens, who had arrived, followed him. With the skip of the music, Antony and Tamsin stepped to the ministers. Uncle Isaac ended with a flourish, and the family moved round to stand in witness.

Mr. Stevens opened with a prayer that meandered awhile. Tamsin's eyes strayed as well, up above the ministers' heads. She'd always liked the great beam's chamfered edge, a line long ago painted red, the color still warm. She thought of the tavern's yellow ochre, and Antony's uncle's sky-blue paint. What had become of it? Mr. Lamb's wandering eye met hers, and it winked. When Mr. Stevens ended a sentence for a breath, Mr. Lamb landed a heartfelt "Thank you, Reverend," and followed quickly with words eloquent and few, about marriage as an earthly substance of divine love.

As above, so below. Tamsin remembered Papa saying it once, on the milldam.

When Mr. Lamb turned to the saying of the vows, Antony and Tamsin turned to one another. Past and present overlay in a moment – the beam of an old house, milldam and night sky, Papa, egret, compass, roses, the captain of a sloop – and all at once she heard him.

"I, Antony, take thee Thomasin to my wedded wife."

She listened, and felt as if standing perfectly at an edge of dry land, when in the exact next moment, with only a single wave, she would be standing in the sea.

"I, Thomasin," she said, "take thee Antony to my wedded husband."

60

THE WEDDING DINNER WAS COD, PUMPKIN, AND SHORE
plum cakes. Afterward, Uncle Isaac settled himself by the hearth
and took up his fiddle again, family resting and listening. When
the bow skipped to the rhythm of "Epping Forest," a half-dozen
Bennetts formed up a circle to dance. Phebe pulled Antony in,
but Grandmother Cat and James said Tamsin must go out with
them, so she did, and they went to the barn. On the pegs where
the coracle and baskets had always hung, there now hung two
coracles. James lifted one down, that looked very different from
the one Tamsin had always touched with wonder. He took the
new one out to lean it against the barn door.

This one –

She touched it. She stroked it, and stroked it again, in tears.
She could not have said whether her tears were of grief or gratitude, as they all came from love. Grandmother Cat and James had
made a coracle for her to take with her to the eastward, covered
with the Devon-red hide Tamsin knew was Ethan's. He had died
of his age in the summer, they said. James stroked the hide too,
and said Ethan's hair would slip and disappear after a while, but
for now –

Crying, Tamsin embraced James and then Grandmother Cat.

He showed her which side of the coracle would be bow and which stern, because of Ethan's hair, and he said to hang and store it dry as best she could. She understood. She lifted and put the coracle up on its pegs again, spread her arms across the hide of the ox she'd always known, and told him what good, long days of work he had done.

When they went back to the parlor, Uncle Isaac was taking a rest with a cider. Seeing Tamsin, he reached for something beside the fireplace and held it out to her – a broad, graceful oar carved of rowan-wood with a pommel at the top, shaped perfectly to her hand.

AFTER A SUPPER OF CORNBREAD WITH HONEY, THE fiddle picked up again, but Grandmother Cat drew Tamsin away, through the kitchen to the lean-to. On the same narrow bed where Papa had been laid out and Sarah born, there was spread a cloak of heavy red wool. Its hood was lined with white linen, the length of its opening bound in black silk.

"Oh, Grandmother, it's beautiful!"

"It will keep you warm in Sawbridge," Grandmother said. "Now let's get you ready to go and meet Antony." She took the pins from the bodice of Tamsin's gown with the fine red stripes, helped her out of it, and untied her petticoats.

"Dear," she said, "let me tell you what my mother told me on the day I married your Grandfather Thomas. She said that for a babe to be seeded in a woman, she must take pleasure in the seeding. Now I do not, in fact, believe this to be true."

Tamsin shook her head, knowing her mother's calamity, and said nothing of it.

"Still, in the embrace of your good Antony, you may take your joy to overflowing." Grandmother Cat's fingers made a dance in the air, like a butterfly. "And should you hope to conceive a child tonight on the hill above the Rowans' Red

Lammas"– her face lit with blessing – "such has been known to happen. There and then I conceived your dearest Papa."

Tamsin's heart was full and spilled over again into tears.

Grandmother Cat loosed the laces of her stays till she could slip them off, and Tamsin stood only in her shift, shoes, and stockings. Grandmother swaddled her round with the long red cloak and walked out with her as far as the rowan trees at the head of the mill path. There she kissed her granddaughter, and Tamsin went on to find her husband.

JAMES AND ANTONY HAD CARRIED A SAIL AND BLANKETS to the hill, laid the sail down under the arbor, and made a pallet of the blankets. When Tamsin walked there, wrapped in red wool, her Antony was already at rest.

"My love," she smiled, "did I tell you that all would be as you'd like?"

"I'll never doubt you again, my Thomasin."

"You'd best not." She slipped off her shoes and knelt to kiss him. His trust pleased her more than he could know.

He drew Tamsin with her swath of red wool under the warmth of his blankets. "What a glorious cloak. Let me be in it too." He slipped an arm inside the cloak and all round the linen of her shift.

"Behold, thou art fair, my love. So saith Solomon the Wise."

Her fingers found each perfect vertebra the length of his back. Years ago in the kitchen, Mother had once said, and Tamsin said it now – *"A bundle of myrrh is my well-beloved unto me."*

He kissed her, murmuring his pleasure of body and holy poetry.

"He shall lie all night betwixt my breasts," she said.

"And so I shall," he said, kissing her accordingly, *"For behold, thou art fair, my beloved, yes, pleasant."*

"What, pleasant?" she laughed. "Only pleasant?"

"Also o ur bed is green," he added solemnly. *"The beams of our house are cedar, and our rafters of fir."*

Tamsin turned soft eyes toward the branches woven above them and corrected the poet-king in a whisper. "Birch."

He looked upward too.

"Dear love," he murmured. "I think sometimes of the mystery of your five moons. In your sampler," he asked, "whyever did you stitch five moons?"

"The moon's changes make the tides," she said. "A little crescent just past new, then waxing ...."

His fingers found and traced a crescent moon.

She hesitated, but went on, "... Full, waning ... then new again."

"I love you. I love you. I love you. Forever, and ever," he said, and the moon grew full. "World ... without end," he said.

Her breath in that moment would not let her form a word, although round and above her and up past the woven birch leaves of the arbor there lifted up what felt to be a fountain, *Amen.*

After this, she knew seed well planted and rejoiced greatly in all the fertile hill.

ANTONY SLEPT AS SHE LISTENED TO THE BITTERSWEET song of September crickets. She would have crickets, no doubt, in Sawbridge, but these she heard now were the crickets she'd heard as a child. They told her she was leaving again in the morning, leaving the farm a second time, this very hill, the Rowans' Red Lammas, millstream and tide mill, the great white egret, the grave of her Papa.

Restless, she got up, wrapped her cloak round her, and walked the rise of the hill, swishing stockinged feet through tall grass. The slight moon was up, a bend of light in a clear sky. Her eyes searched for the Pole Star that Papa once showed a little girl, and she found it. Then fixed below it, a line of stars caught her eye. A graceful curve suggested a thing familiar from years before, and above that dear line, as she watched, a scattering of stars resolved into forms she knew, the spars and sails of a sloop.

The slight curve showed a gunwale and bowsprit that looked to yearn forward, willed by a heart longing to sail. Her own heart lifted and yearned together with the sloop. Rigged above the bowsprit, two jibs scooped space. Certain stars along what seemed the gunwale shed sparks now and then. She thought them swivel guns and laughed at their show. The sloop's one mast held a topsail high, a single-minded awareness. Her own awareness opened high and wide, till she too could watch as if from the sloop's deck. Scanning, she saw no line that divided sky from sea, but flecks of light shone in the dark, as above, so below.

"Tamsin. You can't sleep?" Antony came to her, wearing only his chemise.

She embraced him with her cloak. "My dear, you're cold. I woke and came to look at the stars."

His eyes turned up. "Andromeda," he said. "Fitting she should be here at a coast."

"Andromeda. Is she a sloop?"

"Princess in a Greek myth. The queen bragged her daughter was more beautiful than the daughters of the sea gods, so Poseidon sent a monster to destroy the realm. King and queen, to save themselves, chained the princess to a rock by the sea, so the monster would devour her and spare them. Sacrifice to arrogance and fear."

Tamsin studied the stars in horror. She tipped her head, one side to another, to see – Was that a woman chained to a rock to die for a kingdom? In the dark she saw the rowess Priscilla, her wrists in irons, seated on a horse before a ragged figure taking her for judgment and death at a rock ledge.

She shook the vision from her head. "No," she said, "that didn't happen. She didn't die."

"No, she didn't," Antony smiled. "Perseus flew in to save her. Come lie down with me."

"I will soon." She kissed him.

Stepping out of Tamsin's red cloak, Antony shuddered and went to the warmth of the blankets.

Tamsin stood longer, watching the sloop. Serene in a dark ocean, it never drifted away from the one overboard star that seemed its anchor. The sloop's single mast, rigged one sail fore and one aft, looked to her wingèd, and her arms floated up at her sides. Presently her feet rose from the earth, feathery grasses disappearing below her soles.

This was in no way strange to her, incandescent as she was in the stars of the sloop on the night sea. She held there. Her hands scooped to her belly where she felt – not a quickening, impossible – but a startle as of a sweet wind ruffling a wide, white bloom, gold at its center.

She knew him. She knew his being that was known long ago by Modron of Cornwall. His awareness now vast, she knew his blessing of the child of her body and Antony's, the child that in time would grow to know itself as Christopher did, as earth, sea, space, and sparks of light.

AUTHOR'S NOTE

Once upon a time, I had an obscure fourth great-grandfather named Samuel Pierce, of whom I knew little more than an incorrect birth year. On my circuitous path to his origins, I found his mother Anna Pierce, widowed and remarried with the surname of Mitchell, and his father Thomas Pierce, misidentified as a Unitarian minister. But when I found the brief account, below, in John Babson's writings on Gloucester, Massachusetts, I was captivated by the lives of two bereaved, brave women, my sixth and fifth great-grandmothers, Susannah Warner Parsons Haskell and her daughter Anna –

William, son of William Haskell the third, had a wife Abigail, who died Feb. 2, 1737. He next married Susanna, perhaps widow of Daniel Parsons, Sept. 12, 1739, and [William] died about 1752…. His widow removed from the second Parish to the harbor, and for several years kept a boarding house in Middle street. Her daughter Anna married, Nov. 29, 1762, Rev. Thomas Pierce of Scarborough, Me., who was employed some time as a school-master, before he entered the ministry, and was probably a boarder in the house of Anna's mother. (*Notes and Addi-*

tions to the History of Gloucester: Part First, Early Settlers, by John J. Babson. Gloucester, Mass.: M.V.B. Perley, 1876, pp. 36-37)

In these few words, I felt so much life and intention that I had to read them over and over. When I felt a third woman appear alongside Susannah and her daughter, I realized she was my seventh great-grandmother in another line of my father's family. She was Elizabeth Proctor, one nearly hanged for witchcraft at Salem in 1692. And when I saw the three women braid their lives together, two more appeared for a novel about a lineage, not of witches allied with the devil, but of learned herbalists, healers, midwives, and mystics in an ancient family named Rowan.

Susannah Warner's first marriage was to Daniel Parsons, a seaman, in 1732. Tragically, at least two, perhaps all three of their daughters, died before the age of three. Daniel died at sea of smallpox in 1738.

In the novel's backstory, Susannah's first marriage is to a sea captain, Élie Julien, son of a fictional minister named Ezechiel Julien, who was inspired by a historical person. The French Protestant pastor Ezechiel Carré was from the Île de Ré, off the west coast of France. In 1686, Carré brought dozens of French Protestant families to settle in Rhode Island, and preached sometimes at the French church in Boston. As Britain and France were enemies then, he wrote a politically significant sermon on charity, based on the parable of the Good Samaritan. The Puritan minister Cotton Mather liked it so well, he had it published in Boston in 1689. Ironically, this was three years before Mather's merciless role in the witch trials at Salem.

When the French settlement at Rhode Island disbanded in 1691, Ezechiel Carré disappeared from the historic record. Fictionally, the pastor Ezechiel Julien and his wife Isabelle come to settle at Dorset Harbor, where their son Élie is born and marries, later dying at sea.

Historically, it was Daniel Parsons who died at sea. In 1739, his widow Susannah married William Haskell of the prosperous West Gloucester Haskells. They had six children, at least four of whom survived childhood. William died in 1752, perhaps an unexpected death, as he was not yet sixty years old and had not prepared a will. Now twice widowed, Susannah started over again, but differently this time – and unusually for a woman in the mid-1700s. She left the Haskell house, farm and mill, and moved with her children to open a business at the harbor. What Babson's history calls a boarding house is written in the novel as an inn and a tavern. Susannah's daughter Anna worked with her for a dozen years, then married the schoolmaster Thomas Pierce who was, according to an entry in a minister's diary, a lodger there.

Thomas was from up the coast at Newbury, a great-grandson of Colonel Daniel Peirce who built the 1690 stone manor house still standing at the Spencer-Peirce-Little Farm. (The vowels of Pierce and Peirce wavered for centuries.) Through much of his life, Thomas would have been influenced by the colorful itinerant preacher of the Great Awakening, the Anglican priest George Whitefield, who came and went through Newburyport, preaching out of doors and inspiring several men of Thomas' family. The Pierces helped establish the Presbyterian church in Newburyport, and sent young Thomas to the College of New Jersey, the Presbyterian school and seminary now known as Princeton. In the novel, a book owned by Antony Wingate, entitled *The Preceptor*, was in fact one that Thomas Pierce had during his time at seminary (*Princetonians, 1748-1768: A Biographical Dictionary*). Called to a parish in Maine in 1762, he was ordained at the First Presbyterian Church, "Old South," on Federal Street in Newburyport.

The passionate itinerant preacher George Whitefield was problematic for the decorous eighteenth-century Congregational churches of New England. He remains problematic today for a different reason, as he relied on enslaved labor to staff an orphanage he had founded in Georgia. In the novel, some elements of Whitefield's life are woven into the character of the

Reverend Gideon Lamb – his work at his mother's tavern in England, his piety and vivid preaching, his asthma, his eyes. But Gideon Lamb is a fictional figure set in the Seacoast Revival of New England. He travels only as far as New Jersey to preach.

Tamsin Bennett's relationship with Antony Wingate is based on that of Anna Haskell and Thomas Pierce, my fifth great-grand-parents. Though fictional, Tamsin's love relationships with her cousin James Bennett and Captain Christopher Hawes have historical resonance.

Reading of her love for James, we may think marriage between first cousins was impossible, illegal, but it is legal even now in many states, including Massachusetts. In earlier centuries, with fewer people and less travel, marriage between first cousins was not uncommon, sometimes even favored as a way to keep resources within a family. That said, Puritans disapproved of first-cousin marriage in general, so for Tamsin and James it might have been difficult.

When Captain Christopher Hawes appears at The Rowans in June of 1755, he enjoys Mistress Bennett's *chaudière*, later rowing out with Tamsin to discover a mystical bloom. But 1755 is a fateful year, one of historically grave international disasters. In 1710, the French had surrendered their colony of Acadia, now Nova Scotia, to the British. By 1755, however, the British had found the French population difficult to govern, and decided these thousands of innocent settlers were to be exiled, scattered south into British colonies from Massachusetts to Georgia. Trans-port would begin in October, houses, barns, mills, and churches burnt down.

Then on the first of November in that year, a cataclysmic earthquake struck under the Atlantic. Centered southwest of Lisbon, the quake was felt from Finland to Morocco. This happened on All Saints' Day. When the Cathedral and two hundred Lisbon churches were filled with parishioners, the earth shook violently and stones fell down on them. Fires from the hearths and candles of broken buildings tore across the city. Three massive waves of the Atlantic surged upriver. Most of Lisbon was destroyed, the human toll incalculable.

Seventeen days later, news of the horrors of Lisbon had not yet reached Massachusetts, when another quake struck under the Atlantic, this one northeast of Boston, off Cape Ann. Though not deadly, it was destructive from Portland, Maine, south through Massachusetts, damaging stone fences, brick walls, and chimneys, tipping steeples. Sermons were written, meetinghouses rattled with warnings of God's wrath.

Over time, earthly and human disasters have struck like a bell at this edge of land and sea that we've called Dorset Harbor.

Still we dance. Myth, fairy tale, dream, and love carry us on.

GRATITUDE

However solitary the work of writing a novel may look, the reality is communal. So to my beta-readers Larry Young, Ellie Bailey, and Kathryn Griner, who not only read, but often consulted on eighteenth-century dress, music, and seafaring – even discovering the overgrown graves of Tamsin's forebears – you have my heartfelt thanks always.

Gratitude also to Cam Terwilliger, wise and kind mentor, and to my generous teachers through these years – Nora Corrigan, Marjan Kamali, Tim Horvath, and Alison Murphy. You've given me so much to work with! Thanks, too, to my son Tristan Poehlmann, a writer for young adults, who answered with sage advice every time I asked.

Two writing groups have sustained me – Barbara Hyams' group with the Gloucester (Massachusetts) Writers Center, and Maile Black's group through the Manchester-by-the-Sea Public Library. Warmest thanks to all of you, my neighbors. In a more farflung community, I am deeply grateful for the responses of Lynda Anozie, Mary Margaret Anozie, Laura Gilbert, Carol Ann Groceman, Eleanor Harris, Ben Katz, Kimie Matsudo Kester, Daryl Nardick, and Nancy Wainer.

To my cousinly readers, descended from the flesh-and-blood people who inspired the characters in this novel, I am more grateful than I can say – Mary Murch Sawyer, Candice Sawyer, Brenda Hall, Wendy Smith, Dick Haskell of the Haskell Family Association, and Rick and Natalie Samuelson of the William Haskell House, West Gloucester, Massachusetts.

Since the start of this project, many have graciously shared their wisdom with me – Emerson Baker, Katie Benway, Thad "MacDaddy" Bernard, the Brown Research Library of the Maine Historical Society, Bethany Groff Dorau of the Museum of Old Newbury, Marc Friedman, Lauren Gagnan, Janice Gregory, Allice Haidden, Hannah Harlow of The Book Shop of Beverly Farms, Vijay Joyce of Rekindled History, Marilyn Larson, Charlie Mahaffie, James Sargent, Don Taylor of the Scarborough (Maine) Historical Society, Earl Taylor of the Tide Mill Institute and Dorchester (Massachusetts) Historical Society, Nancy Wainer, and Robin Yasinow.

At last, profoundest gratitude to my publisher Maile Black of Winter Island Press and to the wonderful artist Alex Edwards.